Pashterina's Peacocks

Pashterina's Peacocks

For Storm Constantine

Edited by
Danielle Lainton & Louise Coquio

IMMANION PRESS
Stafford, England

Pashterina's Peacocks: For Storm Constantine,
edited by Danielle Lainton and Louise Coquio © 2021

Cover Art by Ruby
Layout and Cover Design by Danielle Lainton

IP0165
ISBN 978-1-912815-15-9
First edition by Immanion Press, 2021
http://www.immanion-press.com
info@immanion-press.com

For my friend, my confidante, my teacher, my guide, my sister in magic. Your Peacocks have gathered together in their full beauty just for you, in our loss and our heartbreak your dazzling brilliance shines out through the words in this book.
I miss you; we miss you; the world misses you.

Danni, November 21
(Danielle Lainton)

Contents

Introduction

Ian Whates

Storm Constantine is missed.

I'm strongly tempted to leave the introduction there, because as soon as you start explaining something you risk robbing the initial statement of impact and turning its sharp, clearly defined edges into something fuzzy and woolly, but I guess a little more is required. Some context.

I first met Storm at a convention in Walsall in 2004. This was Novacon, which I'd been persuaded to attend by Ian Watson, who was Guest of Honour that year. I can't claim to have been dragged there kicking and screaming, but the word 'reluctant' would certainly apply. Conventions weren't my thing. I knew that with a firm conviction born of complete ignorance. I mean, this was the sort of place where everyone dresses up as wookiees and storm troopers, wasn't it?

A number of people I met that weekend were responsible for changing my mind in that regard, and chief amongst them was Storm. She dressed like a Goth queen, or perhaps a formidable witch from folklore, yet she was intelligent, warm, grounded, and endlessly patient with the convention newbie. I had read Storm's work before this, and knew her to be a fine writer, but never imagined she would become such a firm friend.

A few weeks later, I found myself at the Immanion Press Christmas party, hosted by Storm and her husband Jim, and over the next year or so our paths crossed at conventions, further Immanion parties, and other genre-related events.

It wasn't until I launched my own publishing house by accident that our friendship truly blossomed. I had no idea what I was doing. Fortunately, I knew someone who had been running an independent publisher for years.

"Storm… Help!"

Storm didn't hesitate. From that day forward, she was an intrinsic part of NewCon Press, laying out the text for pretty much every book we published from the second release, *disLocations* in

2007, all the way up to the start of 2020. To put this in perspective, Storm was busy. She had her own writing, her own editing and publishing, her own life, her own menagerie of cats to look after… but she still found time to provide help to a friend in need.

Because of our working together, we had to speak; a lot. Okay, we didn't *have* to speak as often as we actually did, but we both took pleasure in chatting about things genre-related and beyond, and if there wasn't a book in immediate need of layout, one of us would find reason to call the other about something… It's what I miss more than anything: not being able to pick up that phone and just call her.

One of my most treasured memories relating to Storm is a little thing. Not the surreal end-of-the-pier party in Brighton at World Horror Con in 2010, when the bar was free, the food was free, the live band were… interesting, and they opened up the ghost train at midnight; not the book launch and NewCon's fifth anniversary bash in the gloriously Gothic Cittie of Yorke pub in Holborn in 2011, with Liz Williams, Tanith Lee, Anne Sudworth, Ian Watson, Sarah Singelton, Kim Lakin, Eric Brown, Danni Lainton, and so many other fine folk in attendance, where guardsmen from a nearby barracks joined us in the bar for a while in full military uniform, and a man who was being chased by the police tore through the pub to hide in the gents…

No, it was a quiet moment.

The event was my 50th Birthday party, held at the social club in our Cambridgeshire village (the look on the faces of the locals as Storm, Anne, Freda Warrington and more walked through the public bar to the back room in all their finery will always stay with me). The party had largely wound down, and Helen, Storm, Freda and myself were sitting outside on one of the slatted wooden benches overlooking the cricket pitch. The sky was largely clear and the moon full: a harvest moon, and it was surrounded by a halo of glowing light at a slight remove from the moon itself – a phenomenon I'd never seen before (ice crystals, I've subsequently been assured; see what I mean about explaining things?). There was something fae about it, an ethereal sense that the moon had revealed itself this way just for us. I felt at peace in a manner I've rarely felt before, and recall thinking that I could not have shared such a profound moment in better company.

Storm was a wonderful writer.

Storm was a wonderful editor.

But above all else, Storm was a wonderful person, as the anecdotes, reminiscences, and other entries in this volume bear testament.

Storm Constantine is missed. This book goes some way to explaining why.

– Ian Whates
Cambridgeshire
September 2021

Grave's Point

Wendy Darling

We're standing on the scree that is the shore of Narragansett Bay. The stone is sculpted shale, shot through with shades of blue and purple, shimmering with salt water and what must be bits of quartz.

The wind is gusting through our hair as we both look out to sea. Gulls cry as they loft in the blue-gray sky above us. In the distance children squeal as they fly kites.

"You know what this reminds me of?" you say.

And I do know, before you say it. "Cornwall?"

"Well, not exactly, more like Wales. There's actually a city called Newport in Wales, and it's big. This is quaint."

"I'd like to go to Wales one day," I confess.

"It's not far from the Midlands. We could drive there sometime when you're visiting."

I love the ocean, not white sand beaches with azure waters, but rocky beaches like you find in Ireland, Maine, those sorts of places.

"There's a magic in the sea, the waves, the caves," you say.

I look over and your cheeks are rosy. The wind has tousled your hair even more than usual and the colorful ribbons your wear are writhing like snakes. Your eyes sparkle with the light off the water.

I think of the sea dragons you've written about. Princes and mages come to the shore to commune with the elemental powers of the sea and the ancient beasts who hold dominion there.

"I'm glad you came," I tell you.

"I've always wanted to come to New England."

Of course, you never came to Rhode Island, that beach, or New England, where I grew up. You liked reading about it, especially in the books of Alice Hoffman, but you never visited. But I know you'd like it, whether it's the rocky beaches or the hollows of New Hampshire or the Massachusetts woods with their old stone walls. Ideas would swirl in your head and later into stories, the likes of which I could only hope to write.

When I imagined writing this tribute to you, I pictured you in my mind and the visualization that came was you on the beach. My family had a week-long reunion in Newport a couple of years ago and Brenton State Park is one of the places we visited. My sister and brother-in-law brought kites and some picnic food. I tried my hand at flying a kite but failed miserably. I'd forgotten how. Eventually I wandered off down to the shore, taking pictures and collecting smooth, gray stones.

At the time, on that beach, I wasn't thinking of you specifically, but in a way, I was, because you were always in my mind, a part of me. You grew there first through your words, in books and words online, but then flowered when I met you. Your spirit filled spaces in me, guided my perceptions, and steadied me like an anchor.

The fact that you are gone doesn't feel right. We were connected, whether we were actually together or hadn't exchanged a word in months. We could always reunite like no time had passed. But now…. Now that can't happen, and multiple times a day, I think to myself how you might appreciate something or how I could ask you a question, but then realize I can't. It's like you're so close, I can see you, feel you, smell you, hear your voice, but you're still just out of reach.

Some time later we're walking through the muddy grass paths of what was once a grand estate. It burned down and the land became a park. The immaculate gardens have gone wild, rhododendrons towering, vines snaking down from oaks, strangling everything they can get a hold of.

"You know what this reminds me of?" I say, echoing your words.

"No, tell me," you say, bending down to pick up a twig covered in moss.

"The first time I visited, you and Jim took me to Stoke. There were rhododendrons the size of houses."

"Oh, I remember. I don't think I've been there since then. Seems like so long ago."

It was back in 2003, which is after all 18 years ago. "We went to such lovely places. Though to get there I had to ride in the back of the Land Rover."

The great beast of a vehicle only had room for two up front, so I had been relegated to the closed-off back. There were benches, as I recall, meant for soldiers to sit on, I suppose. A single small window gave a view out behind. No scenic ride for me, more like experiencing the roundabouts of Staffordshire in the dark.

"That old thing," you chuckle. "I wonder what's happened to it. Probably scrap."

This conversation never happened, but the visit to Stoke, the lumbering Land Rover, the roundabouts did.

That first visit was magical. Up to that point, you'd existed as someone who wrote books and stories I loved, who chatted with fans over virtual coffee and tea on Saturday mornings, and who, I'm lucky to say, had chosen me to help edit your Wraeththu Mythos, which you were then revising and reviving.

Many times, I've told people the story of how I came to be one of your editors, but I'm not sure I ever told you how very much it meant to me.

You had come to know me as a fan and then, in 2001, as someone who revived the Inception fan and art zine as a web site. In corresponding (aside: authors emailing their fans isn't exactly common), you decided to give me something for the zine: a copy of your reworked *The Enchantments of Flesh and Spirt.* Would I maybe like to read it and then give an advance preview review? Would I ever! That alone was a sign of great trust, because that book was your first novel, and besides that, I could have turned around and shared the file or spilled details. But you knew – through that intuitive nature you used for many decisions in life – that I wouldn't betray that trust, and so you gave it to me.

I ended up doing more than just read it. I marked it up, just because I was already reading it in Word and putting in comments to use in my review. I made corrections, posed questions, made some suggestions. When I was done, I'm fairly sure I sent an email gushing about it and then, feeling cheeky, attached the marked-up manuscript. Rather presumptuous, right? But a day or two later, you wrote me thanking me and saying how I was a great editor. Further, there you were asking if I could I go through the next two books you were revising, when they were ready. I was astonished! But said yes, of course.

Flash forward I suppose about six months, less than a year certainly, and we were instant-messaging when you made another bold proposal: Would I like to visit you? We had been talking about how I was either sick, or upset, or both, and you said you were going to send me long-distance Reiki. Wow, that's cool, I thought – Storm Constantine is sending me Reiki! We kept chatting and then it occurred to you that you could teach me Reiki yourself if I came over. Seriously? Done deal!

So, I got myself some airline tickets and in May 2003, landed in Birmingham. Mutual friends picked me up from the airport and brought me over to Stafford. I think we met up in the Sainsbury's parking lot, of all places. I honestly could not believe I was actually seeing you live, in person. If I blinked, you'd disappear. But no, you and Jim were real and took me to your home (in the Land Rover, naturally). We arrived and instantly I fell in love with everything around me – the house, the cats, watching the trains out the back window, endless cups of tea. And above all, I was in love with you, because you were so much more than I even imagined you would be, could be.

That week, you taught me Reiki and also introduced me to magic. I had never, ever been into that sort of thing until I stepped into the world of your books. Yes, I was imaginative, intuitive, and thought of people in terms of colors and auras, but overall, I was firmly on the side of the rational and an atheist to boot. But with you, I started to consider invisible but real energies, the power of intention, the creation of magical entities. Your living room transformed into a ritual space, with painted signs on the floor when you lifted the carpet, the coffee table becoming a ritual altar, incense burning. You weren't weird or pushy about it; you never insisted I do everything your way or enforced immutable rules. Instead, it was more like you leading by the hand down a forest path, taking me to have a look at some amazing vista or the tree of all trees.

And then there was the magical lair of your office, full of books, cats, and the computers where you wove your stories. You emailed me more manuscripts to read and sitting at a nearby computer, I read and edited. We talked. And talked. When I wasn't writing, I was curled up on the futon, press against the radiator, reading things from your library, like an encyclopedia of standing stones or the history of fairies. Periodically Jim brought in tea, snacks, and it kept us fueled. How cozy it was! How wonderful! (So much so, I never said a thing about your smoking, breathing the sooty air wasn't that dear of a price!)

We repeated this experience numerous times, as I kept visiting every year or so, but that week, when I realized you felt like an old friend, a good friend, was the most magic of all.

We're up on the old fire tower, overlooking the burnt-out carriage house, the forest and finally the ocean. There's no one else around, just a few seagulls passing overhead.

"God, I'm old," you pant, winded from the several flights of steps up to the top.

"I'm not much better," I say. "When I was a kid, I used to race up stairs like this. Back when my family would go camping in the wilderness, where outhouses and fire towers were often the only manmade structures."

"I can't picture that– you, camping. You're such a city girl."

"Oh, it's my favorite place. You on the other hand… can't picture you camping."

"Never!" you agree. "Wet and cold? No, thank you."

I love camping, hiking, and woods, deep down into my bones. You probably would too, but unlikely it's going to happen. Do people camp in England? Maybe, but it's not like camping in Canada. I do think you'd love it. Maybe if someone else rowed the canoe, carried your pack, and cooked lovely meals for you over the fire. At night you'd sleep in a black velvet tent, which admittedly would be hard to find on the way back from the outhouse, but would be pitch black. Inside there would be a feather bed. Maybe a young harish type man playing a flute while another gives you a massage. Owls would hoot, elk would call, and you'd dream of pine trees and glimmering water. Yes, that's the kind of camping you'd like.

You do like it up on that tower. We stay there quite a long time, watching the faraway waves.

I loved working with you on writing. Whether it was reading through your nearly perfect drafts, or going through the edits on my own less spectacular offers, writing was like taking a dip in the sea, a warm sea, not like Narragansett Bay. A sea with brightly colored fish and fields of underwater grass. Such wonders to be seen!

I remember the thrill of those years in the mid-2000s when I was editing the Wraeththu Histories trilogy. You'd email me a manuscript and instantly reading it would become my mission. But not on the computer; I also like to print out what I'm editing. So I'd print out a few chapters at a time on my work's heavy-duty printers, double-sided, small type, so I could edit while commuting on buses and trains. Heavy-duty staples held the pages together as I hunched over your mesmerizing, imaginary worlds, scribbling in my corrections, writing notes in the margins, putting in big check marks around sections I loved. Because I work at a university, people on the bus probably thought I was proofing someone's dissertation, when in fact I might have been reading a rather explicit sex scene between two androgynes who travel into another plane to save the universe. It was a bit of a private joke, doing that work in the mundane world.

Once I finished the paper mark-up, I'd sit down and start working on the Word file. Review tools on, start your engines! Often I'd work with the lights down low, candles lit, because it suited your writing and evoked your spirit. Because of this, I'd have to squint to read the chicken-scratch markings on the paper. But I'd persevere, adding in every correction and including lots of comments. Besides all the proofreading, comments, and questions, I'd sprinkle in gushing complements at certain descriptions, bits of dialog, prose poetry. How could I not? You always told me that most good writers are hard on themselves and underconfident. I'm not sure that applied much to you, but I liked to give you a boost anyway. You work on something so hard, so long, you deserve it.

Something else I remember about your writing is having to deal with your peculiar use of language.

First off, I had to learn the difference between American and British written English. Spelling, punctuation, turns of phrase I wasn't familiar with, and grammar I thought was wrong but which wasn't wrong at all. Probably. At times I'd leave comments saying things like: "I don't know if this is a British thing but…" Maybe in some cases I really did catch an error, but who knows.

A second peculiarity was your vocabulary. Again and again, I'd find myself puzzling over a word and finally pulling out a dictionary. Usually, I'd find that it was some word no one has used in 400 years, or which exists in the magic scene or mythology. You sprinkled them like jewels, though not to show off, but to add another dimension to your already fanciful worlds. In that you were much like Tanith Lee, who's work I also adore. Some people might find your writing overwrought, like baroque jewelry, but then some people just aren't meant for your writing.

On the other side of things is the work you'd do helping me with my own writing. Much of what you edited was stories I wrote for our Wraeththu Mythos short story anthologies. Even year or so we'd put together a collection and I'd manage to produce two stories, the fiction I'd write all year, full of trepidation, I'd send them off to you, basically hoping they didn't suck. Amazingly, you never said they did, not even in a sugar-coated "your story is… interesting…" kind of way. Every time I'd see an obvious reply in my email inbox, I'd take a breath before opening it. And you'd say you liked my work. Or loved it. Which is honestly hard to believe, but I'd take heart and go ahead and make the edits you suggested. Typically I'd accept every edit but ones where you tried to correct my American grammar (yes, it goes both ways).

There were times when it wasn't all praise, because there'd be some fundamental issue that needed fixing. A plot point, a characterization that didn't ring true, an ending that didn't stick. Your suggestions were always spot on. On one particular story, one of the last you edited before you left this world, you really pressed me. I sent in the first draft, and you liked it but there was a problem at the heart of it. One scene just did not sit right with you. I felt trepidation trying to live up to your criticism and I suppose it was justified, because when I sat down to do it, I couldn't carry it out all the way. I sent it back to you imperfect, thinking that maybe I'd done enough and you'd call it done. But no, you did the right thing and told me that I absolutely had to fix that bit. I didn't disagree, but it was hard work. I steeled myself and got it done. Naturally the story went from grade C to B (I don't flatter myself with an A) and that was down to you.

My biggest regret about the work we did is that I never finished the novels I worked on, off and on, during our friendship. One of them was a Le Guin-influenced science fiction tale that probably wasn't "up your street" (Britishism!) but which you patiently read and critiqued. The novel I have more regret over is my Wraeththu Mythos novel, which was set in the foundational, early, wild years of Wraeththu. It's about an industrial band (in an age without electricity) in the mold of Einstürzende Neubaten, with spiked hair, spiked clothes, nasty habits like drinking too much and cursing. Some of my Wraeththu stories, especially the early ones, were way too fluffy, sentimental and soft. For that novel, I endeavored to strip that out. And after several failed approaches, over I think a 15-year period, I finally hammered out five chapters that were decent. I sent them to you and immediately you encouraged me to finish. Immanion Press would publish it, of course. And yet I never finished it, not while you were alive. I have a rather all-consuming job coupled with far too many hobbies, so writing regularly didn't happen. In the month after you died, I made myself sit down night after night to work on it. When I was done, I was happy with it, but then I'd remember how I couldn't send it to you to edit. Not anymore. I wonder what you'd think of it. Hopefully a grade B. Whenever I get around to putting in the revisions several fellow fans generously carried out for me, I'll try to remember all your advice from over the years and get it to a B+.

We're back on the path again, but now it's misting and there are droplets on the rhododendron leaves. Seeing the canopy of oak leaves above us and the lightly used path, I suddenly remember a scene from one of our adventures.

"Remember that time at the castle?"

"Oh, God, how could I forget?"

Big fans of yours managed to pull together a flock of young men to form a group for a LARP. Not sure any of them had ever done a LARP before, but in any case, we all gathered in a very cold castle / hostel somewhere in central Germany. I knew German, but you and Jim didn't, and besides it was cold and none of us knew about LARPs.

"It was good we found the dining hall."

"Place to hide!"

It was a sort of recreated Medieval banquet hall. The food options were limited to I think bratwurst, French fries, beer and mead, but it was enough. A couple of the Wraeththu LARPers snuck away and sat with us.

We ended up exploring the woods behind the castle which, in classic fashion, was up on a mountain overlooking a village. I'm not sure I've ever been in such a – by German standards – wild forest in that country. We went out there to perform some magical ritual, the details of which I forget. One of the Wraeththu boys had sage on him and we burned it while we all touched the ground. There were some serious old spirits down below and not altogether wholesome – or so the Wraeththu boy and my friend Caleb said. We withdrew back into the banquet hall to drink.

"That was a weird few days," I say

"I didn't know it would be like that."

"I had pictured something totally different."

"Like food!"

There was a scandalous lack of food (outside of the banquet hall) and to reach the town you had to descend (and return on) treacherous stone steps. In the snow. Because it was the last couple of days in December.

"You know my place barely had heating," I reminded you. "And the showers were ice cold." Which was why I'd been so grateful you and Jim let me use your shower. The suite you two had in the castle was nice. Appropriately I was the one sort of camping.

"We've been to some strange places today."

"New York City, that gaming con near Bonn—"

"Again, not at all what I expected."

"The best time was Dragon Con though."

2004, when you, Jim and a whole gaggle of British goths flew to Atlanta so we could run our own little track at one of the biggest multimedia geek fan conventions in the world.

"That was fab," you agree.

At last, we make it to the old carriage house. The great home it belonged to was either demolished or burned down or both. The carriage house is slowly disintegrating. The misting has become rain and so we weave our way through fencing and sneak inside. The floor is wet, puddles forming from the rain coming through the broken roof. There are no windows or doors, only archways, and it feels like it's teeming with ghosts. I think of Cobweb, who, in one of your stories, haunts Forever, bound to the house and the land, for decade upon decade.

You are probably lingering around certain places yourself. For one, your house in Stafford. For another, Cannock Chase. And, cheesy though it is, you will always linger in my heart. Dear, dear, Storm.

Home

Fiona McGavin

I have heard it said that home is not a place but is the person who will always take you in no matter you've done. I was hoping this to be true when I turned up on Raehazel's doorstep half dead from my own poisons, with whoever was after me not far behind in the woods.

For a moment I thought it was not the right place. A ruined house stood amongst the pines, roof crumbling, broken windows and ivy smothering walls and windows alike. A garden of feral cabbages and dead hogweeds. *There's no one here,* I thought, *he's gone if he was ever here at all.* But then I spotted the hellebores growing round the door, their winter blooms dying as spring came in. Amongst the ivy there were bare vines of black briony and bittersweet, a few shrivelled berries still clinging to the bare stems: a poison garden lovingly planted for me. I touched the wooden charm hanging round my neck and it felt warm, almost alive. Most definitely, this was the place.

I glanced back to the trees. They were still and silent, but I knew it would not be long before hara and their horses came out of them looking for me. A bird trilled to break the silence. It was not a joyful sound, but mournful and full of longing. I walked through the overgrown garden to the house. As I did so, a feeling of utter sadness and dejection came over me. *Something happened here*, I thought, *something very sad and wrong.* I even turned to leave before I remembered not all wards and warnings are about fear and violence. There are other more subtle ways to keep strangers out.

I was not a stranger. If my charm was right, this was the place. This was where Raehazel was hiding out. This was safety, at least for the time being. I rose my hand and knocked and then leaned back against the wall as a wave of sickness passed over me. If I'd got the dosage right – and I always did – I had maybe an hour before things started to get very bad and very painful. If I was wrong about this place, then…

I knocked again. Something rustled in the trees and I whirled round but it was only a cat, a striped, yellow-eyed thing that stared at me with contempt before slinking off into the trees. When I turned back round, the door was open and Raehazel was standing there, as yellow-eyed and contemptuous as the cat.

"Oh," he said," there you are." As if I'd just popped out for milk for our morning tea.

He hadn't changed. He was as tall and austere as ever. He wore black and grey. His ashen hair was tied back with a simple leather band. All the same, I felt a falling feeling open up inside me at the sight of him.

The trees rustled again. This time it was a huge, brown bird taking flight. Raehazel watched it with more interest than he did me.

"Can I come in?" I asked.

He leaned forward and sniffed the air around me, a slight, puzzled frown creasing his forehead. "You're sick," he said.

I shook my head. "I need an antidote, that's all."

"What have you taken?"

"A mixture: amber-star, bloodshade and greywicke."

He rose one eyebrow in exactly the infuriating way I remembered. "Why would you do that?"

"Can I come in?" I asked again. "I'm tired. I need to sit down."

He stood aside to let me pass. Inside, it was cleaner than the outside suggested. There was not a lot of furniture, no nick-nacks or keepsakes. Everything was grey: grey-washed walls, grey flagstones, shelves of books with neat grey spines with silver writing on them. It felt safe. It was how I'd always imagined death to be: safe and calm, but dull. A place for waiting but not for living.

"Do you have an antidote?" I asked. Somewhere there must be a room full of bottles and jars, leaves and berries hanging in bunches from the rafters, crystals forming in test-tubes and glass beakers.

"I can make you something." he said. "Tell me why you've poisoned yourself. If you want to die, you know a hundred faster and more painless ways to do it."

I walked past him into a sparse kitchen. There was a big table and on it a teapot and a single china cup. The faded pattern of roses painted round its rim was the only colour in the house. Apart from me: I was tattered and yet resplendent in my usual purple, indigo and silver. I sat down in one of the chairs at the table.

"I don't want to die, that's the point," I said. "There are some people after me. I've got this." I took a vial of crystal-clear liquid from my pocket and showed him. "This would kill me instantly, but I figured if they caught up with me, I'd be too busy running, or pleading for my life or being thrown in chains to take it. So, I took something that works more slowly as insurance in case I didn't make it here. I've got an hour left, I think, and they're about half an hour behind me, so you'd better get busy with the antidote."

He leaned on the door post and studied me through those strange eyes. Raehazel, the Prophet, we called him when he came wandering out of the desert all those years ago when the world was falling apart, and no one was sure if it could be put back together again. Those times when some hara became legends.

"Who is after you?" he asked. "What have you done? More to the point, where have you been? You went out one morning to get the newspaper and never came back like a cliché from a romantic novel." For the first time there was a hint of something in his voice, but I couldn't tell if it was pain, sorrow or just curiosity. I was hoping for pain or sorrow. "I waited for you," he continued, "I had other things to do and other places to be, but I waited for you instead."

"I know," I said, "and I'm sorry." I wasn't sorry, not really. I was about to say more when something spasmed inside me and for a moment it felt as if someone was stabbing me over and over again in my chest. I bit my sleeve to keep from crying out and waited for it to pass. If he didn't get the antidote soon, it was going to get a lot worse.

"Who's after you?" he asked again.

"I don't know." I gritted my teeth against the pain. "Mojags, probably. Possibly Gelaming."

"Gelaming?" he stared at me. "What have you done, Liss?"

I closed my eyes against another wave of pain that left me shaking and sweating in its aftermath. "Nothing. Can you just make the antidote and then we'll talk? I promise you."

He nodded briefly. "Very well. Stay here and if you're going to be sick, don't make a mess."

He left me alone while he went to mix the antidote. I laid myself out on the tabletop like a corpse for the undertaker. I closed my eyes and tried to drift with the pain, to accept it and draw strength and power from it. I'm good at that when the pain belongs to someone else. Not so good, it turns out, when the pain is my own.

Old memories flickered behind my eyes as I lay there waiting. I saw him striding out of the desert with his staff and his grey robes flapping about him. He strode straight into our camp without any fear, shouting for water for his pack-horse, and if he knew anything of who we were and our reputation, he showed no sign of it. We didn't know what he was. Kakkahaar, we thought at first, but he wasn't one of them. He wasn't Varr or Unneah and he most certainly was not one of us: Uigenna. He just was. Some hara were born to be great. You know their names: Thiede, Ponclast, Wraxilan, Pellaz and so on and on. He should have been a Heinama, a politician, a war lord or even the Tigron of Immanion himself. Thiede wanted him. He sent Gelaming on their strange horses to fetch him but Raehazel didn't go with them as he was supposed to. He didn't go because the Gelaming only wanted him. They didn't want me. They looked at me as if I was nothing to them, worthless. A vile, crawling snake that wove magic from poison and pain. He wanted to go with Thiede but he didn't. I'd won, but for a long time, I indulged myself in petty little fantasies of going to Immanion and poisoning the water supply. I could have woven such monsters from the energy their screaming and agony cast into the air.

Another memory: another kitchen years later. It was the kitchen in our old house in the city of Nightshade in Garridan. I came in from my workshop and found Raehazel talking in the kitchen to a har with white clothes and a blazing coronet of red hair. Gelaming, I knew that at once and I knew his name too: Thiede. You didn't have to be formally introduced to know who he was. They weren't just talking, they were laughing like old friends, the kind who could be apart for decades – centuries – but still pick up their friendship again as if they'd never been apart. There was a bottle of red wine open, and they were drunk. I stood in the doorway thinking that Raehazel never let himself get drunk. He rarely drank anything more than the smallest glass of wine and left me to get drunk and silly on the rest of the bottle. I had thought I was the only one who could make him laugh with such joy and abandon.

"Who's this?" Thiede asked.

"Liss," Raehazel said. "Liss-am-Carr."

Thiede looked at me for a moment, weighing me up and finding me wanting. "You can do better," he said and turned his back on me.

"I know." Raehazel said softly, and I don't suppose he meant for me to hear. That's the reason why two days later I went out to buy a newspaper and then just kept on walking.

There are two kinds of poison: the quick poison that kills you instantly and forever; and the other slow poison that gradually eats away at you and everyone around you, until there's nothing left of you except the feeling of never being good enough, strong enough, beautiful enough, clever enough. If it doesn't kill you, it scours you empty. I have learned that empty is as good a place as any to be.

The antidote tasted of dirt and soil and worse. I choked as I swallowed it and had to bite my sleeve again to stop it coming straight back up. The actual poison had tasted sweet because I'd mixed it with honeyed milk before I drank it. There's a message there, I'm sure.

While I waited for it to take effect, Raehazel washed up the teapot and teacup and began chopping vegetables. The striped cat sauntered in and he fed it raw meat from the ice-box. The cat ate and went back outside again with an arrogant swagger in its step.

There were voices outside and I sat up abruptly, my head spinning. Raehazel smiled and put his finger to his lips. Through the window, which I realised was not broken on the inside as it appeared outside, I saw hara ride out of the woods and across the ruined garden towards the house. At first, I thought they were Mojags and breathed a sigh of relief but then I saw other hara amongst them. I glanced at Raehazel. He was drying his hands as if nothing out of the ordinary was happening.

The hara walked round the house. They looked in the windows, but they didn't see us.

"I don't like it here." one of them said. "It feels wrong."

"Not wrong. Just sad."

"There's no one here. Hasn't been anyone here for centuries."

"Why does it feel so sad and strange here?"

One of the Gelaming spoke. "Because generations of humans lived here once. Farmed here, lived off the forest, were happy here and now they're gone forever."

"His trail ends here," their tracker said. "He must be somewhere around."

They went to the door. "Liss-am-Carr, are you in there? There's nowhere to hide." But I could tell their hearts weren't in it. They just saw the ruin and felt the sadness. Raehazel's wards were strong enough to fool even the Gelaming. Those waiting in the vegetable patch were stooped with sadness. One of them wiped his eyes with his hand. They walked around for a bit longer calling my name, telling me to come out because they weren't going to hurt me, I'd done nothing wrong, they just wanted to talk to me. Raehazel looked at me and rose one eyebrow again.

"He's not here," someone said. "He must have gone into the trees. He can't be far. Let's get out of here. It's too depressing to bear."

Then they were gone, back into the trees following a faint animal trail until they were out of sight. I looked at Raehazel and grinned. 'That's powerful magic,' I said.

Raehazel nodded. "The sorcery of sorrow. What a pair we are: a sorcerer of sorrow and a sorcerer of pain."

I was feeling much better. A little shaky and weak but the pain was gone and I realised I was ravenous. I wondered if he was cooking enough for two or if he'd just make dinner for himself and leave me to fend for myself.

"What have you done?" he asked. "Who did you kill that's important enough to get Mojags and Gelaming after you?"

"No one." I said. "Well, lots of hara, but none of them are the reason why they're after me. I was in Fallsend minding my own business – you know me, Rae, I'm a bit player, a minor character in someone else's story and I like it that way."

He hid a smile. "Do you? Do you really?"

"I do. I sold some poison to someone who was of interest to the Gelaming: another one like me who Thiede doesn't think is good enough for his sparkling white towers. It was a sleeping draught, that's all. I was careful with the dose and no one died. A day later someone told me friends of the Mojags he'd given it to were after revenge and there were other strangers in town asking questions about me, so I thought it best to make myself scarce."

Raehazel nodded. "Why do you think the Gelaming want you?"

I grinned. "Why wouldn't they? Once I've cleaned myself up, you'll see how magnificent I am."

"Be serious."

"I don't know. To put me in a cage and display me in the marketplace as a warning to others? Look at the wicked Uigenna, poke him with a stick until he bites."

"Maybe," Raehazel said, "or maybe they knew you'd lead them to me."

"Well, they were right for all that they were too stupid to see it when they got here."

Raehazel nodded and turned back to his chopping board. I watched him move. He could make something as ordinary as slicing carrots into an art form: simple, elegant and beautiful.

"You should rest." he said. "There's a room upstairs. Some of your old things are there. I took them with me when I left Garridan. I imagine the clothes will still fit you. I'll call you when dinner is ready."

I stood up. "Thank you."

"Oh," he said casually, "and you should probably know that I don't live alone."

There was no sign of anyone else in the house but there was little enough evidence that Raehazel lived here so I supposed it stood to reason that whoever his companion was would be equally austere. I opened my mouth to ask who he lived with, but a wave of tiredness swept over me and I decided to leave it. I'd either ask him after I'd rested, or I'd meet his companion at dinner. It was none of my business anyway.

Upstairs, I found a small room with a window that looked out on the forest. The trees were close enough to tap at the windowpane and the big, brown bird I'd seen earlier was sitting on a branch staring in at me. It was a kite or perhaps an eagle of some sort. Whatever it was, it was unsettling. I closed the curtains so it couldn't see me anymore. There was a narrow bed with a grey and white striped blanket on it. Hanging from the hook on the back of the door was a purple shirt I remembered as one of my favourites from a long time ago. I found more of my old clothes and a pouch full of my old rings, necklaces and bangles neatly packed in a wooden chest. I'd been like a magpie in the old days, collecting shiny things. Now, the only jewellery I had was the simple wooden charm I wore on a leather thong round my neck. Raehazel had made it for me and given it to me one birthday.

"I know you prefer jewels," he said, "but this has its own magic. It will always draw you home."

I undressed and crawled under the blanket and my last thoughts before sleep took me were to wonder what Raehazel was doing out here in the middle of nowhere, who was he hiding from and who did he live with if he didn't live alone?

When I woke it was pitch dark and long past dinner. I'd been dreaming of Fallsend and the quiet life I'd led there. It was a pleasant dream – the kind of dream you know has no meaning and no point. For a moment I lay in the darkness and listened to the trees tapping at the glass. The house creaked and settled around me and a vixen screamed at her mate in the woods.

Another sound: the faint sigh of breath, a soft rustling of cloth from the corner nearest the door. I sat up and groped for the light. I expected to find Raehazel standing in the darkness but the har who stood there was not someone I knew. He was slender with a pointed, elfin face. His clothes were dark and close fitting. He was not exactly beautiful but there was something arresting about him. He smiled and an arrow of pure sadness lanced straight through me.

"Who are you?" I asked.

He didn't answer but stepped towards me. His feet made no sound on the bare floorboards. Sorrow leaked from his skin and seeped into mine. I wanted to bury my face in the pillow and weep, but I didn't know why.

"You don't remember me?" he said. "I don't suppose you would. No one does."

I shook my head. I considered getting out of bed and going to find Raehazel. Something was wrong here and I didn't like it and I didn't see how it was anything to do with me. I was leaving soon and Raehazel and this strange har could carry on with whatever their relationship entailed.

"I'm sorry. If we've met before, I don't remember."

"Oh, we never met," he said, "but all the same, you had quite an effect on my life. A very adverse effect, you could say." He laughed to himself. "Did you even meet my father?"

"Your father?"

"Ponclast."

I shook my head, "No."

"Ah, so he sent an intermediary instead."

"Your father?" I said again. I tried to remember the history. Ponclast was the leader of the Varrs and he had had a son who'd betrayed him and died. I'd mixed poison for the Varrs on several occasions in those early years. Once, a high ranking Varr had come to me. He was very attractive in a Varrish sort of way, all black leather and silver trimmings. He'd given me a piece of paper with someone's age, height and weight written on it and asked for something particularly nasty, something corrosive and bespoke. I had rather enjoyed making it. I hadn't asked any questions. Why would I? It was none of my business.

"Gahrazel," he said. "My name is – was – Gahrazel."

"You're dead?"

He grinned. "Well, of course I am. The great poisoner, Liss-am-Carr – his elixirs never fail to hit the mark, do they?"

I leaned back against the headboard and studied him. He moved a little closer and I could smell him: lemons and leaves and cigarettes. He smelled young and alive. I wondered if this was part of the spell of sadness that hung around this place and stopped anyone from lingering, but I thought not. Raehazel did not live alone: he lived with a ghost.

"Are you going to apologise?" Gahrazel asked. "Make excuses? Are you going to tell me you were just doing your job and it wasn't your place to ask questions?"

I shook my head. "No, though that's true."

"How much did they pay you?" he asked. He reached for the pouch of jewellery and tipped it out onto the floor. The jewels and metal glittered dully in the lamplight. "Is this what my life was worth? Pretty things? Trinkets?"

"What do you want me to say?" I asked. "I sold them poison and you died. It's what I do. I don't feel guilty about it. I don't care about it. I don't lie about caring about it either. What are you doing here? Are you and Raehazel having some kind of strange love affair? I don't know how that would work, but if it does, then good luck to you. You're not here for me. It's just coincidence that your death and my life have this tenuous link. You're here because of Raehazel. What do you want with him?"

A smile flickered across his face making him look fey and mischievous and another wave of sadness washed over me. In life he would have burned with energy and enthusiasm and ideas. People would have loved him for his kindness, compassion, and high ideals. I would have despised him, but all the same he didn't deserve to have died so young, before he'd had a chance to be anything except Ponclast's traitorous son. The world was cruel, and I was part of that cruelty. Regret mixed with the sadness and for a moment, I felt myself falling into it, before I recognised the trickery and swam back up to the surface again.

"You have a cold, dead heart, Liss-am-Carr," he said and laughed and just like that he was gone.

Needless to say, I did not sleep well after that and I kept the light on. Just before dawn, the vixen started screaming again although this time I was not sure it was a fox. There were words in the scream although I could not make them out. After that, I gave up any pretence of trying to sleep and got up. I dressed myself in some of my old finery: soft leather trousers, purple shirt, a scarf stitched with silver threads wound round my neck, enough bangles and bracelets to reach from wrist to elbow. I jangled and glittered and felt more like my old self.

I padded downstairs and helped myself to some bread and cheese. The cat appeared and I poured milk into a saucer for it, but it just glared at me and stalked away. I wandered out of the kitchen and along the corridor and found the workshop. Raehazel had replicated my old workshop from back in Nightshade. It was neat, tidy and clean. There were shelves from floor to ceiling full of bottles, jars, and boxes, arranged alphabetically and neatly labelled. Other shelves held glass beakers, test-tubes, crucibles, and other paraphernalia. There was a bookcase packed with volumes of mathematical and chemical formulae. A framed chart marked the passage of the moon and stars across the heavens. I stood and stared. He had made this for me because he knew I'd return to him one day. I touched the wooden charm at my neck and it vibrated beneath my fingers. All this for me, for the hope that I'd come home. My cold, dead heart twinged with the longing to mix something – anything. I'd had to leave most of my supplies behind when I fled Fallsend and I missed them. Wolfsbane and belladonna were as much a part of me as anything had ever been.

"There you are," Raehazel said behind me.

I smiled. "You know me. Always drawn to the poisons."

"Not all poisons," Raehazel said, "there is a lot here that heals."

"Everything's a poison if you have too much of it."

"Very true. I trust you slept well."

"Not exactly. I met your companion. Your ghost."

Raehazel frowned. "And who exactly did you see?"

"Gahrazel. Ponclast's son. Apparently, a poison I made killed him."

Raehazel nodded to himself. "Trust Thiede. The games he plays with people."

"What do you mean?"

"I don't see Gahrazel. Why would I? His death was tragic and terrible, but it has no connection to me. I see something else."

I sat down on one of the high, wooden stools at the workbench. "What do you mean?"

"Thiede sends them. They are Thiede in some way. Elements of him."

"You mean what I saw last night wasn't really Gahrazel?"

"It might have been him," Raehazel said. "Thiede can probably talk to the dead. He probably plays with them the same way he plays with the rest of us. What matters is what it made you feel. What it makes you do."

"Nothing." I said defiantly, "It made me feel nothing. It changed nothing."

Raehazel smiled slightly. "But don't you see? You could choose to feel something – guilt, grief, resentment, anger – but you push them away. That you choose nothing is a choice in itself."

I looked away. "That sounds like Gelaming hokum to me. Who do you see?"

"You," he said, "I see you. Or something that looks like you, always walking away from me into the trees. Going nowhere, just out of reach. It's a kind of torture."

"I'm not dead."

"You don't have to be dead to be a ghost."

I didn't know what to say to that. I looked away from him to the shelves of potions and poisons and cures. "What does he want from you?" I asked. "Why are you important to him?"

"Because he doesn't give up. The others who were important to him, he's gotten one way of another: the Tigron and the Hegemony, safe in their ivory towers in Immanion. Orien died, he destroyed Vaysh. He tamed the Varrs, scattered the other northern tribes into nothing. He controls everyone else. Me? I got away. I ran. I didn't play the game. First of all, I vanished into the desert and when I emerged, he found me holed up with some snake-eyed poisoner who could weave magic out of pain, and he didn't like that at all.

You think you're the only one he wants to put in a cage? A gilded cage for me, but a cage all the same."

I frowned, thinking about it. "But why wouldn't you go to him?" I asked. "Why wouldn't you go to Immanion? White towers and luxury and power? All those interesting hara to talk and plan with? Doing something good?"

He didn't meet my eyes. "In the beginning I didn't go because I wasn't sure I believed what he was doing was right. Later, when I knew it was, I didn't go because he only wanted me. Because he didn't want you."

He left the room then. I stayed in the workshop letting the strange energies from the bottles and jars seep into my skin and veins. It felt as if they were recharging me. I heard him moving about in the house and knew he was hiding there from Thiede, doing nothing except waiting for me. And now I was here… what now?

I touched the wooden charm hanging at my neck and a jolt of electricity passed up my arm. *Home,* I thought, *the person who always takes you back no matter what you've done to them.*

We didn't talk of it. Of course, we didn't. Neither of us was the type to talk much of love or hate or feelings. Raehazel had already given too much of himself, and I'd given nothing. The balance between us was all wrong.

Instead, Raehazel made lunch and opened a bottle of wine and we talked of old days and old friends, things we'd done and times when we'd been happy together. The dreams we'd once had and the life we might have lived if one of us had been a better person. He drank only one small glass of wine and I had the rest of the bottle and became quite drunk. I began telling him of a poison I thought I could make that would pass from person to person like the old human plagues from centuries ago and he laughed and said no wonder the Gelaming were after me. He told me the first time he'd seen me moving my arms and weaving dragons, he thought I was making them from thin air. He hadn't realised I was weaving them from the screams of the prisoners in the Uigenna torture chambers. He said he had never seen anything as beautiful as those dragons that flared into life and then disintegrated into ribbons of coloured light a few moments later. I stuck a fork in my arm and made him a tiny dragon of pain that lived and died in the blink of an eye. He laughed and I was glad I could still make him laugh.

I went to bed drunk. I thought he would join me, but he didn't. He was always able to control himself and I knew he went to bed happy, believing that now I was home, there was plenty of time.

I slept fitfully and woke three times in the darkness.

The first time I woke up, Gahrazel was there again. I told him to go away and he did.

The second time I awoke, Thiede was there. He was magnificent, beyond beautiful: tanned skin, white clothes, all that red hair to get tied up in. Arrogance and power leaked out of him.

"Snake," he said, "little monster."

I let the insult wash over me. I knew what I was, and I'd never pretended to be anything else. The way I saw it, there was nothing wrong with me. It was everyone else who was at fault because they were not like me. I was sure Thiede felt the same way about himself, just on a bigger scale.

"Things have changed in Immanion and it won't be long before the waves ripple out." he said, "I'm going away."

"Going? Where?"

He waved a hand vaguely. "Just away. Around. More than ever, we heed hara like Raehazel and more than ever, we don't need hara like you. We have our shadow part in Immanion now. There's no point to you. You should let Raehazel go."

I looked at him and I wasn't sure how much of him was real and how much something I'd made up to help me do what I knew I had to do.

"I mean to." I said.

He smiled. It was like being bathed in golden light. I could have basked in it and I supposed the hara in Immanion luxuriated in his approval like fat, happy house-cats. I might be feral, but I had claws like razors, and I was free.

"The first time I saw you," he said, "long before you knew anything about me and you were just some Uigenna brat with some very nasty power lying latent inside you, I thought: there's somehar who might be a worthy opponent for me one day. I was wrong. You've been nothing but a disappointment to me."

I stood up. I was almost as tall as he was. "You had your opponents. Your Terzians and Ponclasts. They played your game, didn't they? They moved around on your gaming board and you loved it. Me, I just sold some poison to someone and something that was already set in motion moved a little further along. I'm a minor character in your great story and that's all I'll ever be. I refuse to be anything more. *You* don't matter to me."

The third time I awoke, I was weeping: great, body shaking sobs that tore through my body and left me aching and drained. I knew what I had to do. I took the wooden charm from round my neck and let my tears soak into it until the pale wood turned dark. I drew out the pain of having to leave Raehazel again and wove the sorrow and despair of my empty soul into the charm and made it into a thing of power.

I left a note on the kitchen table telling Raehazel to go to Immanion as he should have done decades ago. In the workshop, I helped myself to several bottles and vials of the deadliest elixirs. Before I set off to continue my life as an itinerant poisoner, I put the charm on the workbench so that he'd find it there and wear it round his neck, and always be able to find me no matter what glory awaited him in Immanion. So that he'd always find his way back home.

Everything under the Moon
Memories of Storm Constantine

Freda Warrington

Someone is trying to tunnel under the door. I can hear the *scritch scritch* of claws plucking at the carpet. My watch says it's 6 am; I only made it to bed two hours ago. I try to ignore the noise but it's impossible. One of us has to give in, and it's not going to be the clawed one. It's her house, after all.

I get up and open the door. In comes one of Storm's cats, giving me a 'How dare you lock me out?' glare. Another follows. I leave the door ajar so they can come in and out as they please; I'll get no rest otherwise. My head hurts. I slip downstairs for a mug of tea and a couple of painkillers. Then I slide back into the comfy sofa bed in Storm's study and soon I'm dozing with a couple of cats snuggled alongside.

It hasn't taken long to discover that Storm is practically nocturnal. What we did the night before I'm not sure, but it will have involved friends, wine, and gin, maybe a film, or music, dancing and laughing, perhaps a solstice ritual or a party at someone else's house: sometimes all of the above. Or just Storm and I talking about everything under the moon until the early hours. I tend to wilt and head for bed at 4 am, which I'm sure she regards as a lamentably early night.

I'm awake again by 10 so there's nothing for it but to get dressed and choose a book from her extensive esoteric library. I curl up and read until she's awake; I feel tired yet cocooned by the warm, creative energies of the house, the smell of incense. Occasionally she starts the day with a burst of vacuuming – that's my cue to make the bed back into a sofa and tidy up! We go downstairs and have more tea, with delicious boiled eggs and buttered bread. (We both love eggs). Our conversation is low-key, with some eye-rolling and amusement at nonsense in the newspaper. Then more tea, which we take back up to the study. Sometimes we have topics of intrigue (or gossip) to share; other times she'll sit and answer her emails, or do a little work, while I slump contentedly and read as much as I can of the fascinating book I've 'borrowed'. And we talk writing, publishing, the universe and everything.

Later, one or several of her friends will drop round. Some I know, some are new to me. My own tendency is hermit-like, so I'm fascinated by the flowing group of friends she attracts. All different, all creative in their own ways; in art and music, academia, writing and magic, film-making, sculpting, baking, psychic research, you name it. Storm is the centre. She's interested in everyone who shares her passions, and her interests, both esoteric and far-ranging.

When I eventually head home, I'm generally tired, covered in cat hair, slightly hungover but wildly inspired by her creative energy. There's work to do, stories to tell.

I first meet Storm on 31st October 1987 at Novacon 17, a friendly science fiction convention held in Birmingham, UK. She's very striking: tall, dressed head to foot in skin-tight black shiny stuff, with serious boots and masses of black, white-streaked hair. In the bar, she's surrounded by similarly alternative friends and looks terrifying. Someone's told me she's a writer so of course I want to speak to her, but I'm too intimidated. I'm 5'0" and dressed boringly in something from 'Next' – surely she won't want to associate with someone so dull.

However, a friend assures me she is lovely, and introduces us. And she's right, Storm is lovely. She's friendly, chatty, as fascinated to hear about my work as I am about hers. Over the weekend we talk a lot. We buy each other's books, and I discover the mystical, absorbing world of her most enduring creation: the Wraeththu.

Turns out we have more in common than it appears on the surface. We're the same age (give or take 3 months). We're at the same stage in our careers, being both newly published in the good old days when our respective publishers are enthusiastic about us and our books to come. We're fairly rare, being females in a sea of male authors. We do panels and signings together. We both love writing fantasy, the weird and wonderful stuff of our imaginations.

Over the next handful of years, we meet regularly at conventions, book signings, special events. I'm relieved to learn it's fine to dress in an alternative fashion for cons; no need to look 'smart' for editors! She invites me to her house, where I become a regular visitor and get to know some of her many friends.

What is Storm like? Well, we're all unique, but some are blessed with extra-special charisma. She's warm, magnetic, both interesting and *interested*; she welcomes all kinds of possibilities, all kinds of folk from rock bands to writers, artists, pagans, filmmakers. She engages with creative people and forms collaborations. While I tend to recoil from such endeavours (like many writers, I tend to be shy and solitary), she makes things happen. She's complex, multi-faceted, full of energy – it's difficult to sum her up easily. She loves to party, she loves to talk and to listen. No wonder like-minded people are drawn to her warm, bohemian spirit.

It's true she can appear intimidating; it's her armour as much as her style, because like many of us she has a shy, vulnerable side. As published authors, we have to be 'out there' to an extent, and dressing dramatically (as I find out for myself) tends to command respect and fend off potential inappropriate behaviour from strangers. Storm doesn't suffer fools: at least, not for long.

Yet she has no airs and graces. She loves a laugh, and is the first to laugh at herself too. Sometimes I have Alan Partridge moments – saying the most cringe-worthy thing at the worst possible time – that make me want to crawl under a stone. So to learn that Storm is just as capable of putting her foot in it is brilliant! When she lampoons herself with a mixture of mortification and self-deprecating humour over some embarrassing exchange, I warm to her even more. She's intelligent, fun and witty, with a wicked sense of humour. We laugh a lot – dare I say cackle? – and there's nothing better than an explosion of laughter from her to lift the spirits.

When I need advice, Storm reads my Tarot with spooky accuracy. Sometimes the cards say things I don't want to hear, but she's always right, darn it!

Although friendly, she employs cat-like caution in fully trusting people. She guards her inner privacy fiercely. And that's wise, of course. We go through a lot together, yet it's several years before I feel a change, an increasing closeness; perhaps I'm the one who holds back, not her, but time allows her to see me as reliable, trustworthy, more than a fellow writer. I think we only once nearly fall out over a misunderstanding, but we talk it through and we're in swift agreement: our friendship is infinitely more important than anything that might try to fracture it.

It's January 2021. A message pops up on my Facebook page with the worst news possible: her friend Lou tells me gently that Storm is seriously ill, and not expected to last more than a couple of days.

What?

How could I have not known? I'm in such shock that I bring my husband Mike upstairs to read the message and make sure it's real. Then I collapse. I cry for the rest of the day, and on and off for the days following. I can't stop. I just don't know what to do. I send a garbled but heartfelt reply to Lou, who deserves all the hearts, hugs and love I can muster, because she was one of three who have been caring for Storm throughout her illness.

What are you supposed to do when you learn a beloved friend is dying? I know this isn't about me; it's about Storm, her devoted husband Jim and her two devoted friends, Lou and Danni, who nursed her. During Covid, they formed a bubble; no visits were possible. Would it even have helped her, or me, to visit in such a heart-rending situation? I'll never know. I doubt it would have helped to have me crying all over her. She wants her illness kept secret for now. So I sit frozen, hoping she knows how much I love her and maybe feels the healing light I send with all my strength; hoping she's not in pain, hoping she feels surrounded by a cocoon of complete love with her husband and friends.

But everything inside me feels ripped in half. This morning, a surprise gift arrived; a pink topaz ring set in silver. I like sparkly things, as Storm does. Normally, a new gemstone lifts the heart, but there's no pleasure in it today. Mike says gently, 'It can be your "remembering Storm" ring.' Not that I need help remembering her, but I wear it as I write this. A small connection. Symbols carry meanings that have an emotional force.

I still can't understand how I didn't know she was ill. After doing a lot of work together in 2018, there's been a lull, no pressing reason to keep in touch; I'm always mindful of how busy she is. Scrolling back through her Facebook page reveals nothing, except that she was busy writing and publishing as normal. And then there is Covid, of course. I keep meaning to message her and see how she is… perhaps it's better that I don't. Perhaps it's too hard for her to tell anyone outside her immediate circle. The last thing I send her is lots of love for her birthday, and she sees and 'likes' it. Surely she knows how much I love her. I cling to that.

Two days after Lou's message, Storm is gone. Peacefully, with her beloved soul-mate Jim at her bedside.

As our writing careers move in rough parallel, we have many ups and downs with our respective publishers. There's so much to talk about, and the mutual moaning is so therapeutic! Sometimes she's up when I'm down, and vice versa: do we ever feel a touch of rivalry? I honestly don't think so. I've learned sobering lessons from others about the utter pointlessness of jealousy, and I certainly don't indulge in competitiveness or envy any more – but that aside, we've moved so much in tandem. When I hear that a certain editor won't look at her new work because her 'sales aren't strong enough' – excuse me, what?! – I feel furious on her behalf. When we're both taken on by the same publisher for their new list, we celebrate together. And when the same publisher later dumps the whole fantasy list (including us), we're there to console each other.

So many conventions and signing tours, book launches, outings and parties. She has many other things going on too; a powerful fascination with Earth Mysteries and Angels, Egyptian magic, Reiki, the pre-Raphaelites and much more, all of which feeds into her writing. She certainly lives her life to the full. One time she tells me that her aim is to live with 'maximum pleasure, minimum pain', and that's a philosophy I appreciate.

I spoke of increased trust. This comes to fruition when she includes me, to a modest extent, in her Reiki and pathworking/visionary journeys. She recommends Mike and me to a friend in Glastonbury for initiation into Level One. Later, now a Reiki master in her own right, Storm invites me to join her at Lou's house for Level Two initiation by her and Lou. The experience is incredible. The energies that whirl around us that evening are beyond description. I'm tingling with light and warmth. As we work with symbols and touch and visualisations, the room is completely alive with energy. Was this something supernatural, or the sheer excitement and dynamism of three friends working in harmony? I suspect the latter, but that doesn't make it less powerful. It's absolutely real.

In 1997, Storm and I form 'The Unholy Trinity' with another close author friend, Sue Bentley. Strength in numbers; we hope that three of us will prove more enticing to the media than one. And we do secure a slot in a BBC magazine programme, 'The Eleventh Hour', which sees us being filmed running down the corridors of Stafford castle and talking, by candlelight, about how our 'hobby' (writing) had become our 'full-time work' (writing). This being the BBC (no advertising permitted) we aren't actually allowed to mention our books! So it's unlikely the project achieves much for us, but wow, we had a lot of fun.

As the years pass, we continue to have our individual ups and downs with publishers; they try to push us into more commercial moulds, which is never comfortable. Then there is the 'revolving door' of editors; when your editor leaves, their replacement wants to start afresh, so they feel no loyalty to the existing stable of authors. First our queries go unanswered, then they admit they're not interested in seeing anything new from us, then our particular 'list' is cancelled and we're swept out with the rubbish. If we're lucky (as I have been, at least five times) another publisher will value our work enough to scoop us up for new books. I'm not sure how many times this happens to Storm, but I do know she reaches a point of scorching fury with the mainstream publishing industry. She's had enough of being messed about with broken promises, falling advances, soul-crushing indifference.

So how does she react? Does she give up? Take to drinking and bemoaning the unfairness of it all? No – well, admittedly there is a fair bit of that between us. But then she picks herself up in typically fierce Storm fashion: she sticks two fingers up to the big publishers and sets up her own publishing house, Immanion Press. Immanion begins as a way to reissue her own back list, but expands to publish other authors too, both new and established, and also produces a successful non-fiction occult line.

Storm has written a massive quantity of stories and books, both fiction and non-fiction. Mainly she will be remembered for her stunning creation of the Wraeththu; a new breed of hermaphrodite human that arises from the ashes of *homo sapiens*. This world is an extraordinary blend of science fiction and fantasy; near-future speculation that's down-to-earth, brutal, magical, sensual and captivating. How do you create a brand new civilisation from the ground up? The Wraeththu novels and stories provide one of the most imaginative answers ever. When her characters need gods, they invent their own, much as their human ancestors must have done. When they need magic, they build their own system (which you can learn from the supplementary texts Storm has written). The magic and the gods become real as they are fed by the collective Wraeththu consciousness.

It's hugely important here to note her long-standing creative encouragement of other authors. She taught creative writing. In the 90s, with friends, she set up *Visionary Tongue* as a showcase for new fantasy fiction (I was delighted to be one of the editors). When she noted that many of her fans were writing Wraeththu fan fiction, she did not behave like some well-known authors (who shall be nameless) who tried to shut down this activity; on the contrary, she began publishing anthologies, again with the help of friends, encouraging and guiding these writers, acting as quality control and editor. Imagine the thrill of being noticed by, and working with, your favourite author! Immanion Press gave her the freedom to do this. The freedom, without some editor tutting and telling her, 'No, you can't do that', to jump back into her beloved Wraeththu universe. The freedom to edit and publish unfairly neglected works by established writers; to publish (with consent and cooperation, naturally) anything she likes.

One of the hardest things that ever happened to us was the death of Tanith Lee. Tanith was a brilliant and prolific author of fantastical imagination. She wrote nearly a hundred novels and hundreds of short stories; she had been an early inspiration for Storm, me, and countless other writers. Yet she, too, had struggled. Her sales weren't 'strong' enough; editors, forever under pressure to procure big sellers, had turned their backs on her.

Immanion Press (and other small presses) worked closely with Tanith to reissue her out-of-print work, and to publish the new stories that still flowed from her. Like Storm, Tanith appeared intimidating from a distance; but like Storm, she turned out to be just as warm, friendly, and encouraging to other authors. Many younger fantasy authors came under her wing. To me, she was a legend who became a friend; people loved her.

So when news surfaces that she is ill, there is shock. We hope beyond hope that maybe she can recover. But no; a few months later, in May 2015, Tanith passes on. True to her legend, she is writing and editing almost up to the very end.

Storm gathers together several writers whom Tanith had considered her 'nieces'. We want to pay her a fitting tribute, which takes the shape of an anthology, *Night's Nieces.* A collection of memories, photographs, poems and new stories centred on Tanith Lee's legacy. My story has two lost girls who are fixated on her novel *The Storm Lord*, and even an apparition of Tanith as a guiding light out of the dreadful life situation they were in. The stories we write are each so important. Something to focus on, to feel as if we are *doing something*. At the 2016 Eastercon, we hold a 'remembering Tanith' panel to a packed audience, and smaller gatherings to celebrate her life and work.

Much of my work and communication with Storm over 2015 to 2019 is centred on Tanith. Storm is busy reissuing her work; she ropes me in to write an introduction to the second book of the *Blood Opera Sequence* (*Dark Dance*, *Personal Darkness* and *Darkness I*), and to provide appropriately eerie illustrations for two of the trilogy.

Losing Tanith was so hard. Working with Storm (and others) to remember her helps us all. It helps us beyond words.

Because Storm is such a creative whirlwind, she involves me and her many friends in more amazing events than I can remember. One major highlight is Grissecon, a Wraeththu convention she hosts in 2003. But the pinnacle of everything comes in 2016 with the epic celebration of her 60th birthday. A stunning mansion in Wales, Trevor Hall, is booked for the weekend; it takes spreadsheets to work out which bedroom or suite will accommodate nearly thirty guests! A medieval-style dining hall hosts our nights of feasting. Storm's friends work their socks off to provide food, a well-stocked gin bar, home comforts, plenty of fun and the most astounding birthday cake I've ever seen. It's breath-taking to see so many good friends I haven't seen for months or even years, to meet new people too. So much hugging and talking, laughing and gin-tasting! During the day, we explore the gorgeous Welsh countryside and the grounds of Trevor Hall. In the evenings – we party. We pose for a thousand photographs, a thousand wonderful memories.

Afterwards, I dream about that weekend. I start writing a story about it (still unfinished). It was one of those magical occasions that simply lives in the memory forever.

It never crosses my mind that Storm won't be with us to celebrate her 65th in similar style.

Our work on the Tanith Lee books leads to me admitting that my poor old computer is 12 years old and I really need a new one.

Storm, a keen online gamer, leaps to the challenge with enthusiasm. Don't bother with high street computer shops, she tells me; do what I do, and have this company custom-build a new one for you with all the specifications you need! Naturally I obey; she is wise. She's positively excited for me as I run the specs past her, and past the chaps who are building it. Soon I have a shiny new PC with multi-colour LED lights and all the RAM and processor speed I could desire. Thank you, dearest Storm. What can I do, but name my machine after you?

While we're in the middle of this, we get into one of our publisher-moans; although I still have a mainstream publisher, the war between creativity and commercialism rages on, worse than ever if anything. I'm losing my creative mojo. After a 'long dark teatime of the soul', I've decided to write what I want to write, rather than put all my chips on a year of unpaid work in the hopes some editor will like or loathe it. Storm answers with this message that I'll always treasure:

"It was great to hear you talk about all the sequels for your books you could write. Go, Freda, go! :) Don't look on it as 'no one will want them', but more as 'I'll do better with these if I start my own publishing house' – because that's the truth, anyway. You can design the books to be beautiful, do the covers yourself, as well as put whatever you want into the stories. No more 'helpful suggestions' from agents! And you know, you're right in facing the fact that now we have to pay attention to our legacy and get it out there, because we're not kids any more. That's exactly how I felt about it, and it contributed hugely to me feeling happy and confident about doing it all myself. Just think of all those poor sods still clawing at the doors of big publishers, weeping and lamenting and being ignored. We, on the other hand, are bold entrepreneurs, with the ultimate freedom to do as we like. :)

I really look forward to seeing a story from you for the weird landscapes too."

One crucial thing about Storm is that she's Always There, like a rock. Her own writing, and running Immanion, mean that she spends much of her time in her study; like me, she admits to becoming more 'hermit-like' with maturity, and she loves her home. It's positively rare that she's not at the end of the phone, or quick to answer email. While I'm mindful not to bug her too often just wanting to talk, the truth is that she is rarely too busy for a chat with friends/ fellow authors/ editors/ publishers. We're a network now, beneath the 'radar' of trad publishing, but growing in strength.

So it remains unreal and unbelievable that she's no longer just a phone call away. Often something happens and I think, 'Storm will love that! … Oh.' There's that sense of falling, of missing a step.

Covid prevents us attending her funeral. It's beyond heart-breaking, but to be there and not be able to hug her loved ones, many of whom are my friends too – that would be unbearable. I can't imagine how they all feel – especially those who were with her all the time in her last months of illness. At the appointed time, I shut myself in the bedroom with a memory book of photos from Trevor Hall, a special pendant made for me by my crystal-healer friend, and the pink topaz ring on my finger. I talk to Storm in my head. I think about her friends (our friends), sending warm waves of love to surround them. I cry, I anoint the topaz and the pendant with my tears. I don't know what it all means.

I miss her so much. I can't believe she's gone. We were meant to grow old together! It doesn't seem real, and never will.

The story mentioned above, about weird landscapes, was for a new anthology she edited called *Shadows on the Hillside* (Newcon Press). As ever, I was thrilled to be asked. I didn't dream, at the time, that it would be her last anthology, and the last time I'd ever work with her. No one else involved could believe it either, but what a beautiful project on which to bow out.

I often dream of Storm. We're exploring a spooky old castle, or we're hugging and hugging because we haven't seen each other for so long, or she's trying to stir up some hilarious mischief with her friends. She's always very *Storm* in these dreams.

But my first dream about her, soon after her death, is my most treasured. We're in her house, facing each other across the dining table. She's smiling, laughing at me in a puzzled way; completely bemused that I ever thought she was gone. It was a misunderstanding! Everything's fine. Life is back to normal.

The dream is comforting.

I start reading one of her books on Reiki healing, *Sekhem Heka*, and I can hear her voice, feel her passion for the subject and her light surrounding me. Of course she's still here, in our hearts and souls and memories, in her writing, in her uniquely beautiful way of looking at the world. And as much as we mourn her leaving us too early, that's the price we pay for having known her. To spare myself all the tears and pain, would I rather we'd never met? Of course not. Storm is a radiant soul who changes everything she touches; to have been friends with her for so many years is a privilege and a blessing.

Storm, I'm worried that what I've written here still doesn't do you justice. Is it too little, too much? I don't know, but I've done my best. Once, when we talked about death and the possibility of an afterlife, you said, 'I think people go to the heaven they believe in'. RIP, my beautiful friend; wait for us and one day we'll all dance again under some otherworldly full moon.

End

Silence in the House of Moths

Liz Williams

The House of Birds is never silent; the House of Lions rings with the voices of priestesses, raised in the day-long chants. But the House of Moths is always quiet, filled as it is with the wings of ghosts. Here, children are sent away the day after their births in case they shatter the peace with their cries. When they return, years later when they are grown, they are muzzled for a time, until they learn.

I was one of those children. They did not have to muzzle me for long. Some stories tell of a child who returns to the place of her birth and finds it alien and strange, who does not fit in, who is not understood by those around her. This is not my story. I was an obedient child and grew up into a girl who did what she was told: not because I was cowed or frightened, or because I had no opinions of my own, but simply because my real life was inside my head and there I have always been free, no matter how many chores I had to do in the temple where I spent my early years, or how many hours spent in contemplation of the divine. In the hush of the temple room, where the long rows of girls knelt, bowed forwards with their heads resting on blocks of sacred cedar, the goddess with her lions frowning down upon us, I could do what I liked and go where I pleased. If the goddess knew, she did not punish me. I was certain that the priestesses did not: they held me up as an example to the others and considered me a model student. I think they would have liked to keep me and I would not have minded staying, there in Cybele's house, but the House of Moths required me back again, and so I went.

I was happy in the House of Moths, just as I had been happy in the temple. I had a role, as Second Sister. My eldest sibling Tosay ran the household and allotted tasks to me: embroidering clothes, at which I was good, and preparing food, to which I applied myself with diligence. I also found myself spending a lot of time in the garden, working alongside the ancient gardener, Menred, a woman who had been gardener there since before my own birth. My sister made it plain to me that there would be no chance of my having to

marry and I greeted this pronouncement with relief.
Thus I was content and remained so until the arrival of Suleine.

For Suleine stole my silence.

*

During the first few days of her arrival, I was happy. Suleine was a distant cousin, the daughter of an aunt who had been sent to one of the Dark Sea towns, in marriage to one of the many petty kings who rule that region. I had seen a painting of the town, in the great hall of the House of Moths, depicting a sweep of snow-capped mountains racing down into the sea, with a tiny castellated town crouched between them. It looked precarious, as though the mountains were pausing for a moment, but would then rush on, carrying the town into the waves. I felt sorry for my aunt, and for Suleine. Then, a year after I had come back to the House of Moths, we had word that my aunt had died and her husband, deeming Suleine unsuitable for the marriage market, asked if she could come to us. My elder sister, hospitable and kind, said that she could.

The day of her arrival was hot, the garden steaming after an early morning rainstorm. Droplets fell from the long trumpets of the lilies and the birdsong was hushed, as if in awe.

"The Dark Sea towns are cold, at least in winter," my sister said. "Do you think she will find it too warm?"

"Perhaps if we close the shutters in her room?" I said. "And place a bowl of ice water in it, to cool the air? Even if you are used to the heat, that's never unpleasant."

"Aretrie, that's an excellent suggestion. Could you do those things, while I wait for her carriage?"

I ran down to the kitchen and found a block of ice in the ice store. I struck it with a hammer and it shattered into a hundred glittering fragments, diamonds on the stone flags. Scraping these up, I took a bowl upstairs, then found a jug and filled it. I was about to close the shutters, casting the black-panelled room into dimness, when movement caught my eye.

This room looked out over the city. I could see the dome of the Rose Temple, catching the hard noon light like a great pink pearl. The rooftops fell away, ochre, sand, tawny, fawn, with the occasional splash of rust red tiles, imported across the Inner Sea.

From the bedroom, I could see down a side street to the Grand Avenue and down it, a curtained carriage was coming, drawn by two speckled deer. I could hear the patter of their hooves on the cobbles. For a moment, a face peeped out from the depths of the carriage, moon-round, moon-pale. Then the carriage was drawing up at the gates of the House of Moths. I ran downstairs to greet Suleine.

She was very quiet and meek, a short girl, very stout, with her hair confined in a black spangled net, as woman wear it in the Dark Sea towns. A crystal droplet, reminding me of lilies and rain, hung quivering from it as she alighted from the carriage.

"How pretty," I said, nudging my sister.

"It's a sign she's unwed," said Tosay. "Once they're married, they put a garnet one on the net instead. And when they're widowed, one of jasper."

"Why jasper?" I asked, as the coachman carried Suleine's luggage up the steps.

"It's brown, like the earth into which a body is placed."

It seemed very logical to me. But Suleine's droplet was rainy-clear and it sparkled in the light as she smiled. She looked sweet, it seemed to me. Her smile was shy.

"Welcome," my sister said, and spoke the ritual words of greeting to someone who has never visited before. I echoed them, sounding small and hushed against the distant sounds from the Grand Avenue. Perhaps Suleine thought I was shy, too, for we smiled at one another and said no more. Then Tosay led her inside and the coachman carried her bags up the stairs. We left her alone to settle in, and told her that the noonday meal would be served when the waterclock struck.

"She seems modest and presentable," Tosay said, once we were out of earshot. "Frankly, I was fearing some little madam, all frills and finery and tossing her head. 'Unsuitable for wedlock' can take many forms."

"She gave me a good impression," I agreed.

Over the meal, that impression was secured. This was a speaking day. Suleine spoke when spoken to, proved informative and in fact quite interesting on the subject of the Dark Sea Towns, talked affectionately of her late mother, our aunt, and did not criticise her father, although she would have perhaps been justified in doing so.

"You will have a week to accustom yourself to the House of

Moths," Tosay said. "You will find us quiet, even a little earnest. We have our weekly rites and rituals, in which you will be expected to take part, but our main celebratory cycle, dedicated to Cybele's shadow twin Cymere, is held in the winter. We thus have some months to prepare."

"I understand. I would like to familiarise myself with the rites, since I am to remain here. Besides, I am myself devout. At home we were dedicated to the service of Shtari, but I know a little of Cymere from my mother."

"Of course, she would have told you. But it is seemly that she did not worship one goddess in the household of another. I will give you a set of prayer books and texts."

Suleine thanked her and that was dinner over. She spent the afternoon in her room, but dined with us all in the great hall that evening. By the end of the week, it was as though she had always been with us. She was modest, kind, unassuming. Everyone in the household liked her. I was among them. I would not say that she and I became friends, for I valued my own company too much and we even had a conversation in which, she told me, she was the same.

"My father is overbearing. He told me what to think all the time, and so did my brothers. When my mother died, it grew worse. There was no peace, no peace at all."

I reached out and took her hand, in silence. We gripped each other's fingers for a moment, although some texts do not approve of affectionate touch. But I do not think we regretted it. There was no sensuality in this, only solidarity.

Tosay and I had decided that our next big project must be the sheets. We had many beds in the household, and the sheets were old, dating from my grandmother's day. We had turned them, back to back, and they were good Khemish cotton, but now they were wearing thin. So Tosay sent a servant to the market to make enquiries and at length new sheets were delivered: a big day for the household. Some were white, like snow, and some a pale ivory colour, like an old summer moon. We admired them as they lay draped across the dining room table.

"This is your job," Tosay told me.

"I know. I have ordered new silks. It only remains what manner of design you would prefer: leaves, perhaps, or coral fronds? The woods, or the seas?"

Tosay considered this and we agreed on a compromise, since I liked sea and she liked gardens, and the shadowy woods which fringed the city on the landward side. Half and half, and everyone could choose which set they preferred. The embroidering would take several weeks and I was looking forward to it. We had set up a table for me in the cool of the verandah, overlooking the gardens; I planned to begin early in the mornings, before the heat of the day took the house in its grip.

It was in undertaking tasks such as these that I could truly enjoy my silence. The cast of characters in my head took free rein: I journeyed across the Dark Sea to the steppelands beyond, or went south to Khem and its ancient ruins. I had a company of lovers, friends, beloved companions who had been with me since I was a young girl. I did not know if others had such an inner landscape: it would be childish to ask and would make me seem foolish. As with so many other things, I kept this to myself.

But on the second morning, when I had been sewing for no more than an hour, I found that my silence was absent. I looked up from the embroidery. The garden was loud with birdsong, the doves squabbling on the roof, the rush of swallows' wings in and out of the eaves, a peacock's harsh cry. The high walls, and the magic which played about them, usually kept out the noises of the city but now I could hear all of it: the cries of street vendors, the rumbling wheels of carts, voices raised in anger and argument.

How could anyone work in peace with all this racket going on?

I gritted my teeth and set my hands to the sewing and my mind to my latest adventure, in which I and the man I loved, who does not exist in this world, were setting sail to the Scarlet Isles to reclaim his heritage. But his face, usually so vivid to my inner eye, seemed curiously indistinct, and the sense of the ship, which on previous days had been so strong – the salt wash, the taste of the sea on my mind's tongue, the hiss of the sails and the screams of the gulls – were replaced by the sounds of the mundane world. I flung down my sewing and went back indoors.

During the afternoon siesta, I was, to my relief, able to recapture some of my inner realm. Yet something was not quite right. With some illnesses, one can lose a measure of taste and smell, and this is what had befallen my imagination now: it lacked savour and tang, images only, as if a transparent wall had been placed between my inner people and myself. I could not ask counsel of anyone; they would have thought me mad.

Instead, I went looking, though I did not know what I was looking for. I roamed the House of Moths, restless, seeking, all down its shadowy corridors, shuttered against the heat of the day. I found no answers until I came to the shrine room. Here, I paused at the door for the ritual bow and this stopped me from barging in regardless of who else might be there. So I was able to see my cousin Suleine, crouched like a child before the altar and the smoky image of the goddess, her forehead touching the floor.

An altogether laudable thing to do, but all at once I knew who had stolen my inner quiet. I could feel it inside her, like one of the soap bubbles that small children make with a pot of water. It glistened and shimmered around her, and in it I could see forms. She, like I, was daydreaming. But she, unlike I, was free to do so.

I could not confront her. Did she know? Was there some limited capacity, some household store of dreams which, like sugar in a jar, could be used up if too many spoons dipped into it? I could not believe that this was a deliberate act, unless Suleine was more wicked than I thought her to be.

We were all silent at dinner that night: it was a day for unspeaking. This time, the silence weighed heavily upon me.

And that night, too, I lay sleepless. My inner worlds, a comfort to me in the small dark hours, were no longer available: I saw them as one sees a castle on a distant hill, a little shining image and as inaccessible. Restless at dawn, I had reached the conclusion that perhaps Suleine needed this capacity more than I, that her difficult girlhood had rendered her more in need of the aid of dreams and that the goddess had taken my sugar to give to her in her greater requirement.

When the sun crept in, however, I felt that this was stupid. Thoughts were not sugar, or flour, or anything finite, but a vast realm: after all, the dreams of night were not subject to rationing. Were they?

That night would see the new moon, hence the unspeaking. I resolved to go to the shrine myself, when dusk fell and the call rang out across the city to welcome her. I would petition the goddess then.

In the meantime, there was the day to crawl through. We were relieved of ordinary duties, so I did not have my stitches to remind me of what I had lost, and had to devote the day to cleaning the house to see the new moon in. I met Suleine with our hair tied up in turbans and our hands carrying mops and brooms and buckets. We smiled at one another and were set to cleaning the hall, which we did peaceably. From her manner, her helpfulness and gentleness, I could not see her as some sorceress who had purloined my dreams: this had to be some other cause.

I thought it would be hard to wait for twilight but the day passed quickly enough. This was also a fasting day: the next meal would be served in the morning. This always made me light headed but perhaps that was not a bad thing – it brought one closer to the spirit world, the priestesses said. When the cleaning was done and the final day rite had been said, the shutters opened and the shrine room emptied, I crept back to it. The calls were sounding out and when I looked out of the windows, I saw the crescent moon low above the roofs and turrets, hanging like a rim of gleam in the evening sky. I spoke my prayer to her as much as to Cymere.

When I rose from the floor, I saw that Suleine had entered the shrine room. She came to me and took my hand, squeezing it. Her eyes were full of regret. She made a formal bow, to the goddess and then, strangely, to me, her hands clasped in the gesture of farewell. She put her finger to her lips but I did not know why, since this was an unspeaking day already. Then she sat down on the nearest bench, facing Cymere. I took a step back, uncomfortable and intending to go, but she put out a hand to stay me.

So stay I did, and watched as she gazed unblinking at the goddess. As it grew darker, and the moon's curve grew brighter, so the light around Suleine began to grow, too, until she sat in a pool of pale fire. Squinting against it, I saw a black spot inside the glow, a square, opening suddenly like a window. Through it, I saw the Dark Sea coast, the snowy pine-clad hills running down to the sea. A young woman was standing on a headland, her fair hair in a golden net, a quiver of arrows on her back. She held a bow in one hand and she stretched the other out to Suleine. My cousin took it and the girl pulled her through the window and into the day. She glanced back once and raised her hand, as I raised mine. Then all the light in the room was sucked through the window, like oil down a funnel, and disappeared. Suleine was gone. A crystal droplet tinkled to the floor and lay still. I watched it for a moment, but it remained transparent. It did not darken to jasper.

In an emergency, we are allowed to speak. But it took an awful lot of explanation. I did not want to give away the secret of my dreams; I had not come across anything in the sacred texts which forbade them, but I intuitively knew that they would not be approved of. The priestesses placed a wafer on my tongue, which made it impossible for me to lie, but I told them only what I had seen and since it was the truth, it was accepted. Eventually Tosay and the priestesses decided that, since Suleine had been deemed unsuitable for marriage, that the virgin goddesses had claimed her for their own, that the girl I had seen was one of the Dark Coast deities, the Virgin Huntress, perhaps. There was a sensation for a week or two, and a series of letters to the Dark Sea coast, but Suleine's father had already written her off and although there might have been a question of honour all the same, the priestesses' counsel laid waste to any scandal.

Now, a month later, I sit and sew. My inner world has returned; perhaps the energy that Suleine needed to make her escape has now come back into balance. And with each stitch, I take a step further into my own inner land, have adventures, choose love. I have returned, so far, yet sometimes I see my cousin, in a castle on a hill, tiny as a miniature. She is always laughing. Someday, perhaps, I shall go and visit her.

END

Whistling in the Dark

For Storm, with love and gratitude.

Louise Coquio

I think I am waiting for a sign. Perhaps the answering flicker of a candle in a darkened room, or maybe a fluttering magpie feather twirling its way down to land at my feet when I walk, as I do most days, thinking of her.

As I start working on this piece, it is Lammas in a few days. Storm loved this time of year. She relished the way that the land seemed to lie watchful, causing back-of-the-neck prickles and the sudden, unwanted awareness that everything seemed somehow too still, the land almost sentient. Two years ago, we celebrated Lammas together at dusk in a cornfield, sprawled in the hollows made by the stags who often slept there in the weeks building up to the rut on nearby Cannock Chase. There is a photograph of her taken on that day, looking happy and content, glad to be out in the countryside in the sultry heat. This festival of the first harvest was always important to her, falling as it did, at the same time as the Dog Days and the inundation of the River Nile in Egypt. She had been drawn to this period when working on many of the Egyptian rituals she had devised. As I began writing, and thought of how different this year's Lammas ritual would be without her, it occurred to me that if ever there would be a sign from her, surely it would be now?

We told each other ghost stories, Storm and I. Often we retold the same ones, delighting in the spine shivers and wide-eyed nervousness they conjured within us. Once, closer to the beginning of our friendship, as we told some of our best stories while sat around her kitchen table, over tired and over caffeinated at 3 a.m., we convinced ourselves of an oppressive presence with us in the room. The atmosphere shifted so that we became simultaneously terrified that the light above us was about to blink out and leave us in the sort of unnatural darkness that would have tipped us over from delicious nervousness to out and out hysteria. We decamped to the living room then and laughed at ourselves (in the reassuring glow of every table lamp and available candle) but I think that we spent the following 25 years seeking to repeat the exact same feelings, the thrill and excitement of that particular type of fear, often in our conversations, but also in our various creative endeavours.

Now that she is gone I sense (Imagine? Wish? Will?) her everywhere I go, but most especially here, at Shugborough Hall. Today, during what has become my regular hour of ensuring that I retain my sanity by walking in its parkland and gardens, I sat on 'her bench' and thought of her. It is a wood and metal bench, unremarkable, long enough to seat three people and framed by a trellis of climbing roses and, in its season, dramatic, purple clematis. It is placed to allow a view of the long-abandoned tennis court, since reclaimed by nature, but once used by the photographer, Patrick Lichfield, whose home Shugborough once was. Here, Storm told me, as a wayward teenager, she would roam the grounds with her friends, smoking and drinking in the gardens as dusk fell. On one such evening she had seen Princess Margaret playing tennis here. Back then it was a party house, filled with celebrities and gossip, full of life. When we wandered the grounds together, Storm often lamented the loss of these events and their secrets, as the house was handed over to the National Trust. She felt that Shugborough, and other places like it, had become too sanitised and lost a little of their soul. She wrote about the place a few times. It became the inspiration for parts of Forever, her Wraeththu mansion that echoed with the memories of times gone by, in her story *A Tour of the House*. Storm loved the place and the stories it held within its walls. It was as if she could hear the voices of its ghosts. I admired her ability to find such a rich well of inspiration when she visited properties like it. Stories seemed to find her amongst these old country estates, and of course she would then be compelled to tell them.

Now I come and remember her here. It seems to me that, in the absence of anywhere better to reflect, it is as if she is all around me; on the oak throne where once she posed for photos, in the jewelled flash of blue of the kingfisher on the lake, here by the tennis court, surrounded by the dark, watchful yews that stand guard at the cat monument. Even in the tearoom, as I wait for my coffee to be made, I often think of how passionately she loved coming out here for treats, cakes, ice-cream…she had the sweetest tooth of anyone I'd ever known.

I first met Storm in 1989, the year that I turned 21. My lovely friend Jamie introduced me to her work by lending me the first two Wraeththu novels. I fell in love with them so deeply that I immediately harboured naïve plans about writing a screenplay based on *Enchantments*. Storm humoured me beautifully about this when I finally met her a few months later. It turned out that we lived not at other ends of the country, or even the town, but just a few streets apart from each other. I learned that she worked at the local library, where she horrified some of my mother's more conservative friends with her exotic appearance. When I introduced myself to her, she was gracious and welcoming, inviting me to her home on Ingestre road. Here she lived with a collection of similarly bohemian lodgers and a cluster of adored cats. It seemed such a glamourous place to me – I was entranced by everything; her collection of enormous ceramic cats, the ancient leather bible that she used as a doorstop, the black dragon teapot with its spined tail handle and its mismatched lid topped with the glued-on head of a Jesus statue.

Storm offered to teach Jamie and I to read the tarot cards. She was a natural teacher and taught us to seek out our own meanings within the symbolism and to unearth the story that the pictures told. She read the cards as a writer would, allowing a tale to emerge and pinning it down for the person seeking answers. She was an intuitive and perceptive tarot reader. She wasn't interested in the mundane surface but would instead excavate for the truth beneath. Self-knowledge was her intention for herself and for those around her. As a witch, an occultist, and a Reiki Master, seeking it underpinned everything she did.

She had a quiet wisdom about her. This, and her desire to bring people together, made her the sun around which most of us circuited. In the late 80's and the 90's she was often out in the town, holding court and drawing an ever-widening circle of people into her orbit. In her kitchen, once she had moved to a bigger, but still bohemian house, she kept a typed list of all the different ways her friends took their teas and coffees pinned to the wall. Inclusion on this list served the dual purpose of making all her friends feel flattered that they were important and, ingeniously, ensuring that they were just as capable of making everyone's drinks as she was. Storm really didn't like performing the drearier hostess duties, although of course her home was the hub where everyone gathered and gravitated. She loved to fill it with people - every weekend her living room was crammed with people drinking and dancing. The air would be thick with the smoke of incense and cigarettes. There was always someone asleep on the sofas and floors after such a night.

At the core of her life were her girlfriends. They really were her chosen family; a small, close-knit group of interesting women who met weekly to drink, dance, laugh, cry and often to cast circles, make magic and discover themselves in the process. Life-long friendships were forged at her weekly girl's nights. Such times were taken very seriously; all of us dressed up in our finery and armed with terrifying quantities of alcohol. They were special times with special people. I think we knew it even then. We are lucky to still be able to meet and reminisce about some of the more infamous events from these times.

Storm was a generous artist who loved to work collaboratively and share her work with others. Many of her friends worked with her in some capacity or other. Although I was lucky enough to work with her on a few different projects, it was Wraeththu that captured my heart. I spent hours, over the years, discussing her work with her. I was honoured to be trusted to read early drafts, to contribute opinions and ideas, or just to provide a shoulder to cry on when the words were proving elusive. To be able to do this, as the fan that I am, has been nothing short of miraculous. It delighted Storm to know how loved her characters were, and she was just as inspired by the work of Wraeththu's fans as they had been by her. She really valued working collectively on the Wraeththu anthologies. Some of her most enduring creative collaborations stemmed from these collections. Some of the writers from these projects have contributed to this book – their pieces are beautiful tributes. Storm would have loved reading them.

Storm and I practised magic together, on and off, for 25 years and, for most of that time, we marked out the passage of time together by celebrating the eight seasonal festivals of the Wheel of the Year. In the early years these festivals could be large and raucous affairs. Samhain, in particular, was always a real *event*, with many different friends, drinking and dancing, or even occasionally, fire-breathing. Sometimes we gathered around bonfires in back gardens, sometimes out in the ancient oak woodlands of Cannock Chase and sometimes in the flickering firelight of our living rooms. Eventually a core group emerged; Storm referred to us as her Wyrd Sisters; these were the women who first began performing rituals to Bast and later Sekhmet. They were truly magical times, not least because of the sense of sisterhood they enabled. After every rite we would raise a toast to each other: *I drink to my sisters*. These words will always be powerful.

Like sisters, we sometimes bickered and fell out. There was a period of a few years when we didn't celebrate together at all as our lives took us in different directions but, for the last few years, we had each rediscovered our love of these rituals and of experiencing them together. The group became much smaller, but somehow even more important, as the years went on. Now, we who are left carry on, as Storm asked us to, without her. We mark these familiar festivals with her words, and there is such comfort in this practise. When the circle is cast, it is as if she is close, only just beyond the veil.

Storm knew more than most that words have power. She knew that stories could be used to interpret the world around us, that they could help clarify and make sense of life. She wrote voraciously. She was disciplined and driven, as if the words just had to find their way onto the page. She used to begin a new novel on New Year's Day – feeling that it was important to set her creative intention for the coming year. Even during her arduous chemotherapy sessions, she researched and wrote new Egyptian rituals for us to try out. She was inspired despite her illness. It is hard to accept that her life was cut short before she had the chance to spin the tales that she still had within her.

Her work is an impressive legacy - she wrote so many stories, novels and non-fiction books that delighted her readers and fans. Many of her characters are so vividly drawn that they live on for us: It is as if Pell and Cal still wander the wide avenues of Immanion, or Cobweb haunts the darkest corners of the gardens at Forever. Storm herself can be found within the pages of these books; they are so much a part of her. I am glad that I can pick one up and hear her voice amongst the pages.

It is the other kind of stories that I will miss the most though. The ones that she shared with us late at night, over gin or wine, amongst a cloud of smoke or by the light of candles. These are the stories that live on amongst all of us who are left behind. We tell and retell them. We share them with each other. We laugh and cry, we find comfort in them. Our friendships go on now without her. They evolve into different relationships as time goes on, often stronger and even more important because of the loss that unifies us. None of us forget that Storm sowed the seeds of these friendships. It is our privilege to maintain them. We will remember her this way. I think she would approve.

As I finish writing, the season has turned. When I walked today, I saw this year's pumpkin crop growing in the walled garden - it is not long until Samhain. This year, when the veil is at its thinnest, I will light a flame inside a Jack O'Lantern, place it in my window and think of last year, when we celebrated together for the last time. I feel that Dolores is right in her piece for this book, and that Storm has already embarked on her next big adventure. Still, I'll raise a glass to her and watch that candle flame very carefully. I'll hope that perhaps, one day, she will send me a sign.

Storm Tribute

John Kaiine

Storm and Tanith should have met decades before they finally did. They first bumped corsets in Dublin at an Octocon in 2004. Instant connection. To my memory, they only met twice, but many, many hours and hours of phone calls happened after. They were good for one another. Writing, cats, magic, all of the endless possibilities were talked about and shared. Some recipes too. Also, the state of UK publishing and how badly it treated its authors, either new or Old Guard. Storm was one of the new Old Guard and respected by the likes of Michael Moorcock and Harry Harrison. When Tanith had difficulty in getting published, Storm leapt in and championed her, telling her *'I'd happily publish your shopping lists.'* There really was that much love. One of the many books that Immanion published of Tanith's was Legenda Maris, an anthology of her sea stories. Storm always insisted that *'there was something of the sea about Tanith.'* So, I have chosen this story to swim alongside of them both.

The Sea Was in Her Eyes

Tanith Lee

Day by day the great ship swung across the ocean. She was rigged so full she seemed to carry the clouds above her decks. At first, the passengers had looked up, wondering, at these. Then they looked down and about, and most of them saw the young woman, for she was the only human female thing aboard.

"She's a fine-looking girl, she is so," they said. Her hair was brown and piled up heavily on her head.

She was slender and green-eyed. Her clothes were good, but more than those, they noted three ruby rings on her fingers and the long rope of pearls, nearly long as she was tall, that she wore at night to dinner in the saloon.

"She's alone. Such a girl should have some company," said they.

They generously tried to give her company then, the older men and the younger men, the sailors and the passengers both. She was quiet and graceful with them all, but they slid from her surface as fishes slip through water.

"It's a pity she is a tease," they said.

"She's plain as dough," they said, "despite her rubies and pearls."

"She has emeralds for eyes and a cold green heart."

The sea was wide as the sky, but now and then a bit of land appeared, the thin strip of a coast. Here passengers got off and new passengers walked on. At one land-strip, which had an edging of mountains, a young man stepped aboard, with six brass-bound boxes and a chest, and two servants, two white horses and two black dogs, and an owl that would sit on his arm. His hair was dark and his skin fair. He was handsome, too, and like everything else, his looks came aboard with him.

Half the day he would sit reading, and the other half playing the piano in the saloon. He was rich. A prince, they said.

"Prince Cuzarion," they said, bowing to him. And they tried to win his money off him at cards, or by means of bets and wagers, inviting him to race his dogs against other dogs on board, or to set the owl on some passing gull. But they never won a penny, and the dogs did not race, and the owl never chased the gull.

Sometimes the passengers would tell stories in the saloon after the dinner.

One night the prince, if so he was, told a marvellous and clever story, about a prince who, on a voyage, was carried down into the deep by a mermaid, where he lived with her some while—she having, by then, taught him how to breathe under the sea.

"Is that what you'd like, then?" they asked.

"I am already betrothed,"' said Prince Cuzarion. "Although perhaps I might not mind it, for a month or so."

All this while, the girl had sat in her usual corner, drinking her glass of wine, the rubies burning on her white hands and the pearls weeping down her dress.

Maybe some of them had noticed she would often glance at the prince. Maybe some of them had even seen her gaze at him very long.

So now, one of the other men said to her, "Well, my lady, what do you think of mermaids?"

Although she was so young, she was never discomposed. And now she spoke calmly and clearly, with neither arrogance or shyness.

"I think that they exist," she said, "but they are not as you imagine, being a cruel race, who like to eat men raw and sometimes alive, spitting out the bones to make flutes."

This shocked everyone. The idea itself, and that this young girl should speak of it. So they said no more to her. But Prince Cuzarion, he flipped her one look. It was probably only the second he had ever given her, for she had not taken his fancy, though perhaps he had taken hers.

That night a storm came up out of the sea, boiling and black. It put out the stars and smashed the plate of the moon. That done, it scanned about for something to harm, but though the land was not far off, it did not want the land. Then, it saw a ship dancing along, rigged with clouds, and with lights shining from the port-holes and in the lanterns, and under the howl of the wind fluttered the notes of a piano.

"I'll have you," said the storm, and flung itself forward, kicking the waves from its path.

When the storm hit the vessel buffeting blows, the ship's world went to pieces. Lights and wine glasses and coffee-pots flew one way, and with them the chairs and boxes, and the piano even. And all the passengers. Then everything went another way

There was a great yelling and praying. From the depths of the ship the pair of horses neighed, and above, dogs barked. But in the ship's seams the rats looked philosophically about, for they always knew things might end in tears, and tonight it would be the tears of the sea.

None saw, or if they did they paid no heed, to the slight young girl with her hair blown from its pins, standing on the upper deck, and staring over at the churning waves.

Then the ship split from one end of herself to the other, and everything spilled out into the sea.

That moment, the girl jumped over the side. And if any had spied her, they would have seen she was naked as a knife, but for her ruby rings and the rope of pearls, and her long brown hair.

Cuzarion—and he was a prince—had a great many accomplishments. He had matchlessly waltzed in glittering ballrooms, and faultlessly fought on foot and on horseback; he could play the piano better than most. But swim he could not.

So now, as the cold black water closed over him, he thought with wrathful despair of all he would miss and gave himself up to darkness.

But in the dark, just as the last light in his brain was going out, he felt a cool warmth pressed all the length of his body, and through the shadow saw that a naked woman held him, while her hair swirled round them through the currents like a huge flag. She pressed her lips to his, but all he could taste was salt. Then she blew into his mouth.

"Why have I not died?" Cuzarion presently asked the deeps of the icy sea. But then he thought that probably he had, and just did not know it yet.

Up above, on the surface of the water, which was as tumultuous as the lower reaches were almost still, a curious thing happened.

Among the floating spars and smashed rails, which were all that was left of the ship, amid the turmoil of night and waves, the storm, having successfully broken something, was ebbing away to sleep, but the elements remained all disturbed and out of kilter. Now a lantern bobbed by, still burning in the murk, and you might see two pale horses swimming, led by long brown reins, and it was a girl leading them on, and hair that made the reins. And then several dogs went by, balanced companionably on a piece of stiff sail, and towed along. And an owl perched on a shattered mast, to which twenty men were also clinging, lifting its wings above the brine.

Later, when they had come to shore—and not one of them was lost, although, to be exact, they thought that one of them of them had been—they told this strangest tale. Of a woman in the sea who drew them up from the ocean and hung them out like her washing on the bars and stays and wreckage of the ship. Who bound them there with wet whippy weed from the under-shores of the sea, and pressed, with small slender hands as strong as steel, the water from their lungs, then dragged them in, by a net of weed—and some said of brown hair—to the shores of the land.

There then, in the last of the awful night, men stood by the driftwood fires they had made, wringing out their washing-wet clothes and fear-sodden souls, while the horses stamped and the dogs ran about and the owl dried its feathers. Then rescuers came, with torches and brandy, from the nearby town.

"It is a miracle—is every man here?"

"Every man and every beast. Look, even the bloody rats are saved and brought ashore!"

"No, no," cried one of the servants, "we have lost our prince."

"They have lost their prince."

"And her, we've lost the young lady—" cried another. But when he said this, the rest shushed him.

"She was no girl or maid or lady."

"What then? What?"

"The sea she was."

He woke on a far coast like none he had ever seen, though, being well-read, he had read of such a place, now and then.

Palms like green spiders on stilts swept the sand with their legs. The water was a blue turquoise. Above rose wooded hills, from which blew the scent of orange groves, and the dim ringing of the bells of a monastery on a high rock.

Nearby sat a girl in a satin dress and a rope of pearls, toasting fish over a small fire.

"We're ship-wrecked, then," said the prince. "Only you and I. The other poor devils have all gone down. But I grieve too for my horses and dogs, and the owl. Although perhaps the owl at least may reach land."

"Grieve for none," said the girl, "all have reached the shore, though another shore than this."

"Indeed," said Cuzarion. But a memory was coming back to him, like a remembered dream. "I think you saved me," said he.

"So I did. I saved each and all."

"That is most praise-worthy and talented of you," said Cuzarion, raising his brows. "How, pray, did you do it?"

Then the girl brought him some fish, and he ate this hungrily, and then drank from the bottle of wine she had also set by, which was very nicely aged.

"Did people bring these provisions out of pity for us? And these clothes—this fine shirt and breeches I have on, which are never mine—and your dress, since—I hope you'll forgive me—you seemed without one earlier."

The girl smiled, not looking at him. She put back her mass of hair with one hand.

"I brought the fish and the wine, and the clothes too from chests, out of the deeps of the sea."

"Did you now," said Cuzarion.

"Up from the deeps, out of which I brought you all. It is work I set myself to do."

Cuzarion made no comment. But then he said . "It's a noble thing to be so busy, and at your young age too."

"How old do you make me out to be?" said she, tossing her head a little.

"Oh, a great age—eighteen or so."

"One hundred and eight is nearer the mark."

"Ah."

Then she laughed. "You think I lie, of course. But I tell you true. My name is Elaidh. My mother was a mermaid, and she got me by a human man, and left me in his care, the way the mermaids do, for all that race are female. Then when I was thirteen years old, my mother wanted me, to transform me to her kind, with a long silver tail and hair green as grass. But I loved my da, and so I stayed with him. I thought I should only be a woman, but it seems I have great powers from my mother, though she was cruel, as mermaids are. I am long-lived, and the ocean is familiar to me. I can breathe in water easy as air, and I can give my gift to humankind for a little while, when I blow in their mouths. Also, I can tell the ships that may go down. I walk about the quays, and suss them out. Then I go sailing on them, and when they sink, save everyone I can. With your ship I had great luck and saved every living thing."

"I must thank you, then," said Cuzarion, attempting to laugh, but seeming uneasy. He added, "Do your pearls and rubies come from the sea, too?"

"Oh yes. There are great hoards of jewels and other riches that lie there, mermaid-trove, that I steal from them. My da and I were rich, while he yet lived."

"Yet a pity," said Cuzarion, looking under his lids at her, "that you only blew the breath of life into my mouth. All this while I'd been thinking it was a kiss."

Then she sat back and looked quietly at him.

"Oh, do you see me now?" she asked.

Cuzarion, though a prince, had the grace to blush. But then, he was young as a child beside her.

Some while they were on that coast.

Elaidh taught Cuzarion to swim, and sometimes she would whisper the magic air into his mouth so he might swim under the sea, but not very far down. Even so, he saw wonderful sights there. Peculiar creatures that moved about below the rocks, and mysterious plants and corals, and fish of rainbow colours.

By day, he and she would swim then, or walk about the country. Going inland, they went by mustard fields and fields of lavender, and on the hills the bees rose in clouds, just as the fish rose in the sea at their passing. Now and then they met with people, who spoke a language Cuzarion, for all his education, did not know. But Elaidh knew it. She told him frankly she knew by now most of the languages of the earth, for she had journeyed nearly everywhere. "There's no land," said she, "the water cannot take me."

In a village under the monastery rock, they went into a cool blue church whose walls were figured with saints. And Cuzarion was amazed Elaidh could do this, and more amazed when she bowed to the cross, for he had heard mermaids, and their kin, could not have one single thing to do with God.

As time went on, Cuzarion began to think less and less of who he was, who he had been, his other life. He thought more and more of Elaidh. And as he thought more of her, he saw her more and more clearly. At first she seemed plain, but very graceful. Then she seemed lovely, and then beautiful. At last she seemed the only living thing, so that if a bird exquisitely sang, somehow it was Elaidh, and when it flew, it was Elaidh. And the dawn was Elaidh, and the evening star, and the moon.

"I should like to stay with you," said Cuzarion, "for ever."

"That is hardly possible," said Elaidh.

"Because you will never die, and I shall?"

"One day I shall die."

She led him into the wood at dusk. The grass was thick with clovers and warm still from the sun. They became lovers with finesse, and ease, for each had been a lover before.

And at first Cuzarion was most happy. But then, he was less happy. He became content, then static, then restless. And Elaidh became again only beautiful.

"Elaidh, I must get home. How long have I been away?"

"One month," said she.

"So long—it seems only a day or so—"

But she knew he lied.

"You'll understand my difficulty," said Prince Cuzarion. "My father is old and gives over much of the running of things to me. Besides—I was to marry."

"She'll be that impatient." said Elaidh. From her face you could tell little, only perhaps that she had spoken in this way before, once, twice.

"Yes, she's a royal girl, and she will be very angry."

"What is her name?"

"Oh—some royal name Sapphyra, that's her name."

"Will you not give her up," said Elaidh, "for me?" But she spoke in a light and mocking manner, and Cuzarion smiled.

"Would that I could," he said. "Kingdoms depend on it."

"Go up to the monastery, " said Elaidh. "Say the sea cast you here, but now you'd be going home. The priests are wealthy and wise and will find you a ship."

"Come with me, Elaidh."

"I? Come with you where, and to what?"

"In my own country—maybe we can make an arrangement, you and I. It's not unknown. I must marry the princess, but even so, there will be times when I can get free of her."

"No, then. I will not be going with you for that."

Cuzarion was sorry. He felt badly about himself. And so he walked off through the fields of mustard and lavender and mint, and among the olive groves where, as the soft wind blew, every leaf flashed, like the silver tails of a thousand fish.

When he came back near evening, Elaidh was not there. He searched a long while, even standing at the edge of the dark blue sea, calling her. But she was gone. She was gone for good. After a day or so, he walked up to the monastery where the priests were gracious to him, for he was a prince, charming, and well-read.

The ocean is not made of tears, though one might think it. No, it is the other way about, for the water of the sea is in us, in our blood, and when we cry, we cry the sea's own salt water.

The princess whose name was Sapphyra, had herself done some crying, but that was now over. She had a fair face of sharp features, and raven-black hair.

"How good it is, to see her cheerful again," said her maids. "A year ago, when she thought him dead, she grieved so." They did not add that while she grieved, she had pinched and slapped them every day.

Now the princess, and her three highest attendants, were gathering flowers, in the palace's wild gardens that ran to the shore. In one more day, Sapphyra would be married to the Prince Cuzarion, and the garlands—which others would weave from the flowers—were for her wedding: A quaint custom.

"Who is that?" said the First Attendant, straightening up with her armful of lilies.

"Some great lady," said the Second Attendant, "standing by to watch."

"She's only a girl, she is," said the Third Attendant.

Then Sapphyra turned and looked.

There the woman stood, under a tamarisk tree. In the sunlight, she shone like a church window. Her gown was silver, there were diamonds in her hair, and on her fingers three red ruby rings of incalculable price.

"Good day, madam," said Sapphyra, feeling quite undressed in her embroidered morning-wear.

The woman nodded. "You are the Princess Sapphyra?"

"I have that joy."

"Long then, may you be joyful," said the woman.

"But let me ask," said the princess, frowning somewhat, "your own name, and your purpose."

"My name is Elaidh, and my mother was a mermaid. I am here to offer you my wedding-gift."

A great silence had fallen in the wild gardens. Even the daylight nightingale had left off her song.

"A gift? Why should I deserve one from you?"

"Ah," said Elaidh, sadly, "you must take my word for that."

The three Attendants were in a fuss.

They bustled about, and everywhere flowers fell from their hands and out of their gilded baskets. But Sapphyra said, "If I should accept your gift, how am I to receive it?"

"You must come down to the shore," said Elaidh.

The Attendants did not wish to. But Sapphyra took hold of them and shook them.

"Do you know nothing? The mermaid-kind are wealthy beyond all thought. And see—the gems all over her—why, even her two shoes are studded with pearls."

"And why should she need shoes," said the Third Attendant pertly, "if her mother was a fish?"

But Elaidh was walking slowly away by now, and Sapphyra soon followed. The Attendants unhappily went after.

The sea came gently to the gardens, it was there an ocean of low tides.

But Elaidh stood, with her pearl shoes in the water. "Now, princess Sapphyra, you must be brave, and trust me. For I'm set to show you an astonishment of this world, which is a treasure-hoard of the mermaids. But to see it, you must come down with me, under the waves."

At this, all three Attendants began to scream, but such silly little screams, like operatic mice.

Besides, Sapphyra turned and slapped them. One! Two! Three! After which there was only snivelling.

"They must come down too," said Sapphyra, spitefully.

"Very well," said Elaidh.

So she stepped up to each of the women, and kissed her on the lips, and as she did so, into each of their mouths she blew her pure salt breath.

This dazed them a touch. So, when she walked out into the sea, they went after her, lifting their skirts foolishly, to keep them dry, until the water closed over their heads.

Down and down sank the princess and her maids, after the swift form of Elaidh—who seemed to fly through the water.

The light left the sea. It grew dark and then black. But everywhere in the black it was lit up by gleaming objects, some of which were stones, or plants, and some of which were glowing fish with eyes like candle-flames.

Huge rock-faces rose about them, and from the ledges of these, bloated shapes sometimes launched themselves, and flapped off like crows. Then they came into an orchard of corals, which were all in razor blossom.

Now and then Elaidh spoke to Sapphyra and her ladies, and through the sorcery of her breath, or her mind, they heard her, although they themselves could not utter at all.

"There is a giant octopus," said Elaidh. "Never fear him, he knows not to be discourteous to me." Or, "Look there, the wreck of an antique galleon." The octopus was a cause of discomfort to the princess and her ladies, though he did no more than blink his eye at them. The galleon filled them with terror, for the bones of men lay over its decks, and even the figurehead had become a skeleton.

But then Elaidh led them through a forest of tall seaweeds, every one of which was like a long, six-fingered hand. And then they passed through a tunnel of the rock, and coming out, they were in a vast cavern, elsewhere open only at its top. But somehow, through this opening, miles up, the sunlight entered, and came down and illuminated the space, and the floor of fine, moon-white sand.

Sapphyra and her ladies stopped, balanced in the sea, and staring.

"Here," said Elaidh, "as I promised you, is a treasure of the mermaid-kind."

On every side went up heaps and actual towers of riches, such as would surpass the trophy chambers of an emperor. There were caskets and chests of golden coins and silver, and cascades of pearls, emeralds and diamonds. There were statues of solid gold with eyes of opal, and unusual artefacts of gold, one of which was a model of a golden palace, very intricate, and large enough a child could have played in it. It had windows of carnelian, amethyst and chrysoprase, and roofs of polished ivory.

The ladies seemed to forget their terror. They floated to and fro, handling things and exclaiming silently, so crystal bubbles blew out of their mouths like words.

"You may take anything you can carry," said Elaidh.

At this, Sapphyra strove to pick up the gold palace, but Elaidh came to her and pressed her arm. "For you, princess, there is another treasure."

Then Elaidh drew Sapphyra aside into a second cave. And here Sapphyra lost all her composure. For from the floor to the ceiling, the cave was piled with jewels of a shining, heavenly blueness, some set in gold and some strung in ropes, some burnished, and some cut so they had become like stars of the northern pole. And some were larger than a man's hand. They were sapphires.

"For your name," said Elaidh. "Take whatever you want."

Then Sapphyra made an apron of her skirt, and she darted about the cave, until she had gathered everything she could, and rather more. And still she was digging out rings and necklaces and putting them on, tying others into her corset ribbons and her black hair.

After a time, however, a louring weariness seemed to overtake her. She sat down on the sand, holding the treasure to her. Then she spoke to Elaidh, and though no words were to be heard, Elaidh heard them.

"Madam," said Elaidh, "it is a great disservice I have done you, although I did it without malice, or intent, without thinking. Listen now. Keep these jewels from your husband, the prince. Then, when a time comes that what you wish for most you find you do not have, put on some of these gems, and go to him. Then he will give you back what I have taken from you. And if it is really mine, it is also his, and shall be yours."

Riddles! said the crystal bubbles from the lips of the princess.

But the next moment Elaidh raised her up, and gave her a push that sent her spinning, and Sapphyra found, to her indignation, she was rushing out of the cave, and up and up through the light-changing water, with the three Attendants whirling around her. Until all four broke the skin of the sea, and fell out on the sands of the earth. And there lay the tame wild gardens of the palace, and all around the gold and jewels that had tumbled from their skirts.

Years passed. To the prince and princess they seemed only a few in number. So that, should they add them up, they were startled always. To others, the number of the years was more than twenty-five.

They were not often together, the prince, the princess.

She would be at cards, or at her dressmakers, or she would be lying on her sofa, eating something that had to do with chocolate. Or in the theatre, in a dream.

He would be riding, and then he would be aching from the ride. He would be up all night to drink or gamble. Or, now and then, with one of the scatter of his mistresses. Or he would play the piano in the echoing marble music-room of the palace, surprising himself by how often his fingers stumbled on the keys.

There was a solitary odd story told of the royal couple.

At the start, for a decade, almost, they had been childless. Then one day the princess had given birth—astounding the physicians who had, it seemed, burst in too late to do more than ponder the flawless child—and shake their heads over its largeness and the adjacent slenderness of the princess, which had persisted throughout her term, right up to the morning of the child's unheralded appearance.

Once, at a dinner some months later, the princess had drunk a great deal of champagne. Pointing at a sapphire necklace she had on, she exclaimed, "Do you see this? This is the reason for my child." Which was thought, by the assembly, very daring, perhaps rather too bold, and also most curious.

More curious still was the truth. But there came a night the prince told it to his heir, the son the Princess Sapphyra had shown to him that morning, eighteen years before.

The boy entered the music-room, and found his father, the prince, seated there at the piano.

Cuzarion was no longer young. His hair had turned grey, and though his court, and the mistresses, still lauded him as handsome, it was a sort of handsomeness which might have looked better on a statue than a man.

But the boy—oh, the boy. He was like the morning sun, so young and straight and fair, his hair the light brown of acorns, his eyes the green of apples. In honesty, he resembled neither his father nor his mother, the princess, at all.

In the tradition of the royal household, the prince's son had the same name as his father, just as the prince had had his own father's name. Cuzarion, they were all named that.

"Cuzarion," therefore said Cuzarion, to his son, "I've called you to me to tell you a tale that you will think a lie. Or else you'll think I have gone mad."

But Prince Cuzarion's son, Prince Cuzarion, smiled kindly at his father.

"No, sir. I would never think that."

"Well, then, we'll sit here. Let me tell it through, and then decide, for you have reached a proper age, both to hear it, and to judge."

Then the elder prince spoke of the voyage he had made those few years, more than twenty-five, in his past. Of the storm and the sinking ship, of how Elaidh had saved him and every other living thing aboard. But then he told of how he had loved Elaidh, and lain with Elaidh, and presently left Elaidh to come home and resume his life. To do him credit, the elder Prince Cuzarion did not paint his love for Elaidh as anything more than it had been, the passion of a month, nor himself as any more than he was, a man capable only of a month's fidelity.

And the younger prince listened gravely. Even when his father explained how Elaidh was a magical being, the daughter of a human man and a mermaid of the deeps of the ocean.

Then the elder prince mentioned his marriage to the Princess Sapphyra. That it was pleasant enough. That it went by. And that one day he found her sobbing, and she said, "We have no children, you and I."

"And we had done everything that humans may do," said the elder prince, "to ensure a child between us. Yet none arrived."

"But then I did arrive," said the young prince. "It is most sorry I am, to have kept you and mother waiting."

"My son," said the elder prince, "you were born of a spell. You are my child, it is a fact, but not the child of the princess. The mermaids have their children by another means. It is the father brings them forth, having carried them a while, without knowing it. It seems Elaidh visited the princess before her wedding. Elaidh gave her sapphires, for her name, from the depths of the sea. And one night Sapphyra came to me in a necklace of these jewels. Later, as I slept, I dreamed of Elaidh, and in my sleep I possessed Elaidh as a man possesses a woman. And when I woke, the sheet was damp from my lust." He glanced here at his son, a little afraid to have embarrassed him. But the younger prince was not ashamed. Still he sat gravely, listening, as if in his heart he somehow knew it all.

"Sapphyra too," said the elder prince, "lay in the bed that night. In the dawn, a ray of sun fell on the coverlet. Then she and I woke, for something stirred on the mattress between us. And when she threw off the covers, a baby lay there, white as the sea-foam, and clean as the morning.

"And this was I?"

"And this, my son, my mermaid's son, was you."

"Then," said the young man, "Elaidh is my mother."

"So she must be."

"Shall I ever meet her?"

The eider prince sighed. "Perhaps. I hope you may. But I think it will never be in my lifetime. For I think I shall never meet that lovely girl again, she that was the evening star to me, and the flight of a bird. She that I forgot then, as I forget now how to play my piano, and everything—but her."

But the boy was in a sort of trance, and could only look glad, thinking of his new history. He said, "How shall I know her, if she should come here?"

"Ah," said the elder Cuzarion. "Easily enough. She will look, I think, just as she did. Eighteen she will look, your own age now. For her kind live long but never grow old. And she is in her colouring also like you. Her hair is brown that has a spirit of green in it. Her skin is clear as waters."

"And since she is half mermaid, how will I notice that?"

"As I did, my son, if I'd looked as I should. For though she shed no single tear, the sea was in her eyes."

Storm Constantine was a force of nature and of super-nature. She made myth. Psycho-sensual goddesses, ghosts and gods. Her writing shaped mountains, swamped oceans and hearts, gave mystery and hope, burnt the skies and stars. And, in person, she was amazing; fun and funny company, caring, *real* and so full of insight and tales of weird life. She has now joined the immortal pantheon – among others - Angela Carter, Leonora Carrington, Mary Shelley, Tanith Lee.

Storm and Tanith, company for one another now. Two Wise Women sitting around the campfire, surrounded by cats, drinking gin, nattering, laughing, making stories, making magics, weaving words and worlds, watching over future scribes.

Storm: Taken from the world but not the Earth.
She was our glorious, much-loved friend and I will always miss her.

Gouache & Watercolour

Paula Wakefield

It was already a mourning sky when the end was confirmed and from my isolation sick bed I watched frail snowflakes fall, melting before they landed.

*

'Am I dying?' she asked me one early Spring afternoon when we'd curled up in sunlight and fur rugs on her divan, with her cats.'

'We all are, my darling.'

'But, am I now?'

'No, you're not.'

'When do you think…'

'I don't know, Love. It's happening to us all.'

'Yeah, but…'

'You're probably a bit ahead of the rest of us. You always were'

'What do you mean?'

'– ahead of the times, ahead of the publishing world, ahead of the pack.'

'I was, wasn't I!'

And we disgruntled the cats with our cackles.

Storm Constantine was streaks of iridescence ahead. Careful and cavalier, kind and occasionally condemnatory, especially about anyone who might injure, by word or deed, members of her clan. She was daring and she could be defensive. Wise and wistful, vision guide, creative mentor, Reiki teacher, boozing buddy, sharer of secrets, drunken dancing partner, fellow feaster of words, work companion, word painter, occasional ostrich, latterly self-named mushroom, empathiser, extraordinary editor, faithful friend, puller of thorns, dreaming companion, spitter-of-feathers, my mantic mistress… she was, and is, so much more but, speaking only for myself, attempting to tell, I stutter. I can't say/write her loving, loyal, wonderful, magnanimous, shining self. *You'll love, 'mantic'.*

We sometimes talked about how writing can be like breaking rocks. This is breaking my heart, again, more. Soon, I think, it'll be a bag of gravel. But in my ear She's whispering, 'Go on, swing the hammer, don't be scared, make use of the hurting, anger, love.' Always love. 'But be careful with your back!' She had my back, always… blood and bone beloved. *I'm growing blisters, Storm.*

Outside my garden room door there is a besom propped in a large old chimney pot. It's there just in case she's ever in need of a bit of our favoured form of transport. It points skyward and one day she'll invite me on another, a different, a new, undreamed of journey, perhaps.

*

Once upon a time (as everyone who is in-the-know knows is the very best way of all ways to begin a story) I spotted her, (how could I not?), from the windows of my digs, walking, gorgeously exotic and commanding, down one of our mundane roads. My breath? Away of course!

Later, only a couple of years later, when we were introduced, I had forgotten my first Storm sighting. Not because she was less visibly striking, (and by this time her public, writerly persona, was even more well-known) but, partly, because she was more than approachable. She was welcoming and embracing, and so lovely, as in: someone I could come to love: unassuming, jokey, generous, a well-read film fan, down to earth and esoteric… herself. In our early days we often communicated, dallied and dreamed, in smoke signals, wine, and gin before it became nouveau niche. Little could I guess at that first meeting (although I might have intuited it) that she would come to call me, Wyrd Sister. Not that we always saw eye to eye or enjoyed all of the same things. But a life-long preoccupation of mine that Storm took much pleasure in, and which was only one of our many fascinations which contributed to drawing us close, was my love of, and familiarity with, nursery rhymes, and over dinner one evening when we were swapping pieces of delicious lamb beautifully cooked by Jim…

'I'm Jack Sprat,' I said.

'You can't eat fat!' Storm responded, passing me her veg'.

'Eh?' said Jim.

We recited the rhyme to him: Jack Sprat could eat no fat / his wife could eat no lean / so betwixt them both / they licked the platter clean.

Jim grinned. 'I'd have eaten the leftovers tomorrow,' he said in his phlegmatic way.

We loved our cats, she loved and privileged my child. We grew to love 'new' others, and I still do, thanks to her.

Another truth be told about the event of my introduction to Storm; at that time, I was in a post-birth fog. Storm was curious about information she could make imaginative use of in her writing and her writing worlds. Her technical knowledge of English was only one of the skills that made her an excellent editor, despite her lack of formal further and higher education. Stafford Girls' High School stood her (and Carol Ann Duffy) in good stead. She had passed her eleven plus exam, I failed mine.

Storm side-stepped my mundane politics but we agreed that our academic experiences illustrated the absurdity of selection, of all academic exams. Storm's political views (if certain of her feelings and thoughts can be described as such) were mostly expressed in her writing where earthly matters: identity, hope, love, desire, betrayal, knowledge, ownership, injustice, wars… the strengths and frailties, the ugliness and beauty of body and spirit were painted with her fantastical brush, par none. We would have had a good chat about how that phrase seems, at some point, to have been glossed from 'bar none'. *'Would have had' – past tense, type 3 conditional phrase; now that conversation won't happen with You.* A fraction of my loss, and nothing to do with having no lack of other erudite companions.

From the start of her story-making work she pushed at the binary boundaries that narrative drive seems to demand of characterisation and plotting. She would later make good literary use of my birthing story. Those were the days of floppy discs and perforated edged printing roll. It all seemed very cutting-edge and ah, the joy we shared in our recollections of sniffing the sweet but faintly sharp-edged scent of purple-pink mimeograph ink, in our adolescence, before photocopiers. We were part of yet another revolution.

We agreed we had been too careless about our youth and, in maturity, we lost little of the tenderness that continued to sometimes render us vulnerable, despite encouraging each other to grow thicker skins. But we realised our sensitivities were blessings as well as a curse and, as the years disappeared in front of us, we needed to apply a little less balm to the other's emotional bruises. Growing older together, we bemoaned the physical changes ageing causes; we imbibed (such a Storm word) less alcohol and drank more tea. Sometimes we felt we were becoming antique, but Storm had always valued technology and the imaginative and practical possibilities its progress offered. In her workroom she used a sculpted ergonomic key board that her fingers flew across, click-clack, click-clack and before we knew it her proliferation had worn away the letters. No matter, she touch-typed in and out of her realms.

Boundaries are never static, they are always, even if imperceptibly, moving. But that first meeting with Storm was a tectonic shift, and another universe was formed. Over thirty plus years we grew our worlds, designed our architecture, tilled our sisterhood soil and sowed seeds of friendship that continue to help me through her leave taking of us. *But you are still here, Storm, in these words, in our thoughts, in the gravel of my heart. So many ways. Always.*

butbut BUT! BUUUUT!

Certain losses make grieving a greedy process. *I don't want to only remember, recall sharing with You the scent of leaf mast, peppery beech and oak on Cannock Chase, musty dust on old books, thick-pages almost felted, their first-cut frayed edges softened by age.* So much shared, so much emotional and psychic shorthand, so many touchstones: differently deprived childhoods, mad or neglectful parents, the sanctuary of hedgerows, copses, wasteland, pools, derelict buildings, fairy tales, films, myths and legends, magick, history, historical novels, ghost stories, clothes, friends, adversaries, lovers, old musicals, – yes, musicals, South Pacific was a Storm favourite, and in the past we'd washed quite a few men out of our hair. The list goes on, Arthur Rackham illustrations, the pre-Raphaelites, Marie Spartali Stillman, Moreau, the Four Marys of the Bunty girls' comic, the young teen magazine Jackie, Marc Bolan…

The warp and weft of individual memories is unique and although one's experiences might resemble the shades and textures of some, perhaps many, others the threads of reminiscence shared and re-spun, then woven again with a beloved have a supplementary inimitable pattern and texture. Her warp, my weft. Mine, hers, ours.

So I want more. *I want more with You!* Grief is selfish. *I want to see, not just in my mind's eye, the liquefaction of your clothes, and the delightful contrast with your backpack, and your huge, heavy boots.* Later they became too heavy and *you wore slippers. It was ok, my love, you'd already made you mark. More than one. And they were always lovely slippers!* Grieving is a type of hunger and it is painful because it can never be satisfied. Our cherished, powerless memories are never, ever enough; in fact, they intensify our cravings.

And then there are regrets. I'd wanted to take her to Venice, the peacock-coloured waters would have reflected her luminance. In some of my grieving fantasies She and I, in a gondola, of course, glide past palazzi pointing and playing with our black and purple masquerade masks. We drink from age clouded Murano wineglasses, thick as cataracts, and her heavily lipsticked mouth leaves dangerous kisses on the rim of hers. There are no vaporetti disturbing us. We call out to and laugh with ghosts flitting in and out of the shadowed calétte; we lust after the courtesans' shoes while they mock our youthful naivety. They leer and jeer, and heckle as we pass, be-gowned as we are in our net curtains, bits of velvet, flounced and frilled things, jumbles of costume jewellery discarded by adults in the childhood dressing up boxes that we both had; ten little-girl miles apart, waiting for each other, taking refuge in our imaginations. She is lustrous. Her hair grows and overflows the sides of the boat mingling with the ripples the stirring oar creates in the aquamarine, cobalt, indigo…

With Storm, I travelled to Egypt before I actually set foot in Alexandria, Cairo, Karnak, the kings' valley, Luxor, Saqqara, before I had floated down the Nile on a Pterodactyl-sail Felucca. In reality Hatshepsut's temple was bigger, but less mysterious, than the building I visited during one of my visionary quests with Storm. The landscapes she conjured were of out of this world and her imagination travelled farthest when she was at home with all her familiars around her, or close by.

*

We were not prepared, none of us, for such an early, irrevocable departure. Immediately after Storm and Jim were informed of her premature destination they came to tell me. Like the planet, my world became scorched and scourged as if by drought, or else it felt torn apart by hurricanes, and submerged by dread and tears that would not, could not be checked. I am not exaggerating. Storm was much too far ahead and no amount of gentle magick could slow down this momentum even though the rest of us worked our wands to splinters.

So, little did we know or guess that Storm's body had been dissolving this-world boundary for some time. Now she had shape shifted for good. Somebody, somewhere, sometime said/wrote that there is nothing to writing, you just open up a vein and bleed. Here is the vein. Out of isolation I made it, crone-like, on the arm of my now adult son, to her funeral. It had started to snow again, at a time and on an occasion that would be a tired trope in fiction but here none of it, neither occasion, grieving disbelief, nor snow could be edited out. I wore a peacock feather that she had long, long ago given me, but back home, in bed again, I realised it had gone. Here is the blood. I was distraught, I'd lost one of her many treasured gifts.

No, Louise said… it's not a loss, it's significant. Louise, her friendship, and her family, another of the incalculably valuable and greatly valued offerings from Storm Constantine, along with Jim, Deb B – now Deb C, and Danni. I drifted off, yet again, into post Covid sleep but this time with the feeling that Storm was brushing my cheek with the peacock feather.

She remains iridescent. Look carefully and you might catch a glimpse of her in the blink of a cat's eye. Sometimes I catch a whiff of smoke that must be from her cigarette. Somewhere, she pulls a talon loose, drops it, *this way*. There is a scale she has scraped off, visible in a stream of moonlight, when the time comes. She is still leaving gifts, and clues, and one day we will catch up with her as we never could here.

And she left me a bequest: you.

Ends.

"For Her Light"
The Nephilim of Storm Constantine

Deborah Cartwright

An extract from the testimony of the temple scribe Ashur Ninku, 'The Coming of the Watchers' Mesopotamia, circa 4000 BC:

The strangers came, and they were not like us. Something else, but wearing the skins of men, the eyes of men, their hands. We took to collecting the sound of them in our flesh, the aorisms of power, without substance, yet entirely substance, an unexplained integrity of sound. In these waveforms of kelestic symmetry, we felt the remote passing into the definite. We saw the wings of change form within the ichor of their sound; a thick smoke, sweet upon the tongue, curling into unimagined shapes that suggested surrender, ecstasy, pain, renewal.

We learned the names of these strangers, the ancient names of the Sumerland; in this place, on this earth of now reality, the names are different, but the old cadences can still be uttered, chanted; they will still vitalise the call.

We stand together in the wildest places of the earth, and form the forest of hands against the black sky, stretching up, reaching for what is ours to take, yet never to attain. Our bodies begin to pulsate to a subliminal rhythm and we feel the imminence of contained energy, soon to be released. We dilate our throats to the air and resonate the ancient names.

We convoke the Nephilim, and they come to us, strangers with the eyes of men...

The above passage was written by Storm Constantine in 1991 for the cover of the album Earth Inferno, by the dark, gothic band Fields of the Nephilim. It is a piece that evokes the deep mystery and power, not of ancient gods, but of real beings, maybe a mysterious lost race. It conjures thoughts of people who are not quite human, who are instead something else, something 'other'. It is a quintessential, much-overlooked, piece of writing from Storm, which for reasons that will be explained here, presents more of the truth of what the Nephilim and the Watchers actually were than many other academic descriptions. Storm wrote this passage for Fields of the Nephilim just two years before we first met. She would have been entirely unaware that at the same time, I was involved in revelational research into the origins of the fallen angels, the so-called Nephilim, or Watchers of myth, that they existed not as some ethereal spirit entities, or long-forgotten deities, but as a living flesh and blood prehistoric race.

Storm and I eventually met through a mutual friend on a bright summer's day in June 1993 at her Victorian home in the Midlands of England. I sat in Storm's gothic sitting room as she poured tea from a dragon-shaped teapot. The head of the dragon on the lid was broken off and had been replaced with the dismembered head of Jesus from an old, garishly painted icon. The whole room exuded this fantastical yet subversive ambience, as did Storm herself. Clothed in a flowing, richly patterned frock, with her long, dark hair plaited with ribbons, I felt an immediate kinship. I had been in her house for only 10 minutes but was already utterly captivated not only by her exotic beauty, but by the welcoming warmth and rapt enthusiasm she exuded towards me and my then partner, Andrew Collins. "So, tell me all about your research into the real fallen angels?" she said.

And so, it began. But where to begin now? To tell the story of our shared life and work; the magic and mystery of a passion that bound Storm and me together for 27 years? Like Storm, this passion for the forbidden and subversive in the mythic past began in my childhood. I was very young and barely in junior school when my 'sympathy for the devil' first developed. "Mum, why does everyone hate the devil?" I asked after coming home from my first day at Sunday school. "I don't really know," she replied disinterestedly. My mother was not religious at all and had not wanted to send me there. Rather, I had insisted because my little friend had pleaded with me to go with her. "The teacher said that he got thrown out of heaven just for asking God some questions. Well, I feel sorry for him, it's not fair," I continued, "God is a nasty meanie, and I don't like him!" And that was the end of my attendance at Sunday school. But it was not the end of my life as a heretic invested in understanding the forbidden side of ancient myths.

By the time I was 21, my 'sympathy for the devil' had turned into avid research through my relationship with the then Fortean, paranormal and occult writer, Andrew Collins. Anyone who knows of my relationship with him, will know that it could not be described as particularly ordinary. This is because we were not only romantic partners, but magical ones. I was born and grew up with the gift of psychic intuition, displaying consistent visionary abilities from the cradle. These abilities were at a level enough to create strange paranormal events in our home when I was just a baby. Eventually, when I was around 6 years old, these 'gifts' ensured my parents and grandparents joined the Spiritualist Church and the Theosophical Society, and changed their whole lives to try and find answers. Although my father eventually became a spiritual medium himself, I knew that this was not the right path for me. I asked too many questions and was too much of a critical thinker to ever fit into any one religion, movement or organisation, however esoteric it might be. I wanted knowledge. I always had. I desired nothing else as a young person but knowledge of origins, of culture and of human power more than I wanted anything else. On this ambition, Andrew Collins and I were perfectly matched, and fate bound us together in 1989.

Through our joint investigation methods, both Ashmolean and intuitive, we became convinced that the fallen angels described in The Book of Enoch had actually existed as a real culture in the history of early civilisation. The first and oldest fragments of this Apocrypha date to around 300BC and is named as The Book of the Watchers, originally The Book of Giants. The term 'Watchers' in Aramaic comes from the root 'awake, watchful' and in Greek, *egregoroi*, or Slavic, *grigori*, which translates as 'those who are awake'. This first part of The Book of Enoch tells the story of how some of God's angels were dispatched to earth by God himself to 'watch' over humans. However, they soon began to lust after human women and eventually defected en masse to take human wives and illicitly instruct humanity in the technologies of weaponry, building, agriculture, astrology, astronomy, the movement of the celestial bodies, writing, cosmetics, art, the knowledge of enchantments and the magical signs of the earth. The book describes how this knowledge was forbidden as humans were 'meant to come upon it over time and not have it foisted on them all at once'.

The hybrid offspring of these unions between Watchers and humans are named in the text as the Nephilim. In The Second Book of Enoch, these Nephilim are described as giants 'their size being greater than that of the great cedar'. The account in The Book of the Watchers is associated with the Bible passage in Genesis 6:1-4, which speaks of the 'Sons of God' instead of using the term Watchers:

'When men began to multiply on earth and daughters were born to them, the sons of God saw how beautiful the daughters of man were, and so they took for their wives as many of them as they chose. Then the Lord said: "My spirit shall not remain in man forever, since he is but flesh. His days shall comprise one hundred and twenty years." At that time the Nephilim appeared on earth, after the sons of God had intercourse with the daughters of man, who bore them sons. They were the giants old, the men of renown.'

The Book of Enoch was first translated into English by Richard Lawrence in 1820. As a subversive text that describes the 'fall' of a group of rebel angels who set up a kibbutz-like 'haven/heaven' of progressive culture on a mountainside and taught human women forbidden knowledge, it makes a rip-roaring read. As a Hebrew text excluded by the early Church as canon in the New Testament, The Book of Enoch also changed everything when it was finally translated. From that time, this idea that angels as immortals walked and lived amongst us began to infiltrate and influence early Freemasonry and other esoteric fraternities such as Rosicrucianism. Although the canon of these fraternities has been somewhat constructed from the foundation of this suggestion of secret, original knowledge, the concept that angels were real flesh and blood, however, is not one that became commonly or widely accepted, and is still not today.

The earliest record of other beings passing forbidden knowledge to humans that precede the Old Testament and the Apocrypha of The Book of Enoch, is the Sumerian Enûma Eliš. This is a series of seven clay tablets of cuneiform writing, dating to around 2,000 BCE, which present specific creation myths. The name of these tablets, *Enûma Eliš*, is after its opening words, which mean 'on high'. These writings record the story of a group of demigods called the Anunnaki. The word 'Anunnaki' derives from 'children' *na*, of the 'sky father' *Anu*, and 'Earth' *ki*. The translation then is literally Anu-Na-Ki: Heaven-Children-Earth. Like the fallen angels described in The Book of the Watchers, they were recorded as being ancient demigods who had come from a high place down to earth to give knowledge to humankind.

The Enûma Eliš was recovered by archaeologist and cuneiformist Austen Henry Layard. In 1849, Layard uncovered the tablets in fragmentary form from the ruined Library of Ashurbanipal at Nineveh (now Mosul, Iraq). The first translations were published in 1876 and they record that these demigods, who lived on high, are noted to have supposedly brought advanced knowledge of civilisation to humans. Like the Watchers of The Book of Enoch, this was knowledge such as engineering, maths, agriculture, astronomy, medicine, tool and weapon-making, written language and science.

Storm was familiar with these Sumerian myths before we met in 1993. By then, she had already made the connection between the Watchers of The Book of Enoch and the Sumerian Anunnaki in her own search to find out more about their giant offspring called the Nephilim. Inspired by the passage in Genesis that describes how these strange and otherworldly giants had 'appeared on earth', she had pondered on what made them 'men of renown' exactly. She told me that she had been fascinated by the idea that the term 'men' had been used, which clearly alluded to them being actual flesh and blood giants and not just mythic or fairy-tale ones. She was also captivated by the idea that this mythical race of demigods had actually been able to breed with humans and give birth to a new race of unique and powerful beings who were not quite human, who were still 'other'. Storm did not undertake any further academic or anthropological research into the Nephilim but was inspired to champion the existence of this lost race in her fantasy creation of the race known as Wraeththu. This was a fantasy race, as any of Storm's readers will know, of beings who transformed humans with their unique physical traits and revered powers. Storm's famous Wraeththu novels tell of how they emerged as something 'other', their appearance on earth heralding a period of immense cultural change for humans. Exactly as the Watchers and their offspring, the Nephilim of prehistory, had done.

The Watchers and the Nephilim, these 'children of the sky', have been remembered or revered throughout the history of many global religions and movements. They have been thought of as gods, angels, djinn, demons, ascended masters, giants and even ancient aliens, but for Storm, they were the Wraeththu! Unsurprisingly, very few cultures after the Sumerians themselves regarded them as an actual flesh and blood population of terrestrial origins. Any record of them existing as archaic hominids that developed and advanced quicker than perhaps other populations during the stone age was largely lost by the new era.

Since Layard's discovery in 1849, many antiquarians, explorers, Assyriologists and archaeologists took up the interest and continued to work on both the translation and fieldwork of Babylonian and Assyrian civilisation. It is from the first work of Layard that other researchers such as Assyriologist George Smith, E. A. Wallis Budge and other early Western antiquarians became engaged in the search for the origins of civilisation. Ultimately, it was the work of Budge and Layard that inspired Zechariah Sitchin to first publish his pulp newsstand paperbacks in the 1970s and create the ancient astronaut fantasy idea of the Anunnaki. This idea has since had a 21st century revival in modern cult, rhetorical TV shows like Ancient Aliens.

Scholarly researchers who were also influenced by Layard and his work were Dr Jeremy Black and Dr Christian O'Brien. It was this latter researcher who is of the most importance because he focused specifically on the Anunnaki as a lost terrestrial, archaic population with advanced knowledge. In his 1985 book, The Genius of the Few, Dr O'Brien laid out the unique idea that the Watchers and the Nephilim of ancient mystery had been a living population instead of a myth. This work carries his prehistorical research back to 8,000 BC when a group of sages known later to the Sumerians as the Anunnaki, or 'Anannage' as he translates it, came to be known to the early people of the Middle East as the 'Shining Ones'. O'Brien describes them as a population that settled into a fertile basin within the mountains of Southern Lebanon. Here, he presents this unique prehistoric culture as living on a mountain, in a kibbutz-like settlement of advanced and progressive culture, which he terms *Kharsag* from the Sumerian term *Hursag*, variously translated as meaning 'mountain'.

This concept that the myths of gods, angels, demons, giants, fairies and ancient aliens were all inspired by a real memory of a lost race, one that had actually birthed our entire civilisation, was to take a permanent and strong hold upon Andrew and me at the start of the 1990s. Such was this hold that we became determined to find them and set about this by undertaking some rather unorthodox methods. Andrew would put me into a trance state and then regress my mind back, back to a time when the history of human culture was just beginning. I saw many fantastical and strange things during these regression sessions: images such as megalithic enclosures open to the starry sky, human figures adorned with black feathered cloaks, arms raised to the heavens appearing like giant birds, the scent of almond and the deep vibrating sound of throat singing are just a few of my enduring memories of those sessions. Although these trance journeys of the early 1990s were not without dangers, and physically took a toll on my health, they were not without reward. Amongst all of the fantastical imagery, there were enough small nuggets of useful information for Andrew to apply further academic research to and begin historically and anthropologically to piece together the fragments of what this lost race could be. Despite Dr O'Brien's conviction that his 'Anannage' had been based in Lebanon, the regressions were pulling me time and again to the region of South-East Turkey instead. We eventually came to believe that this was where the real centre of the Nephilim culture at its height had been located. That somewhere near the borders of Iraq, Turkey and Syria, the paradise of *Kharsag* was waiting to be found.

Furthermore, we were gaining the increasing conviction that the fallen angels of the Hebrew apocrypha, the Watchers and Nephilim of The Book of Enoch, and the Anunnaki, or Shining Ones of the Sumerian Enûma Eliš, were a fragmented memory of what had really been a sophisticated shamanic culture existing around 15,000 years ago in the Mesolithic period. The visions were showing us that these figures were practising a form of shamanism based on animism. This is the belief that all living things, and even inanimate things in nature, have a soul or spirit and are connected by consciousness. It became evident that the Nephilim had perhaps been a kind of shamanic elite in comparison to contemporary hunter-gatherers of the early pre-pottery Neolithic period. They were an elite, we thought, that possessed sufficient technology and knowledge to eventually catalyse the Neolithic revolution in the Near East at the end of the last ice age. More importantly, after a closer study of shamanic traditions in Anatolia, Andrew was able to form the hypothesis that the Watchers as flesh and blood humans had been remembered as 'angels', purely because they had specifically practised a form of bird shamanism.

It made complete sense that a prehistoric population, their appearance recorded as otherworldly, very tall and ceremonially dressed in feathered cloaks made from the 8ft wingspan of giant vultures, would have had a huge impact upon ordinary hunter-gatherer peoples; enough for them to be remembered as a form of mythic being. From this, it is quite feasible that any memory of these ancient bird shamans, men with wings, could be passed down through millennia to eventually be recalled as 'angels'. Andrew's further research also proposed that this lost culture's shamanic animism was a sophisticated practice that measured and recorded the movement of the celestial bodies and revered the astro-ritual death journey via the spirit forms of carrion birds. These particular birds were important because they symbolised death/rebirth and acted as psychopomps for souls to enter the celestial realms in the stars.

All of this we told Storm on that sunny day in her house in 1993, over tea from a heretic teapot. Storm was enthralled, and it was not long before the suggestion of a new set of fantasy novels based on this research into the Watchers was a working idea. Storm was keen to use all and any of the material from the regressions that had no use for the hypothesis of Andrew's work. As such, once picked clean of any useful academic content, my visionary content came to furnish Storm's fantasy series published as the Grigori Trilogy, which included the titles Stalking Tender Prey (1995), Scenting Hallowed Blood (1996) and Stealing Sacred Fire (1997). During those years, Storm and I would spend long periods devising the characters and plots, pouring over magical philosophies and building an entire world where the Grigori and their offspring, the Nephilim, could return to the modern human world and once again propel humankind into the fate of their future knowledge.

Part of the visionary work that was not verifiable by Andrew in the early 1990s concerned the idea that there had been a migration of the Nephilim culture around the globe. The material had shown that the Lizard Peninsula in Cornwall had been a place where they had arrived upon the shores of the most southerly point of prehistoric Britain. This is a place called the Lizard in Cornwall and naturally, we took Storm to visit Kynance Cove there for a short research holiday. She was immediately entranced by the astonishingly vibrant coloured rocks of the cove. Blood red, black, gold, and luminous green adorn all the cliff faces and rocks of that area. It is a unique colouration, specific to a group of minerals called serpentine, the name originating due to the minerals presenting the texture and colour of snakeskin. Serpentine is a rare mineral colouration in rock that can also be found in the Middle East today, in an area that would once have been Kurdistan, the original homeland of the Watchers and the Nephilim. If they had arrived on the shores of prehistoric Cornwall, perhaps they would have viewed it as a sacred place, a place that reminded them of home and of the power of the earth.

Kynance Cove became a sacred and magical place for Storm, a place where she found much of her own power and inspiration. Together, we would explore its sea caves, feeling as if we were walking through the body of a giant and archaic snake. The haunting magic of that coastline captivated her completely and some days she would weep from the effect of its beauty. For it was, she told me, a place where she felt whole instead of fragmented and powerful instead of powerless. It was the first place where she felt connected to the land, to others and most importantly to herself. Storm had found her Elysium and together we made real magic there over the years.

'We stand together in the wildest places of the earth, and form the forest of hands against the black sky'

Today I am still honoured to have given her such a gift. It is a small return for all that she had given me.

The results of all my work with Andrew and his academic research were published in 1996 under the title From the Ashes of Angels. However, immediately after finishing the research and Andrew obtaining a new book deal with Penguin to publish it, our romantic relationship sadly came to an end. The synchronicity was not to end there though because, in exactly the same month that Andrew began writing the book, in 1995, the first archaeological spades were going into the earth at a site called Göbekli Tepe in Southern Turkey. What they discovered was not to be announced to the public until the year 2000, but what was discovered was to vindicate our work entirely.

Built at the end of the last ice age, Göbekli Tepe is a 12,000-year-old series of mysterious stone temples in a large megalithic complex. Its discovery is one of the greatest challenges to 21st century archaeology because it is 7,000 years older than the Great Pyramid and Stonehenge. The temple enclosures are made up of a series of strange buildings and rings of T-shaped monoliths, all built with stones weighing from 10 to 15 tonnes. The stone monoliths are also elaborately carved with bas-relief images of ice age animals and human forms, which show a level of sophistication and artistic achievement unmatched until the rise of the civilizations in ancient Sumer, Egypt and Babylon much later.

Göbekli Tepe is now recognized as the oldest stone architecture in the world. After its announcement in the year 2000, Andrew wasted no time in visiting the site as soon as possible to discuss its meaning and purpose with the archaeologist who had discovered it, the late Klaus Schmidt. There were no doubts in Andrew's mind that this whole astonishing complex had been built by a highly sophisticated culture with a knowledge that was mind-bogglingly in advance of other hunter-gatherer populations of the same period. There was also no doubt that as a physically real complex, this was the work of builders that were therefore equally physically real and that they could only be the Watchers of The Book of Enoch.

Andrew dedicated a whole new project to it, focusing on understanding the meaning and purpose of Göbekli Tepe within the framework of his earlier work on angels as a prehistoric, shamanic population. The results showed that it was built as a reaction to a global cataclysm and that the temple enclosures served as a gateway and map to the sky-world. This is a term used by shamanic cultures worldwide for all the celestial bodies and the realm beyond the earth's atmosphere. Surviving shamanic tribes today still revere the sky-world and see it as a place of first creation, which can be reached through a soul journey to bring back knowledge and power from the stars:

...'we raised our hands skyward against the black sky, stretching up, reaching for what is ours to take'

By analysing the exact alignments between star constellations and the megaliths in the enclosures at Göbekli Tepe, Andrew concluded that this soul journey was made via a bright star in the constellation of Cygnus. The results of this work were published in 2014 under the title Gobekli Tepe: Genesis of the Gods – The Temple of the Watchers and the Discovery of Eden. Although Andrew and I had gone our separate ways, our search for the Nephilim and their forbidden knowledge had never ended. The discovery of Göbekli Tepe eventually brought us together again, as research partners, in 2011 and at that point, it felt like our search was only just beginning.

We had been right about where they had been located all those years prior but there was more to discover about who and what they were exactly.

In the early 21st century, the advent of a new scientific discipline called paleo-genetics, which is based upon a method to extract DNA from fossils, was to change everything known about prehistory and the origins of civilisation. The Max Planck Institute for Evolutionary Anthropology in Leipzig sequenced the genome of fossilised Neanderthal bones for the first time in 2008. In 2010, the results of this sequencing shook the world. The revelation that unfolded was that when Homo sapiens left the African continent and entered Europe, they had interbred with different species of other archaic hominids that had already been in Europe and Eurasia for 200,000 years. The DNA results showed that not only was this inter-breeding successful, but the resulting hybrids were also eventually to become ancient modern humans. The evidence was clear that all modern humans, with the exception of a few African ethnicities, possess between 1 to 20% Neanderthal DNA.

Following the Neanderthal revelation, The Max Planck Institute was to go on to discover an entirely new species of an archaic population as well. A new species of archaic hominid that they named the Denisovans. This name derived from the cave called 'Denisova' located in Siberia where the fossil bones of this hitherto undiscovered species were found. The sequencing of these fossil remains, a finger bone and a molar, revealed not only that this archaic population was of a large stature, but that South-East Asians, Native Americans, Tibetans and Australasians have 1 to 5% Denisovan DNA. It appeared that the Denisovans may well have been a race of 'giants', who were engaged in interbreeding with both Homo sapiens and Neanderthals. However, they were also much more highly advanced in technology than even the Neanderthals. This is indicated by the artefacts found at Denisova Cave in the same layer as the bone fossils. These are artefacts of exquisite artistry such as drilled stone jewellery and adornments, and even fine bone sewing needles. The evidence so far indicates that the Denisovans lived in Eurasia and North-Eastern Europe up to around 50,000 BC, when as a pure species they became extinct. However, like the Neanderthals, their DNA lived on in their hybrid children, the 'Nephilim'.

This new revelation of archaic hominid interbreeding in 2010 clarified mine and Andrew's original hypothesis that the Anunnaki, the Watchers, the Shining Ones, were a cultural oral 'myth memory' of a lost prehistoric race. What we knew now was that this lost population had been Denisovan and Neanderthal human hybrids. Not angels, not djinn, and certainly not aliens. Rather, these ancient modern hybrid humans, these 'Nephilim', had existed in Europe and Eurasia from 50,000 down to around 10,500BC as a population formed from the offspring of Homo sapiens with Denisovans and Neanderthals. Andrew's hypothesis is that the human hybrid culture who were the builders of Göbekli Tepe were all of tall stature; around 7 to 8ft tall, with red hair and an elongated cranium, traits inherited from their archaic Denisovan and Neanderthal genome.

'The strangers came, and they were not like us. Something else, but wearing the skins of men, the eyes of men'.

Recent archaeology has demonstrated that palaeolithic settlements of these hybrid cultures in Eurasia possessed sophisticated tool technology. Evidence to date shows that they created: an obsidian industry and trading commerce throughout the Steppes and ancient Anatolia; made drilled jewellery, fine needles, tailored clothes with elaborate beading; cultivated plants, herbal medicines and drugs on a large scale; domesticated wild horses and wolves, thereby beginning the evolution of the domestic dog in Siberia. They also built highly accomplished stone buildings, temples and monuments such as Göbekli Tepe, Nevalı Çori and Karahantepe in the Şanlıurfa province of Turkey. All of these sites contain buildings that demonstrate an advanced knowledge of the celestial movement of heavenly bodies and constellations in the cosmos. The utterly astonishing thing is that some of these achievements were as early as 50,000 years ago! It is not difficult to see how the Neanderthals and Denisovans interbreeding with incoming Homo sapiens and passing their advanced knowledge down to them and their hybrid children is the exact story of the Watchers in The Book of Enoch and the Annunaki of the Enûma Eliš.

All these new facts about the real existence of a Nephilim culture are fascinating. However, it is only through the mythic traditions of surviving tribal cultures in Eurasia today, and not archaeology or paleo-genetics, that demonstrate perhaps what the metaphysical knowledge and 'magical' abilities of the Nephilim culture may have been. Many current shamanic traditions talk of the first peoples, the ancestors, who are described as having had extremely developed animal-like senses. Oral traditions record that they lived not in separateness from nature and from the animal kingdom in the way that modern humans do. Rather, they lived connected to all living things and were not only in tune with the natural, unseen forces of the earth but had mastery over them. Shamanic cultures today believe that these archaic ancestor gods could actually communicate with animals, become one with them even, to see and experience the world as that animal. It is said that they learnt from animals how to make rain, read the stars, control the weather, locate underground water, migrate and navigate to find new settlement locations, and transcend physical matter through soul journeys to the sky-world to bring back knowledge.

These abilities may seem fantastical, or mythic, but it could be supposed that they were originally innate to archaic hominids like the Neanderthals and Denisovans. It is not beyond reason, or science, to speculate that these may have been natural, innate abilities that were lost over millennia through genetic selection, mutation, and the gradual dominance of the modern human genome. This is an idea championed by the late Neanderthal researcher and author Stan Gooch in his 2006 book, The Dream Culture of the Neanderthals: Guardians of the Ancient Wisdom.

With both seemingly magical powers and advanced domestic technology, this Anunnaki culture marked themselves as the 'super elite' amongst the hunter-gatherer peoples of the Mesolithic period in Central Eurasia, until around 10,500BC when a large cataclysmic impact event devastated their culture. Many anthropologists and historians today are now exploring the hypothesis of the greater antiquity of civilisation and the idea that these lost palaeolithic cultures were remembered as gods by the first Bronze Age civilisations.

More is being discovered every year about this astonishing lost culture of hybrids through new scientific and archaeological methods. The journey of discovery is certainly not over yet. I, for one, want to visit Siberia and discover more about their power and philosophy directly from the amazing shamanic peoples, like the Buryats, who still inhabit the area. My search today is for what we may have lost as a culture and a species. Just as Storm pondered on the meaning of 'men' mentioned in that passage from Genesis many years ago, I want to think about lost knowledge we may once have possessed and archaic abilities that have largely vanished through genetic mutation. The knowledge these brought has now faded into mere belief, superstition, and religion. In our modern world, it is for the very few to claim the ability to feel the electromagnetic fields of the earth, to divine the presence of water, to journey to the spirit realms and communicate with the unseen, to foretell the future, to create rain, affect weather and possess the powers of animals and the natural world. These abilities now seem only a legend or a ludicrous fantasy.

For Storm, however, there were no lines between fantasy and magic. For her, magic was always a very real force in the universe. Not in a card trick kind of way but as a force of the human mind. The force of consciousness itself as an intentionality, or 'will' to effect change: change in the self and in the environment. Like me, she had possessed a fascination with how humans had first learnt this occult art and how they had come to inherit even the idea that such powers existed. Origins! It had always been about that: the origins of human mind magic. It had long captivated us both and we had found it in the prehistoric shamans we call the Nephilim.

Storm was never a religious person. Despite being an occasional practising Wiccan, she never believed in gods or goddesses in the way that most modern neo-pagans do, as higher beings existing in 'spirit' only. Rather, what we both believed in, was the hope that the gods had once been real. Only in recent years did the penny drop that many animistic and shamanic cultures around the world have always known this. It is kept as sacred memory and not religious belief by tribal cultures that the 'gods' were once living, that they walked the earth, and that we are their physical children. This idea that our origins and civilisation, our history as such a diverse population, emerged from something physical but not merely modern human, still something strange, something 'other', was the pervasive passion of our lives. For Storm, it was almost a sign of the sacred. It was an obsession that found its expression in her creation of the Wraeththu.

In a way, the endeavours of Storm and I were a kind of will for the Nephilim to return, these 'strangers with the eyes of men'. Our work both together and individually, our collective 'visionary tongue' if you will, was a kind of evocation to bring the ancients back to life in the minds of readers, either as fiction or as fact. And, in a way they did answer our call. Storm lived to see the revelations of science and archaeology in *convoking* them, in bringing them back en masse. It had been her recent wish to begin a new series of novels where the Nephilim as otherworldly human-hybrids and the Wraeththu come together in a magical, visionary journey to discover origins and forbidden knowledge. It is an idea that, for her light, I hope this tribute will ignite.

'We convoke the Nephilim,
and they came to us, strangers with the eyes of men'.

Bibliography:

Black, Dr Jeremy - The Literature of Ancient Sumer (Oxford Library Collections), 2004.

Budge, Wallis E. A. - The Seven Tablets of Creation, The Babylonian Legends of Creation, 1921.

Collins, Andrew - From the Ashes of Angels: The Forbidden Legacy of a Fallen Race, 1996.

Collins, Andrew - Göbekli Tepe: Genesis of the Gods: The Temple of the Watchers and the Discovery of Eden, 2014.

Collins, Andrew - Denisovan Origins: Hybrid Humans, Göbekli Tepe, and the Genesis of the Giants of America, 2019.

Gooch, Stan - The Dream Culture of the Neanderthals: Guardians of the Ancient Wisdom, 2006.

Gooch, Stan - Neanderthal Legacy: Reawakening Our Genetic and Cultural Origins, 2010.

Paabo, Svanto - Neanderthal Man: In Search of Lost Genomes, 2014.

Layard, A. H., Nineveh and its Remains, 1849.

Layard, A. H., A Popular Account of Discoveries at Nineveh, 1852.

Layard, A. H., Inscriptions in the Cuneiform Character, from Assyrian monuments, discovered, 1860.

L. W. King, Enûma Eliš: The Seven Tablets of Creation, London 1902.

O'Brien, C.A.E. & O'Brien B.J., The Genius of the Few, Wellingborough, 1985 (Revised edition by Dianthus Publishing 1999).

O'Brien, C.A.E. & O'Brien B.J., The Shining Ones, Dianthus Publishing, 1999 (Revised edition by Dianthus Publishing, 2001).

Smith, George - Assyrian Discoveries: An Account of Explorations and Discoveries on the Site of Nineveh, During (1873 to 1874), 1875.

Smith, George - The Chaldean Account of Genesis, 1876.

The House that Never Was

Graham Phillips

I am a non-fiction author and researcher into historical mysteries and the unexplained. Storm often used to accompany me during my investigations, the subjects and sites involved inspiring the settings for several of her short stories. Astonishingly, some of these daytrips became real-life paranormal adventures, the most unusual involving a visit to the old country estate of Ranton Abbey in Storm's home county of Staffordshire. "Unusual" is not a word Storm herself used to describe our experience there. "Utterly bizarre" is what she called it. However, before recounting this weird episode, I should first outline the background to our visit to Ranton Abbey.

In AD 913 the site was the location for one of England's most crucial battles, when the English warrior queen Ethelfleda led her army in a decisive victory over the Danish invaders. The battle of Ranton marked the beginning of the end for Viking rule in central England but cost many lives on both sides. It is said that for years afterwards the sound of battle could often be heard at night on the heathland of what later became the Ranton Abbey estate. The Abbey itself was founded in 1150 as an Augustine priory, but in 1536 the English King Henry VIII had the monks forcibly evicted when the property was seized by the Crown. Henry, who had broken away from the Roman Catholic Church and established himself as head of the Church of England, had no love for the clergy and ordered that any who refused to leave, or hand over the monastery's wealth, be severely punished. This was happening to monastic communities all over England, but at Ranton the monks were said to have fiercely resisted, and many were slaughtered by the king's soldiers.

The abbey was abandoned and left to fall into ruin until 1820 when the property passed into the hands of Thomas Anson, the first earl of Lichfield, who demolished the old ruins and built a large hunting lodge on the site adjacent to the monastery bell tower, the only part of the original priory to still survive. No sooner was the hunting lodge, known as Abbey House, built than rumours of strange happenings began to circulate around the nearby village of Ranton. Servants at the lodge reported hearing mournful chanting and witnessing the appearance of spectral hooded figures. Indeed, these manifestations of what locals believed to be the spirits of long departed monks, so frightened those who worked in the building that servants refused to remain after dark. Claims of ghost sightings, unaccountable sounds, and poltergeist activity continued right up until the Second World War when troops from the Free Dutch Forces were quartered here. They too reported peculiar activity, including the unexplained movement of objects, eery noises, inexplicable sounds said to resemble harsh breathing, and menacing dark figures moving along dimly lit corridors. Ultimately, in 1942, Abbey House burned down under mysterious circumstances and today only its ivy-covered ruins remain.

It was back in 1982 when I first visited Abbey House with seven others. The building, which belonged to the late Earl of Lichfield – Patrick Lichfield, the Queen's cousin, and famous photographer - stood in a remote location surrounded by deer-filled parkland, accessible only by a narrow dirt track around a mile from the nearest road. It was a shell of a building, divided into numerous roofless rooms and passageways, below which the dank cellars remained virtually intact. We arrived just as the sun was setting, and that evening those present witnessed some of the weirdest happenings any of them had ever experienced. It began with a strange, laboured breathing sound coming from one of the rooms, for which no explanation could be found. Other noises were heard by most of those present, including whispering voices, banging on the walls, and the occasional cry that sounded unlike any identifiable creature. Weirdest of all, three of the party swore they saw dark humanoid figures moving in the shadows, and one even claimed to see what he described as a dark amoeboid shape moving down a corridor towards him.

It was almost four decades later when I again visited Abbey House, now accompanied by Storm, who thought the place might be an ideal setting to include in one of her works. By this time, the Ranton Abbey estate had been sold to a private investor who had preserved the parkland as it had been in Patrick Lichfield's time. (By the way, the entire estate, being privately owned, can only be accessed with permission.) The ruined hunting lodge, considered too dangerous to enter, was now surrounded by a high wire fence, the dilapidated building appearing almost resigned to its remorseless decay. Ivy cascaded down the outer walls in a tumble of greenery, while undergrowth covered the floors, and brambles partly obstructed the glassless and frameless doors and windows. Small animals could be heard scurrying amongst the vegetation within, whilst every so often plaster trickled from the brickwork as birds flew to and from nesting holes in the crumbling walls.

Storm and I were kindly shown around the exterior by a member of the estate staff who was fascinated to hear of the peculiar happenings of 1982. As no one had been allowed inside for longer than the man had been working there, he knew nothing of any recent paranormal phenomena associated with the ruin. However, when Storm told him that she was a novelist and was looking for an appropriate location for a supernatural tale, he immediately suggested another building on the Ranton estate; it was just a couple of miles away and there would be no problem going inside.

We followed his Land Rover along a winding dusty track until arriving at a large house, partly surrounded by trees, that we had been told was a half-converted manor dating from the nineteenth century. We were now deep into the estate, even further from any road, town, or house, surrounded by fields where cattle grazed, and scenic countryside upon which the sun shone brightly on that warm mid-summer afternoon. Peering in through the windows, the interior of the building appeared unaltered from Victorian times, its walls covered with dark oak wainscotting, and ceilings decorated with elaborate white plasterwork. Our guide unlocked the main entrance and we followed him into a spacious hallway, from where oak panelled doorways opened into various rooms, and a grandiose wooden staircase before us led to the upper chambers.

Storm was thrilled by what she saw. Much of the original furniture - faded mahogany cabinets, which may once have proudly exhibited expensive chinaware and other luxury ornaments; seats, now covered in mould; a couple of Greek-style busts on darkened wooden plinths; and old coat stands all remained in situ, as if untouched since the last occupants had departed long ago. The air hung heavy with the musty redolence of age, while the uneven floorboards creaked with our footsteps. Storm and I were led from room to room of the ground floor: what was once the lounge, still housing a stained leather sofa which had to be well over a hundred years old; a gaming room with a broken billiard table leaning against the wall in one corner; a dining room with the pitted remains of a once magnificent dining table, below an extravagant glass chandelier that still hung from the ceiling, the whole scene bathed in multi-coloured sunlight streaming in through a stained-glass window depicting a kneeling angel with hands clasped in prayer. Dust motes danced in the air as the place echoed with Storm's voice asking why the house remained empty. Leading us into the kitchen, still containing its original cast-iron aga. on which stood an old kettle, half eaten by rust, the man explained that the building was being converted into apartments back in the 1960s when the property developer went broke. The place had remained untouched ever since, evidently because new government legislation had imposed conservation orders on such properties.

Upstairs, the scene was in total contrast. Here the large, once stately bedrooms had been partially transformed into tasteless 1960s studio flats. Sickening psychedelic wallpaper; orange, pink and yellow skirting boards; purple door flames; aluminium picture windows; and plain hardboard doors with transparent plastic handles. Each room had a small adjoining kitchen with laminate worksurfaces and fake-tiled flooring, and a bathroom with toilets, baths, and sink units fashioned from what seemed to be sickly green plastic. The building was like some wacky cake with two completely conflicting layers: one floor, a decaying remnant of Victorian grandeur, the other fixed in some grotesque Hippie-era time warp. Storm was transfixed. The crazy juxtaposition inspired her, and the idea for a short story began to take shape in her mind. "Is the place haunted?" she asked our guide.

"No idea," he answered. "At least, no one has lived here for years to report anything."

"But I thought it might make a good setting for a novel." She said.

He remained silent for a moment. "If you want ghosts, there's another building like this elsewhere on the estate that's more in its original condition. That *is* said to be haunted." He had no idea what the haunting was supposed to entail but promised to make enquires. Storm asked if we could see the place right away, but the man explained he had an imminent appointment and offered to take us there in a couple of weeks.

So – you may be thinking – what was so bizarre? Well, that happened when we next visited the Ranton Abbey estate a week or two later. With both Storm and I having a free day, we called the same estate employee and asked if we could visit the second manor house he'd mentioned. He told us that, as he also had a light workload, he would be delighted, and we arranged to meet at Abbey House later that day. When we arrived, things immediately got weird.

Our previously jovial guide seemed somewhat confused that we greeted him warmly: on the previous visit, the three of us had spent at least two hours talking generally about all manner of things, even exchanging humorous anecdotes. It seemed, that from his perspective, he was meeting us for the first time. Storm and I exchanged puzzled glances when he told us that he only had a short time to spare, as he was expected at a meeting. Hadn't he, just an hour or so earlier, said he was free all day? But it was when Storm brought up the subject of the second manor house that we really became confused. The man had no idea what we were talking about. There was only one such manor, he explained, and offered to take us there. By his description, he was clearly referring to the place we'd previously visited. When I reminded him that he had already shown us around that building, he seemed to have no recollection of the occasion whatsoever. Although totally mystified, we decided not to question him further as he appeared anxious to get moving, presumably to avoid being late for his meeting.

"I think he's been told to not show us the other manor," Storm suggested, as I drove us along the track we'd taken a couple of weeks earlier, following the man's Land Rover.

I frowned. "What, since this morning?"

Storm shrugged. "He probably asked permission and was refused."

"So why not just tell us that? And why's he taking us to where we've already been. It's as if he doesn't even remember us."

When we arrived at the same deserted manor we had visited previously, I was shocked to see that the entire place was now boarded up, with windows and doors all covered by heavy metal sheeting. Storm was dismayed. "It must have been vandalised since we were last here," she said.

I breathed a sigh of exasperation. "And they probably blame us. No wonder we're not being shown the other place."

At first Storm agreed, but then thought for a while. "Then why agree to meet us again and bring us back here?" she said.

I agreed it made no sense. It made even less sense when, before we had the chance to question him, the estate worker explained that he was running late and told us we were welcome to remain here alone. "Just follow the same track back when you're ready to leave," he said, cheerily, before driving off. *Nothing* was making sense. If he had been refused permission to show us the second manor, why claim there was no such place? And if we were being blamed, directly or indirectly, for vandalism, why was he happy to leave us here alone? And most peculiar of all, he didn't seem to remember us at all. As it turned out, he didn't.

I bring in here a relevant episode that occurred some weeks later when two friends, Angeline and Chris from the USA, visited the Ranton estate in the hope of investigating the ruins of Abbey House. They knew absolutely nothing of Storm and my experiences – indeed, the account has never been published until now – and they were only familiar with the events of 1982 published in one of my books. They met with the very same man who had twice met with Storm and me and were shocked when the gentleman seemed to have no recollection of ever meeting us. He knew nothing of the strange events witnessed by my companions and I four decades earlier, even though Storm had spent some time telling him all about it while I was taking photographs of the crumbling building and the remaining monastery tower. Furthermore, even though we had told him we were both authors and showed him our websites on Storm's phone – by which he had seemed impressed - when Angeline and Chris hoped to jog his memory by explaining that we wrote books, even that apparently meant nothing to him.

Back to the main story. You may still be thinking that there's nothing that unusual about Storm and my experience at the Ranton estate. The hard-worked estate employee may have simply forgotten - maybe he entertained a lot of visitors. Perhaps he *had* been instructed to show no one the second manor. And conceivably the owners had coincidentally decided to recently board up the building we had been shown around. However, as we approached the house, we noticed that the metal sheeting, boarding up all the doors and windows, were covered in rust. And on closer examination we realized that even the heavy bolts that held the sheeting in place were rusted. Astonishingly, the place had clearly been boarded up for ages. Yet just a couple of weeks before, all the doors and windows had been visible, and the estate worker had easily opened the then visible main entrance door with a key. With no way to get inside, we phoned the estate office and explained our situation. It had indeed been securely boarded up for years, we were told, and there was no possibility of entering. In fact, it had remained that way for so long that no one in the office had any idea what the present interior was like.

So, what had happened to Storm and me? It certainly wasn't some manner of weird, shared vision. There's no doubt that our tour around the inside of the half-converted manor house had really occurred. I had filmed the entire thing on Storm's mobile, and she copied the footage onto her PC before deleting it from her phone. We viewed it several times. Oddly, it seems to have vanished. I'm sure I had a copy on my own laptop, but I can't locate that either. I still desperately hope it will show up.

In conclusion: As I have been unable to contact the gentleman who showed us around the estate to obtain his permission to publish his name, I have omitted his identity from this account. Nevertheless, since our last visit, both Storm and I spoke to other members of staff who attested to the fact that the strange manor house has been boarded up for many years and that there is no way we could have been inside. Moreover, there is no second manor. Storm was contemplating adapting the bizarre episode into a novelette when she sadly passed away. And I decided it was just too unbelievable to publish as a true story – until now. So, what on earth *had* we experienced: a time warp, another reality, some type of Brigadoon? Maybe, now that Storm has entered the great beyond, she knows the answer to this extraordinary mystery.

Storm Constantine, I miss you and our adventures dearly.

Cinderkin

Justina Robson

Orders run down from Queen to Chamberlain to General and so on like rainwater running down glass. With an uncertain series of dashes and some minor deviations, that is, as drop meets drop, waits for support, plunges onward, runs out of impetus and then waits for the next surge. The surges are all created by the ebb and flow of misgivings (let's not call them fears, because that is undignified) and those are the result of a long history going back so far that anyone studying all its details will become and remain mad, lost in the labyrinthine library, awash in lore and jottings of who did what to whom and why until they lose their mind entirely. But you can't be alive in Zathria and not know some of the rules and contingencies that dictate your life's path, and at different levels this plays out in different ways. One thing is certain, if an order requires a journey which ends in Vanazon, then you should do all you can to escape being on the sharp end of it.

Such an order has been given. A Princess, one of six, don't fuss, not such a loss, still got five more where that came from, is to be sent on a marriage mission. The full dowry, the whole shebang, not an inch of effort is to be spared. There will be maids and servants, dowry, of course, some diplomats probably now writing their wills with shaky hands, some other sundry retinue of people that the castle administration will be glad to get shut of and of course, all the horses and vehicles necessary to accomplish a journey of speed and safety to Vanazon. Yes, that's right. To Vanazon! For a wedding!

No wonder the Master of the Queen's Horse has gone deathly pale. Somehow, somewhere, she is sure, there is a plan within a plan within a development that has brought about the notion that a marriage to someone in Vanazon's royal house is going to fix up the tenterhook agreements of peace between the two nations. Nation is pushing it. Let's call them principalities. The human world is small, self-aggrandizing. Principality will do. They make up in culture and viciousness what they lack in area. To Vanazon! Let all rejoice at the prospect of a newly ensured peace. Although there is plenty of chance that none who go will return in the same number of pieces. What idiocy is this?

There's perishing lack of news at the lower levels. Nobody knows a thing. Not the butler, not the candlesticks guy, not the woman who does the fireplaces, not her sister with the dodgy hip, not the talking dog that sometimes gets up to the top floor by 'accident'. He was sleeping in one of the hayricks on the day this was hatched. Only Fixwhit the privy executive (yes, toilet-cleaner) has an inkling because he was doing third floor gutters a week ago and overheard someone saying that this is a matter of playing on the vanity of a certain Vanazon princeling who has some kind of influence with Ears That Matter. No matter. The order has come. To Vanazon!

Thank goodness, the Master thinks, that she is not really, not honestly, not properly expected to go in person on such an auspicious occasion because there will be a great need for horses for the remaining court and the five staying-right-here princesses. So that's at least ten horses of special character and conformation and none of them lippy. Only she could assure such continuance of service. Yes.

But for those on the bottom there's no escape. Drowned by compulsions is where you'll be, regardless of who did what higher up the chain. Master of the Queen's Horse isn't at the bottom, but stable-hand definitely is, and that's where Shalaz has wound up after a long series of events of no note, bounced from pillar to post by the whims of others due to what he looks like, and where he might've come from, though nobody knows for sure about that; he's just one of many who walk out of the forests without a history anyone's willing to ask about. A lack of sponsors and patrons and a lack of any desirable traits, plus a few undesirable ones, means that stable hand is about the best he could aspire to. And in places other than Zathria, much less than that. In fact, the closer you move towards the human hub of things, to fiefdoms encircled by other human holdouts (or, if you are human, kingdoms, strongholds, outposts, forts) then aspiring to life itself is fairly ambitious for such as he.

The Master of Horse, Yvrielle, hired him last so he should go. She hired him out of kindness because he was a destitute and he's from the forest and he's got the marks of a Cinderkin, whatever you want to say about it possibly not being that and being fox instead, and he doesn't talk. All these things mean he was beholden to her, humble and cheap. Also, she would never admit, he's good with the horses. Very good. Strangely good. With the horses. In a way that makes her feel that if he were noticed by Eyes That Notice her position might become a little less certain, so it is really best, for the sake of the safety and wellbeing of everyone in the party, that he be assigned the task of caring for the horses and etcetera on their journey to Vanazon. They are sending five excellent horses, plus less excellent ones which can be fancied up to look good and will survive the journey of several days' steady progress along rough roads. It stands to reason that she ought to send her best groom to keep up the pretence that the quality of the steeds is better than it is. Definitely.

High in the castle itself, on the fourth floor, in the tower that faces out over the wilds towards the rumoured sea, the Princess In Question is looking out of the window, wishing that *looking* was *flying*.

The forest, against which Zathria is a stalwart human stronghold and frontier of civilization, starts as scrubby wilds about ten miles distant, where the farmland and the hunting grounds peter out into a series of little bothies and a patrolled region called The Break. The Break is five miles wide and circles three-quarters of Zathria's border with what the Princess suspects is all the authoritative security of a chocolate fireguard.

Princess Ven is what passes for an expert in The Wilds. She immersed herself in independent studies and field research (wandering around with a notebook) after exhausting the Castle library and tutors on all they knew about being born as a middle-ranked female into a family of inherited power in an uncertain world; a world which didn't show any enthusiasm for alternatives to its current organisational model. It had been a disappointing road to say the least. The Wilds however, because so few facts applied to them with any consistency, offered a vast opportunity of some kind of discovery, escape, promise – all the vague possibles which ordinary life seemed equally destined to withhold.

Scholars of the Wilds are many, but actual information is on the skimpy side due to so few hands-on researchers ever returning to deliver their papers. It is therefore a pastime in which one can sit at home while producing a huge amount of lurid speculation at leisure, knowing that nobody will manage to find any solid evidence to dispute your wisdoms. The perfect pursuit for a lady intellectual, if Zathria had that kind of society, which it does not, all its purposes being pragmatic (meaning greedy) or warlike (also meaning greedy). The King has no time for higher thought or messing about with woodlands and the Queen's opinions remain a mystery as she's had the sense never to put one forward.

Wilds and Break aside, the rest of Zathria's border is a gateway to civilization, of a sort, pointed towards softer landscapes, bigger towns, wealthier marketplaces. The human world sees itself as a network of marvellous invention and safety locked within a much larger barbarian waste of near infinite mass, which they pretend to have no fear of by deriding it and employing a vast number of priests and witches. The embers of older civilizations poke up from the land at certain points, hinting about previous world masters. These are variously worshipped, or sometimes demonised, which is the same thing but with more drama. Princess Ven has written, scathingly, about this in an obscure journal of wit and observation – The Scandalous Riddle - which has sporadic circulation throughout the realms and perhaps upward of twenty regular readers. Her theories are variously mundane and placating if required for state purposes, because at least three of the regular readers are court spies, though the same theories are bleak and horrifying in her private notes where she faultlessly records her actual thoughts in the form of watercolour paintings.

The paintings are code which only she can understand. To the untrained eye they look like botany life studies.

She generally writes too much, is the consensus among the witerati, but the Riddle needs column inches and contributors keep going missing. Sometimes they migrate to more lucrative journals although none of those make it into Zathria as distribution isn't worth it for so few subscribers. The Riddle comes as an insert with her father's regular papers. He takes all the publications from the rest of the world, as a standard practice, but doesn't read them as all his news is delivered by the Vizier and the Priests. He leaves his copies in the library, pristine, in case someone visits who needs convincing that he's a man of learning. They stay for a couple of weeks and then are used as firelighters in the kitchens. Ven is the only one who reads them. That's how she found the Riddle in the first place.

Zathria, seen by its citizens, is a proud, fierce nation-state in that it survives perilously and has few natural resources worth squabbling about. Princess Lora is the oldest princess at a venerable twenty-one years old. Her marriageability is the heart of its most worthwhile product, the feud with Vanazon, which has bred tales of assassination, spying, daring do and scheming for over two hundred years and is showing no signs of dropping in value as a way of fundraising for the royal purse. This particular wedding idea is a new venture, threatening to disrupt this status quo with a peace in which only the peasants and sundry animals stand to gain.

Vanazon has offered its finest son in some obvious scheme which nobody can get to the bottom of. Prince Veher is known on the battlefield as a tall, typical soldier type, no obvious physical defects and plenty of vim. He's twenty-five and still alive in spite of countless attempts to review that situation. He is reported to be the healthy, outdoors sort who doesn't bother with court life other than to raid the prettier ranks of it for entertainment. In short, he is a typical, boring Prince, the kind that any King of the Zathria/Vanazon type longs for as either a son or a son-in-law. No imagination to speak of. No ability to out-manoeuvre the old man, easily disposed of if circumstances call for it. As a result the Zathrian Vizier is convinced the offer is ludicrous. It's a plot to lure Lora out into the dangerous territory between the two places where something will undoubtedly happen. Something of a Very Bad nature. Oh Woe! But despite this it's going ahead.

Princess Lora is not going, though.

Princess Ven is going. That's the master stroke at work here.

Even the Cinderkin can see the kind of minds that have hatched this idea.

It's possible that Ven will be the heart of a new plot to infiltrate and overthrow the Vanazon royal family, scheming Zathria's ascendance as a demure sleeper agent – and at the very least her children will be a constant bulwark against real danger. But as she herself is the only one capable of planning and executing something that subtle or ordinary this is unlikely. Instead, the intolerant reputation of the Vanazon court towards anything like an opinionated, educated woman suggests a lot of other things will happen. Very Bad Things. But, if you are the Zathrian King spoiling for a fight and low on funds because you have spent everything on the army, Good Things. We can't say Very Good as that might imply he doesn't care for Ven in a sufficiently seemly way. A generous spirit could assume that sending Ven is merely intended as an insult. One more poke in the many monthly poking sessions that riddle the joint affairs of the two warring courts. One outcome is certain though. Ven will not return to Zathria, and nor will any lasting peace accord.

Never say never though. Perhaps they will meet her, show her great dishonour and send her home. Surely some of them will see that as the double whammy – more insulting to return her unharmed as unworthy of a gesture of war. Your feeble attempt to insult us insults us! Years of backstabbing lead to exquisite sensibilities when it comes to paranoia and interpretation.

The Cinderkin has seen them all, but thankfully has never been involved in any way. Until now. And that brings him a problem which he is going to have to resolve extremely quickly. If Ven leaves Zathria then she will take her journal with her and that particular book is his entire reason for being in the human world in the first place.

Tabah, also known as Ember to Wildblood kin, wandered. He was looking for poultice herbs if anyone asked, and picked them if he saw them, but in fact he was wandering with the sole purpose of figuring out what to do in the hope that something would occur to him if he only kept moving forwards. The Break was the least likely place to meet another person unless you went to a guard bothy – he had a route which avoided all of them and most of their sightlines – and unless you hoped somehow to bump into Princess Ven, who was also known, in her outdoor disguise for the purposes of fooling guards, as Beibei the witch of Green Owl. Green Owl was the least significant of the witchclans and the least likely one to cause any interest. The disguise was superficially good and would have worked, except that everyone knew it was Ven. Tabah wasn't sure if Ven knew this. He wasn't sure how much Ven knew about anything, given he didn't know her and had, aside from a couple of times he'd held a horse for her, never got close enough to ask. In particular, he didn't know if she knew what was in her journal. It wasn't the kind of thing a human could know unless they were some kind of adept and Zathria was the place you went if you didn't want to find one of those.

It was possible though. Queens dallied in the summertime woodlands during ceremony season as much as the next woman. Wildblood roamed about the place at all times. Romances happened. Kings needn't know. They particularly needn't know about certain books that might be in their unvisited library collections, secreted there by wildblood persons for the sake of securing them in a safe place where safe meant safe from wildblood sorcerors rather than humans.

No human could have read it, so that wasn't the problem. The problem was that the book belonged to Her Darkness and Tabah was one of the guards of Her collection and he was reasonably sure, beyond all doubt, that it was the book that Princess Ven had discovered some years ago and, taking it for a blank book of empty pages, had made her personal journal out of it.

Now it was too much to hope for a chance meeting in which somehow an entire relationship's worth of trust and understanding would take place in minutes and the book be re-secured. A quick run through her usual paths convinced him she was more likely indoors, possibly confined due to the circumstances, and there was no chance of him getting close to the book this way, nor close enough to warn her about the book itself. Zathria's crushing dullness and intense human presence was a brilliant hiding place for it as it rendered the thing itself quite dormant. But once beyond the border there was no telling what it would do and, if it did anything, there were plenty of hunters out there willing to do whatever it takes to get their hands on it. Zathria and Vanazon would be inconsequential to them.

He managed to circle the outer castle grounds. The book gave off a tell-tale hum of potency that was strong enough to convince him he had located it in the Princess' Tower, high up, where the second rank of windows dared face the Wild. He thought he could glimpse a figure behind the glass. On the crenellated ramparts just to the tower's side, guards in Zathrian blue patrolled. There were more than usual, that is to say there were some, so clearly they had been placed there to ensure Ven didn't try to escape.

If the book survived all the way to Vanazon then he would be forced to turn back and it would be effectively lost. Vanazon was as enthusiastic about witches as Zathria was lukewarm. They would find the book and take it. Enough of them held high positions in court that getting it off Ven would be no problem. And they might be able to read some of it.

Tabah didn't know what was in the book. He was destined to guard it at Her Darkness' displeasure for the crime of dallying with one of her personal court. That displeasure might last years more, decades more, a lifetime more. There was no way to tell. That he had been part of her personal court at the time and therefore the entire business seemed whimsical and cruelly unjust was par for the course with her. Even so, he was desperate to please her. To fail at this simple task would confirm his permanent expulsion – he'd leave out of shame.

But. Ven was in the tower with the book and he was outside on the ground and tomorrow they left for Vanazon. It was all getting a bit late in the day.

Steal it? No chance, she kept it on her person. He would have to get past too many people, had no reason to go in, would not get out. He wasn't that kind of Wildblood.

Spirit it away? Again, wrong kind of Wildblood for that. No witches worth the salt it would take to be shut of them remained in Zathria except for Mildew Most, and she was only here for her vineyard. Even if she knew how to translocate objects, it wasn't certain the book was one of those things that could be moved that way.

Hire another Wildblood to risk their necks for it? Fleert was the only one with a chance, but she was too young for Tabah to want to involve in anything genuinely dangerous. Better Fleert stick to tormenting the astrologers. Plus she was a ward of Her Dreaming and if that went badly…no, that wasn't possible either.

Burn down everything except the book? Possible, but Her Darkness would take a much dimmer view of starting a war with the humans than she would about overdue books. Even lost books (temporary) and incompetent courtiers.

But on the journey anything could happen, couldn't it?

In the Tower, Princess Ven looked down across the swath of the Break and saw someone standing far below, near the thistle meadow, where she had built a bower (called it a bower, that is, but really it was more like a child's fort of bendy sticks) and liked to sit there to think her Real Thoughts. Whoever it was wore a cloak and hood, so they were unidentifiable even if her eyesight had been that good. They seemed to be looking at the Tower.

In her arms the large, leather-bound journal suddenly shook. No, it quivered, with an eager vibration which reminded her instantly of Sabre the cat when he had stalked and waited and was preparing to pounce.

She screamed and stood up, dropping the book onto the window seat cushion where it fell lightly and settled a bit too slowly for an ordinary book, and was silent.

'Milady!' her maid, Mym, came rushing in.

'Nerves,' Ven said quickly to forestall her, clutching her own elbows to prevent herself from shaking. 'I need wine!'

'Yes'm.' The maid hurried out. Her own face was splotchy and pale because she had to go too, but Ven didn't know how to help with that any more than she already had. They were both prisoners of the situation and that felt very like an execution. It was, at least as far as she could tell, an end to her pleasant, if lonely, life.

But now. The book.

She stared at it suspiciously, then dared to move closer again so she could look down through the leaded glass.

The figure was gone. A few deer moved about in the scrub, but nothing human was visible out there. Not that this was convincing of much. There were hundreds of places to hide. She watched for as long as it took the maid to return and then absently poured a glass out and drank it, poured another and handed it over to the equally silent Mym who drank it at the same determined pace before refilling it and handing it back.

Ven considered for the hundredth time how she might get out of the tower and into The Break. If she could make it there she could make it to the Wilds, she was pretty sure. And then what? Was it really preferable to risking it with Vanazon?

'I don't know what's out there,' Mym said, following her mistress' gaze to the darkening woodland where the sun had begun to cast orange and red across the leaves as it went down.

In spite of all her research, Ven didn't know either. She considered, self-pitying, that perhaps she ought to have spent all that time studying actual known politics and culture instead. She'd always relied on Mym for that, though.

It was technically time for ladies to retire for the night, but neither of them made any moves in that direction. They had no intention of wasting the limited hours of freedom, such as it was.

'Maybe some bandits will come and rob the coach,' Mym said

after a minute.

'It will probably be assassins,' Ven said. 'Did you pack the poison?'

'Of course.'

They had discussed escape many times, and every possible scenario and many impossible ones and both were sure of one thing. If it was assassins or bandits or robbers or any kind of Very Bad Fate Apparent manifested, then they were going to be sure to have the final escape of a potent poison to hand so neither of them had to suffer some worse situation than death. Still, talking about it as an actual possibility was chilling. At least Ven knew her poisons and could ensure a fairly painless exit. It seemed pitiful to have only that to look forward to.

She looked down at the book again. It hadn't made any untoward movements or noises since that one time. She wondered if maybe her increasing terror had made her imagine it, or somehow do it herself. Perhaps she was falling into fits slowly. With caution she sat down by it and put her hand on it. Nothing.

Come on, she thought. Be something. Be something! Anything.

But the book was its usual self.

'Do you want your inks, M'm?' asked Mym. 'Or we could read a story.'

'No more stories,' Ven said. 'Just pack the ink up. We have to be ready.'

She sat with her wine and tried to pick out the stars as they appeared one by one.

Mildew Most was standing at the junction where the cart track that led to her hill vineyards met the much weedier and less hospitable cart track on her own land. She was tall and strong and with her arms folded and her feet planted wide she commanded the twilight in its entirety as she watched Tabah gallop up. On his black horse, in his black cloak with his arms and hands and face all 'soot-marked' with his natural colouring making him appear as a shadow he would have been terrifying to an ordinary person, but of the two of them it was Mildew whose presence was the more powerful by quite a long way.

'Took your sweet time,' she said as he kicked his leg over the horse's mane and slid down to the ground.

The horse, without saddle or bridle, walked off a few yards to wait, puffing and snorting. Steam rose from its flanks into the cool air. Flies gathered swiftly.

'I only found out yesterday,' he said.

'Been news here for two days.' The witch regarded him with contempt.

'Yes, but you have the King's Ear,' by which he meant she could hear all that went on if she wanted to.

'And what've you got? The Donkey's Arse?'

Tabah said nothing, put back his hood and shrugged off the cloak, letting it fall to the ground, and with it all the bindings that kept him human enough to pass for merely ordinary Wildblood. He had the same kind of colouring as a buckskin horse, with dark brown fading to soot on his arms and legs, like opera gloves and stockings, and some soot around the eyes, end of the nose and mouth, giving him a slightly skull-like make up. The buckskin part was a glowing gold and across all of him were the sigils and writing of the Wild, lit up, as if from internal candlelight, where they kept him firmly written into the human shape. His stable clothes of rough dark shirt and half breeches were still straw-and-hair covered and his hair, like the mane of his horse, had been brushed but fallen back into tangled ways on the journey. It seethed a little, as though it was alive. His brown eyes remained hazel as if to make an extra point as he stabbed a finger at the character writing on his arm and glared at Mildew, 'No magic near the book, see?'

'Really?' Mildew said. 'That's why the book woke up this afternoon is it? That's why you're here now, coming to ask me to do something like I can just wave a magic wand.' She gestured with one finger in the air, making a very rude sign.

She was as tall as he. Feathers and bones were braided into her grey streaked hair, along with hanks of various other things that might have been trophies, or were possibly collectible items she just happened to like, including a Fiavian hussar's red uniform tassels and most of a white heron, including the beak, which hung lowest of all against her belly. Her clothing, also a fairly standard peasant drab, but in fine materials, gave her a housey mousey look beneath the hair which made it all the odder. She was handsome and compelling, like some kind of dread headmistress.

There was no question that Mildew was not her real name. She was, what most people in Zathria dismissed as 'bit o' Wildblood' which usually meant someone had once seen a Wildblood a few generations back. In that sense nearly everyone was Wildblood; in the sense that meant it was exotic, powerful, potent and desirable. Just enough Wild to be talented, not enough to be repellently weird. Except that when this was said of Mildew it was said defensively, to ward off any kind of Attention From Aspersions which Mildew might take offence at, should any hint be given that she was probably more of the 99 percent Wildblood category, or possibly that she was the author of the entire category taking an inexplicable turn as a lowly vintner. Mildew Most was her human trading name. She made the most excellent wines – and was indeed a master of mildews, moulds and all kinds of other things that went into or out of wines at various points – and she was the backstop of the Zathrian economy so 'bit o' Wildblood' was as far as anyone was going to go in that direction.

For now though, Mildew was in her resolute dame form. Heron beak, tassels and all.

'I came to ask your advice,' Tabah said, cowed as he knew he would be. The wand thing was unnecessary, but a bit of a joke. He felt her grudging acceptance.

'Wasn't you that set it off, then?'

'No.'

'You didn't even know until I said it just now, did you?'

He sighed. 'No.'

'Huh,' Mildew said, looking contemplative. 'Well, doesn't that just take the custard.'

'Should I retrieve it and take it back to Her?'

'Maybe. Can't have it lying about in the wrong hands,' Mildew gave him a pointed look.

Tabah scowled, 'It was safer if Ven had it, I thought, than if it was just in the Library. If she had it to herself then I knew where it was, there was no danger someone else might find it and carry it off or try to burn it.'

'Burn it?'

'There's a trend at court of using the pages of magical tomes as cigarette papers. Among the young men.'

'Onionskin papers I assume?'

Tabah shrugged. He didn't know paper.

'Barbarians.' This of all things seemed to spark something in Mildew. Her attention, which had been reviewing affairs with general disgust, sharpened itself. Then, 'Do you know which book it is?'

'No,' Tabah said humbly. 'She told me never to mind that. I was just to keep it safe until she said otherwise.'

'And she sent you here?'

'No, I chose Zathria. I could have gone anywhere. But not a place of power or near one.'

'And this mission of yours started when?' Mildew glanced at the stars.

'On the Pass of The Iron Dogs.' He didn't understand this digging at the past suddenly, but as Mildew was his only hope of advice he stuck it out, even seeing where it was all going.

'And why did she choose you?'

He mumbled something and looked away at the suddenly very interesting overgrown hedges where thick bundles of sweet hawthorn flowers were now the only other things clearly visible in the weak moonlight.

The reaction was not what he had expected and he had been expecting a deepening of her contempt. Instead, she snorted. 'You. And Fires of the Lightning Strike?'

This wasn't the kind of contempt he'd expected. 'Yes me. Why not me? What do you mean?'

Mildred waved her 'magic wand' hand at him, encompassing all he was, had been and would be, and wrapping it up in a big parcel of Hell No.

'Hell yes,' Tabah said angrily.

'Hell No,' Mildew said. 'No offence.'

'Offence taken. Also. Yes. I wasn't imagining it. She sent me out here when she found out we were…' but he broke off, not sure suddenly of what they were, exactly.

'Taking it up the arse from a higher power doesn't mean they're into you. Figuratively speaking,' Mildew said. There was a tinge of pity in her voice that made it all the worse although he knew most of it was meant to throw him off guard so he revealed more than he ought to.

'It isn't like that.'

'Court life is always like that,' Mildew said. 'Never mind. It's not a reason is what I'm saying. It's not a reason to send you far away on a fool's errand.'

'She was pretty clear about it.'

'I'm sure. And you were so fixed on your feelings that you

bought it.'

'Fires and I…'

Mildew held up her hand. 'Don't. For both our sakes.'

Tabah stood his ground. He felt his lower jaw jutting forwards. 'Have it your way.'

'So, you leave the court with the book. You bring it here. You hide it where nobody will touch it and you wait,' Mildew said. 'For eternity, as far as you know. Because you touched the Fire and you are now being burned and that makes sense to you. Her punishment feels right. All that importance. But. How long until Ven picked it up?'

He'd got the measure of her stabs now and focused only on the other things. 'A year maybe. Two?'

'How did you know she had it? There she is, a girl in her own home, you're all the way outside in the stables, you never go into the Library.'

'I…' he paused. Something, for the first time, felt off.

'How did you get the book in to the Library?'

'That was easy. I said I found it on a bench where Princess Ven had been reading a few hours beforehand and I asked one of the scullery maids to return it to the Library.'

'Because a scullery maid knows all about the Library.'

'She knows where it is and she can go there without looking suspicious!'

'Or she gives it to the Princess, because it's her book.'

'But she didn't have it.'

'How do you know that?' Mildew sighed the sigh of someone leading a horse to water.

'I'm bound to the book, all right?' he said and saw the look of sly triumph crease into a smile on her face. 'I know where it is. I just know.'

'I see,' Mildew said. She turned and started to go back up her track between the vineyards.

'Hey! Wait! You have to help me! I mean, please.'

Mildew stopped. 'Who bound you to it?'

'My Lady Darkness.'

Mildew started walking again, slowly, stolidly, the walk of an old woman, which she wasn't. 'Can't help you, Ember. But I can tell you. It's not what you think it is.'

'Mildew, please!'

She was lost to sight in the overgrown lane. He ran after her, faster than she was by far, but the lane was empty. The wind stirred the thorn and the leaves on the vines.

'Shit!'

There was nothing for it but to reclaim the grazing horse and his human cloak and return to the stables to wait for morning.

The caravan set off late and progressed slowly, moving at the speed of a hangover, since most of the participants were all much in the same boat as Ven herself – disposable – and knew it, so they had taken best advantage of their departing evening's feast. Only Tabah was clear-headed. And the horses, of course. Fortunately there was nobody on the roads once they'd cleared the town and they were soon well on the way to the ferry post at Brine Marsh, where a very long estuary met its match in a very long river and spread out into a series of thickly wooded and treacherous bogs. A lot of work had provided a cut-through, first on platforms and then by ferry which crossed the brackish stream at the point where the banks were firm for most of the year. Merchant traders from other nations preferred to pay local Zathrian couriers from the point of the far bank but all business was stopped for the day to allow passage of the royal party so, as afternoon came slowly on, they passed camp after camp of grumpy looking men, idling about smoking and gambling wherever the ground was stable enough to hold them and their carts.

Ven felt sick to start with because she had stayed up late drinking. Mym was no comfort, huddled in her own problems, the only mercy was the covered carriage which let her have a soft bed upon which she could roll around feeling miserable in private, occasionally stifling the urge to heave as she was tossed this way and that by the carriage suspension, bumping against the padded buffers and wishing she had drunk water and chosen to ride instead. Definitely tomorrow she would ride and enjoy whatever moment could be enjoyed in that rather than bounce about like a bread roll in a too-big bag. The day was also hot and the carriage airless. The morning suffusion of elderflower remedies meant there must be stops for ladies to make water, requiring the erection of a temporary tent and the digging of a temporary privy atop which a folding seat was thrown so ladies did not fall in said hole. Formal clothing dragged that out for ages with all its fussy fastenings. Flies bit and stung, without any regard at all for pomanders and tincture of viperleaf. The maids in the second carriage were all surly and resentful and made no effort to help anyone but themselves. No doubt their minds were fixated on the possible fate of ladies' maids who find themselves in trouble on the roads or handed over carelessly to the whim of foreign powers, which is mostly what tried to occupy Ven's mind, so she didn't blame them. She blamed her father, and men in general. By the time they reached the ferry with all the horse fussing and negotiation and whatnot that had to go on she was tired though, and headachey, and too miserable to care who was at fault. Just let this disgusting journey be over.

Tabah walked near the back of the line. He had had to exchange his decrepit cloak for a royal tabard of Zathrian colours which felt very much like a targeting assist more than a matter of pride at that point. From villager to traveller to guard nobody seemed to hold out the demanded hope of peace, instead watching the progress with a business-as-usual impatience, cross with the level of wealth they were seeing moving along the road, and none of it headed their way. The King's reputation was the only thing that kept them civil. The ferry crossing occupied all the afternoon. He had to give his full attention to keeping the animals peaceful, moving back and forth across the churning brown waters until every one of them had made it across.

The far bank brought with it a sense of safe distance. The silent convoy became louder and rowdier as drinking started again and the guard cheered up at the thought of camps, nightfall and being away from the tattling tongues of anyone connected to the King. They made good time and the first camp was set and waiting for them within the fringes of the Auburn Forest – technically Zathria but really a strip of the wild that crossed down through Zathrian held territories, before branching out again into full dominance of the Southern Reaches. It was not much more than ten miles broad and the only barrier of any significant note between them and a long, tedious trek to Vanazon. Cutthroats, bandits and whatever wildlife might loiter would all be here, among the trees. Thus the edge camp had been built as a permanent waymeet and was fiercely and well defended by an entirely different group of guards to the kind found at the court and the ones accompanying Ven's progress.

In stark contrast to the day's works, the camp personnel were efficient, strong and organized. Of Vanazon agents, interlopers, hidden plots and any untoward things there was no sign. The evening came on "quietly" with the chorus of bug and frog. Tabah knew that Ven had left her carriage for one of the sturdier huts only because he felt the progress of the book moving slightly left to right as he groomed the last horse. For all that Mildew had said about the book waking up there was no hint of life from it all day and that continued into the evening.

Then he noticed the shadows. Motes that could easily have been mistaken for the flicker of firelight or foliage were breaking off from their origins and moving together through patches of darkness. To a human eye they would have been unnoticeable, but he saw them clearly because he recognised them. This was Cat In The Corner, a servant of Her Perspicacity, and they were here for only one reason he could think of: the book. They were using their most stealthy form. Probably they wouldn't build enough reserve to transform into a solid state for a while yet, but soon they would, especially as the night deepened.

If they were already here, then much worse would be on the way before dawn.

Tabah made a decision he hoped he wouldn't regret.

Princess Ven was wrestling the rings off her fingers. Her hands were sweaty and the sickness of the day had transmuted seamlessly into sickness of pure fear as she had formed a plan during the afternoon. She'd fallen into a stupor after the ferry crossing and woken up a time later with the leather book satchel under her face and when she opened her eyes and came to herself everything had changed.

Well, nothing. She was still in the carriage and it was moving. Mym was propped in the corner staring greenly through a chink in the curtains, her nose outside. Harness clinked. The carriage trundled. The mumble-voices of the guard came and went. Hoof and stone and metal shoes clacked in irregular jolts.

Ven stared at the pretty white damask of the carriage interior. She was keenly aware of her movement through space; a body moving between two junctions, an object of small power being handed over, a floating unknown of little significance, that might be set alight or crushed as leverage in a larger game, a vessel of possible futures for other beings, born to die and be traded on and on into the future in the rounds of a ceaseless struggle which had no meaning or significance at all.

Everyone was implicated. Some had power – her father, Vanazon's Emperor (as if you could be an Emperor of something that could be ridden across in three days), a host of other men of various colours, weights, types, temperaments scattered here and there, all different, all the same in their fealties and loyalties and bands and hierarchies. Even the bandits had gang rules, codes, laws like hammers to bash them into line. Ven saw the hammers and the line, saw herself being swung to tap something else into place; felt herself smashed into her present shape. Her mind, that had spent its time focused on obscure writers, difficult subjects, arcane texts, wildflowers, ladies' occupations to pass the time between pain and death – was now betraying her by exploding all of this, which was known but hidden, into full and inescapable view. It wasn't that she just saw it. She had become it with a force that defied all of the efforts of her foremothers to smother, deny and crush it back, because once it is seen it cannot be borne and they must bear it and go on for they had no choice. They saw, they buried under tapestry and weaving and alms and court politics and they forgot. They had their own hammers for forgetting and crushing and bashing what they must carry into a tight, small ball, curled up and held inside. And now, in her sleep, it had been born.

She stared at the damask and listened to the carriage and sat and was jolted about, spine loose, sore from the hours of constant joggling. She opened her mouth and let out her first scream, silently, because who could or would understand such a thing and she must not scare the horses, and felt her hand on the book satchel. The satchel was open and the book had slid part way out. The leather of the satchel was smooth and warm, stiff and firm. The leather of the bookbinding was thin, pliable, cool, like the skin of a bent knee on a summer day in the shade that you touch unexpectedly and find taut, alien, colder than you think it ought to be but unmistakably alive.

She thought of her mother who had not come to see her off because she was ill with one of her long headaches and couldn't be removed from the bedchamber or suffer any kind of light. Ven had loathed and despised her at the moment of departure.

She looked at the damask, but the horror of knowing would not recede, in fact it grew. Land, animals, people, everything churned like the wave of soil under the plough, going up, coming down, crushed under, cut raw to the sky, and she would not escape, like all of them, for she was prisoner of her helpless body, that guilty body, which had put her here and not there, a lottery token on the bad turn of the tide, dictating that whatever she might have been, this is all she could have. But she could see what others had.

Her father's face, that intake of breath through his nostrils as he lifted his chin with its jowls quivering as he jutted his lower jaw and pushed out his lips in some kind of ham parody of fortitude, that said she'd get no mercy from him but, at the same time, invited all eyes to consider what a grand sacrifice he was making, the terrible suffering he was bravely stuffing down inside for the sake of the people, for his wife, for himself, that poor, noble, lonely fellow with the weight of so much responsibility upon his shoulders, trying to keep them shored up by filling his ribcage with air to puff it, his belly with ballast to always bring him upright, park him like a giant, solid rock upon which all craft would be smashed to matchwood. This was what he had built, this rightness, and he was proud. What she did only mattered because it might shine light favourably or disfavourably upon his bulwark. She did not exist as a person, but then again, to him nobody did because this is what it meant to be King. She'd admired his fortitude in that moment, too.

In this new vision he was a wooden doll, a nothing, his strings jerking him around. Inside the doll, a sad, small creature was rattled; a dry pea in a bottle. Across the world of men a thousand wizened things were drummed against their prison walls and altogether made a rushing sound like an angry churn of flies.

Beneath her fingertips the book's skin warmed and shivered. The shiver continued, regardless of the carriage's jerks. After a moment she realised that it was purring.

After a second more she began to stroke it, as much to comfort herself as for any semblance it might have had to a cat, and that was very little. But she felt the purr become more approving, satisfied.

The terror and horror began to recede, and in their place came knowledge.

When Mym put her head back into the carriage she saw her mistress sitting bolt upright, her hair loose from its bindings in a dark nimbus around her head, probably due to the damp and the sense of thunder in the air which always did that to girls with curls. For someone who was daydreaming Ven's eyes were strangely fixed and focused. When they turned suddenly to rest on her Mym jumped involuntarily.

'Mym,' Ven said. 'When we arrive you must insist upon a great celebratory feast. We have supplies for it. Spare nothing.'

'Yes'm,' said Mym, who had been waiting for the inevitable change of her mistress' ways once they were out of range of the castle and hoping that those ways would remain kind and shy as Ven had always been, not capriciously terrible as they might turn, for many good reasons. This was only medium strange for someone with the possibility of turning truly odd and she was relieved so she ignored the fact that she had the distinct sensation that Ven's journal was somehow looking at her and that whatever she did next was going to be the deciding factor in whether or not she survived the night.

Mym put her nose back out to see what was going on and pretended none of that had happened. The mind did ridiculous things when it was discomfited and in the dregs of drink, she reminded herself. One more reason to stay detached from whatever was going on, no matter how much she thought her heart was going to break with it. People did things wrong. They died. People grew up, they had to do what was expected of them or pain and violence followed. These things happened. Life was like this. Make do and get on with it. If Ven wanted a party she could have one. Wasn't like any of this rabble was going to say no to it and it was the only chance she'd get, poor thing, even if she lived to marry in Vanazon or whatever came. And for Mym, the worst would probably happen, but you had to keep going towards it, keep on moving to it, as if you didn't know. Nobody would let you off. All their lives depended on it.

Ven heard Mym's thoughts as clearly as bells, though they wouldn't have been hard to guess in any case. Impelled to act in any way at all just to break the horror, she moved across to the door and yanked the curtain apart on her side, against all protocols, sticking her head out to see for herself where they were.

At that moment one of the guard was hurrying past to get to the front of the line. No, not a guard, she thought, after a second's confusion caused by his lack of armour. It was the Wildblood who held her horse for her when she went riding, and collected it when she returned. And he wasn't human. That was clear as day to her now. His appearance was as close a replica of a human being that he could manage, and it wasn't an illusion, but there was more than that. She couldn't see that more with her eyes, just like she hadn't seen the facts of her life so clearly in her mind before, but the knowledge seemed like a vision because she 'saw' that he was bigger and more strange than any human in the line. She saw that he was made, in one plane, of fire.

'Ember,' she said, nearly soundless, her mouth experimenting with the name but it was right. It was completely right.

He turned back to glance up at her.

She snapped herself back inside the carriage on reflex, anticipating a telling off, but of course there was no governess present, no mother, no sister, and Mym was lollygagging out the other side.

Half-trapped beneath her leg on the seat cushion the book gave a firm, muscular flex.

Ven's mind was racing so fast she could barely make sense of it. One part was reaching for her journal and inks, to record these incredible developments, making plans for papers, for essays, for talks she would give to audiences of professors. Another part was cringing away from the journal with a visceral horror. Another part of her was wondering what she could do with all this knowledge at this moment – there must be more, she must pursue it! She must find a way to talk to that Wildblood. The book had reacted to him twice. They were connected. He must know something about it. And yet another part was sickened with terror that if anyone found out about any of this she would be exposed, shamed and horribly punished. Certainly Mym would, too, and perhaps the entire company on the journey. Her father hadn't known about her activities at home because he hadn't cared to. The Wildbloods in his household only existed as their own form of politics, to keep safe from the Majesty of the Wild. They were, to him, a kind of hostage. He could easily read treason into any of this and, given his temper, he would.

She didn't even squeak. If anyone had seen her pale face, fixated, glassy eyes and frozen posture they would have instantly known a mortal dread upon her. But nobody did see and it couldn't last forever. The carriage went over a rock as it passed through the camp gates and shook her out of it. She found her hand on the warm skin of the book, a fingertip caressing its velvety surface and finding, at the edge of the binding, the sharp corner of a paper sticking out of the pages.

Without looking down she picked the corner up and brought the item before her face. It was a folded paper with her name inked on it in her mother's shaky copperplate script.

She was about to unfold it when the carriage drew to a halt and boots crunching on gravel were followed by a sharp rap on the door. She shoved the letter back where it came from and the journal back in its satchel as the sergeant-at-arms said, 'We've arrived.' She heard and felt the bump and fuss of the steps being put in place. Giggles and unladylike voices from the rear carriage announced the maids' glee at finally being able to get out. Mym, gathering her things together, and Ven's, rolled her eyes. She began to chatter about the party times that the maids and guardsmen had been planning since the day this trip was put on the calendar, all the life and freedom denied them by the round in Zathria to be seized in the narrow days of the trip back and forth. Mym was making all the noises of professional disapproval in a prim, and somewhat disappointed, way.

'But Mym,' Ven said after a suitable time. 'Why don't you join them? You should. Vanazon could be terribly…boring for you.' And by boring they both knew what was meant by that. Ven had seen for herself a window, and wasn't about to waste it. 'Once we've settled in and I have my dinner you are free to do as you please. Just be back by the morning in time to get us ready for the travel.'

Mym's practiced first objection, one of several that must be acted out, was cut off as the door was opened and a gloved hand offered to assist Ven out into the sunset light. She took it and stepped out into the fresh and cool evening air. The solid wooden huts of the camp, the tower and the wall of spiky posts were all dwarfed by the encroaching clouds of the tree canopies all about them. Above that the mackerel skies showed a magnificent backdrop of mountains beyond.

It was a frustrating length of time meeting and greeting the camp dignitaries, formally accepting welcomes, going through the motions until at last Ven was able to be alone in her quarters – a perfectly good, solid room with a clean bed, a desk and a wardrobe – and at last open the folded letter.

"My Dearest Ven. You are in grave danger. The sergeant-at-arms is a pawn of the Vanazian state. This journey is the King's opportunity to rid himself of everything that vexes him at once. You must leave at the first chance. I have paid the keeper of the horse to ensure the best steed is available for your escape. But I do not trust her. It is likely she will betray me to the King sooner than relay my command. Therefore you may be on your own and can waste no time looking for allies. I have placed letters of note inside your book satchel, as I know you would never leave it. Uncut jewels and valuable spices are stitched within a set of plain clothing I have had packed at the bottom of your chest. I believe that Mym at least is faithful. Poor Mym! You cannot save her, so do not waste your chance in trying to find a way. Get to horse. Ride east. The countries there have a slim respect for women you will not find elsewhere." There was no signature, only the ink mark of the Queen's ring.

It was by far the longest communication Ven had ever had with her mother. The gesture itself, so dangerous, was more than enough for her to feel all the sudden loss of a love like that and for a few minutes she couldn't speak, but then the door opened and Mym came in, ushering two sweating and cursing guardsmen as they lugged Ven's chest of valuables, dresses and gifts into the room. Mym hastened to unpacking as soon as they were gone.

'I think,' Ven said, finding that her voice had become that of a mouse somehow. 'That I should ride tomorrow. Perhaps I ought to talk to the master of horse.'

'I think that's a very wise idea,' Mym said, choked up as she heaved the enormous weight of the wedding dress aside onto her own smaller bed. She wiped her eyes on her sleeve. 'Perhaps you ought to practice a few canters on the lane tonight. To be sure you can control the beast. Before they're all drunk as lords. I'll call him.' She darted out.

Ven had never felt scared like this before in her life. The note. The journey. The thoughts. But worse than that immediate terror was the sudden vision that no matter what happened now her life was over, as anything she'd valued in it would be taken anyway, even if she made it to Vanazon, married and was not murdered in some plot or other. She'd led the life of a neglected child, which had sometimes felt very lonely, but which now looked like a golden era of heavenly peace.

She looked down at the journal. She knew its every scratch and mark, the place where the lining was coming unglued a bit from repeated openings and being braced firmly while she wrote, the torn page, the soft edges of the not quite matched places, the blue and white of its stitching. She knew every word of her own tiny writing and line of her sketches. She felt afraid of it now, but also angry, because it seemed like it had betrayed her, by pretending to be a book when it clearly was something else. She'd put her heart and soul into it, every dream and hope, every minute of her time. There had been, lately, a sense that she was putting herself into it, to try to save that piece of her, when she must lose everything else. That feeling had spurred much of her Wildblood research – that and a fantasy that somehow she could become known for it and taken up to the great colleges of other nations and could escape that way, if only she could discover something and prove her worth. The world, a power there, would notice her. The journal had meant all those things. And now it was turning against her.

She withdrew her hand from it slowly, watching it as she would have watched a dangerous creature.

There was a rap at the door, Mym's triple threat knuckles, very quiet, very fast, because she was nervous. It opened without pause and Mym came bustling in, ushering the taller figure of the Wildblood stablehand behind her.

Ven, still wearing her travelling dress, stood up rapidly.

The Wildblood was tall and dark, his livery somewhat awkwardly worn in a way that suggested he didn't care for it. She saw things that were not, and had never previously been there, about his person – some kind of antlers, a mantle of thorns, a trailing cape of shadows and, at the edges of his eyes, the glow of a banked fire's deepest heat. She knew it wasn't there because she could also see him the person and that was the usual Wildblood human, oddly coloured, with the movements of someone who doesn't want to draw attention. That was all very usual. The ghosts of other things were new and they were, she was certain, created by the book.

He glanced at her and then immediately his gaze went to the place on the bed where she'd been sitting.

All the mummery and chitter she'd been fumbling through to get out what she wanted to say went out of her mind. 'What's going on?' she said instead. 'What have you got to do with my journal?'

He looked at her with his jaw a bit slack for a moment and she saw he hadn't expected candour. He sucked in a breath, looked at Mym who was goggle-eyed and also, weirdly, glaring at the same time; both petrified and threatening. 'I'm it's guardian,' he said. 'It belongs to Her Darkness and I was sent to prevent anyone reading it.'

Ven stared. 'Reading it? There's nothing in it!'

He lifted his hand and she stepped forward protectively, between him and the book. His face wore a look of concern but he retreated and confused her. He held both hands up in the universal unarmed gesture.

'If I may have it, I will show you.'

She looked at Mym who shook her head, helpless. 'I…I..didn't know it was hers. I thought it was just an empty notebook. I didn't mean to ruin it! I swear!' How childish and silly her voice sounded to her now, as if any of those things would matter in an adult world. They'd never mattered to her father or anyone she knew. What was done was always faulted, however ignorantly or innocently it had happened.

To her surprise the Wildblood backed a little more and somehow hunkered a little, although he couldn't be smaller. The essence of antler and mantle receded to a fine skin of shades. 'No, no. I understand. Please.' He held out his hand. Asking for the book.

Ven wrung her hands together. She felt that the book was all she had left, but now it was also a kind of evidence against her. She didn't know who Her Darkness was, because the named and documented Wildblood were so few, and they didn't speak much of anything that made sense to humans when interviewed about their lives. But it sounded somehow a lot like the way people said her father's name, or title. Only more so. Not the kind of person whose book you ought to be defacing.

'I…' she looked at Mym, but Mym was shrunk and small on her own bed with fear, a kind of desperate hope in her face as she looked to Ven to lead them out of this. And Ven was shaken, because Mym had always been so pragmatic, so everyday. Mym was the last person to dwell on fear and the first to do what had to be done.

(He has to tell Ven about Mildew)

'If you don't hand it to me of your own free will, I cannot take it. Because now it is yours,' Ember said.

'And aren't you free now?' Mym braved. 'If you were the guardian but she's got it anyway?'

'If I was free then I'd be gone,' he replied. 'Trust me, nobody wants to be gone from here more than I do.' He let his hand go down and sighed. 'I am the prisoner of this book. I am bound to it, like a page.'

'What for?' Mym again. Belligerent with anger that was the outer skin of her fear. Ven loved her.

'Yes, what for?' Ven said, folding her arms as if this was a major point in a distinguished argument before some board of judges.

'I...am not sure. I loved someone in the court of the dark queen and she bound me to this book. The connection, the reason – they all say I have displeased her. But I don't see how.'

He related, piece by piece, his encounter with the witch, and concluded, 'So, you see. Maybe you're not the only one feeling damned.'

'And can you read the book? Even if I'm not supposed to? Why would you make a book and not want someone to read it? What's the point of putting it out there if you...if you are...was she hunting? Is it a trap?' Ven's mind, freed from a bit of its fear, had begun its usual process of wandering and linking. 'Was she testing?'

'Let me read it,' he said. 'I have a feeling that I was meant to, but I never tried it, because...' he hesitated.

'Because,' Ven said, 'you always believe people like Mildew Most, and you have faith, and you are loyal to Her Darkness and don't doubt her either because she's very powerful and you're scared. Or because she's really wise and you feel stupid around her.'

The dark eyes of the Wildblood looked at her sombrely. 'Yes,' he said. 'That's true.'

Ven reached behind her and picked up the journal and held it out to him. 'It takes one to know one.' She let it go, desperate to hold onto it, desperate to see what was on those empty, bare pages that she couldn't read.

He took it and opened it. Her little paintings, pressed flowers and decorated margins looked back at him, nothing else. He leafed through it a bit and she saw her essays, her doodles, her diary...

He smiled. 'I think she will like that.' Then before Ven could speak he clicked his fingers and the lamps in the room went out. The window shutters had been closed against the storm outside. They were suddenly in almost total darkness save for the slightest chink of light coming from beneath the door where the stone was worn on the lintel. That and the glowing writing on the pages of the open book. It was faint, hardly more than moongleam, but the marks of the ancient script were there in long, connected lines.

Of course, Ven thought, feeling so stupid. A book written by Darkness can only be read in the dark. She moved closer. At this range the light of the ink shone on her own figures and made them faintly visible too. She heard Mym squeak with a terror she was smothering with her hands and then saw a hand that was long, fine and elegant, and not belonging to Mym or to Ember, reach out and delicately turn the page.

'My dear,' said a voice from over her shoulder, not where any head should be that belonged to that hand, 'Ember is quite right. You have improved my little book no end. And for that I shall grant you a request.'

'You sent it on purpose,' Ven said, stock still, daring hardly to breathe, the words hardly whispers as they came out.

'Only one suitable for running wild would ever touch it,' the darkness said from the far corner of the room, seeming as though it was looking around, facing away from them. Then it was back, close to her cheek. 'And only one faithful and strong would never try to read it, even when he could. But life is short. What will you ask of me?'

'To change the world, make it fair, make it better.' Ven had had this wish so many times that she didn't even have to think to know what she wanted to say.

The shadow paused in its examination of the book. The fingers traced the edge of a lily where Ven had written extensively about her frustration and despair with the life of women, in the castle and beyond. 'That is beyond my power,' said the voice. 'I suspect it is beyond all powers. But if you like you can join us beyond the limits of that world. In the darkness things may be remade into shapes of their own making, their own dreaming. In time the wild blood can run strong enough to transform you into a creature that will no longer be bound by these foolish visions, never tormented by the likes of men.' And Her voice on that final word seemed to consume the very idea and melt it, as a snowflake melts on the tongue.

Ven gulped. 'What about Mym?' Not just because Mym was there, listening. Because it wasn't fair, not right, to leave her to what must come in the wake of her desertion. Mym would be blamed for everything. That was the Zathrian style of operations. Probably one reason they'd been left in this room. At any time someone could 'discover' their treason, being alone here with Ember, and have it as a reason to do whatever they had planned for their advancement, or the advantage or disappointment of some King. There was no end to the opportunity.

'No!' Mym gasped, astonishing her. 'No! I can't. I won't go with them. I've got me Mam to think of. I've got a man back in…please, Ma'am.' The raw fear had changed her.

As usual, Ven hadn't thought far enough.

'Then I'll have to stay,' Ven thought aloud, feeling the cold grasp of terror and failure both. She would have leapt at the chance to leave but her death was, after all, assured. Here, or in some nightland far away, there was only time between now and then, and it would be better short and true than long and full of regret.

'Perhaps,' the voice did not sound at all convinced. It became mocking, playful, 'But what a pity to lose you. If only one of us could call on a faithful friend to cover our escape into the night. Ember. But be quick. The sergeant at arms has almost drunk what must be drunk to do what must be done.'

The lamps came back to life and in their light all shadows fled leaving the three of them in the weak but gentle gleam of the burning oil. Ven rushed to Mym, who was cowering.

'Gods forgive my cowardice!' Mym cried. 'I'm so sorry. I can't. I can't go. I'm afraid! But you…' she convulsed into a paroxysm of grief and regrets that Ven was unable to comfort.

'Mym,' she said sternly. 'It was my choice.'

'Ladies,' said the Wildblood. 'Say your goodbyes. If you will come, Princess. Ven. Then come to my side. We will be leaving. Mym, good servant, be out of this room within the minute if you wish to see your man again in this life.'

Ven, still in her travelling clothes, hardly light but also, without much in the way of anything else, looked about automatically for the book satchel. It was on the edge of the bed, buckled shut, and heavy when she picked it up in a way that suggested the book was there, or something was there. Something that growled as it slapped against her leg through her coat. Mym's collapse was so unexpected, she could hardly bear it, but she seized Ember's hand and with the other opened the door.

'Move, Mym!' and then, without a backward glance, she was

floating with the speed of her descent of the steps of their hut, strangely light as though she was made of smoke, the camp barely visible, shrouded by the same smoke that hid her from their sight. All she felt was the fierce, hot grip of the Wildkin and the pulse of blood in his palm, matching hers, as they ran.

The charm faded quickly. They had barely gone around the post of the gate when she was suddenly and rudely back in her very tired and normal form, getting wet as rain began to fall unevenly from the blackened sky above. A wild excitement and a terrible foreboding warred for control of her. She was only not sick because she was trying to see so very hard, looking at Ember as the last hope.

'It's not easy,' he said. 'I was human once. We should go further away.'

They hurried along the road in the rain for a few yards until they reached a tiny animal track that turned up into the trees on the hillside and then there was no more thinking because it was too dark to see and she could only stumble after him, slipping, and holding his hand. 'What's not easy?' She was whispering but he heard her.

'The change,' he said.

'How?' she asked, feeling rain run down her nose.

'Open the book,' he said.

In spite of the weather she managed to get it out of its satchel. She opened it at random, light from the pages filled her face, and the book read her.

Ember was nervous too. Not because of the book or the humans – now that the book was reading there was no trouble to worry about for Ven or him in that respect, they wouldn't get caught – but because he didn't feel sure that Fires was going to show up. Ven was right about him, which is why he'd helped, and she was probably right to throw shade on Mildew, but one thing you could be sure about when it came to any Wildblood was their changeability. Fires was all he could think about as the skies glowered and the rain came in larger drops.

Then the air felt dense and heavy, charged with a terrible possibility. In the reflected light of Ven's astonished face he saw her hair rising upwards, one strand at a time, felt the sudden inner burn of a Wildkin manifesting.

'That bloody maid just wouldn't leave,' said a droll, dry voice at his side and at the same moment there was a flash that made the world stark white and a crack that split the air and all their eardrums with a painful stabbing. A moment later the thud of an explosion rocked the ground. And then heavier bits and pieces of Ven's old room came splintering in a hail of wood through the sudden downpour.

There did not seem to be any bits of Mym.

Fires of the Lightning Strike was in their most quiet form, ashy grey, tall, with a shock of hair that fluttered like old rags. They smiled at Ember with a row of glowing red-hot teeth. 'Time we were off, I think.'

Screaming and shouting were coming from the camp.

Ven looked up from the book. The light from the writing faded away, leaving her in darkness, and she closed it with a snap. 'Ink and dreams is all we are made of,' she said. Her Darkness was a mist of lamp black among them.

From the pages of the book the drawings of the little flowers, the birds, the small creatures, the horses and the deer, all the many small doodles and the large paintings swept up and over Ven's arms, covering her from head to toe, their line and colour sinking into her like water into paper. The words of her hopes and fears, the idle musings, the stern essay notes, these rushed through her, finding the deep ink of Her Darkness and writing themselves in an ever-shifting narrative within her bones.

'At last,' whispered the Darkness. 'Someone to talk to. Come. Time to show you what the Wild is made of.'

And in that moment Ember and Fires became their equine forms, and Ven a black bird of scribble and ink, a crow she'd once drawn and coloured. The book, the satchel, her clothes were written on her, ready to be told, but for now she flew on midnight wings, untouched by the rain, for she was already an imaginary being and made of the Wild.

She circled the burning guard camp, and when she had seen Mym, safe and sound, and that nobody had been badly hurt, she circled high enough to see the trail of the burning-eyed horses and followed it, far away from the reach of the ordinary world.

Until she turned off and watched them race away, job done. Fire and Ember belong together in the hidden twistiest and truest paths of the spirit, wound in poetry, they are for a different future.

Her business is hardly finished. A day to the East is Zathria's castle, dour and glum. Night wraiths lie like the dregs of battle upon its gutters, soaking up the steady diet of quietly held miseries that must accompany the rule of ruthlessness, reason and power.

It's the hour when the wine is pressed out of the soul. And a crow, very large, towing lines of inky words behind it, like the tail of a grim peacock, made entirely of omens, cuts its silhouette against the stars. Do you remember, oh my mother, when we looked at the stars together, so icy and so far, so free in the unfenced sky?

It circles down, words falling from its feathers, striking the roof, soaking the stones, rushing down the mouths of the gaping gargoyles into the rooms, into the furnishings, onto the walls. Pictures appear, huge, spectral with wobbly, watery colours. Here a kingfisher. There a clutch of daisies with the words, 'Common Daisy' and that's true enough, but then it also says, 'Sweetener of Old Wounds.' That's new. That kind of new is everywhere coming into being.

The spells fall and sink into the house under cover of Her Darkness. They create couplets in the bedrooms, pithy one-liners in the privies, jokes in the kitchen, a brimming cauldron of power in the dining room. The dungeons bloom with black roses that are edible and good. In the kennels the dogs chase the fattest rabbits. The horses dream of meadows. And on the balcony, a sleepless woman, her grey hair coming loose from its braid, stares out at the world in the direction of Vanazon, and sometimes down at the long drop to the courtyard's moonlit flags. But we mustn't jump, must we? There's still the others.

Girls above in their bedrooms dance with princes and princesses, and everyone is a prince, and everyone is a princess and nobody must marry, only dance and enjoy a glass of champagne, the smile of a friend, the touch of a flower upon the edge of their noses as they come close to the brimming bouquets. A boldness fills the dreams, a sense that there are no shortcomings, no mis-steps possible here.

But on the balcony the words creep slowly, carefully, winding around the columns and the balustrade. People can't be taken to the Wild. They must long to go, until the longing is stronger than all other things, until they are consumed by the desire to know.

The words form a vine, upon which flowers, in the sunlight

appear fine and yellow, and in the night strange and luminously white. There are thorns, subtle, and tipped with particular inks. It grows up from the balcony, along the face of the castle, to the rooms above, and down among the wistful wisteria to the servants below. As it is made of ink and words it will not be seen by anyone who doesn't study hard. As it is made of ink and words it can be read in the way one smells a beautiful bloom.

Ven watches her mother wring her hands, rest her fingers on the rail, wince and snatch her hand back with the prick of a thorn and then look up in wonder as she hears Ven say, 'I am free.'

Later a crow visits Mildew Most's house and leaves a calling card upon the step.

Crow is the first shape. Crow sits on the roof and sends tendrils of words down to the library and sucks the pages dry. There will be others. There will be much more. But in good time. For now there is ink and wings in the darkness.

On Storm

Neil Gaiman

Storm entered my life like a myth. It was a Fantasycon, in Birmingham, and when I arrived at the convention the word was already on the street. Robert Holdstock breathlessly told me the story in the bar: There was an author who had been Found on the Slushpile (which already made her mythical and magical) who had been brought to the convention by Futura. She wrote novels about the Wraeththu, non-gendered post-human creatures, and, Rob told me, she appeared to have arrived with some of the people she wrote about: people whose gender Rob was unsure of, but who he thought were astonishingly attractive.

I said hello to Richard Evans, then an editor at Futura, later my editor at Gollancz, who wanted to know if I'd met Storm yet, and who took me over to meet her. She was, unquestionably, the best-dressed person at the convention, possibly the best-dressed person in Birmingham, and she had magnificent, enormous hair. I was, of course, intimidated. But then, Storm was funny, and friendly, and nice, and remarkably Down to Earth for someone who looked so magnificent, which meant that we became cheerful convention friends. It was the smile that did it, I think. An open, friendly, occasionally wicked smile that meant that you knew you could trust the person you were talking to.

As the conventions went on, we would find each other in bars, and settle down and catch up. The beautiful, semi-imaginary people she had brought with her to that first convention seemed to fade away, to be replaced by real people.

And pretty soon, we were Guests of Honour at conventions all around the world, and Storm being there the other Guest of Honour meant that I could relax, that I knew there was a friendly face, someone who had known me forever, or more or less, someone I could just sit and talk and drink with and hug and be, well, normal with. It could be anywhere in the world – I remember arriving exhausted after a long journey, in Perth, in Western Australia, and seeing Storm, and knowing everything was all right.

When I was anywhere near Stafford I would see her and Jim, I was impressed when she transitioned into the publisher role, when Immanion Press became a real thing. She never seemed to age, not in the way that some of us do. She was always poised, always funny, always there. The smile was as open, as wicked, as real, as it had been at the start.

About a decade ago, she wrote to let me know that she was a scent addict and loved Black Phoenix Alchemy Labs scents. I wrote back, to tell her that I had lots of their prototypes living in my basement, and would be glad to send them her way, and did. I loved being her undercover scent-dealer, and loved knowing that I was making her happy.

I was shocked hearing that Storm had passed away. I'm not sure I'm used to the idea yet, or that I truly believe it. She seemed eternal, and mythic. The last time she wrote to me, was to tell me that she had loved a book of mine. "Thank you for the words," she said. "Each one tasted lovely." It was a perfect Storm sentence. It started off here, and then went somewhere I wasn't expecting, but which felt delightfully right. And somewhere I could see her smiling.

New Words, Old Songs

Nerine Dorman

It took me the better part of a day to finish piling rocks on top of Jehanna's cairn. It was hard labour, made harder still by the splinters of grief that brought me up short. Only yesterday, she'd been well. We'd talked about extending the wattle-and-daub walls of the outer shrine. And this morning she was gone. Slipped away in her sleep so that when I'd come into her chamber to bring her morning tea, she'd lain there, stiff and cold, her skin like wax and her eyes staring into eternity.

Jehanna wasn't *that* old, or rather she hadn't been completely ancient, but she had admitted to seeing more than sixty summers, and she'd been around during the Before, so she knew many things that I didn't. She'd still had hope that we would be able to claw our way out of the rubble of society, but some of the things she spoke of were so strange, so impossibly outlandish, that there was no way I could ever see people flying in the sky in metal tubes with wings, or even communicate over long distances with the tablets some folks still had – quite dead, really. No better than black mirrors with cracked screens. I have found some of the larger ones useful for scrying, and that is about it.

There had been no one to help me wash her and wrap her in her shroud. I had entwined late-blooming jasmine in her hair and painted her eyelids with kohl, the way she said the ancients in faraway Egypt used to. Thankfully, I could get her eyes to stay closed with a judicious dab of the gum we used for our book binding. I couldn't bear the dullness in her pupils. It was like she still saw me, despite the impossibility of the matter.

I was able to heft her mortal remains onto an old blanket, which I then used to drag her out of our home and a short way up to the cemetery with all its little mounds and bread-oven style mausoleums. No one from the village down by the river came to help me. It's as if they knew and would have nothing to do with Jehanna's passing. It was all on me, her acolyte.

Tomorrow was the holy day, and they'd come visit the shrine as if nothing was the matter. I knew this in my heart of hearts, and I was not ready to face them. What I was grateful for throughout the rest of the day was that there were stones aplenty. The farmers bring these as offerings, for we always have need for our dead. The ground here is hard, and there isn't always time to dig a grave – especially in midsummer when flesh spoils so fast.

But this was late winter, and a bitter wind howled down from the crags, and one of the hunters had told us that there were still pockets of snow up on the Wolfberg. Only by late afternoon, did I catch whiffs of decay from Jehanna's cairn. Or perhaps it was merely my imagination. I hated the thought that I covered her over with so much rock, that her body was returning to the earth – so hard, with not even a bed of soft straw. Not that comfort mattered to the dead, but it did to me. This last indignity stung me like a wasp.

But I'd sooner cover her over with her new home of rocks than let the jackals and other scavengers have at her. Down the valley, by Algeria village, they expose their dead to the birds. Sky burials, they called it – a custom from the Before, it's said. The mere thought turned my stomach. The few times we'd gone downriver for trading, I'd seen their Place of Bones, as they call it, but never ventured close. I fancied I saw skulls leering at me from the ground. Or maybe it was just my overactive imagination.

No ravens would peck out Jehanna's eyes, and jackals would have to look elsewhere for a meal. By the time the moon rose fat and orange, and the last light bled from the inky sky, the skin of my hands was raw and abraded, but my work was done. Jehanna was gone to the arms of the Goddess, and I was alone.

Usually, we'd greet the night and put out the lamps in the shrine and close the doors of the Goddess's sanctuary. But for the first time in years, decades perhaps, no one had opened Her home for sun's first light. I was too tired, too sad, and too numb.

I hadn't even been able to cry.

Oh, we'd been called upon to offer last rites for our villagers. In my sixteen years, twelve of which I'd served under Jehanna, I'd observed nine people pass from this world to the next. I'd dried their loved ones' tears, heard the heart-rending keening and sobbing as the last rattling breath was offered. I'd embraced those shaking with grief until their breaths evened out and a measure of comfort passed from one to another.

Yet there was no one to do the same for me.

Even Indygo, the caracal Jehanna had hand reared as a kit, who occasionally deigned to be seen around our sanctuary, was conspicuous in her absence. I'd have thought the cat would at least offer her last respects. But then again, these beasts so beloved of our Goddess are notorious for their fickle natures, and semi-wild ones like Indygo even more so.

My grief was a heavy rock fallen from the mountain and resting precariously on my chest so that it was hard for me to draw breath. Any moment now, I expected Jehanna to berate me for not having lit the lamps or having cooked supper. Instead, I curled myself into her bed and pressed my face against her pillow, that still retained the bitter herb scent of her hair and that muskiness that was uniquely hers. Her chamber was bigger than mine, and I supposed it was mine, now. Along with her duties to the Goddess and to our community. The immensity of it all weighed even more than that precarious rock, and even as I tried to bury myself in Jehanna's bedding and unwish myself from existence, I couldn't escape this new, terrible reality.

If I dreamed during that first night of aloneness, I did not recall the fragments as I awoke the next morning at the first pipings of the birds. I breathed, tangled in Jehanna's bed linen, and the weight of her passing shattered me anew.

Yet my work would not wait. Yesterday had been an anomaly, a catastrophe, but I could not allow myself the luxury of slipping. Today was the holy day, when our Goddess would hear the petitions of her people, and the task fell to me to get everything in readiness.

I hurried through my ablutions and broke fast on old bread and a cup of red tea.

The food was ash on my tongue, and the tea did little to warm me. I would have liked nothing more than to sink back into Jehanna's bed, but the Goddess needed me more. Who else would sweep out the shrine, place fresh beeswax candles in the sconces, and light the incense so that lazy swirls of blue-grey smoke twisted into the rafters where speckled pigeons perched?

Jehanna would sing the adorations as she worked, and usually I added my voice in counterpoint. Now, I had to sing her part alone, and my voice was feeble and scratchy in the chamber. Dust motes floated in the air and caught the first rays of the sun as I laid down the reed mats then drew fresh water. I had time enough to gather proteas from the veld nearby into the sanctuary.

I had watched my mistress about her task many times. The familiar words rolled off my tongue as I opened the double doors to the niche to expose the golden flesh of our Goddess to the sun. But the words rang hollow, even as I bathed her limbs and dried her with clean linen.

Her leonine features were flat, dead, to my eyes, when in the past I'd fancied that Her quartzite-and-garnet gaze would follow every movement, her lips curled in a mysterious feminine smile.

At her feet sat little figures Jehanna told me were her kittens, but they looked misshapen to me this morning, childish lumps only vaguely representing the forms they were intended to represent. In one hand She held the symbol of life, and the other was raised in benediction.

"Why?" I asked Her. "Could we not have had more time?"

She did not answer me.

Midmorning, the first of our community arrived for the Blessings. None looked askance at me that I was all alone. None asked after our priestess. Instead, they filed in meekly, and placed their offerings before the sanctuary: cured meat, smoked trout, flasks of mead, preserved fruit, and vegetables in glass jars. Offerings for the Goddess that would also feed me. More food than I could eat in a week, to be true. But in return I was to bestow upon them the benedictions of our Goddess.

I lit the incense, I shook the sistrum, and I led their worship in the standard call and answer. I was accustomed to Jehanna's voice ringing out, the subtle magic of her words throbbing in against the rafters and teasing forth a sense of awe, that the Goddess was near, that She was padding among us on velvet paws.

Jehanna's words on my tongue and lips felt…wrong. Instead of flowing forth smooth, water over river-tumbled stone, they were jagged edges that jarred. Splinters stuck under fingernails. Empty. A travesty.

I was hollow. Nothing. Going through the motions while I was certain that the people under my care were merely humouring me. My service to my people faltered at key points, where uncomfortable silences wedged fingers into the cracks. That joy, that bliss of the Goddess I was accustomed to feeling when Jehanna called upon Her, was missing.

More than once, a few startled faces glanced up, but I soldiered on, even though it felt all wrong.

Somehow, I maintained my façade of priestess until the end of the service, when the last congregant had stepped forward to drink from the chalice and allowed me to anoint them with the sacred oils.

The final part, where I drew in the web of power – in this case I had to try hard to pretend that it was working – and the last of the congregants filed out, was the worst. I stood, arms stiffly raised, palms up, my breath hitching with ragged inhalations and exhalations.

People chattered brightly among each other outside, the moment they passed through the pylon and headed back down to the oak-shaded village. I lowered my hands and sank to my knees, all but blinded by the rectangle of daylight that glared into the shrine.

The frescoes about me, with their myriad gods and goddesses, spirits and other entities, seemed to judge me with slanted eyes, and found me wanting. It felt as if our Goddess, too, glared at me from the safety of Her sanctuary, yet I lacked the strength to get up and close the double doors.

"I can't do this," I whispered.

No one answered. I really was alone.

Fraud. Failure.

How many times had I supported Jehanna? I knew all the words without having to dredge them up from the murks of memory. Why were they robbed of all meaning, now? Had Jehanna taken something vital with her when her spirit had fled?

What would Jehanna do, in this situation?

Before Jehanna was priestess here, it had been Khanyisa. I'd never met her, but I often placed offerings on her cairn, out of respect for what she'd taught Jehanna. Her teachings had lived through Jehanna and had fallen to me, a thin filament of knowledge spun through the decades.

A fragile thread, indeed, if it could be snipped so arbitrarily. And its weight was more than the craggy red sandstone heights that encapsulated our valley.

What would Jehanna have done in my situation? She must have had a day like I had, where she stood alone and weighed down by sorrow. Jehanna had made it all look so effortless, be it sweeping out the shrine or offering last rites for the transition of one belonging to our community.

We should have had more time for the passing down of the fire, the stories, the knowledge. But it is not for mortals to dictate the warp and weft of their wyrd. And the gods move in ways that are larger and more encompassing than our lives.

The walls grew too close, my breath too short.

I needed silence, space.

Call to me from beneath the stars, and I will answer.

Where this thought came from, I knew not. Perhaps a random scrap of wisdom or our Goddess whispering in my heart. Often, at night, Jehanna would go out. She never would say where, and she'd return before dawn to chase the cobwebs out of the shrine's corners and sing up the sun.

All I knew was that she took the goat paths, armed with only a stout stick and her jackal-skin kaross. Even now the kaross lay half-across the foot of the bed, and the stick leaned in the corner by her door.

The idea took hold, like a dog worrying at a bone, even while I went through the motions of caring for our – my – small garden and fed the poultry. By the time the sun had slipped past its zenith, the notion was fully formed.

I had no one to ask permission of save myself, so after a meal of day-old bread and cold red tea, I took up the stave with its carvings curving sinuously around its length. The kaross, that still smelled of her, I threw over one shoulder, and I trod upon the paths.

It was late-afternoon as I ascended from our sleepy little hamlet by the reed-fringed river. Speckled pigeons were sharing their gruff, *rhoo-rhoo-rhoo*, and the shadows were painted long. My way took me between wind-scoured tors and pillars of stone, as I ascended the rough ridge that would bring me to the plateau that skirted the Wolfberg. Above me was the heights in red ochre sandstone, frowning down on me and all but glowing in the westering sun.

I had no firm plans about where to go, and I said a silent prayer to our Goddess, to show me the route, and of my own accord my feet found the track that made its way to the cracks. As a child, I'd gone up there with my friends, where we'd crawled and clambered an improbable playground of tunnels, ledges, and boulders. It was possible to follow two of these narrow ravines and make one's way all the way to the top of the mountain, though I'd never gone all the way myself – it was not safe in these leopard-haunted wilds.

Not that one of the big cats had ever taken a human in living memory, but they frequently took unguarded livestock, if given half the chance.

I paused at a large, flat white rock the size of a small cottage, its base furred with vivid green grass. This was the last place to find sweet water, and I filled my canister and paused to look down on our settlement. Little thatch-roofed homes huddled beneath scraggly oaks, and thin fingers of smoke were curling upward. Already a chill clung to the air, and I pressed on. It was foolishness to venture forth at nightfall, especially a woman alone, but I had to have faith that our Goddess would watch over me.

I recalled the easier of the crags from years gone by, and I was grateful that my instinct guided me along that path rather than the other, where there were precipitous scrambles, difficult to navigate without help. Soon, it was as though I was being squeezed between two sheer walls of stone, and each footfall slapped small echoes. Here, my breath misted before my face, and when I looked up, I could discern the first faint pinpricks of stars in a dusky heaven.

"What are you doing?" I asked myself.

"I don't know."

I could turn around any time I wanted to, but I didn't. It would only emphasise my failure, and I fancied I could hear Jehanna tutting and telling me not to be such a weak-livered fool.

Sometimes we need to travel outward in order to journey inward, she had said.

Often, I had not even known she was gone. I'd be opening the shutters and feeding the poultry, and she'd come striding back. Perhaps her face would be paler than usual, her eyes wide and staring, as though she saw beyond the fine mesh of flesh and bone. A feyness would cling to her that would eventually dissipate with the noon-day sun.

She'd become Jehanna again, laughing and singing, and ready with her smile and her subtle teasings whenever she felt I was being too serious.

I never forgot that *other* face of hers.

Would that I knew what she found. What she did.

I simply had no idea.

I may well be walking to my death.

Yet in walking, there was a particular rhythm, of drawing breath, of putting one foot before the other so that the muscle strained and pushed. At some point exhaustion, hunger, cold – all discomfort faded, to be replaced with the novelty of new sights around a bend. A particular gnarled cedar tree, lightning struck and clawing at the sky. Or a lazy adder, sinuously winding across one's path. Or the chittering of the tiny bats, skittering hither and thither. Wonder all about, in the tiny details one might ordinarily ignore.

My path became glittering white sand, and I emerged from the channel of stone onto a plateau of wind-hissing mountain reeds and bizarrely contorted rock formations. Here something that looked like a sleeping dragon, there something I could best describe as a crowing rooster, a sleepy-eyed puppy or a truncated bridge. Now what?

The trail continued to wind its way between the outcroppings, between stands of old-man cedars and the occasional cairn built by other travellers. It became something of a game for me, to find a stone and clutch it while I hiked until I reached the next cairn and placed my own offering on the carefully constructed pile.

I was here, this said. *I am marking this way so that others may follow.*

Some of the piles were so old, they were shrouded in lichen. Perhaps even from the Before times.

I supposed none of that mattered now, here.

A brilliant green star flashed across the sky, so low that I fancied I could hear its faint roar as it burnt up as it trailed to the horizon. For the duration of its passage, the rocks and vegetation about me were painted in an eerie green glow. I paused, my heart thrumming wildly, my mouth dry from more than thirst. Never in my life had I ever dreamt I would see something like this, nor had I ever heard anyone tell of such a phenomenon.

Then a nightjar took up its bell-like, repetitive *weeoop-weeoop* call. Mountain reeds slithered and hissed with the chill breeze that cut right through the kaross. What was I doing here? What was I searching for?

Jehanna had often talked about finding my inner quiet, but I was terrible at meditation. Always I'd sit, and one part of my body would start cramping, itching, or going numb. Or a fly would crawl on my arm so that the tickling of its tiny feet would drive me nearly mad.

I was lucky if I could get through a quarter of an hour of sitting in stillness, let alone the hours Jehanna managed, where her breathing would grow deep, and I'd find myself mesmerised by the even rise and fall of her lungs. The way her face was tilted slightly upwards with a quirk of a barely there smile curling one side of her lips.

She used to say that our Goddess spoke to her, came to her in dreams or her dream-quests. I was lucky if I recalled even the faintest echo of the dreams I'd had the night before, let alone recall them with any degree of depth, breadth and colour, the way she used to.

Would that we'd had more time, perhaps I could have made my breakthrough. And she would have been proud of me.

"All within the fullness of time, dear heart," she'd tell me, and always with that enigmatic smile and her laughing eyes.

I was nearing seventeen summers, damn it all. Most women my age had one or two children and a husband. What was I but a failed priestess?

So, I walked, and my feet no longer felt the stones on the quartzite-strewn path that gleamed beneath the stars. The cold was magnificent, and each breath drew it deep into my lungs so that it felt as if my very core burnt with icy flames. When I paused to sip water from my canister, the chilled liquid made my teeth hurt.

And then I saw it – an arch, *the* arch – set upon a ridge, and gleaming in the night as the ruddy moon pressed its skull-like features up from the east. Had I come this far already? Our hunters and rangers often spoke of this rock formation. It was said to be a holy place, hollowed out by the fist of a forgotten god from the Before, when he was angry with humanity. The impossibility of stone was tiny in the distance, but unmistakeable.

My pulse quickened. This, here, was why I had come this far, to see this landmark, to be able to tell others that I touched the very rock that made a graceful bow. Yet it was one thing to see the intended destination, and quite another to push on to find the strength to reach it. Now it was as if the cold, which at first had spurred me on, now leeched all the strength from my limbs. I trod with numb feet and marrow-deep exhaustion. My doubt whispered that I should rather have made this journey during the day, and better provisioned, too, and that I would find my death here on this mountain this night.

Why not sit a short while, catch my breath? Rest a little. Why was I putting myself through all this pain?

But no. Even with the tears running freezing tracks down my cheeks, I pressed on, though every muscle, every sinew protested with each step I took.

If I sat down now, on some convenient rock or sheltered in the lee of a hollowed-out tor, I'd fall asleep, and all the effort I'd gone to would have been a waste. After an interminable march, my path wound its way up the ridge and the arch, which until now had been my beacon, slid behind the fortifications of stone at its base. Here the wind mourned and hissed through the vegetation, and jackals added their ululating, eerie cries to the night, singing to the moon over the bones of their kills. One wrong step now, and I would offer them a fine, if stringy, repast. Though what they would make of my kaross, stitched together from their brethren, I had no way of knowing. There would be no one to save me.

Not even our Goddess – she was of a mind that we need to be the answer to our own prayers. That was one of the first lessons Jehanna had imparted.

Yet here I was. Had she, too, walked this path before?

White quartzite pebbles, round like dove eggs, lay strewn on my path as it brought me to the summit. The ascent had helped somewhat with the cold, and I wiped the perspiration from my brow and pulled the kaross tighter. Only a little further now. It couldn't be much longer. And then, from behind an outcropping, the arch revealed itself, a window opening onto the plains to the east, through which countless stars glittered. The moon was now at its zenith, so that it bathed my entire world in its cool, pale luminescence, and softened all the edges. I saw well enough that I almost didn't miss having a lantern, and of their own accord, my steps hastened over the remaining intervening distance.

I clambered up onto the terrace, and the view opened for me, as though I were standing in the Goddess's window and was no longer encapsulated by rocky heights. A great plain stretched out to a distant range of mountains, and now that I was not focusing on where I placed one foot ahead of the other, I had the leisure to take in the immensity of the star field above and around, scattered with uncountable points of brightness.

Jehanna had told me that each of these were suns like our own but immeasurably distant. She once drew pictures of what she called the planets circling our sun, and where our sun – a star – was in relation to the others. Her explanation made my head hurt, but by the same measure, I couldn't believe that these were the souls of the departed, gazing down on us – like some of our people believed.

I wasn't the first to wash up at the base of the arch – I found a niche, somewhat out of the wind, where previous travellers had packed a circle of rocks where traces of ashes yet remained. Someone had put down silver stoebe, so that the foliage had compressed into a prickly bed, which was far preferable to seating myself on the cold, hard ground. There was a small comfort to be drawn from the knowledge that I was not the only one who'd been here, and that others passed through from time to time. Perhaps I was lucky that I was alone for what remained of the night, so that I could do my work.

For it was work, self-work, and a challenge I had to face without anyone else to guide me. I felt somewhat foolish for seating myself cross-legged, Jehanna's kaross draped over my shoulders and snugged around my body so that the icy night didn't steal the last of my warmth. My teeth chattering, and shivers wracking my body, I started with the breathing, and wished that at the very least that I had a cheerful flame to offer a modicum of warmth. Yet it was almost as if I could hear Jehanna chiding me for wishing after indulgences.

My thoughts skipped and skittered, a handful of pebbles tossed into a river pool whose mirror surface was marred by flurries of cat's-paws. I was all too conscious of the ache of my legs and feet, the way my extremities were prickling, of the way my ears were now pained. At times I thought I heard something, and I'd spend long moments peering out at the darkness beyond my shelter. Nothing, of course. Not a leopard or painted wolves – not that we had the latter here, but I'd heard tales about the dangers they posed to lone travellers beyond the mountains.

Added to that was the frustration of fretting that dawn would come before I'd achieved this journey on top of the external one, and my concentration slipped between my fingers like the tadpoles I'd hunted as a child.

Concentrate on your breathing; hear your heart beat. Focus on the tip of your nose, where the air rushes in and out. Breathe slowly. Every time you get distracted, focus your attention back to the tip of your nose.

That's what Jehanna would always say, but it never stuck. When

I tried to think of my nose, and the air rushing through my nostrils, I'd develop an itch on the back of my neck, or a small stone would start pressing under my left butt cheek. And then I would be worrying about something I'd done or said a week ago. Or end up thinking about chores I'd left undone.

For how long I sat, I was unsure. It was as if my body gradually disappeared. I wouldn't say that I was falling asleep, because I was still very much aware of the wind in the mountain reeds and the way it keened around the edges of my tiny shelter.

Breathe in. Hold. Breathe out. Hold.

And existence fell away without warning.

I could only describe it like slowly sinking into a fathomless black pool, with the light gradually dwindling above me until everything was blackness. The next I knew I was trudging through a landscape entirely unfamiliar to me. A thick mist enveloped everything, so that all was immersed in a kind of nowhere twilight. My bare feet sank up to the ankles in thick, black mud that made awful sucking sounds every time I dragged myself forward step by step. Instead of the heath, reeds, and protea bushes I was accustomed to, I was wading through lush green grass and bushes with bright yellow, pea-like flowers. The air was thick with moisture, and I made my way gradually uphill, with a rushing stream tumbling over a set of terraced falls to my left.

So much greenery, so much water – where was I? How had I fallen from night-time on the mountain to this?

But it was best to continue. My route was measured by the gaps between the grass polls, and I recognised stands of poplar, so there was something familiar to grasp onto, though these poplars looked far more verdant than the scraggly stands I'd seen along the river. Tall, weathered fingers of grey rock poked up at the sky, easily three or four times taller than a man, so that it seemed as though I were ascending a series of stepped crenelations.

I feared that this new journey would continue indefinitely, until I dropped into a narrow glen where the thin, slatey ribbon of a watercourse snaked between stands of venerable oaks whose lichen-furred boughs arced towards each other. And that was when I saw *her*.

Jehanna.

Only she appeared unlike I had ever seen her before, younger. Her long dark hair fell in lazy waves to well past the small of her back, and she wore a black fur cloak that reached her knees. The fabric of her dress was midnight, made up of ragged lace like I'd seen in dresses from the Before, but so much of it, layered like cobwebs that clung to her form. Her eyes, as per usual, were darkly outlined with kohl and her lips were painted in with the same shade, so that she appeared almost a mummer, her skin pale as though she had daubed it with clay from the riverbed.

She half leaned against an oak, watching me, her gaze inscrutable.

"Priestess!" I rushed to her, but I slowed once I realised that her expression remained impassive, with none of its liveliness.

"Why have you come here?" she asked. "This land is not for you."

"I needed to speak with you!"

She cocked her head, and a tendril of hair slid over her shoulder. "Is that so?"

"I never got to say goodbye?" I was so unsure now, my heart pulsing sorrow while my limbs trembled.

She offered a one-shouldered shrug. "Life isn't fair, but you shouldn't have come after me. If you keep following, you'll end up so far from your body that you'll never find your way back."

"Where are we?"

"The Borderlands."

"The world between waking and dreaming, life and death," I whispered.

Jehanna's lips twisted into a half-smile. "Good, you've remembered something, after all."

"But I'm not ready to be alone."

"Neither was I when my teacher passed over."

"I don't know what to do." A ragged sob escaped me. "I don't have the right words. I did the blessings on the holy day, and it…" I searched her face even as I struggled to shape the words just right. "The magic was gone."

At this, she laughed. "Oh, my sweet, sweet child. Those were *my* songs. You need to make your own."

"But didn't your teacher hand them down to you? Aren't we supposed to preserve the traditions? You were always going on about not forgetting."

"The words of another won't fit in your mouth," she said, but not unkindly.

"You never taught me that!" I hated the whining tone in my voice.

She arched a brow. "It wasn't something that I was ever taught, either."

"I'm not ready to be on my own. There's still so much I need to learn."

"Oh, my dear heart, when my teacher passed, I wasn't much older than you are right now. And I wasn't ready, either."

"But you were the best!"

"And I was your only," she said. "You have nothing and no one to compare me to. We do what we can with what we have. And where we don't know, we search deep within ourselves, and we ask the Goddess. And if we are still enough, patient, we will hear Her voice. And, more often than not, she requires of us to be the answers to our own problems." "Then why have a Goddess in the first place? Why bother with our rituals, our adorations?"

"It reminds us to look beyond ourselves, that there is that which is greater than we are, so that we tread lightly where we go, and respect all that which is around us. Don't fret about my words. Understand what it is I've taught you, about the role we play within our community, as priestesses to offer comfort, to mediate, to remind others about looking at the will of the divine."

"So none of it matters? It's all just pretty stories we tell ourselves?" My frustration was quick and hot within my breast.

"The world is a harsh place. If what we do makes it easier for others to live in whatever threads there are allotted to their wyrd, then it is our Goddess-given duty to do what we can to serve others, and in so doing, serve Her. You wouldn't have sought me out in the first place if you didn't already hear Her call. But our time of parting has come, and you must create your own path, that is uniquely your own. I may have written my words on your heart, but now you must write your own on the hearts of others."

"But I don't know what to say?"

"This is why you must find your stillness. The moon cannot reflect in a pool whose surface is marred by ripples, whose depths are stirred up by currents from your thrashing. The picture will be shattered into thousands of pieces. I never lied to you when I said this path won't be easy."

I opened my mouth to ask yet another furious question, but she placed one cold index finger on my lips to silence me.

"Find your stillness. Then you will find your words. Not mine. Mine are gone with me, but you will find that they have left small impressions that will remind you of what we shared. And that is how it should be."

This was not the answer I'd wanted or expected.

"I'm scared of being alone."

At this, her smile grew a little broader. "As we all are, but you come into this world alone. You leave it alone. It is as it always has been and always will be. And I am never far." She touched my collarbone, and the skin there tingled. "What we shared will always be here. And if you need to speak to me… or the Goddess…" Here she gave a soft snort. "You will find your stillness. And while you won't always hear the answers you want, ten to one you will find some wisdom. I hope." She cocked her head then, listening, but if there was a sound, it was only she who could hear it.

She straightened, regarded me. "It is time now. Dawn is coming in your world."

"But…" She faded into yet another swirl of mist even as I watched, leaving behind only the bitter green scent of crushed herbs and musk.

I shivered, and even as I did so, I was drawn back, spiralling into wakefulness. The mists grew thicker, until there was only darkness.

I shuddered and blinked open my eyes. At some point during the night I'd curled up onto my side into a foetal position, Jehanna's jackal-skin kaross pulled around me tightly. But there was no denying the coldest hours of the night, and the fur and my makeshift bed did little to prevent the autumnal chill of the pre-dawn hours.

A true dream, then. There was no denying it. I could still hear every word she'd spoken, though they brought little comfort. But then even Jehanna had suffered a loss such as I had, hadn't she? And now I must make my own story from here, even though the hollowed-out grief inside me gnawed and gnawed at my heart.

Shivering, my teeth chattering, I rose carefully, grasped Jehanna's stave and wrapped the kaross close to me. I went to sit on the flat rocks at the base of the arch, watching as the inky cobalt bled to pale dove grey, and the stars gradually faded into the firmament. Kestrels swept about the heights, dipping and swooping, and I knew it was time to return.

By the time the arch had vanished behind me, and my body had warmed up somewhat from the hike and the rising sun, my hunger swept past my sorrow, and lent determination to my stride. There was work to be done.

It was past noon by the time I stumbled into the settlement.

Though it had been more than a day since I'd eaten, and it felt as if my stomach adhered to the back of my spine, I was curiously light, filled with energy. Every small detail, from the leafless banksia rose twining over the porch of my cottage – *my*, not our – to the little grey waxbills flitting across my path stood out in sharp relief. I was not quite ready to visit the shrine yet. That moment would come. For now, I was content to throw open the shutters and take a broom to the peach pip-studded dung floor. I aired out all the bedding, dusted and wiped down surfaces, burnt some impepho herbs to clear the air.

I still saw Jehanna's hand in everything, but instead of that being a deep well of sadness for me, I had peace with it. Jehanna's hands had guided me until but a few days ago, and now it was my turn to move things forward. All things ended. New things began. The ache of this truth was dull, but every breath I drew, every shift of the sun in the sky, took me further and further from her.

After a late lunch of greens from the garden fried up with eggs, from hens who were severely put out that I'd not been there to feed them or let them out of the coop in a day, it was time for me to pay my respects to Jehanna.

I bathed myself, pulled on a clean shirt and leggings, and after selecting a generous spray of jasmine, I made my way up to the cemetery, with the setting sun slanting my shadow until it was an alien thing running ahead of me.

Indygo made her appearance, and trotted slightly ahead of me, her long black ear tufts twitching this way and that as she listened about her. She was very much a case of 'touch me with your eyes only' but for some reason, today, as I stood by Jehanna's cairn and had no words, she entwined her ruddy-furred body between my legs and purred louder than I'd heard her before.

Others had been here, in the interim, and small offerings of old coins, poppets, bunches of proteas in old pottery jars, had been placed about the space. This gesture from our community brought fresh tears, and I stood there a long time until the skin on my cheeks was dry and tight.

The rumbling from my stomach reminded me that it was time to return, for I had neglected our Goddess this past day, and at the very least this evening I'd need to make some offerings and explanation. She'd understand. She'd forgive this one day that I'd been gone.

Stars were prickling the dove-grey sky by the time I pushed open the doors to the shrine. Old incense hung heavy in the still air, and I lit only the votive lamps on either side of the sanctuary. I would not open the doors, for tomorrow morning I'd bathe Her, offer her fresh linens and food, but I could still sing an adoration.

I stood before the sanctuary, closed my eyes, and tilted my face upward as I began a song. The melody was one Jehanna had sung for many countless occasions, a minor key filled with sadness and joy, and the notes lifted to the rafters like ravens spiralling on thermals. The words, however, they were new, my own, and I knew then that the words would be different each time I sang until I wove the pattern in them that was truly mine.

For now, it was sufficient to sing the lament of those lost and those found, and the love that stretched beyond the boundaries of this world and the next.

I sang until my voice was rough, and when I turned, I discovered that I was no longer alone.

Elsa, the miller's youngest, stood at the door. She had a cloth-covered bundle in her arms – what looked like a crock.

"Can I help you?" I asked.

"My ma said I must bring you something for dinner," said Elsa. "But I am sorry if I disturbed you… I didn't mean. But I've never heard that sung like that." Her eyes were suspiciously bright in the low light.

"They are new words," I said without any shame.

"They are beautiful." She made to place the crock on the ground by the door.

"No need, come. I'm done here. You can bring that to the cottage."

She gave a sharp nod, and I snuffed the lamps.

We walked the short distance to the cottage, and Indygo rushed on ahead of us, clearly sensing that an opportunity to mooch for treats lay ahead. I could smell the rich, meaty stew right past the lid and the cloth, and my stomach gurgled loud enough for Elsa to hear. We traded a glance, and we both giggled.

"Have you eaten?" I asked her as I lit the lamps in the kitchen.

The girl shook her head. A small weevil of guilt nibbled at me. They'd probably given a more than generous portion for me.

"Will your ma get cross if I share my meal with you?"

A shrug.

"Come, sit." I gestured at the chair I usually sat in by the small, rickety table.

She obeyed, and watched while I placed the bowls and cutlery, and ladled out sizeable portions for both of us, along with a small glass of red wine each – from the libations bottle, but I doubt the Goddess would begrudge us this small indulgence.

We ate in silence once I'd blessed the meal, and this time the words rolled off my tongue with meaning. Elsa was young, maybe ten or eleven. On the cusp of womanhood, and I caught her glancing at me with awe. Which was amusing, because she was only a handful of years older than I'd been the day I'd found my way to Jehanna's doorstep.

Once we were done, and we'd both sipped the last mouthfuls of wine, Elsa asked the question I'd known she would the moment she'd acquiesced to my dinner invitation.

"Will you teach me to sing like you do, for the Goddess?"

Pashterina's Peacocks: For Storm Constantine

Ruby

A charming vortex of hair, ribbons, beads, tie-dye and velvet, drawing you in, all the while knowing that you will certainly feel the absence when that intoxicating gaze falls on someone else and you are released...still, worth it while it lasts. Once experienced, it's never forgotten.

Over our quarter century creative relationship, I didn't meet up with Storm nearly enough times in person. It's a deep regret which is my fault alone. Shyness doesn't begin to come close in description, I'm somewhere beyond that. Storm was slightly amused, or perhaps simply bemused, by the extremeness of my affliction, but always patiently accommodating. I hope I thanked her enough in the many and lengthy email exchanges we shared throughout the years.

I can't put an exact date on when I first discovered Storm's books. In the early 1990s I bought the Tor Wraeththu omnibus (lured in by the cover of course) at Forbidden Planet in London. On the train home I noticed it was signed by the author, oblivious then to the future significance. I do know that I read either Hermetech or Sign for the Sacred first (again it was the lush covers that called to me). All those decadent and jewel-like, stand-alone novels of that era that primed me at that most impressionable time of coming of age. Wraeththu (along with many other adventures) waited in the wings.

I've always liked to draw. It never seemed strange to me to draw characters from books I liked. What *was* strange for me was to write to an author's information service, to send illustrations with the hope of them being printed in their actual zine, to risk them being seen by actual people. I have no idea what possessed me. Some spell in Storm's writing perhaps, as from that moment I was set on a path. I found a warm welcome at Inception from the inestimable Vikki and Steve, unconditional support from the fabulous Eloise

Coquio, soon to be presiding over the unique melting-pot that was Visionary Tongue, and indeed in plentiful supply from Storm too, with her becoming a kind of protective patron. And I wasn't the only one to be taken under her raven wing, she naturally and instinctively surrounded herself - like a queen holding court or Sarah Bernhardt hosting her salon - with interesting and talented people. A ferment of creativity, encouragement, magic, intrigue and toast. Through Storm I met a coven's worth of amazing writers and artists (including one of my absolute favourite people on this planet, for which I will always be grateful). The rest – the fantastic cliché that it is – is history...

Storm seemed to me at once down to earth and yet otherworldly plus, of course, very, very beautiful. Like a character from one of her stories made flesh, of any author I can think of, she would be the most at home in the many Worlds she created. And what Worlds they are...

Renunciation

Ricardo Pinto

THEY LAY OUT THE INSTRUMENTS before the Candidate. A mask of bone-plaster cast from his own face. A bowl of white jade inscribed with the glyph, *absence*. A mirror more reflective than water. A reliquary of silver for the removals, a weeping eye embossed into its lid. A pair of four-fingered gloves. Stoppered bottles of green jade. A bowl of obsidian, its rim carved into a snake devouring its own tail. An obsidian blade small enough to fit in his mouth. A huge bronze bowl, brimming with water brought hither from the far away sea. Four small pots of precious iron on a brazier, bubbling with oil. A set of pincers. Two gouging spoons, each paired with a sliver of obsidian. Two coring screws: one curving slightly right, the other slightly left; each paired with an obsidian blade.

The Twelve regard him with the empty pits of their eyes, their lipless mouths severe in their pale, cracked, leathery faces. Triangular holes frame the roots of their nostrils. The childlike figure of a homunculus stands before them wearing a silver blinding mask. One of the Twelve stretches out his hands—cloven from missing middle fingers and knuckles—and coils them around the homunculus' throat. His thumbs work at its neck, and a liquid voice sounds from behind its blinding mask. "I speak, who went first into the Void. Though the Renunciation was decreed as punishment, we came to understand it to be a liberation: a doorway between this world of lies to that other that is perfect and unchanging."

A heartbeat's pause.

"Do you choose to submit to the removals, and so to join us fully in our realm of Thought?"

The Candidate answers as in a trance. "I so choose."

Another of the Twelve unstoppers one of the bottles and pours its liquid into the white bowl. He offers the bowl to the Candidate, who accepts it and drinks.

The Candidate disrobes and sinks to the floor. The Twelve kneel around him, clasping his head and throat, his shoulders, his hips, his wrists. As the drug seeps into him, it numbs their dry touch, and he feels that he might float up through the ceiling and dissipate into the sky.

They hold the bone-plaster mask before his face. The bleaching paste smearing its interior gives off a vapour that stings his nose and eyes.

"Close the portals of your face," says the liquid voice, "breathe deeply and hold."

He obeys, they fit the mask, and his face heats as if it has been turned up too long to the sun.

The mask peels away from his face with a sucking sound. "Open your eyes." He does. The mask is in flames. "So too the face you have no further use for is consumed." And, indeed, as he watches the mask burn, his face feels on fire.

"Behold the outer wall of your mind." They hold up the silvered mirror. His face, reflected, though of a man and not a youth, is recognisably the one he had before he became an ammonite. He watches its porcelain smoothness begin to crack, and the spot and bar tattoos of his grades and results fade like sun-kissed frost.

"Matter lies. You are freed from those judgements."

The cracks widen, until it seems his face must shatter, but instead his skin softens, rucking like ageing leather.

They shatter the mirror. "Be dead to this world, live clear in the other."

One of the twelve pours a smoking fluid from another bottle into the obsidian bowl. As they offer it to him, he runs his finger around its serpented rim. The caustic vapour curling up from the bowl nips his nostrils and stabs ice up into his head.

"Free yourself from the seductions of perfume, from the revulsion from stenches."

Hooding his eyes, he brings the bowl close enough that its fumes envelope him. He breathes deeply, drawing the cold fire up the tunnels of his nose. Its tendrils push up around his eyes and into his forehead; an exquisite, shimmering pain blossoms within his head. A hand grips his chin, and, with a flash, the meat of his nose is sliced off.

"Breathe!"

Unrestricted by nostrils, his breath inhabits the vast, dizzying gape of the new hollow in the middle of his face. Around its margin, pain smoulders.

"Be free of the error of speech, the intoxication of taste."

They prise his mouth open, reaching in to pincer out his tongue. Cloven hands grip his forehead and chin. With a cut across the root of his tongue, the tension is gone. He chokes on sudden blood.

"Drink but only into your mouth!"

He angles the bowl up to pour its acid, and his mouth ignites.

"Spit out the impurity."

He vomits out the liquid, pebbled with teeth, feels his lips fraying; his mouth is a ball of flame.

"Drink of the night-black sea."

As they yank his head back again, he glimpses, through tears, the bronze bowl tipping above him. His mouth and face cleave an ocean wave. The deluge quenches the fire in his flesh, then ebbs.

They surround him. One presses a hand against his chest as if to stop his heart beating its way out through his ribs. In the reliquary, his tongue lies in its own blood.

"Be free of Matter's deluding forms and colour."

They hold his head, and a spoon approaches his right eye. "So the sun was made." He feels the spoon slide into his head; a twist and the eye is out. "So the Moon was made." They gouge out his left eye. He is entranced by a meshing waft and weft of light. Mesmerising patterns evolve, even as he is aware that his eyelids are being trimmed to the bone. They angle back his head and pour fire into the pits. They tilt his head forward, and the burning oil weeps down his cheeks.

"Be free of the lying whispers, the corrupting music, the unbearable clamour of this world."

Somewhere, a vast bell stutters and chimes. A remote sting as they have his ears off. A crunching and squelch as the screws spiral into his ear canals. The shudders in his skull as they draw out matter, like snails from their shells. They lean his head first to one side then the other, pouring fire into and out of the throbbing holes they have bored.

Their hands draw away, leaving his head a ruin devoured by fire, its windows still smouldering.

Black silence. As the memories knotted into his stomach threaten to come undone, he clamps them tight; shimmering hysteria gnaws at the edges of his control.

He recalls his teacher's borrowed voice: *That first waking is the moment of greatest peril.*

He curls his mind tighter around the terror, feeling that he is a seed in an infinite nothingness.

Try to recall the sublime beauty of the procedure.

The procedure. Every fibre of his thought wraps the ravening memories at his core; if they should break loose, they may devour him.

Remember, the body is the anchor.

His body, he still has his body. Hardness is pressing on his heels, his calves, his thighs, his buttocks, his back, his shoulders, his . . .

Snatches of memory, impressions, shocks, horror—all threaten to tear free. He squeezes that churning chaos until, sure that he can hold it, he resurrects himself, from heels to head, filling the Void with his human shape.

His breath lifts his arms that are crossed over his chest. They fall. They rise again. They fall.

Under his wrists, his heart is pounding.

His head! He kills that thought.

To make space real, he dares to shift his body. He raises an arm, but almost immediately encounters a solid, smooth surface above him. He is in a capsule: a sarcophagus of bone. He resists a frantic impulse to break free. Embodiment is the anchor, the foundation, the earth from which he must grow.

His teacher had said: *To cling to materiality, is fatal.*

But, as he seeks to crush the terror of what he has become, the Void seeks to crush him. Squeezed between those two infinite pressures, he is nothing more than a membrane.

His teacher had said: *After the body, the breath.*

His breath flows fast and deep into his head, into the ruins of his head. *So much air!* He is a scooped-out man drowning in air. Seeking respite, he shifts his breathing to his mouth but discovers that it has become an alien cavity.

He snatches back his breath and endures it flushing in and out of his hollow head. He slows his breath to a thread and, thus tethered, he dives into the Void.

Before its terror can extinguish him, he imagines the Hidden: a cube floating in the night. He rotates it, gazing upon its sides, each more familiar than his own lost face; each a square bisected into two of the triangular hierarchies of the twelve Domains. Within each triangle, shapes corresponding to the lores are arranged in exquisite geometries that describe their connections to each other.;

these shapes are the locked gateways into the mnemonic structures secreted within. The Hidden is a crystalline architecture of wisdom constructed by the Wise. It is a cage for imprisoning the world.

He turns away from the cube and yanks himself back along the thread of his breath to his body. Its man-shape is there to receive him. He moulds himself back into the shell of his being. The terror must be faced—he must touch the truth of what he has become.

He recites the first two lines of the catechism:

The punishment is liberation.

From lies to perfect truth unchanging.

Reaching up with both hands, he finds not his face but a strange landscape of ridges and rucks; a leather mask through which he faintly feels his fingers' touch.

As he approaches the place where his nose had been, he recites more of the catechism, repeatedly:

Free from the seductions of perfume, from the revulsion from stenches.

He traces the triangular rim of the new opening into his head. Daring to explore inside, he touches the vertical bone of his nasal septum. Breath torrents around his fingers.

He jerks his fingers out. Sweating, he rolls his head as each breath roars in and out of his hollow face. He closes what mouth he has left, quenching a scream.

Thought births Matter.

Order quells Chaos.

Certainty conquers doubt.

Through the uncanny contours of his new face, he perceives a waft. Air moves over his hands as if wings are beating over him.

A pebble pushes past the tattered edges of his new mouth and settles on the stump of his tongue. Dissolving, it releases a shrill bitterness that he recognises: a pellet of the elixir; a promise of near-immortality.

A touch to his hand makes him shudder and recoil. It was the space between his forefinger and middle finger that was touched: the prearranged sign. He releases a long sigh: this is his homunculus.

The belt that secures him in the capsule peels away, exposing a band of sweaty belly to the chilly air. Straps peel off his thighs and shins. He pulls his knees to his chest—his flesh as stiff as unkneaded dough—and clamps his aching arms around his shins. Other hands rock him up to sitting. Cold sweat sheathes his back.

The hands help him swing his legs over the rim of the capsule, guiding first one foot, then the other, down to an icy floor. He rises, swaying, grateful for the hands steadying him. A heavy robe settles on his shoulders, wraps around him, tightening as belts are pulled and knotted.

When his homunculus draws his hands up to clasp its neck, he gently meshes his fingers over the little man's throat. He and the homunculus have done this before many times, but now this warm column of flesh feels like a rope, rising from the pit he is in, up into the living world. He delights in the pulsing under the skin.

When the throat begins to vibrate, he throws back his head in ecstasy. He remembers who he is, straightens and thumbs into the neck: *repeat.* This time he attends to the vibrations in the throat: *Immortality.* He freezes: the Grand Sapient has come himself. If he fails this test, he will be destroyed. How long has the Grand Sapient been present? He reviews everything he has done since he awoke; when he recalls that he had almost screamed, his stomach clenches.

His homunculus' throat vibrates again: *The Grand Sapient will verify your removals.*

He releases his homunculus, dropping his arms to his side, submitting to the Grand Sapient's touch. Two cloven hands settle on the crown of his head like a cap. They separate, caressing down the sides of his head; with no ears to interrupt them, their passage is smooth. They cup his chin, the fingers resting on his neck. The thumbs meet to push against his skull, where the bridge of his nose once sprang. Separating, the thumbs trace the edge of the hole in his face, meeting again on the cleft above his lips. As the thumbs invade that part of him never before touched, he shudders, enduring their journey up the inner walls of the cavity, their pressing on either side of his nasal septum and gently waggling it.

The thumbs retreat, the hands sliding away from his chin, the fingers coming to rest along his jawline. The thumbs cross each other to touch the corners of his ruined mouth. One thumb feels along the new upper margin of his mouth, while the other feels along the lower, revealing the ragged tissue where his lips had been. Reaching the corners of his mouth again, the thumbs stretch it so wide, that he fears that what is left of his lower face must tear.

The thumbs creep inside his mouth, inflate his cheeks, run over his upper, then his lower gums; they roll the moist stump of his tongue and leave.

The cloven hands clamp the sides of his head. As the thumbs circle the rims of his eye sockets, he clings to the edge of what he can bear. The thumbs thrust in, and his hands jerk up to grasp the wrists of the Grand Sapient. He pants, enduring the excruciating presence of those thumbs where his eyes had once been. Finding some dregs of his strength, he forces himself to release the wrists. The thumbs push into the back of his eye sockets erupting red spirals, blue diamonds, gold filaments. When they withdraw, he sags, whimpering.

The hands grasp the back of his head, and—greatest torture of all—the thumbs invade his ear canals, winding into the grotesque twistings within his head, producing infernal rustlings, disjointed squealings. Maddened by a feeling that his head is infested by worms, he grinds his gums.

When the thumbs eventually pull out, he crumples, moaning soundlessly.

He becomes aware of an insistent touch on his hands, and clasps again the neck and throat of his homunculus. Its throat vibrates, but he is too disorientated to comprehend.

The sequence of vibrations repeat: *the closure of your senses will now be tested; you must confess the slightest sensation.*

Moist substances are put into his mouth in sequence and, when each makes no impression, he expresses this through his homunculus, who responds, in turn: *Not vinegar; not honey; not salt; not fish.*

A slight heat on his face. *Anything?*

Nothing, he says.

Not flash, declares the homunculus. *Not cymbal, not gong.*

He counts his breaths, waiting.

Have you questions?

He thumbs his homunculus' neck, and it says for him: *Those random colours, random sounds when you probed the cavities?*

Chimera that will fade with time.

His homunculus swallows, and he counts more breaths as he regains his composure.

At last, a cloven hand cups his chin, a finger settling against the artery in his neck.

The throat of his homunculus vibrates again. *Are you sane?*

His mind is a mirror reflecting the Void. *I am sane.*

The cloven hand disengages.

Welcome to the True Land, brother.

The gale pouring past him confirms that he is standing atop the Pillar of Heaven. Had he his eyes, he would be seeing the bowl of Osrakum below and, beyond its Sacred Wall, the Land spreading vast. Around him, his brethren are ranged in mute witness; for all that, he feels utterly abandoned. How he yearns to fly free into that airy void.

He has just come from communion with his masters. They opened for him some portals into the Hidden. Mind in mind with them, he glimpsed, for the first time, the glorious, shimmering, mnemonic structures of his chosen Domain. They were nothing like what he had imagined; nothing like the world of Matter that he has forsaken. The Hidden is truly an alien world beyond the dreams of men who are blinded by their senses; if he possesses the greatness of mind that he believes is his, he may yet add to its perfections.

But, before he can properly begin that work, he must—unmediated by drugs—endure the Seals of Renunciation; the doorway he has passed through—from Matter to Thought—must be locked behind him with pain.

He kneels and, trembling, reaches out for the posts. Sliding both palms over their grain, he splays his fingers. The chevron-irons rest on the back of his hands. A vibration in the stone under his knees is the warning from a silver-shod staff. He struggles to null his mind.

Clack! Hammers strike the irons, jointing his middle knuckles with their fingers, snapping their tendons. Agony shrieks at the gaping heart of each hand; warm blood wells from the wounds.

The staff strikes a second warning. Frays of panic escape the clench of his control. The branding iron sears into his forehead—even to his skull. Screaming soundlessly, he struggles against the instinct to pull away. When the pressure of the iron releases, he lolls forward, rasping a silent groan.

When the staff strikes a third time, he snatches together the shreds of his composure, summons what strength he can and stumbles to his feet, raising aloft his forked hands.

Blood threads down his arms. His stigmata form the angles of a triptych of pain. Now he is fully Wise.

Soon they will come to fetch him, and he will sleep until the Rains come. He pulls the reliquary out from his robe by the cord from which it hangs. He traces the weeping eye moulded into its silver lid, clicks it open and feels inside. When he touches the hard, dry pellets, he is filled with wonder: how mysterious that these morsels of meat had once conferred such astounding miracles as sight, hearing, taste, and smell. Quelling grief, he slips the reliquary back under his robe.

He feels his way across the summit with his feet. When he reaches the edge, he curls his toes over the sharp rock. Before, he would not have braved such a vertiginous height. The south-west wind beats against him. His robe tugs at his belly and chest, and flaps at his back. The wind cools and soothes his wounded hands and dulls the burning in his forehead. It judders the rims of his ear hollows and plays in his eye pits. He opens his mouth, letting the wind caress its scarred interior, and imagines that he is singing.

A Short Memoir of Storm, and Wet Weather

Ian Watson

Almost anything in this memoir may be inaccurate! By now I've realised my fallibility.

Has the Pope realised hers or his? Infallibility only extends to faith and doctrines, consequently a papal person cannot proclaim that the whole world shall understand Portuguese, for instance. Probably this is a bad example.

Initially, Storm created Immanion Press to restore her own backlist to print. Amazingly generously, she then offered this benefit also to her chums, of whom I was privileged to be one, although I never knew her as well as I would have wished, due to being marooned for years surviving by writing science fiction and fantasy in an isolated Midsomer-like village, all be it with fewer murders.

Immanion Press required a huge amount of skilled work on Storm's part; I reciprocated in part by editing novels by newer authors whom Storm took under her wing. Thus, there were handsome books to sell on suitable occasions.

And lo, a suitable occasion presented itself when the county of Staffordshire's annual agricultural show decided to feature one marquee within the showground focusing not on comely cows and fleecy rams and rousing fiery roosters, but upon arts and crafts, including fiction.

I drove to Stafford the day before the show, as did Mr. Big Ian (Whates)—I'm Wee Ian—and in my memory we helped Storm and Danni and Jim set up the Immanion table in the arts marquee before locking down for the night. Possibly we then went to an art deco cinema in Stafford's main street, converted into a pub although retaining the ranked interior. Followed by an Indian, inevitably. Was this the same evening when, ambling back to our hotel, Big Ian collided with a lamppost and bent it? To be strictly fair, Big Ian denies this—but he'd have concussion afterwards, *wouldn't he*, so how can he be sure?

Overnight, prior to the county show, there came a Storm. A Bad Storm, not a Good Storm. A Storm of Thunder and Lightning accompanied by a Tempest of Rain. Due to the weight of water sloshing about, the marquee failed at one end—*our* end—and, like a dam breaking, a flood came pouring down upon the Immanion table. Next morning, we turned up to confront wet ruin.

But lo, the organisers declared that insurance covered this inundation! As a result, Immanion received the full cover price of every single book upon its table. Immanion Press sold out totally! (Or soaked out.) Never before had there been such a sales triumph at a public event. (Or at least I supposed not.) Calloo, callay. We roamed around amidst the beef-faced farmers, carefree, admiring the scrubbed and beribboned pigs in their pretty little pens.

Storm kindly republished four of my out-of-print novels in lovely editions, and also, in 2004, she published the first UK edition of my novel *Mockymen* which until then only had a 2003 first edition hardback from Golden Gryphon in the USA. I myself must have read my completed novel at least three times including proofing and whatnot. The guys at GG had read it at least twice. Diligent US reviewers devoted quite long reviews. Yet Storm alone was vigilant enough as an editor (being an author too) to notice that when in Chapter Whatnot one significant character asks another significant character, "But how will I recognise your brother?" the answer ought to be, "Because you met him in the previous chapter, imbecile, a few pages ago!" Well, that clunk was bandaged successfully thanks to Storm, so that the ebook, available through the Gollancz Gateway, is the only true and correct text, being the Immanion text. Incidentally, Storm generously let Gollancz use her own pdf for free. She was that kind of person.

And while we're on the subject of weather and rainstorms... Out of the goodness of her heart, Storm also helped out with practical matters regarding Big Ian's NewCon Press, for which I was doing assorted editing, and which published fresh fictions by me during the 21st Century, without which I might have lost my authorly voice (so to speak). Consequently, it was highly appropriate that when Big Ian and Wee Ian planned our most ambitious SF convention yet in October 2008 (NewCon4) along with other members of our Northampton SF Writers Group, we invited Storm as a very special guest.

Our venue in Northampton was the sizable former fish market, converted into an arts lab plus craft shops and café. Due to all the former dead fish, its floors sloped for hosing away scales and tails. Overhead, excellent ventilation was open all year round, uncloseably so. Hence no heating existed in the vast L-shaped hall. To hold a convention there in October, with typical UK weather for autumn... hmm, dodgy.

To survive, we needed an Indian summer all weekend. We needed vindaloo-level weather (and no monsoon)...

Now I discreetly confess to having some control over rain, provided that I concentrate and can see the sky intermittently. Or at least I like to think this is so, and on occasion, sceptics accompanying me have been amazed by sudden sunlight when I have spotted a crack in the blackest clouds and prised it open. TV Weather forecasters scratch their heads in bewilderment. However, I only control *rain*, and I must put the rain which I displace somewhere else, which may result in unfortunate flooding in some other unprotected location.

For NewCon4 I duly concentrated all my energy—and indeed the sky remained a tropical blue all weekend (apart from at night) accompanied by a heatwave. However, when Storm arrived at the Park Inn where we were putting guests, when she opened the door to her room, and before she could take a step further, the entire ceiling crashed down followed by thousands of gallons of water, destroying bed, room, and everything.

When later Storm made the connection with whatever I'd been up to in my simple-minded way, she explained that, as a Chaos Magician, she had effectively 'earthed' all the weekend's potential water which I was displacing away from the fish market to protect us from rain and cold.

Truly, Storm was a magical person.

Goddess of the Seven Stars: The Rebirth of Sobekneferu

Andrew Collins

In 2017 cinema audiences were treated to the latest reboot of the classic horror movie franchise featuring the resurrection of an ancient Egyptian mummy. Titled, inevitably, The Mummy, and starring Tom Cruise, it was an action-packed thriller that sees the resurrection of a princess named Ahmanet who wreaks havoc across modern-day London before being finally defeated. She, however, is just the latest incarnation of a fictional female character that first appears in a novel written by celebrated Irish writer Bram Stoker (1847-1912).

Entitled *The Jewel of Seven Stars*, the book tells the story of how an ancient Egyptian queen and sorceress named Tera is able to live again through the daughter of the Egyptologist who finds her ancient tomb. When first published in 1903, the book's dramatic ending was deemed so shocking that the publisher asked for it to be replaced in future editions with one more suitable to its somewhat sensitive post-Victorian readership.

Who exactly Stoker's Queen Tera might have been, historically speaking, has intrigued both admirers of the Irish author's works and Egyptological students for a long time. Even though this is always assumed to be Queen Hatshepsut, who ruled Egypt during the country's New Kingdom for six years circa 1479/1473-1458/1457 BCE, there is today growing evidence that Queen Tera was based on someone else altogether. That person was ancient Egypt's first *official* female ruler Sobekneferu (written also Neferusobek). She ruled the country for just four years at the end of the Twelfth Dynasty, circa 1798/1797-1794/1793 BCE, and yet her legacy has been far reaching and continues to be felt today.

Egypt's Twelfth Dynasty (1976-1794/3 BCE) ended the country's Middle Kingdom. Four of its eight kings all bore the name Amenemhet, honouring the god Amun. Among them was Amenemhet III, Sobekneferu's father, who reigned circa 1843-

1798 BCE, and her brother Amenemhet IV, who reigned for nine years immediately before Sobekneferu.

Inscriptions bearing the name both of Amenemhet III and of Sobekneferu suggest co-regency, while some scholars have proposed that following her father's death she entered into an incestuous marriage with her brother (Gillam, s.v. "Sobeknefru," in Erskine et al, 2013).

Beyond this everything is unclear. All we do know is that, as her name suggests, she was devoted to the crocodile god Sobek, and that she continued to be venerated as a living god long after her death.

Bust of Sobekneferu on display in the Louvre, Paris. Credit: Wiki Commons Agreement, 2020.

The Real Queen Tera

So how can we know that Sobekneferu was the inspiration behind Stoker's Queen Tera in *The Jewel of Seven Stars*? The story tells us that Tera lived approximately "forty centuries" ago and was the only daughter of King Antef, who reigned during the Eleventh Dynasty. Now, there was indeed a king named Antef who ruled during Egypt's Eleventh Dynasty circa 2130-1991 BC. In fact, there were four kings all named Antef who reigned during this dynasty. Yet none of them had a notable daughter fitting Queen Tera's description.

Bringing us closer to an identification of Stoker's Queen Tera is the statement that in her tomb, "Prominence was given to the fact that she, though a Queen, claimed all the privileges of kingship and masculinity. In one place she was pictured in man's dress and wearing the White and Red Crowns. In the following picture she was in female dress, but still wearing the Crowns of Upper and Lower Egypt." This is a major clue as to who Queen Tera might have been, for Stoker would have been aware that Sobekneferu was the first royal female to wear the crowns of Upper of Lower Egypt. This was three centuries earlier than the reign of Hatshepsut, who even today is cited as the main inspiration behind Stoker's Queen Tera (see, for instance, the introduction to Penguin New York's 2008 edition of *The Jewel of the Seven Stars* by Kate Hebblethwaite).

The connection between Stoker's Queen Tera and Hatshepsut is generally based on a few salient points. Hatshepsut's tomb was found in 1902, the year Stoker wrote his book. Clearly, he would have been inspired by stories in the newspapers referring to this great discovery, especially since Hatshepsut was one of Egypt's few female rulers. Moreover, Hatshepsut unquestionably wore the White and Red Crowns of Upper and Lower Egypt and was certainly represented both in male clothes and also in more feminine attire, all just as Stoker writes regarding Queen Tera.

There are problems, however, with these statements. Firstly, Hatshepsut ruled Egypt as much as 500 years after the intimated "forty centuries" ago that Stoker tells us Queen Tera lived on earth. Moreover, even though Hatshepsut's tomb was discovered in 1902, it was at the time of minor interest since it was found to be empty, plus news of its discovery did not reach Britain until 1903. Even then it was only featured in academic journals, and not in the national newspapers of the time. So it is extremely unlikely that Stoker will have known of Hatshepsut's tomb prior to the publication of his book.

Like Hatshepsut, Sobekneferu had herself ruled both Upper and Lower Egypt and was also depicted both in male attire and also in more feminine clothes. So identifying Hatshepsut as Queen Tera is more difficult than you might think.

What is more, there exists a tentative link between Sobekneferu and a king named Antef, Queen Tera's fictional father. A king list known as the Royal Tablet of Karnak, the details of which were readily available when Stoker wrote his Egypt book, shows a king named Antef ruling immediately after Sobekneferu, something that has led some commentators to suspect she might have been married to him (Macnaughton, 1932, 157). Could it have been *this* King Antef that was the inspiration behind Queen Tera's father? Once again, Sobekneferu becomes a better fit to Stoker's Queen Tera than Hatshepsut who hasd no connections with a king named Antef.

Bram Stoker tells us that Queen Tera saw her future destiny as being determined by the stars of the northern sky, in particular the seven stars of Ursa Major and the constellation of Draco. Sobekneferu would have been interested in these same sets of stars through her veneration of the crocodile god Sobek. In ancient Egyptian astronomy the crocodile was shown clinging to the back of a female hippopotamus, or as part of a hippo-croc hybrid called Reret. The ancient Egyptians identified this composite sky figure with the stars of Draco, which was seen to control the movement around the northern celestial pole of the stars of Ursa Major. Indeed, seven stars were generally shown on the body of the crocodile on the hippo's back, arguably for this very reason.

The Deep Bosomed One

Sobekneferu is herself connected with the hippo goddess in an inscription on a limestone block fragment found at the site of the Egyptian Labyrinth. This was an extraordinary funerary complex constructed at Hawara in the Fayyum Oasis, some 65 miles southwest of Cairo, by her father Amenemhet III. After his death the Labyrinth was transformed by Sobekneferu into a temple to which representatives from all the districts of Egypt would come to pay their respects to the god Sobek. Alongside Sobekneferu's name in the inscription from the Labyrinth is mention of an obscure goddess named Dhdh.t (Dehdehet), which means "to hang down low" or the "Deep-bosomed One," a reference to drooping breasts.

Since the hippo goddess in Egypt was shown with long drooping breasts this name almost certainly refers to her, either in her form as Tawaret or, more likely, as Meret-Weret, which means the "Great Flood." She was a patron of the region, her name referring to the region's Lake Moeris (modern Birket Qarun), beyond which was situated the town of Shedet. This was the site of Sobek's main temple as well as a royal palace that almost certainly became Sobekneferu's personal residence.

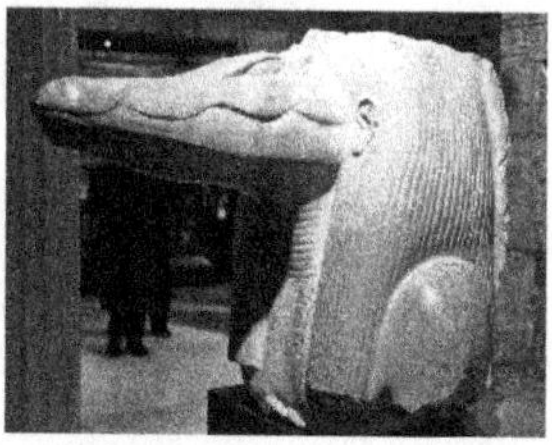

Head of the crocodile god from the site of the Labyrinth at Hawara. It dates to the reign of Amenemhat III. Credit: Wiki Commons Agreement, 2020.

The hippopotamus goddess Tawaret. Was she the mysterious goddess revered by Sobekneferu? Credit: Wiki Commons Agreement, 2020.

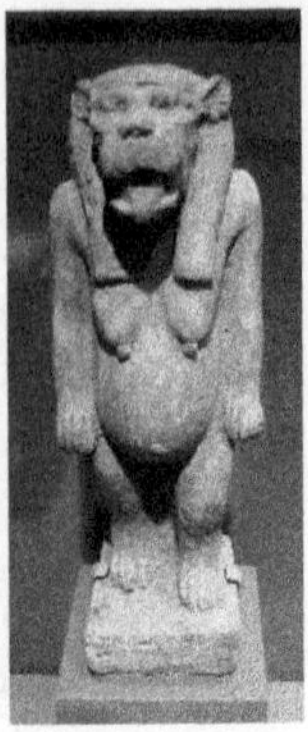

Goddess of the Seven Stars

Through her connections with the crocodile god and hippo goddess we can be pretty sure that Sobekneferu's gaze at night would have been toward the northern heavens. There is, however, an even more specific link between the female monarch and the ancient cosmologies surrounding this region of the night sky, and through this an even closer link with Stoker's Queen Tera.

In his two-volume work *The Book of Beginnings,* published in 1881, mythologist Gerald Massey (1828-1907) wrote extensively about the universal belief among ancient peoples of a cosmic ruler governing the turning of the stars about the northern celestial pole, and in doing so governing cosmic time. He wrote that in ancient Egypt this primordial deity was personified as the hippo goddess Tawaret (he spells her name Tuart). Since the movement of the seven stars of Ursa Major around the celestial pole was seen to be under the control of this cosmic genetrix symbolized by the stars of Draco, Massey repeatedly refers to her as "goddess of the seven stars."

Massey goes on to single out queen Sobekneferu as the ancient Egyptian ruler responsible for reviving the cult of this age-old stellar genetrix. For him she became the earthly personification of this cosmic deity who governed the seven stars of Ursa Major. These are ideas echoed by Stoker in *The Jewel of Seven Stars,* when he writes:

I have been looking over the writings again; and I find that in seven places round this corner [of Tera's tomb] are the symbols of the constellation which we call the Plough, which Queen Tera held to rule her birth and her destiny. I have examined them carefully, and I notice that they are all representations of the grouping of the stars, as the constellation appears in different parts of the heavens. They are all astronomically correct; and as in the real sky the Pointers indicate the Pole Star, so these all point to one spot in the wall where usually the serdab is to be found! (A serdab was a small room or niche in an Egyptian tomb reserved for the internee's lungs, liver, intestines, and stomach, which would have been placed inside four so-called canopic jars.)

In addition to this Massey writes that a word used to express cosmic "time" in the ancient Egyptian language was "Tera." Was this one of the reasons why Stoker called his queen by this name, since she was the embodiment of cosmic time? Almost certainly the answer is yes, and it should be pointed out that no such astronomical associations can be attached to Hatshepsut.

Although there are no records saying that Bram Stoker was familiar with the works of Gerald Massey there is every reason to believe that he came across his books through connections made with the London occult scene. Having read about Sobekneferu's apparent connections with the cosmic genatrix that Massey calls the "goddess of the seven stars," a term, by the way, unique to the writings of Massey, he devised the character of Queen Tera.

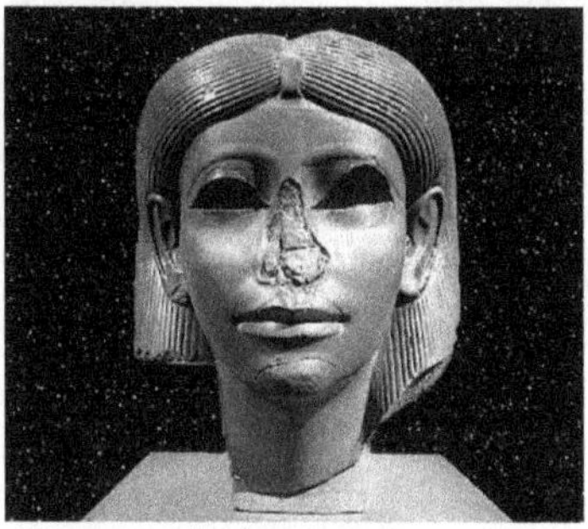

Head of an ancient Egyptian royal daughter dating to around 1850 BC and thought to show Sobekneferu. Currently in the Brooklyn Museum, New York. Credit: Rodney Hale/Andrew Collins.

The Plot (Spoiler alert!)

There were, however, other inspirations behind Stoker's creation of Queen Tera in *The Jewel of Seven Stars.* The book tells how British Egyptologists Abel Trelawny and Eugene Corbeck were able to uncover Tera's sarcophagus in Egypt's "Valley of the Sorcerers," which along with Tera's coffin, her intact mummy, and various other items from the tomb, are shipped back to England.

We are told that on entering the tomb Trelawny and Corbeck had fallen into a trance-like sleep for some days during which time

Trelawny's wife dies giving birth to a daughter who is named Margaret. When she reaches eighteen, her father once again falls into a deep sleep initiating an investigation into his condition by the police, medical doctors and a suitor of Margaret's named Malcolm Ross. Gradually, Margaret begins to change from a sweet demure young woman into a powerful, confident person. This change in personality coincides with her being overshadowed by the spirit of Tera, the queen having performed dark rituals before her self-induced death to ensure her resurrection in "a land under the Northern Star," in other words the British Isles.

After Trelawny regains consciousness, he understands what has to happen, and so he, Corbeck, Ross and Margaret move the sarcophagus and its precious contents, along with the other items removed from Tera's tomb to a house owned by Trelawny somewhere on the rugged coast of Cornwall in the southwest of the country. Once there, everything is set up in a cave beneath the house that has been decked out to replicate Tera's tomb. Here they perform what is described as the "great experiment," its purpose being to release the queen's spirit from an ancient Egyptian statue of a cat so that she might live again. At the height of the ritual, as a fierce storm rages, all hell breaks loose. A window shatters, blowing out the lamps and plunging the cave into darkness. When a light is finally lit everyone except Ross appears to be dead.

Seeing Margaret lying on the floor, Ross picks up her limp body and carries it into an adjoining room. Setting her down, he leaves her there, only to find her body missing upon his return just minutes later. In its place is Tera's marriage robe, which the queen was found to be wearing when the mummy had been unwrapped earlier that evening. Next to it is found the titular Jewel of Seven Stars, a finger ring containing a large ruby engraved with seven stars, which had been found in the tomb. That's it. That's the end. So disturbing was this deemed by the book's publisher that they made Stoker change the ending in subsequent editions. Instead of Tera possessing Margaret's body and disappearing mysteriously, the evil queen is defeated; Margaret marries her suitor and all live happily ever after!

Florence Farr and the Egyptian Adept

The manner Bram Stoker has the character of Margaret change

from a somewhat meagre young woman into a strong empowered female is today considered to be one of the first literary portrayals of what in late Victorian England would come to be termed the "New Woman." This was a movement spearheaded by independent women demanding radical change in the way they lived their lives. Unquestionably it was a principal inspiration behind the feminist revolution of the twentieth century.

For the male dominant society of the Victorian era the growing reality of such empowered women was seen as an enormous threat to their world. Stoker may have wanted to embody some elements of the New Woman movement in his portrayal of Margaret's transformation. This seems especially so in the knowledge that Stoker is thought to have used the ideologies of the New Woman movement to create the characters of Lucy Westenra and Mina Harker in his earlier novel "Dracula," published six years earlier than *The Jewel of Seven Stars* in 1897. On this basis, I suspect it was the remarkable achievements of strong empowered women like Sobekneferu, Egypt's first female ruler, that Stoker wanted to compare with those advocating the New Woman movement.

The Florence Farr Connection

This knowledge also now helps us to identify the real Margaret Trelawny, for her character is almost certainly based on a remarkable woman named Florence Farr (1860-1917). She was a British West End actress, composer, director, and member of a well-known occult society named the Hermetic Order of the Golden Dawn. Stoker unquestionably corresponded with Florence Farr and almost certainly knew her personally.

At the time of writing *The Jewel of Seven Stars* Stoker was business manager at London's Lyceum Theatre, the lessee of which was Stoker's actor friend Sir Henry Irving (who, incidentally, was the role model for the character of Dracula in Stoker's novel of the same name). Not only did the theatre become a hive of social activity involving key figures from London's occult scene, but Farr was also working at the theatre in charge of the performance, direction and musical composition of plays.

Florence Farr was a leading advocate of the Victorian New Woman movement, and incorporated some of these ideas into ancient Egyptian themed plays she wrote during this period. This is important, although even more significant is that during the

1890s Farr began channeling an ancient Egyptian female spirit that came to be known as the Egyptian Adept. Contact with the spirit had come originally from a mummy in the British Museum belonging to a "chantress of Amun" named Mut-em-menu (Tully, 2018). Through repeated communications with the Egyptian Adept, Farr came to believe that the entity was a personification of her higher self, quite literally her "ka," or "sister" self (in the ancient Egyptian language *ka* means "soul").

An illustration by H. M. Paget showing Florence Farr as Rebecca West in Henrik Ibsen's "Rosmersholm." Credit: Public domain.

So influential did Farr's contact with the Egyptian Adept become that Samuel Macgregor Mathers, the then head of the Golden Dawn, officially recognized this spirit entity as a "Secret Chief," believed to be guiding the organization's destiny from the astral planes. So much interest was there in these communications from other members of the society that Farr created an offshoot group to specially concentrate on the Egyptian Adept's instructions from beyond. This was called "The Sphere" and during communications the Egyptian Adept would speak of how the powerful ancient magics of her native country would soon be revived through the work of Farr and her colleagues. Inevitably, some members of the Golden Dawn objected strongly to the growing influence of the Egyptian Adept, seeing these communications as a threat to the order's status quo.

News of the growing discontent surrounding Florence Farr's channelling of the Egyptian Adept would inevitably have reached the ears of Bram Stoker through one of his contacts in the Golden Dawn (he himself was never a member of the society even though this is often stated in books). Almost certainly this would have influenced his decision to create a female character in which a powerful ancient Egyptian spirit gradually gains control not only of her life, but also that of those around her. This then was almost certainly the genesis of the plot's main female character Margaret Trevelyn/Queen Tera.

Ancient Egyptian Females on the Big Screen

Across the years there have been various cinematic adaptations of Stoker's *The Jewel of Seven Stars*. They have included 1970's Curse of the Mummy, a made-for-TV film release forming part of British TV's Mysteries and Imagination anthology series of classic horror and supernatural dramas. This followed very well the Victorian theme of Stoker's book, with Isobel Black ably playing Margaret Trelawny/Queen Tera. Then came 1971's "Blood from the Mummy's Tomb." This was Hammer Horror's own unique take on the story. Set in the modern day with flash backs to ancient Egypt it is seen by many as the perfect horror adaption of Stoker Egyptian novel in which Valeria Leon plays Margaret Trelawny/Queen Tera.

The Awakening

It was not, however, until 1980 and the release of the Orion/EMI film The Awakening that Stoker's Queen Tera came much closer to being identified with the historical Sobekneferu. For the movie, which starred Charlton Heston as the main protagonist, Egyptologist Matthew Corbeck, Queen Tera is renamed Kara. She is said to have ruled as queen of Upper and Lower Egypt "3800 years ago," the *exact* timeframe of Sobekneferu. I see this choice of date as no coincidence, implying that the screen writers had done their homework and realised that the only female monarch that matched the fictional narrative of Queen Kara was Sobekneferu. However, since they did not feel Sobekneferu's name was snappy enough, they went instead for Kara, one half of the queen's throne name Sobekkara.

In the film, it is Corbeck's daughter Margaret (played by Stephanie Zimbalist) who is very gradually possessed by Kara's spirit, this being the inevitable consequence of her father's discovery of Kara's tomb 18 years earlier.

Margaret's full transformation into Kara is completed inside a London museum as Corbeck tries to resurrect the long-dead

Egyptian queen by performing a ritual involving her mummy. He dies in the chaos that ensues. The film's final scene shows Margaret, now as the queen herself, standing before the tall columned doorway of the museum, a snarl on her heavily Egyptianized face as she stares out over the city's nocturnal skyline contemplating how she will begin her reign of terror over this new world she now finds herself within. Interestingly, this final scene from the film was missing from the American release, which had the movie end with the resurrected Queen Kara watching Corbeck's death; a strange echo of how the ending of Stoker's original novel was also censored.

Artist's impression of Sobekneferu by London artist Russell M. Hossain. Credit: Russell M. Hossain.

If we skip over the 1997 film Bram Stoker's Legend of the Mummy, which was a pretty mediocre adaption of *The Jewel of Seven Stars,* directed by Jeffrey Obrow, we come finally to 2017's cinematic blockbuster "The Mummy," directed by Alex Kurtzman and starring Tom Cruise and Russell Crowe. Although Bram Stoker's novel was not credited as being the inspiration behind the storyline of this film it is obvious it was, a fact that has not gone unnoticed by movie critics. This seems obvious from the fact that The Mummy was to be the first of many movies in Universals' Dark Universe. This would have revolved around an extended universe featuring all the studio's classic movie monsters including Stoker's own Dracula, Mary Shelley's Frankenstein, as well as Wolf Man, the Phantom of the Opera, and many more. Due, however, to the extremely poor reception of The Mummy, Universal's Dark Universe was shelved indefinitely, with only 2020's The Invisible Man being considered part of this franchise.

There is, however, a nod to Sobekneferu in 2017's The Mummy.

The ancient Egyptian princess brought back to life following the discovery of her tomb (the role being played quite brilliantly by Algerian actor, dancer and model Sofia Boutella) bears the name Ahmanet. This is very obviously a simplified form of Amenemhet, the name of Sobekneferu's father and half-brother.

So if Bram Stoker was looking toward any ancient Egyptian royal female on which to base the character of Queen Tera in *The Jewel of Seven Stars* it was almost certainly not Hatshepsut. Although she was a very important Egyptian ruler who came to wear the crowns of Upper and Lower Egypt, there is nothing about her life that fits with what we know about Queen Tera. Only Sobekneferu, ancient Egypt's first female ruler, fits the bill with regards to Tera's interests in magic and ancient astronomies.

This brings me to the life of my great friend Storm Constantine, which this present volume so eloquently celebrates. Her interests in ancient Egyptian magics, expressed through book like *Bast and Sekhmet: Eyes of Ra,* co-authored with Eloise Coquio (1999), and *Sekhem Heka* (2008), were inspired at least in part by her love of Bram Stoker's book *The Jewel of Seven Stars.* Storm was fascinated by the idea of a revival in ancient Egyptian magic brought about through a strong empowered figure like Queen Tera, who she knew full well was based on the life of Sobekneferu.

What Storm did not know during her beautiful life is that one of her favourite spots in Britain—a wild, rugged bay on the Lizard peninsula in Cornwall named Kynance Cove—was the inspiration behind Kyllion Cove, the location of the cave that Bram Stoker has Queen Tera resurrected in *The Jewel of Seven Stars.* This was something I found out just months after her death in early 2021. It was thus with this in mind that myself and some of Storm's friends said our final goodbyes to her in a touching Egyptian themed ceremony at the very spot where this Egyptian queen had herself been born again in a fictional manner perfectly befitting the dark, rich fantasy inspired world Storm brought to life in the many great books that will forever keep her memory alive.

Bibliography

Constantine, Storm. 2008. Sekhem Heka. Stafford, Staffs., UK: Megalithica Books.

Constantine, Storm, and Eloise Coquio. 1999. Bast and Sekhmet: Eyes of Ra. London: Robert Hale.

Erskine, Andrew, et al. 2013. The Encyclopedia of Ancient History. Hoboken, N.J.: Wiley.

Ferguson, Christine, and Andrew Radford eds.). 2018. The Occult Imagination in Britain, 1875-1947. London: Routledge.

Macnaughton, Duncan. 1932. Scheme of Egyptian chronology with notes thereon. London: Luzac & Co.

Massey, Gerald. 1881. The Book of Beginnings. London: Williams and Norgate,

Stoker, Bram. 2008 [1903]. The Jewel of Seven Stars. New York: Penguin.

Tully, Caroline. 2018. "Egyptosophy in the British Museum: Florence Farr, the Egyptian Adept and the Ka." In Ferguson and Radford, 131-145.

Andrew Collins is a history and science writer. He is also the co-author with Storm Constantine of the book *SHE: Primal Meetings with the Dark Goddess,* published by Megalithica Books in 2018. He is currently working on a biography of Sobekneferu, Egypt's first female pharaoh.

How A Teleporting Bookshop Took Me Somewhere I Never Expected

Fiona Lane

Sometime around the end of the Eighties, I did something I had never done before. I went out and bought a copy of a book I had already read. To be wholly accurate, I bought *two* books I had already read. I had previously borrowed both of them from the local library, and dutifully returned them, just as I had done with every book I had ever borrowed, since the first time, at the age of five I had entered a dark, wood-panelled room smelling of lavender polish, clutching my dad's hand and my new library card, and returned clutching the illustrated tale of Old Dan Tucker.

These books were different, though. I *had* to own my own copies, so I could re-read them in their entirety at my leisure, or pick them up and enjoy favourite passages over and over again, the pages falling open at exactly the right place without me even having to look, because I'd been there so often, and they knew what I wanted. I could even doodle on them if I wanted, without the stomach-churning terror that had afflicted five-year-old me when I accidentally circled some of the text of Old Dan Tucker and realised, moments later, the awful sin I had committed. (I hasten to add, in order to forestall the stifled gasps of shock from those to whom doodling on a book is a crime of unspeakable hideousness, that I am not a serial book defacer, I just wanted these books to be *mine*, in a way that borrowed library books never could.)

The books were "*The Enchantments of Flesh and Spirit*" and "*The Bewitchments of Love and Hate*" by Storm Constantine. Both their baroque titles, and the author's unusual name, marked them out as something different from the run-of-the-mill volumes shelved next to them in the Science Fiction and Fantasy section of the library - disappointingly small, back in those days before the film version of Lord of the Rings devoured everything in its path and made the genre cool.

But a book is, of course, far more than just its title, or author's name, or its pristine, unsullied, un-doodled pages. It's the world the book contains, and what a world these books brought to life! Later, attempting to proselytise on their behalf to friends and acquaintances whose lives I was sure would be immeasurably enriched by reading them, the words "magic hermaphrodite sex" may or may not have been employed – and I could tell by the quizzical reaction that this was not the single most convincing phrase I could have used – but my clumsy description was miles apart from what the books were actually about - '*No, really, you have to read them.*"

Reading them – which I'm glad to say at least a few of my targets did – parachuted you into a fantasy world populated by characters which were so very, very real. Here were characters which did not merely walk off the pages, but came singing and dancing down your street, kicked in your front door, moved into your spare room, put their feet up on your coffee table, hogged the tv remote control and drank all your booze. What's not to love?

So I bought the books, but that presented me with another problem. At that time, I was aware that *Enchantments* and *Bewitchments* were the first two parts of a trilogy, with a third still to come. Far from being disappointed, I experienced a warm, fuzzy feeling just thinking about this. It was like having Christmas to look forward to. In February. You must remember that, back in the days while we were all sitting around waiting for the Internet to be invented, we didn't expect instant gratification or next day deliveries. Entertainment was not on tap twenty-four hours a day. There were only four channels on tv. I was a patient and humble book-buyer, content with my inner glow of third-part-of-a-trilogy anticipation. Until I got to the back page of Bewitchments and found that the *third book had already been published!*

That was it! I stood up, shook my tiny fist at the heavens and declared "This book shall be mine! And I mean Right Now!"

Well, no I didn't, obviously. I would have been sectioned if I had. I did the rather more sensible thing, which was to go to the nearest bookshop, quaint analogue money tokens in hand, and attempt to purchase the volume known as *The Fulfilments of Fate and Desire.* Which I failed to do, as they didn't have a copy. No matter, other bookshops existed. All of which also were devoid of my prize. Things were looking bad. I couldn't afford a plane ticket to London. Jeff Bezos was still working in banking. What was I to do?

As it happened, I spent that Christmas with my parents who lived in Glasgow. Glasgow is the largest city in Scotland. I mean, it's not London-large, but it has shops. Lots of shops. Bookshops. A Waterstones bookshop. A five-floor Waterstones bookshop. The largest bookshop in Scotland. Surely I could get a copy of *Fulfilments* there?

Fighting my way through the Christmas crowds on Sauchiehall Street I found the Waterstones and made my way eagerly to the Science Fiction and Fantasy section. Disappointingly small in those days, although still finding room for the latest edition of Lord of the Rings. But not, however, for anything by Storm Constantine. I checked the "C" section several times, and then all the other sections, just to make sure, but this grand and glorious Waterstones, flagship of all things bibliophilic in Scotland, contained no *Fulfilments of Fate and Desire.*

"Drat." I said. Or a word of that approximate length and shortness.

Mightily disappointed with life in general, and Waterstones in particular, I left in a huff. But, as I exited the mighty Waterstones onto a smaller side street, what did I notice on the other side of the street, but a small, independent bookshop?

(Yes, you probably have an inkling of which way this is going, but humour me, okay?)

So, in I go, into the Small Independent Bookshop, and seek out their SF & F department, which turns out to be one single shelf, right at the back, half empty, with only about a dozen or so books on it……one of which was *The Fulfilments of Fate and Desire.*

That moment, when you get the thing you really want…

(It was even better for me than it was for you reading about it here, just so you're aware.)

So I took my prize home, back to my parents' house where I was spending Christmas, and tried very hard to not read it too fast, and failed dismally at that, and didn't care one bit.

However, there's a small coda to this story. Some time later, the next time I was in Glasgow, I went to look for the Small Independent Bookshop again, and it was gone! Vanished! It was as if its entire purpose had been to sell me that copy of *Fulfilments* and then, primary mission accomplished, teleport itself back to whichever dimension it had appeared from in the first place. Or, maybe, it had just found the competition from a five floor Waterstones, still squatting on the opposite side of the road cracking its knuckles menacingly, too much to cope with. But I know which version I prefer to believe!

And that was the story, with a surprise twist ending, of how I came to buy a book. But oddly enough there is a second chapter to this story which I ought to relate since this is supposed to be about Storm Constantine after all.

Time passed, the Internet was born, Jeff Bezos went into commerce and Waterstones gained an insight into what it's like to be a Small Independent Bookshop on the other side of the street. Storm wrote more books, which I added to my collection - thankfully without the trauma associated with getting hold of a copy of *Fulfilments*. I loved all her books, but the characters from her original *Wraeththu* trilogy were still living in my spare room, and by now they'd finished the beer, had raided the kitchen for gin and pretzels and were partying to some really loud music. But still no new Wraeththu stories came from Storm to answer the most important question posed by the very last full stop in *Fulfilments*.

What happened next?

I wasn't the only reader tormented by this question, and I wasn't the only one who sighed dramatically and muttered to herself "*Right, I'm going to have to do it myself!*"

Back in the early days of what has become known as 'Fan Fiction', many authors weren't quite sure how they felt about it. Quite a number were worried about legal ramifications. A few were actively hostile. Storm was not one of those. She encouraged it from the start, perhaps having the vision that others did not, to see that it could be a very positive thing, both in promoting the original author's work, as well as providing a creative outlet for their fans.

As it became known that Storm was generally well disposed towards these activities, people felt encouraged to do so, and soon there was quite a collection of stories online based on her world, and the characters who inhabited it, authored by a wide variety of talented enthusiasts. And me. Writing the stories in itself was fun. Having people read and enjoy them online gave me the added bonus of feeling unusually pleased with myself. Occasionally I wondered if Storm herself ever read any of the stories. If she'd perhaps ever read any of *my* stories… It seemed unlikely, because the accepted wisdom concerning fan fiction seemed to be that authors should avoid reading it in order to steer clear of any conflict of interest. Still, a girl could dream, couldn't she? I mean, how cool would it be if the very person whose work inspired your own writing was to read it?

One day I received word that Storm was putting together a collection of stories based on her Wraeththu world, and that she had read one of mine and wanted to include it.

That moment, when you get the thing you really want…

I will state now that it was better, by some margin, than the time I found the copy of *Fulfilments* in the mysterious vanishing bookshop in Glasgow!

It was actually quite extraordinary that Storm was so ahead of the curve, that not only had she given her blessing to online fan fiction, but she was now going to publish it herself, through her own publishing company, instigating the *Wraeththu Mythos* series of stories set in her Wraeththu worlds.

In truth, there should have been nothing startling about this – spinoffs from popular tv series, films and books, produced by established professional writers, had long been a thing, but Storm's act of taking the strange little community of fan fiction writers under her wing and befriending them, encouraging them and giving them a platform, was genuinely revolutionary.

More anthologies of Wraeththu stories followed, and I was lucky enough to be able to contribute to each one. I counted myself even luckier when she asked me to write a full-length novel. I was a bit daunted to begin with, but Storm was hugely encouraging, making it sound like no problem at all (perhaps one of her more creative tales) and, once it was written, she set-to with her formidable editing skills to lick it into shape. I loved getting her feedback. I loved her funny, pithy comments and the genuine talent she had for offering truly constructive criticism and making it sound like the highest of praise! I learned a great deal from her about all aspects of writing, and a good many other things besides. (Not least, after many early years spent reading horse-related fiction, what a curry comb actually was.)

She also took care of all the other little aspects of publishing which I had no idea about, didn't seem fazed by the hat obsession in my authorial self-description and generally was just the sort of person I had hoped she would be. It's often said that you should never meet your heroes, and in these days of the sort of democratisation of relationships between the famous and their admirers that the Internet has facilitated, many people have ruefully come to acknowledge the truth of that axiom. Storm, however, was the glorious, shining exception to that. She didn't disappoint me. Quite the opposite. When, all those years ago, I first pulled a copy of her book from the library shelf and was intrigued enough by the curious synopsis of its contents on the inside cover to take it home, I never imagined where it would lead. But I'm glad it did.

And, of course, there is a third, sad chapter to this otherwise uplifting tale. The last time I heard from Storm, I had just submitted another short story for the upcoming new Wraeththu anthology. She was very enthusiastic about it. She said she *adored* it. Can I say that, or will I get sent to my room without supper for boasting? I don't care. It made me happy. It still does. When the anthology was delayed, I just thought it was the usual internecine problems associated with publishing. And then came the sudden, shocking, totally unexpected announcement in January of this year that she had died.

It's hard to quantify what I have lost. I was not her family, and I never, in fact, got to meet her in person, although I always thought I would, some day. I had daydreamed occasionally of how we'd meet, like old friends, and laugh and drink gin and swap witty stories. Or, more likely, Storm would be witty and welcoming to this funny wee Scottish wumman, and I would just sit there looking a bit flummoxed, wondering if my hat was on straight. (I'd even got as far as thinking about what I would wear for the occasion, so I wouldn't look quite so dull and ordinary next to Storm and her vibrant ribbons and braids.)

I am sad beyond measure that it can never happen now, and that there can be no more new stories of the worlds she created from the pen of the person who knew them best. There's a hole in my life, and something has ended. And yet, something continues, in the people she inspired and mentored. When you touch other people's lives, and bring something good, something positive to them, that's a kind of immortality.

And just perhaps – given her wild imagination and belief in the existence of other worlds and other realms - she isn't gone at all. Perhaps she just popped into a small, independent bookshop one day, searching for a rare volume, and it then accidentally teleported itself back to its home dimension… Whichever dimension that is, I hope she's writing stories there!

Storm

Kim Newman

I've spent a lot of time not writing this piece.

I'm doing it now, well after midnight – because if I don't, it'll melt away before it gets set down as words.

Of course, I want to be a part of this book.

But I'd so much rather not be writing a memorial piece – because I'd so much rather Storm hadn't died.

What I'd like to write about her …

… is one of those program notes that goes in a convention booklet when a Life Achievement Award is being given out.

An account of her life and work and the effect she had on people … her wicked humour and her kindness, the latter quality much rarer than the former in our field. Her commitment to what she wanted to write, because she understood there were people who wanted more of her, more from her, even when the business side of writing did its best to put her in a file and leave that file on the shelf.

Her style, in several senses of the word.

Even her name, the name she chose – with a hint of threat, but also with warmth, humour and ambition. A natural event of great force. An imperial association. A by-line and a promise. A declaration of purpose.

Storm Constantine would not be silenced.

She imagined people could be better, different, never dull.

She is a person you miss when they're out of the room or no new writing comes along for more than six months … so imagine how you feel when she's off the planet.

Good. Sweet. Strong. Talented.

They're called stars because they shine so bright. Sometimes, they shine in the Stephen King sense. Sometimes, just because they exert such a force that planetary objects revolve around them.

Successful in all sorts of ways, some hard to measure but impossible to ignore, Storm nevertheless deserved so much more.

I'm sorry for us because she isn't here.

When she was, she was wonderful.

Islington, 1.43AM, August 2021

Sun Kissed

J.E. Bryant

The light breeze surmounted a series of eddies that had kept it at bay offshore, then pulled their vortices into its wake as it headed for the beach. It grew stronger with this robbed energy and pushed forward to the rising heat from the white gold sands of the island kingdom of Wasaruna. Up the gentle incline of the beach it breathed, blowing a fine hail of scintillation before and behind it, again gathering power from the up currents that lifted it over snaking dunes. Basking spear billed birds blinked at its passing and considered hitching a ride inland, but the breeze was still hardly more than a cooling instant in the heat of mid-morning. They turned their heads back to the sea as it slipped past them.

Before it now was the fetid tree line of the jungle, a bank of baffling foliage that would dissipate any momentum. The breeze, about to resign itself to its fate, was caught by a sudden easterly that came floating into its side steam. The newcomer, almost spent, gathered with the former and, in the mergence, found new vigour and a fleeting companionship. Together, becoming one, they curved west and down towards the port of Coracor. Clement yet storm ravaged, this industrious trading post lay caught between the realm of men and the hidden denizens of the sea.

The low, whitewashed buildings of the port's outskirts quickly gave way to the taller quay houses, their two-storey shapes festooned with drainage pipes to feed storm waters back to the sea. In the relative calmness of this day the narrow, cobbled streets provided the perfect landscape for the breeze to channel itself and whistle through. A tumbling scrap of sack cloth here, a flapping of a merchant's canopy there. Did the ale house fisherman exclaim blessings to the crustaceans as they clutched at their hats, or was that just a trick of the wind? A wind? Could it call itself a wind now?

It flew from the port, its momentum gathering as it skimmed past the high cliffs to the west. A swooping bank propelled it around an eroded spit and back into the neighbouring bay. It hopped rocks covered with yellow lichen that longed for the return of the rain, and bore down upon a couple of ancient fishing sheds.

The tar clad structures were huddled so close together they could have been mistaken as a single building. Both faced seawards, with only a stove shelter obscuring the view of the lapping waves from their adjoining fronts. Together the sheds were cordoned off from the clustering trees by a wide triangle of prayer ribbons and flag, one building sporting a disproportionate number of windows than its companion.

A woman stood in front of this humble abode, a child supported across her chest and waist. Her body was draped in an ankle length cape roughly woven form the teased sea grass that grew upon the dunes. Beneath it she wore light clothes suited for swimming, a bone handled sea knife dangling from her belt. It was to her the wind was drawn. It fluttered all the written pleas of the flags and lifted tresses of long black hair across her face. She might have pulled her cloak tighter around herself if it had been any protection against the elements, but that was not its purpose. Instead she turned her face to greet the wind, the hair clearing from her noble features, and drew upon its welcome coolness to prepare the skinny boy for the afternoon's work. She lowered her son to the ground.

The wind easily outpaced the two of them, skipping across the waves, leaving mother and child as they strolled across the shore hand-in-hand. The boy looked up at his mother in her strange cape and wondered, not for the first time, what she always looked for on the horizon. In turn, Popana Lilly Gilori had learned not to dwell too long on that distant seam between sky and sea.

She smiled down at her son, "Time to find out what the sea has for us today."

A girl from the port was getting married. She had turned up shy and anxious at Popana's door a week ago, wringing her hands more out of nervousness at meeting the outcast than any fear of her approaching nuptials. She was pretty, in her own way, Popana had thought, but there was something probing about the girl's questions that soon turned her cool appraisal to irritation. The girl would no doubt go back to her tattle tale circle with embellished stories of the mad widow and how she was best placed away from the port and wandering eyes of the menfolk. Popana did her best not to react. She had lived years now with the stigma of being an attractive woman with child whose husband might be lost at sea.

"I wish you to make me the two necklaces of Lackli." The girl had said as she stood well back from the door to Popana's home, her fidgeting blunting her manners. "You made similar for Manakee and her husband, and they are still very much in love. So, I think what they say is true, there is power in your work."

Popana considered the girl's words in cool silence. Despite the implicit barbs of the catch-all 'they' and 'their' bringing images of marketplace gossipers, work like this was appreciated - although a few more coins in her purse would inevitably lead to another dreaded trip into Coracor. Anlap, the trader, was always fair to her and appreciate her craft, although his wife continually found reasons to be in the store whenever she called. Distrust and whispers dogged Popana's every step in the port. At least here to the west she was free of that, for the most part.

She felt a light pressure at the back of her long skirt as small hands worked their way across the fabric. Her son, Loroc, peeped at the visiting stranger around Popana's thigh. The girl in the sun outside started at his appearance, the shift of perception written on her face. Popana sighed slightly. Many times in his mere five summers had her son been the bridge between the fiction of beach combing outcast to something more human, more real. Here she was now, a mother.

"Your son?" the girl asked barely hiding the surprise in her voice.

Not wanting to be drawn into personal matters, Popana traded a question for a question, "People think there is power in my work but there is no greater power than love itself. So I ask you, do you love your man?"

The girl gawped, either shocked at such a bold request or still unsettled at seeing the child. The question remained hanging between them alongside Popana's indifference until the girl composed herself.

"Merium loves me very much. He has delivered some beautiful gifts to my family and he plans to become a merchant. We shall be very happy together."

"That is not what I asked." There were times when being labelled the outcast played to Popana's favour, and this was one of them. "This conversation," she continued, "is already outside the boundaries of life in the port in more than one sense. What is said here will go no further. Do you love Merium?"

The girl blustered, but then recognised the seriousness behind Popana's demand. She looked at the ground, her cheeks colouring.

"I do."

"Good. That is good. Come then and see if anything interests you."

In one practiced move Popana picked her son up from behind her and placed him on her hip. He hid his face in her dark hair, his sun bleached blonde a stark contrast, just like his father. Loroc loosened his tanned arms and half turned to give the visitor a cautious appraisal.

Closing her home behind her Popana stepped forward, the woman beating a hasty retreat off the veranda and onto the sand. She then led the way to the neighbouring hut and opened the wide double doors to let as much light in as possible. The weather stretched wood complained as she pulled, and the gathered sand made perfect arcs on the floorboards as the doors swung free.

There was her workshop as she had left it, unchanged, not at all interesting or exciting to her familiar gaze, but that didn't stop the heartache of showing this space to someone new. Seeing it fresh through their eyes, wondering at the organised chaos of it all. Her tools, the hand cranked stone polisher, even her work bench, all had been bought or constructed side-by-side with her clever husband. She held herself for a moment, pushed down the welling tears, the desire to cry, how can he be dead when he still lives here? That etcher there? Traded for our own home-grown spices. That stool? Effrain had used the joiner's lathe and had turned the legs himself.

Popana recalled the anguish of her self-imposed exile from Coracor's rapier tongues, of having to stack all of these precious mementoes on the cart that had taken her and Loroc from the port. So many consequences set in action by Effrain's disappearance. Composing herself, she left this all unexpressed and merely pointed to a board where some of her recently finished pieces were hung on display.

She'd take them to the market in a week or so, weathering the frowns of the port folk to deliver them to her old friend Anlap. Hopefully he'd already sold some of her previous items and she could restock her larder with something other than dried fish and forage. The girl stepped forward to see.

"I can make them bespoke too," Popana said. "But that will cost you more, and I need to know your tastes. Plus it takes time. Time to gather, to carve, to polish, to set."

The girl, finally finding herself on familiar territory, leaned in as she would at the market place and scrutinised every piece. Her head began to bob and weave like a bird looking for grubs and Popana was forced to look away, her critical gaze directed back towards her homestead. The union of Lakli was a solemn bond, but this girl's scouring eye seemed more focused on not appearing to be less than her friends when it came to wearing the piece in public.

"There's no rush," Popana said, and turned her back on the hut and the girl, the horizon calling to her as it always did.

The showing of the workshop bought the conflicting thoughts of her husband to the forefront of her mind. These odd rituals she had fallen into since his disappearance always underlining his absence. She'd learned, over the years, that she could only interrupt the thought processes, not stop them until they'd run themselves to completion.

First the facts, spilled over in seconds yet limpid clear at each point in this perpetual, torturous pilgrimaged.

Thankfully she'd been awake and nursing their son when Effrain had risen to leave for the harbour. Nothing portentous about this final morning together, maybe a moment when he'd considered the sky from the kitchen window and mentioned how the clouds looked strange in the emergent dawn. Nothing more. His parting words a simple, "see you later my love." Then he was gone.

There were three of them on the boat that day. Effrain captaining two junior crew; young men still at home with their parents and unmarried. Not that their being without partners made their disappearance any easier on the families. In fact, Popana remained unsurprised at the anger the mothers had eventually directed towards her. Concern, then grief, then smouldering resentment calcifying into suspicion and rumour. That made a bleak kind of sense, she thought. What didn't was the crew's disappearance. Their boat was a good one, their skills at the catch already noticed among the hawkers at the fish market. They had also weathered the elements for three summers now and had been at sea in storms before.

There was talk from the other crews out that day of the speed with which the weather had turned. It wasn't a rolling storm front, they had said, rather a huge high cloud that seemed to drop onto them from above. A heavenly thing that led to hand wringing about angry deities and fresh ceremonies and offerings cast by the superstitious from the harbour walls.

Her husband's boat was further off than the fishing flotilla chasing a shoal of surface feeding fan-tails, so said those who were there. The young and fool hardy, the old sea salts had embellished the story from the safety of their ale houses afterwards, so Popana now had no clear idea of what actually happened.

When the storm dropped, visibility failed every vessel. Cut off, boxed in some said by cutting, icy sheets of rain. Those caught on the edge turned their prows towards the brighter skies behind, but all suffered as the waves grew gigantic around them, smashing the cross beams, tearing the sails and tugging the rigging into whipping tentacles.

The soft clink of bead against metal brought Popana back to the moment. The girl behind her had picked up, and now held, the delicate intricacies of one of the necklaces. It was a shell, coral and green stone piece that the craftswoman in her was proud of. Popana needed the coin, but if the girl chose that particular item of jewelry... She turned away and looked again at the shore, the shallows and then, inevitably off to the horizon. The mental dirge of her husband's vanishing picking up where it had left off.

Speculation and fantasy were in her wheelhouse now, with Effrain taking the lead role. Not solid and strong as he once had been, but something malleable and wild, a figure in a constant state of flux.

At times she imaged a blow to the head that had caused him to lose his memory. He had been plucked out of the water by a passing merchant and was now desperately trying to piece his life back together in some neighbouring harbour. Or perhaps the storm swells had deposited him on one of the many smaller islands that littered the archipelago. She pictured him felling trees with makeshift tools and building a signal fire. In her darker moments she gave way to her deeper conviction that he was drowned. Eyeless and rotting he lay on the seabed, a clinging film of silt his shroud, his beautiful features ravaged by hungry dwellers of that stygian limbo.

Desperation had transmuted itself into numbness. Her continual searches of the sea perpetuated, but she no longer felt that old stinging pang, the instinct to rush to the docks to wait every time a mast appeared on that oh so familiar horizon.

"I like the structure of this one, but the colours in this. Is it possible to combine them?"

Popana returned her full attention to the wares and considered the woman's words.

"I can dismantle these two and make you one necklace. Just the one, though. Do you see? If you wish for two identical ones, I'll have to create another to match. Or, perhaps you could choose another different one for your partner?"

"Hmmm," the woman nibbled her lip in thought. Popana continued down the path of dissuasion.

"I'd have to travel up coast to the black foot divers. You see the centerpiece? That's fretwork sawn out of a black foot shell. This will add time to the crafting and, to be realistic, cost."

The woman's stare told Popana her tactic had immediately failed. Stubborn pride, hard won among her peers no doubt, glinted behind those ambitious eyes. She could afford Popana's services and she had summoned up the courage to come and see the crazy woman in good time. Her partner would love her forever and their matching, beautiful necklaces would be the talk of Coracor.

"Yes," said the woman twitching in place. "I'd like that. How long will it take and, as I can see no indications on any of your pieces, how much will it cost?"

"My time and my materials… 125 talari should suffice," Popana went in as high as she dared knowing that this woman wouldn't be happy with the starting offer.

"I'll give you 80."

"That's 40 talari per necklace," Popana responded. "That's the price of something with much less craft and care. It'll take me two days to travel to the black foot divers and back alone. Of course, if you want to take your custom elsewhere."

"I didn't say that," the woman's tone wasn't indignant. She was merely playing a part, constructing a story to be told to her friends later, about how she managed to haggle two 100 talari necklaces down to half that price. Popana in her turn was calling her bluff.

The woman could wait until a trader turned up with jewelry, or she could hire a seat on a carriage to the capital, but being the only jeweler on this section of the coast had its advantages.

The back and forth between the two of them continued long enough for Loroc to become restless and for Popana's arms to tire. She settled on 105 talari and an agreed delivery date that was comfortable for both parties. The woman, who finally revealed herself as 'Lilith', seemed pleased with herself. She nodded once in agreement and then hitched her skirt hem in one hand before trudging away across the sand.

Popana placed a relaxing Loroc on the ground and looked after the woman.

"Well, little one. Would you like to go and see your friends tomorrow?"

*****

She and her family had never been robbed, they had never been waylaid by bandits on the road, nor had they been attacked by any of the larger animals that prowled the southern coast. Of course, there were stories of all of these misadventures happening to others and, moreover, being embellished in the retelling. It was the underlying loss of Effrain, however, that left her with an unshakable unease. She was physically taller and stronger than most of the women her age and, in her more willful moments, she could easily dismiss her fears as being ridiculous exaggerations based solely upon wild conjecture, not facts. And yet, the niggling power of these fears was pervasive and somehow seemed to inform almost everything she did.

So now she, in the early morning light, gathered all her jewelry and secreted it throughout the lining of her carry basket before stepping into her good walking shoes. Her hand brushed against the sea grass cloak that hung on the door of her workshop as she locked it, the touch triggering her to wonder where best to use it to harvest the corals, shells and stones she'd need for the commission. A thought best kept for her return, she realized, as she began to bolt the shutters.

Loroc, untidy and rubbing his eyes, didn't complain for his part. The promise and excitement of visiting the black foot divers was enough to propel him from bed and into the carry basket along with their simple provisions for the road. He'd soon be too big for carrying Popana realised, wondering where she might find fair for a wagon in the future. She knew he could and would walk when she tired, but was still happy to be carried.

One night away from home seemed such a short amount of time, but there was no room for error in Popana's life. She had no family, no real friends now and no other means of supporting both Loroc and herself. No surprise then that planning and double guessing had become her unwelcome credo. She'd done well to listen to their combined voices thus far, and this imagined success only compounded her caution. She wiggled the carry basket onto her back, checked all of her supplies one last time and then set off, the wide brim of Loroc's hat tapping against the brim of hers with each passing step.

*****

The sun rolled across the sky, warming them on the early part of the journey, then making the road toilsome as it reached its zenith. In turn, the road rolled beneath Popana's, and occasionally Loroc's, feet with only the odd trade wagon for company. These rattled in the ruts of their forerunners, signalling their appearance either behind or in front of the walkers, and then taking an interminable amount of time to finally catch up and pass them. Sometimes the wagoner would slow and match pace with Popana to chat, other times a simple salutation of the day and a nod was all she received.

By mid-afternoon, the path to the village of the black foot divers appeared on their left, and they followed its circuitous route down to the clustered homes and fishing huts. Loroc raced ahead, eager to find where the village children were playing and to join them, leaving Popana to quell her mild anxiety at his departure. It was a welcome return for her, despite her mixed feelings about the Lilith girl and her commission. At least the job motivated this trip today and a chance for to feel the only real sense of adult companionship left to her.

The village elder accepted Popana into her kitchen as if she had never been away, her ragged smile making her eyes sparkle. She was preparing the evening meal and pointed, with a hooked knife, to a bowl of vegetables that needed to be washed and cut. Popana took her carry basket from her shoulders and propped it by the door, then moved into effortless synchronicity with the elder's kitchen work. The old woman's gnarled hands moved with skill from beneath the edges of her light shawl, her white head bobbing over the gathered pots to sniff and taste.

"The children are practicing their breathing skills with Geron. Loroc will have fun," the old woman pressed a hand onto Popana's arm knowing the other woman would want to leave and check on her son. "Stop your worry," she said. "It is a calm and sunny day. Geron is our strongest swimmer and the practice will not stray from the shallows. They all get to blow bubbles at each other under water too. It will be fun, and I need you here." The elder banged the edge of a bubbling pot with the side of her spoon to emphasise the point and to halt further discussion.

They sat at the kitchen's table when all the meal's preparation had been completed, sipping some herbal infusion of the elder's concoction. Sweet and aromatic, it immediately seemed to lift Popana's tiredness from the road.

"So what brings you here?" The older woman peered over the top of her cup.

"A commission," Popana said, resting her forearms against the sand smoothed boards of the table. "I can't forage as deep as your divers, and fresh black foot shells are less brittle when fret sawing, so here I am. I've bought some items from my collection and my tools. I can trade and mend in exchange."

The elder dismissed her offer with a flap of her hand.

"You're always welcome here Popana. You know that. Yes, some of the village will trade for your wares, but the offer of a place in our community stands. Your skills could be taught here."

"The harbour is where I do most of my business…" Popana tried to explain once again, knowing the elder would dismiss these words.

"What is one day more travel to get to the market? Your work is in demand and the people of Coracor will come to you. I know you have to make a living, but that burden would be lessened here."

"It is my home, our home. Loroc needs something stable, something regular. To move…"

"You say 'our' home and I understand. You are like a lighthouse keeper. You need to keep the beacon tended in the hope that Effrain will one day find his way home. Maybe he will. Or maybe your heart will mend and you'll come and live here. We are in no rush." She paused to let the commitment behind her words settle in before continuing. "Now, tell me of your last trip to the harbour. What's happening there these days?"

Later, Loroc slumped into the hut that had been set aside for them to sleep, his words a jumble of news and stories, his limited vocabulary straining to give more detail to Popana's questions. She cleaned him up and tucked him into a bunk and still he chattered; about the other children, about the practice but mostly about Goran and what a skilled swimmer and shell diver he was. He yawned and chatted some more. Yawned again and then fell fast asleep mid-sentence.

Popana slipped into the bunk beneath him. It was a cool night and she was tired from the journey here, but Loroc's tales of Goran and the elder's invitation weighed heavy on her heart. Her son would thrive in this community, he could benefit from having men in his life as well as boys and girls his own age. Her home and her workshop still called to her, though. They had help define her very being in the dark months without her husband. The old woman was right. Together these buildings represented a beacon of hope, not a memorial. Not yet.

*****

The morning was busy for both Popana and her son. She wished to get her business concluded as early as possible while, in turn, there were still more adventures to be had for Loroc before the heartache of heading back on the road home.

With her mending work done Popana set time aside to consider the clean, but still fresh, black foot shells that were offered in trade. Their individual and unique inner markings caught and reflected the light in a halo of colours as she tilted them this way and that, imagining how they would cut and what pattern would preside on the centre piece she would create to match the other.

"A gift," the village elder handed over a neat package of her dried tea when the time came to depart. The old woman held Popana's hands in hers around the bundle.

"Think on what I said," she fixed Popana with a powerful yet kind stare. Then she waved off the children who had come to make Loroc's leaving all the more difficult. "Come along, come along, I need you all to help me. Let these good people go without your gawks and cries burning their necks. The sun will do that for them on the road.

Mother and son turned and walked away, Loroc sad at first then tired from the morning's play, his small and sinewy frame easier to shoulder once he settled and dropped off to sleep. Perhaps it was the added weight of the traded shells, or perhaps he had gorged himself on the ample and varied breakfast, either way Popana's feet dragged and she struggle to keep up the pace that had brought them to the village in such good time. It was harder to leave than to come, and she wondered on why the weight on her legs and feet was now matched by a weight deep inside her too.

She walked for as long as she could with Loroc asleep and then stopped for a short break as he woke. Together they digested their food then resumed their journey, Popana letting her son walk even though that slowed them. Hand-in-hand they wandered to the side of the well-worn cart ruts and watched as the sun move over head and then behind them. Their shadows stretched forward, their hats creating two strange creatures with willowy bodies and large round heads. Then these faded to a greyish blue as the early evening set in. It was almost dark before they spied the path down to their home.

*****

Popana paused and stretched, the remaining twinges from the road worrying her shoulders as she worked. She looked over to where Loroc played with his toys in the shade, wondering again if she was doing what was best for him. Quiet, introverted, lost in a playful internal world all morning, the absence of the other children written throughout his muted behaviour since rising. She sighed. She would go and play with him later. Right now the best thing she could do for them both was finish this centrepiece while the light remained perfect for such detailed work. She gently rethreaded the precious blade of the fret saw and went back to the delicate thrum of her cutting.

She'd selected a shell with the most interesting patterning at the hump of the carapace and removed this section for the fine work. She'd learned from bitter failures to leave the crusty outer covering alone until the pattern was set, and then to clean and smooth from the outside in. The nodules were harder to cut through, risking the expensive blade with every stroke, but they gave strength to the piece until it was ready to be polished and smoothed. On this one, Popana had marked out a spiral in the style of the symbol of Lakli that was represented on its partner. The pattern curled towards the centre of the piece, but spiralled here in the opposing direction. She was pleased with that moment of inspiration that led to this mirroring.

The days fell back into the natural rhythm from before their trip. In the morning, while the light was strong, Popana worked, then they ate and rested before she schooled Loroc in the afternoon. A week had passed by the time she finished the new central piece, and it took another day to replicate most of the necklace Lilith had taken a shine to. With the almost complete piece nestled upon her ringed fingers, Popana looked to her sea grass cloak and thought where she might collect the remaining stones required.

The cloak was an idea that had come to her in the depths of grief. One day she had waded out to the shallows in search of food, her feet bare and careless of the hidden spine fins that could sting from beneath the sand. Her body going through the motions as she hid her wailing, internal monologue from her son in the carry basket. She had dragged her sea grass bag behind her, throwing the odd handful of shellfish in when she discovered them. Surviving, masking her anguish, half-mad with sorrow and wandering through the shallows, oblivious of beauty around her plodding feet.

That day they had returned home and she had set Loroc back down in the shade with his toys before going inside to cook. She dumped the sea grass bag onto the table and slumped into the chair next to it. Making sure she still had a view on her preoccupied son, she had leant back from that precious sightline and took up her silent sobbing once again. Head in her hands, the odd, involuntary gasp or sniff the only indication that she was in pain, the salt of the sea air on her skin mingled with the constant flow of her tears. Popana had already learned that it was best to cry herself dry, to empty as much grief as she could in these grasped moments of privacy so she could fake wellbeing for Loroc later.

Her head sunk to the table and still she cried, waves of grief that crashed against the shore of her being, making her think that this torment would never cease until, with a moment of surprising clarity, it did. She had opened her eyes in that instant, her view of the sea grass bag made fantastical through the lingering tears. A sinuous and bejewelled thing it lay there, coiled in upon itself, sparkling and glinting in a most puzzling manner. Popana had to blink repeatedly to understand what she was seeing. There, set in among the fibrous threads of the bag, were a collection of beautiful stones, dead corals fragments and shells. A near circular pebble of sea polished glass drew her eye, and the craftswoman within her surfaced, taking inspiration about what to do with this wonderful discovery and the potential it offered.

At first she'd woven bigger bags, but there was still a balance to find between trawling for items of interest and a growing Loroc who didn't always want to be confined to the carry basket. There was no way she would leave him unguarded on the shore, and so the straps to the bag had become longer and she had tied them to a spare belt. The results, though, remained variable and Popana realised that the wider the area of the bag, the greater the chance of finding something useful.

Bit by bit, with each experimental form, the bags transformed to fish tailed mats and then, finally, to the cloak. She was happy then for the first time in an age, the rope fat hem becoming water logged and drawing a cloud of detritus into the higher webbing of the garment, Loroc able to be carried, to wade, to sometimes swim alongside her.

Popana came back to the here and now, the memory fading as quick as it had come. She needed to find more of the softer green stone which was much easier to drill for the beads of the second necklace. She stood and pushed thoughts of how she had created the cloak to one side. Grabbing the heavy garment from its peg and their sea shoes from a box near the door, Popana stepped from her workshop and called to Loroc.

It was past noon but the heat was still strong and the night a long way off. The clouds were isolated and bore no news of foreboding weather as Loroc jumped up and held his arms out to be carried, the sight of the sea grass cloak delighting him. As Popana held him she consulted her mind map of the waterfront before her, a playful wind doing its best to break her concentration by playing with her hair. There were many areas she had trawled already but, as with the farmers inland who moved their crops from field to field, she knew that it was best to allow the sea to replenish its collected gifts. Her gathering had not been as bountiful of late, and so her scope had expanded as she ventured further into the shallows. There was one place that she hadn't explored before, an expanse of sand that ran between two fingers of the reef. She placed Loroc back onto the sand and decided she would go there.

They reached the shore and Popana crouched in the gentle waves, submerging both sets of shoes until the soft leather of the uppers became pliable. Then she sat in the water, slipping Lorco's on first and then her own.

They paddled together for a time, Loroc as cheery as ever in the cooling joy of the sea, kicking up spume and squatting to look at the shapes in submerged sand. They moved deeper and began to wade. Deeper still and, with a hand braced under his belly, Popana let her son splash about for a while, flexing his swimming skills. He tired and reached for her already out of his depth, his wet arms clinging around her neck. She started in surprise as he flicked his head to remove the wet hair clinging to his face, then moved the boy to her hip and began to peer down into the undulating world below her.

They'd gone out further than she'd expected when she looked back towards the beach. It was narrow here between the banks of coral to either side, but there wasn't anything that caused her too much concern. She glanced behind and saw the cloak splayed under the water, the hem defining a pleasing arc against the pebbles and sand. Returning to the view ahead, Popana spied a glint of something greenish a pace or so to her left. Hopeful of swift rewards, she stepped towards it… and dropped.

She was underwater. But how? Her instinct was to hold Loroc away from the problem and she could still feel fresh air on her wrists and around his body. She'd stumbled. All she needed to do was stand up. Her feet sank into the soft sand below her and she felt a harsh tug on the cloak's ties at her neck. She couldn't stand. The water must be deeper here, she thought, some trick of the eye when seen from above, a hidden dip she had stepped into.

Popana was a skilled enough swimmer to control her breathing, but the panic remained real. She let the tiniest breath bubble away from her mouth and reassessed the situation. She strained again and again the harsh tug across her neck and throat. The cloak was caught. It was caught. Caught. Had it billowed wider as she sank and reached out to snag one side or the other?

Loroc began to wiggle in her hands, his thin form slippery and warm as opposed to the cold world she now inhabited. His wiggling increased. No, Popana thought, no dear heart wait. I have to think. Think. Another puff of precious air rippling her lips, the weight of needing to breathe and rising panic constricting her chest. One breath, the water scorching her throat and they would be done for. She looked up at the indistinct Loroc above her and thought, not like this, not now.

His insistent struggling freed himself from her grasp and a new level of despair pushed her pounding heart to new levels of stress. He was free in the water. A slimy hand touched her face, too small, too deep. Popana flailed trying to push Loroc away, back to surface. Another, bigger pop of air escaping from her labouring lungs. Backwards. Could she clamber backwards?

A red blur was seeping in at the edges of her vision. She tried to take a big step back up the incline, but the bank of sand gave away against her pounding heels. Think. Her mind struggled with the word, then the need to gasp fresh air became all her being. Her eyes were filled with water, above her the shape of a struggling Loroc, in front of her the open sea, an unclear impression of the world rolling away from her to the where the island fell away.

The drop. Open water, vast and uncaring. A figure there? Someone coming to her aid? A shadow in the water, made of kelp yet square shouldered. A curve of volcanic rock? Large, strong obsidian hands raised palm first towards her, seaweed tassels flowing like immature wings beneath the driftwood arms. Another ripple of lost breath obscuring the view, more red now than murky blue. Her sea knife. It was at her belt. If she could reach it… Too late. She had to breathe. Now.

The figure's hands seemed to be pushing towards her, pushing the sea towards her. How futile, she thought. She was almost oblivious to Loroc's returning hands. His hard pinch on her nose, his sudden appearance in front of her. Not like this, not like this, not…

His little face filled her vision, his lips pressed to hers, a final farewell jostled by her last breath escaping around them as she exhaled. She breathed in ready for the water, the choking struggle, the end. Instead Loroc blew out all of his breath into her. Small, salty, confusing, but enough to wake her. He swam up and away as

Popan's hand moved expertly to her knife. Loroc returned, held her head in his tiny hands and gave a blurry nod. His lips on hers again. Popana breathed out around his cheeks and then took another sip of air from him. The hilt of the knife in her hand. The blade to her throat turned towards the deep. A cut, a push and she was clear eyed nad staring at the sky. Gasping, heaving, hauling every piece of the air around her into her painful lungs.

Back upon the shore, an odd calm replaced the fear and the tears of gratitude they'd both shed as they'd dragged themselves up the beach. They sat caked in sand, Popana behind Loroc, both facing towards the point of their lucky escape, both lost for a moment in relief.

She relinquished her grip on him and began brushing sand from his back. She thought back to the shadow in the water and shook her head, dismissing it, her hand carving strokes across her son's miniature shoulder blades as she did so. In that dismissal Popana felt something release, a letting go of the stress of the moment and a realisation of the significance of that letting go. She imagined the sea grass cloak billowing under the water where they had discarded it. An amazing thing for a transient moment, and now a bad idea being unwoven by the tides.

A vision came to her then, uncalled for and powerful. All these thoughts, always plaguing her, never spoken but irresistible. A sunset, then, on this beach in the future. Her son, a man sat as he was now, staring out to sea. The embers of a low fire glowing nearby, illuminating the twilit scene. Coiled across Loroc's back and over his shoulder was the sea serpent tattoo of the sailors, black against ruddy, fire-lit skin. Popana couldn't see its head nestled upon her son's breast, guarding his heart, but she knew it to be there. In the vision, she placed a hand upon his slim and strong shoulder and knew that the moment in the water when he had freed himself and rescued her, was just the first letting go of many. A wind pulsed down upon them for the shadows inland, waking the fire, lifting a school of darting embers up, up into the unknown.

Storm

Michael Moorcock

I remember the first time Linda and I saw Storm and Co enter the lobby of the Brighton science fiction convention, like an exotic cloud of Goth splendour, immediately brightening the place up. For us, she looked the way all outstanding fantasists should look! We were vastly cheered up by her presence alone, not to mention her exceptional and original talent. When the moment came, she was the only author I wanted to collaborate with, and my expectations were exceeded. Below is an extract from our novel, Silverheart, which is, to my mind, the best tribute to Storm.

Extract from Silverheart:

"You did only what you had to do, played your part," Max said. "It was necessary."

Care for her, Lord Iron said.

"With all my heart," Max replied.

He withdrew his awareness from the dying Lord's mind and opened his eyes. The first person he saw was Rose, her face. Even in grief and suffering she was beautiful, and it was not simply a surface beauty. "Do not fear for your father," Max said, "He is at peace."

Rose stared at him, mute, her face pale.

"Do not fear me either," Max said, "What you see before you has a short life this day. But the man I am within it will live on. We will live on."

He gathered Rose to his breast, enfurling her in his copper feathers. He could feel her living warmth, smell the strength of her spirit. Holding her in his arms, he opened his wings, which beat upon the air. "Let us enjoy this while we can." He bore her high above the reborn city. They flew on magical wings, sure in the knowledge that the word was new and innocent below.

They flew to the highest point, where the Jewel of All Time spilled its life-giving rays all over the city.

They flew in joy and in love.

To fulfil their fabulous destiny.

Rishi Reiki

Paul Weston

It may be a surprise to some that a Goth Queen, who wrote novels about vampires and fallen angels, would be interested in the subject of Reiki. It can seem very much a fluffy New Age kind of thing, often linked with crystals, Ascended Masters and so forth. Storm Constantine had a little to say on her initial experiences with it in the 2002 article *Reiki's Fire* that was included in her *Whatnot's and Curios* anthology. It was my great pleasure to have helped set her off on this journey. Primed by her experiences, she went on to investigate the Sekhem system, producing the definitive work on the subject in 2008. Between the two, sits a fascinating adventure. The core of it will take barely half a dozen paragraphs to describe, but it was so dense with multiple associations, it will require the rest of this article to do it justice.

Reiki is a Japanese healing system, something that can supposedly be transferred to someone through a mysterious process known as an attunement - an odd affair involving the recipient sitting with eyes closed whilst having their head and hands blown on. After that, a permanent connection has supposedly been established with an energy that could manifest as heat, or even cold, through the hands, in a way that could be felt by most people they touched. This energy could help with a variety of physical and emotional conditions. The Ki in Reiki is the Ki or Chi in martial arts, Tai Chi and so on. A Japanese man named Mikao Usui had founded the system in the nineteen-twenties after a mystical quest and experience on a holy mountain. There were different levels or degrees. With the second, it was possible to send this force at a distance to people, and even situations, through the use of particular symbols. Rooms could be filled with it. There were all kinds of options.

Japanese sources were discovered and investigated. One of the most notable researchers was Frank Arjava Petter, who presented the results in a book called *Reiki Fire*. Working in Japan itself, he found the grave of Usui, met members of his family and a Japanese Reiki society that was unknown in the west. They had raised a ten-feet-tall memorial to Usui, in a Tokyo cemetery, that has an extensive inscription full of biographical detail.

Usui studied world religions deeply. It is also said that he had great knowledge of medicine and 'fortune telling'. He travelled outside of Japan, to western countries and China to study in some way, but no details are given.

It is clear that Reiki emerged from a zone with a very distinct flavour of the peculiar forms of Japanese Buddhism that, like its Tibetan counterpart, carry forward many archaic strata from earlier indigenous practices. The holy mountain of Usui's retreat was Kurama, near Kyoto. There is one main temple towards the bottom and various others on the route up. It was inaugurated in the eighth century AD. A priest named Gantei climbed the mountain, led by a white horse. Bishamon-ten, spirit of the sun and protector of the northern quarter of the Buddhist heaven, enlightened him. Gantei founded a temple which has been used by various sects since. Another temple on the mountain honours a kind of trinity of forces. Sonten is a supreme deity. He came to Earth from Venus, descending on the mountain in the form of a being called Mao-son over six million years ago. His mission was the salvation of the human race. As part of this, he became one with the spirit of the planet and still resides inside an ancient cedar tree, emanating force out into the world. Sonten manifests as Love, Light, and Power. A shrine on the mountain top is supposedly sited on the very spot that Sonten descended.

Kurama temple literature contains the Usui Reiki Master symbol, which is obviously Japanese script. It is used to represent Sonten. The depiction of the Love aspect of the trinity resembles another of the Reiki symbols.

Usui had undertaken a twenty-one day fasting retreat on Kurama and, so the story goes, on the dawn of the final day, saw a bright light in the sky that moved towards him and enveloped him. In this light he saw again the symbols he had studied in the temple, and now somehow fully understood their use. Returning from the mountain, with healing power in his hands, he embarked on a programme of good works, serving the poor and needy.

The exact date of this is unclear, but he did open a clinic of sorts in Tokyo in 1922 and would go on to help victims of the devastating earthquake that was soon to follow there. He became moderately famous, and invitations came for him to travel around

Japan to spread his knowledge and the Reiki blessing. Over 2,000 people were taught by him. He died in 1926. Reiki passed from Japan to Hawaii, and from there gradually moved across the world

One of the most useful perspectives I had for understanding Reiki was provided by Storm's friend, the writer Andrew Collins. After the Green Stone saga, he became interested in seeing if he could find similar phenomena to psychic questing in other historical periods and cultures. The Tibetan Terma tradition provided the most fruitful material. Buddhism was brought to Tibet in the eighth century AD by the great adept Padmasambhava. To say this being was a bit of a paranormal force would be an understatement. He was toting quite a package of empowered teachings and energies. In fact he didn't think the Tibetans were ready for the whole deal, so he withdrew some of it from circulation in a variety of increasingly strange ways. In the most simple examples, he might take a scroll of teachings, a statue or a ritual artefact, and hide them in a cave behind some rocks or bury them in the ground or some such. This was consigning them to the element of earth. A fire concealment would literally mean incinerating the material. Water would require casting it into a river, waterfall, or sacred lake. For the element of air, a true shamanic sorcerer's performance was required, whereby Padmasambhava threw something up from his hands and it dematerialised. These elemental treasures, known as Termas, went into a kind of suspended animation, awaiting the time of their return.

In the centuries ahead, unusual visionaries would be inspired to find them. These characters (called Tertons) would often seem a bit crazy. They were often mystics who didn't conform to normal monastic-type patterns. Strange dreams, omens and visions of saints and deities, would lead them to particular places. The earth element retrievals are comparatively straightforward. The Terton would rummage around some rocks in a cave and uncover a scroll or statue. One of the most famous scriptures in the world, the so-called *Tibetan Book of the Dead*, is considered to be a Terma treasure found in such a manner. It is believed to have been written by Padmasambhava. Modern textual analysis suggests it dates from the time of its alleged recovery but the belief remains. The other elemental retrievals are weirder by far. A Terton may build a fire and then reach into it and pull out an artefact. Likewise a waterfall or lake. And thin air.

Most rarefied of all are the "mind treasures" that disappeared into the element of ether. These were whole teachings on consciousness, reality, and mystical processes of attainment. They weren't just verbal formula and ideas. They were charged with blessing power, alive with energy for transformation. Anyone receiving such a teaching in a ceremonial empowerment would find it coming to life within them if they upheld the necessary practice. Tertons might suddenly get a complete download from a wisdom deity and something forgotten had returned to the world. I came to believe that Reiki seems to be an example of a mind treasure.

On New Year's Day 2000, I initiated Andrew Collins into Reiki One and Two together. He experienced a massive download of information about its antecedents and planned to write a book intended to be called *The Divine Fire: In Search of the Origins of Reiki, Buddhism and Eastern Asceticism*. For a while, he and his closest associates carried out psychic questing style meditations to try and access more information, with some very interesting results. Sadly, he could not interest a publisher.

With *The Divine Fire*, he was hoping to investigate whether the mystic consciousness found in Hinduism, Buddhism and its Tibetan variants, had antecedents even further back. This took him back to areas he had presented in *From the Ashes of Angels*. Since his investigation of the Terma tradition, Andy had been greatly interested in Dzogchen. This Tibetan Buddhist teaching could perhaps best be categorised as a kind of Tibetan Zen or the Upanishadic non-dual Hinduism whereby a limitless void is recognised as the omnipresent universal consciousness from which all form emerges. As with all the Tibetan teachings, some beautiful forms lead to that formlessness, and Dzogchen seems to carry forward aspects of the pre-Buddhist Shamanic Bon teachings.

The eighties had seen the notable Dzogchen adept Namkhai Norbu become prominent. The teaching had apparently originated in a place named Xanxun or Zhang Zhang. Norbu was a scholar as well as teacher and he helped promulgate studies in the topic. Xanxun was supposedly a pre-Buddhist kingdom, located broadly in the area of West Tibet, where the Holy Mountain Kailash is located, and Ladakh. It had expanded to reach the edge of Turkestan and even to the borders of Iran. In 2000, Andy was willing to contemplate the possibility of a strong Iraq connection.

Through Namkhai Norbu, he also became particularly

fascinated by the concept of the Rainbow Body. Following successful adherence to certain practices, it is possible to dissolve apparent separation from one's true form, what could be termed the Enlightenment Body, the Rainbow Body. The Tibetan accounts differ from those of the Hindu adepts and demonstrate hints of a more archaic shamanism. At death, the body of an advanced practitioner may shrink. Coloured lights may be seen around it. Some fingernails, toenails and hair might be all that remains of the physical form. The greatest of all adepts may have a fully functioning Rainbow Body without physically dying. Whatever the case, the light body persists and does its thing in other realms, perhaps helping nudge some mind treasures through.

As Reiki spread globally, variants began to emerge using different symbols. Kathleen Milner stated that one such group originated from the Indian guru Sai Baba. Many attested to the power of the system, but then Sai Baba's organisation disclaimed any connection. American Reiki Master and researcher William Rand developed what he called Karuna Reiki from it and this remains the most widely disseminated form.

The standard Usui attunements are commenced with the so-called Master symbol, something primarily in Japanese kanji script and featured in Kurama temple literature. Two of the other symbols in the system are seemingly odd and out of place against it. Likewise, the Karuna attunements are driven by a Tibetan symbol with an accepted history and a wide set of associations, but feature other seemingly unconnected symbols.

It is sufficient to note here that the Tibetan symbol refers to a diamond thunderbolt ritual weapon of ancient provenance wielded in Hindu texts by the God Indra. The Tibetan form is of a short double-ended five-pronged club with a sphere at its centre. This sphere symbolises the emptiness of the true nature.

For a few years I found myself getting a range of attunements from wandering freelancers, including the Karuna symbols. After Storm Constantine and Debbie Cartwright had received what might be termed conventional Reiki from me, it was felt that it might be interesting to see how this other system might land with them, so we set up a weekend in Glastonbury in November 2000 to find out.

The result was remarkable and fascinating, demonstrating for me the potency of group alchemy when a suitably unusual cast of characters is assembled. It felt that things that were in my mind but never mentioned contributed to what unfolded. Debbie was certainly aware of Andy's *Divine Fire* project earlier in the year and it's possible that a little of the material hung in the airwaves as well. The core was a visionary realm accessed by Debbie and made the centre of an experience of a whole system that Storm would develop and call Rishi Reiki. I have long felt that it sits intriguingly alongside their interaction on the Grigori trilogy.

Some more introductory contextualisation is necessary for full appreciation. For some time I had been giving considerable attention to material in Geoffrey Ashe's books *The Ancient Wisdom* and *Avalonian Quest* that linked certain aspects of the Glastonbury mythos within a postulated ancient wisdom package. My summary and expansion, largely written in early 2000, features in my *Mysterium Artorius* and *Avalonian Aeon.* It was a journey that went from Babylon to the Altai mountain range, thereby prefiguring in certain respects a unique odyssey that Andrew Collins would also make over a period of decades

Ashe went in search of the sacrality of the number seven, seen so prominently in the Book of Revelation, and championed by HP Blavatsky. Jerusalem had been considered by the Jews to be the centre of the world. It was literally the place where the process of creation began. The centre of the centre was Solomon's temple. Everything about it was designed to embody divine laws. The ceremonies that took place within it didn't just reflect God's work, they helped to harmonise the world with it. At the base of the temple was a rock that was supposed to be the first piece of solid matter made by God. This made it the navel of the world. Even stranger was the belief that the hill where the temple stood, known as Zion, was the highest point on Earth. This is particularly odd as the nearby, plainly visible, Mount of Olives is obviously taller. The world was considered to be flat and circular with a mountain at its centre. There are perplexing anomalous references to this mount in the Old Testament. Psalm 48, verse 2 refers to *'Mount Zion in the far north'*. Why the north?

Closer investigation reveals that the Babylonians had revered the number seven before the Jews. It seems that some of their ideas were passed on during the formative process of the writing of the Old Testament, in the time of the Babylonian captivity. Some academics argue that the Babylonian numerology stems from their knowledge of the planets, which they counted as seven. This list consisted of the visible planets of pre-telescope days, Mercury, Venus, Mars, Jupiter and Saturn with the addition of the Sun and the Moon. It seems however that the list was manipulated to align with an already established sacrality of seven. The Sun and Moon were not always included in planetary counts. Other cultures numbered them differently.

In Babylonian sacred culture, seven appeared as part of a complex of closely connected concepts. In the city of Babylon was a circular 250 feet tall, seven-tiered ziggurat, known as the Etemenanki, *"the Temple of the Foundation of Heaven and Earth"* and the *"Mount of the Mountains of all Lands."* It was considered to be the centre of the world, the point of creation and its cyclic regeneration. On its summit was a temple where the climax of their New Year ceremonials, the *Akitu*, was acted out between the king and a priestess who represented the goddess. It was believed that through the ziggurat's centre ran a mystical axis, a "bond" or binding post, connecting the realms of earth, underworld, and sky. The heavens rotated around its top. Here was one area though, where there seemed to be a discrepancy between mythic and physical reality. Anyone standing on the top of the ziggurat and looking up to observe the sky could soon see that the pole star pivotal point was not directly above but off to the north. The World Mountain temple seems to have been a model of an original located elsewhere.

Earlier Mesopotamian cities had similar ideas. Ziggurats had seven levels. The Sumerian capital Nippur's temple was known as the *"House of the Mountain"*. The city had a wall with seven gates. There were also significant sevens in the Sumerian Underworld, into which their "bond" or binding post, of cosmic unity extended. They feature in one of the most famous stories of the ancient world, the descent of the Goddess Innana, who became the Babylonian Ishtar. She encountered seven judges, at seven gates, who demanded that she remove an item of clothing at each until she reached the heart of the underworld naked. The motif of the septenary path that reaches a centre by a difficult route suggests comparisons with labyrinths. Whilst the Sumerians clearly influenced the Babylonians, the mystery of the displaced centre of the heavens remains. The two cultures occupied essentially the same geographical region. The pivot of the sky would still be somewhere in the north.

Seven appears in the context of the sacred centre, the creation point, the heart of the world, both above and below ground, at Jerusalem, Babylon, Nippur and the Greek Delphi, which Ashe also examined in some detail in *The Ancient Wisdom.* It is not omnipresent throughout the ancient world but further examples of the familiar package of symbols do occur in some far-flung locations.

The idea of a World Mountain as centre and starting point of creation, is widespread in Asia. It is best known as the Mount Meru of Hinduism, often portrayed with seven tiers, that has the familiar celestial pole star axis through its centre, around which the heavens revolve. Remember that in Jerusalem and Babylon, the temples were not physically aligned in such a way, hence the need to somehow identify them with a prototype in the north and thereby partake of its archetypal potency. Meru was not believed to be located in India but to the north, where the migrating Indians had originated from. Ashe wondered if the references to *"Zion the far north"* were suggestive of a diffusion of a set of ideas from a point of origin connected to the Meru mythos.

In ancient times the polar constellation was Draco, the dragon serpent. The sky revolved around it. Finally, through looking at the heavens, Ashe found his source for the mystique of seven. It is in the seven stars of the constellation of Ursa Major, the Great Bear. Its stars circled about the centre of the sky and could be used to locate it. It therefore will always be in immediate proximity to the axis of the World Mountain. Nations which had early versions of the sacred seven cultural package lived in latitudes where the constellation was always visible. It disappears in the later forms of Hinduism, as the Indians travelled south and it vanished from their sky. Ashe delivers detailed evidence of the significance of Ursa Major in many cultures down through the ages. The Sumerian Nippur was considered to align with it. Babylonians called it the bond of heaven.

The Hindu sacred texts known as the Vedas are indubitably a part of the wisdom tradition of humanity. Just how ancient they really are is a perennial topic of contention. They were probably written down between 1500 and 500BCE but undoubtedly preserve far older material

The Rishis were inspired sages of the Vedic era, composers of the sacred texts. They came to be considered as semi-divine. Many names have been preserved. They weren't all men. The lore surrounding them is diverse. One particular group have unique importance: The Saptarishis are seven sages who are definitely not human, and oversee different epochs in the vast Hindu time cycles. In some versions, their ranks change in accordance with that. They reside somehow on seven-tiered Meru and connect with the seven stars of Ursa Major. This lore brings us back to the idea that the roots of the culture lay at a more northerly latitude earlier in time.

The Vedic scriptures, although available to us as written texts, are intended to be chanted aloud. Some are accompaniments to meticulous ritual procedures, fire ceremonies and so forth, honouring archaic deities. One such figure was Agni, whose very name means fire. He has three levels of manifestation in the human realm, as Fire on Earth, as Lightning in the atmosphere, and as the Sun in the sky. In this, he becomes associated with the rainbow as an emanation of sunlight. Some iconography gives him three heads to express this. There are depictions of Agni with seven rays of light or flame emanating from him. The number seven is associated with him as having seven tongues (indicating how easily he consumes sacrificial butter given to his fire) and in sometimes driving a chariot pulled by seven horses. He serves as a messenger, a link, between the human and divine realms, and his rites and priests facilitate that process. He is present in every home hearth and funeral pyre. Agni would later become increasingly internalised and his fire linked to inner yogic processes. He remains present in the lamps of the Hindu Diwali festival.

There is certainly a link with archaic Iranian strata that feed into Zoroastrianism fire ceremonies. Agni was even portrayed as a bird like the famous Garuda. In *From the Ashes of Angels,* Andrew Collins had made much use of the divine bird stories, including Garuda, to indicate the possible presence of a memory of the Watchers so, coupled with the fire ceremony connection, we have at least a subtle nuance of Storm and Debbie's wider concerns being present and suggestive thereby of intriguing continuity to tease out.

The early Hindus thought of Ursa Major as both the Seven Rishis and the seven bears. Geoffrey Ashe recognised a kind of riddle here that seems to be asking, who can be both a bear and a seer? The answer is a shaman. From there, he proceeded to the climax of his journey. He was led into the Siberian realms of the

Altai mountain range, with its sacred Mount Belukha, and archaic shamanism. In this region can be glimpsed the oldest currently discoverable forms of the complete seven package. Mammoth ivory carved with seven circles of dots was discovered at an Altaic cave burial.

The shaman represents the earliest religious specialist. Generally speaking, the most powerful are born, not made. A series of common events in their early lives mark out a specific developmental syndrome. Intense psychic experiences may make normal life unbearable and force upon them a kind of dissolution of their personality. This can take the vivid form of dismemberment as limbs are torn asunder and fed to fierce demons. Some unfortunates never get beyond that. The ideal result sees the candidate put back together as a fully functioning shaman. They are able to demonstrate incredible abilities. In many cases they will carry the complete oral traditions of their tribes, memorising mythic sagas, plant lore, law codes and so on. They will act as mediators with the ancestors and deities. Most importantly, their acceptance will be determined by their abilities to successfully function as healers and to help the tribe in their everyday tasks of hunting animals and generally finding food. The shaman will often magically identify with an animal and wear its fur. It's all very well having weird experiences where you believe that you've left your body and can locate a lost animal, or find a grazing herd for the hunters to attack, but if it doesn't turn out to be true they won't pay any further attention.

In the visionary world of the shaman can be found recurring motifs that are immediately familiar from the quest for the sacred seven. There is a world tree, an axis that connects the three realms of underworld, earth and heaven. It's sometimes pictured as a pole holding up the sky. The north star is pictured as immediately above. The shaman travels up and down it. It seems to be very much connected with the World Mountain concept, with its levels and orientation to the pole star. This geography can be specifically internalised so that the shamans align their spinal columns with the world tree. The ascent of its different levels seems to prefigure the yogic chakra system. Mircea Eliade argued at length that yoga has clearly evolved from shamanic roots. Shamanic lore often talks of a paradisiacal lost golden age, when their powers were greater, and humanity as a whole was closer to the divine. Mount Meru was later located in esoteric texts as within the body of the yogi.

In the Altai region there are significant sevens associated with these three zones of the shaman's universe. In the underworld, the lord of the dead lives at the bottom of seven levels with his seven sons and seven daughters. Geoffrey Ashe disagreed with authorities that believe the Central Asian shamans were influenced by India and Mesopotamia in their use of the World Mountain and the number seven. He maintained that the transmission of ideas was in the opposite direction.

The Altai region has also been the focus of another immense quest centred on the fabled realm of Shambhala. Somewhere in the mountains of Asia, perhaps in mysterious Tibet, was a valley where a group of sage immortals hid away from the world and engaged in secret great deeds for the good of all. Occasionally a worthy few would make contact with them. They can be compared to some extent with the Seven Rishis.

Shambhala represents a living and vital reality for the Tantric Buddhists of Tibet and Mongolia, who believe it to be the home of a system of secret wisdom. Some of this is embodied in the teachings of the Kalachakra, which means "Wheel of Time". Its origins are believed to predate Buddha, who visited Shambhala himself to be initiated in its mysteries. On the one hand, it has a tangible physical location, but also strange qualities which can hide it from the profane, making it all but invisible to the outside world. Its pilgrims are somehow summoned by subtle inner means.

In modern times an Agni Yoga was founded by Helene Roerich, wife of mystic painter and explorer Nicholas. A definite Blavatsky wannabe, in 1920 she had gone out at night into Hyde Park in a deliberate attempt to try and set off a similar encounter to the one reported by HPB there, that set off her alleged contact with Himalayan masters. As far as Helene Roerich was concerned, she succeeded, making contact with the very same 'Master M' and went on to, in modern parlance, channel a teaching she called Agni Yoga, taken to mean a path to mergence in divine fire. An epoch of divine fire is upon us and a spirit baptism in the same is available through the cultivation of mental ethical physical disciplines. The planetary consciousness can be transformed.

The Agni Yoga literature would expand into a corpus running into thousands of pages. Some might find it a tad bland. Beyond that, further channelled messages of Helene would be the driving force for the immense Roerich mid-twenties expedition into Central Asia in search of Shambhala. It reached the Altai Mountain area in 1926. Regardless of any Tibetan focus, this Siberian realm can ultimately be considered to be where the great odyssey was leading.

I would add my recently acquired knowledge of Usui, and the vision quest culture of Kurama, into this cross-cultural World Mountain package. Seven Rishis in the stars. A being from Venus touching down. An ancient mind treasure activated in the modern world.

Dion Fortune, who had a home in Glastonbury between the wars, wondered, in the 1934 *Avalon of the Heart,* if the terracing on the Tor might have been deliberately sculpted in remembrance of a prototype holy mountain on some other continent. She had Atlantis in mind, but the general idea would prove to be fruitful in later speculations. Geoffrey Ashe believed that the terracing was a unique form of the sevenfold Cretan labyrinth that can also be found amongst the Hopi. This formed part of the Seven mystery. It's yet another contentious but fertile idea. Ashe wondered if the Altaic cave burial discovery of mammoth ivory carved with seven circles of dots represented an early stirring of what evolved into the septenary maze design?

The Ancient Wisdom and *Avalonian Quest* also featured the work of the remarkable Stephen Jenkins, author of *The Undiscovered Country*, who had worked as a teacher in Mongolia and been initiated into a type of Tantric Buddhism that included Kalachakra Shambhala teachings. High-ranking Lamas told him that a European had visited Buddha. They believed him to be a Celt. He received Shambhalic initiation. In the midst of this mysterious episode the "presence" of Shambhala was transplanted to Britain. Apparently the Lamas had been deliberating about the whole business for at least a century. They stated that Shambhala once had a literal physical existence in the Celtic Britain of the last centuries before Christ. In *The Undiscovered Country* Jenkins puts forward the possibility that it was actually Glastonbury. There's not exactly a lot of archaeology to back this one up, but it is a marvellous mystical, poetic idea that sets the mind off on strange, suggestive tangents.

Ashe and Jenkins raise the possibility that something of the Central Asian ancient wisdom package made its way to Britain. The

Glastonbury landscape seems to speak eloquently of it once the code is broken. The Tor combines many of the familiar motifs. The alleged septenary spiral maze appears to have sculpted it like a ziggurat. It could easily accommodate World Mountain concepts. There seems to be an association of both paradise and underworld around it. The mythology of Arthur and his return is not unlike that of a Shambhalic warrior named Gesar Khan. Ursa Major has been known as "Arthur's wagon" and his very name is generally taken to mean "Bear." The Celts originated in Asia. Their Druid religious leaders evidenced definite Hindu and shamanic elements.

In his 1990 *New Light on the Ancient Mystery of Glastonbury*, John Michell portrayed Arthur as a title that kings held down through the centuries from shortly after the last ice age. He would have been the earthly embodiment of a stellar deity. *'Arthur was the spirit guardian of those islands, the keeper of the Bear and also the leader of the bear hunt. His legendary adventures were ritually enacted as the tribes moved around the central pole of their territory, imitating the revolutions of the Great Bear around the pole star. Their totem was the bear; the image of their chief god was Arcturus and the Great Bear constellation, and the title assumed by their leader was Arth Fawr or Arthur'.*

Michell was led to this idea through his investigation of the mystery of Glastonbury's seven holy islands. As far back as the Domesday Book, seven island hills in the Glastonbury area were given special legal status. They were free from taxation. The King himself had no power over them. The site of the Abbey itself was one of them. The others were located at Beckery, Godney, Martinsea, Meare, Panborough and Nyland. Small chapels were placed upon these outlying hills, which the Abbey maintained. The mystery is what was special about them. There are plenty of other hills in the vicinity and a number of them are larger. Looking at their position on a map, John Michell saw that they seemed to form the image of the constellation of Ursa Major. The Tor was the pole star Draco, around which they revolved, and may have been seen as Arthur's father, Pendragon, the dragon's head. It is perhaps not a huge surprise that Michell's ideas are not exactly academically sound but, once again, they set the mind off in interesting ways

This was all part of my recent mental furniture on that weekend in November 2000 and what followed carried enormously rich associations and nuances. Debbie Cartwright's visionary abilities were fully switched on, and what she experienced became integrated into the Rishi Reiki system that Storm developed. The scenario was sufficiently striking and potent to be worth repeating here independently of any attunement procedure and use of symbols, as it can serve as potential inspiration and connection. It was written down by Storm at the time and is presented here in essentially the same form.

You find yourself a short distance from an ashram temple. A group of archetypally venerable ethnically Indian figures, with long white hair and beards dressed in saffron robes are there to meet you. These are the Vedic priests who mediate between humanity and the Rishis.

They lead you towards a conical beehive shaped but with a small entrance that requires ducking down to pass through. It is the lodge of the rainbow body, the place where they ascend to commune with the hidden masters and also perform the funerary ritual of the rainbow body with those whom have died

A low tunnel opens out into a circular conical roofed room. The walls are daubed with an ochre coloured paint and there is a raised dais in the centre. You are asked to sit on a domed pillar of rock in the middle of the stone platform. Underneath this is an opening from which rises the pungent smoke from burning aromatic plants and herbs. This serves to help facilitate a changing state of consciousness.

Around the edge of the circular room sit a group of more holy men. Their leader stands before you and a fire is lit around you. You are now encompassed by a ring of flames but it does not burn you or even overwhelm you with its heat. The holy men begin chanting a mantra. The chief priest before you now holds his arms outstretched with upward facing palms that emit a calm orange flame. Through this fire, he will impart to you the power to transmute your energy body and ascend to cosmic heavenly realms

The priest now raises his right hand and closes his fist over the flame. As he does this, the flame in his left hand begins to burn more fiercely. He reaches out with this fire as if to offer it to you, but as he does so, his thumb and index finger turn and join to form a circle, his other fingers splayed behind it. Within this circle you can see the flame burning, horizontal now. The priest then intones a naming mantra and the deftly blows through his circled fingers sending the flame shooting towards you. The jet of fire enters into your body at the solar plexus. He has imparted to you a particular ray of the sacred force of Agni, the cosmic fire of the universe, which brings being and form to all things incorporeal.

As you look upon the fire surrounding you, you see that it is now changing colour through the spectrum, from crimson to red to violet. You yourself are now a rainbow of the seven holy rays of Agni and have achieved the living holy state of rainbow body, for your etheric body of light has now been transmuted to align with the cosmic spectrum of power.

Glastonbury Tor was clearly visible from the window of the room in which this vision occurred, the same room in which I had attuned Andrew Collins, and recently expended a lot of mental energy writing my summary and expansion of the Geoffrey Ashe material.

Looking out of my window at the Tor when my guests had departed, taking in all of the associations, was a rich experience. On the night of the previous New Year's Eve, the 1999 biggie, the Tor terraces had been memorably lit by innumerable torches so a very potent vision of a possible past was widely visible. The septenary labyrinth was certainly real that night and I had a lot to bring in with it from Geoffrey Ashe and John Michell. I vividly imagined Ursa Major brightly shining above. The scene readily rippled to briefly reveal a Babylonian ziggurat transparently essentially occupying the same space across the Tor. I seemed to focus in on tall viper-visaged figures on its summit. Diamond thunderbolt lightning, Pendragon power, struck the World Mountain tower on the Tor, on the ziggurat together, opening up a mind-treasure transmission from the sages in the stars, through their ashram outside of space-time. There we were with the Rishis. It was all a huge unity in the resplendent overflowing Void. Then the sequence reversed as I came back through to my living room.

I had become accustomed to thinking that way. How would I classify such thought processes? Was I accessing some kind of truth or was it fiction? A reverie? Thanks to the example Storm had set with how she had developed the inspirations from Andy and Debbie on the Watchers into her Grigori trilogy I wasn't overly troubled with such distinctions. It was magic in the truest sense of the term as far as I am concerned, and it was alive and fruitful with eerie power in the way all the best literature should be.

Nearly twenty years later, the dynamic that has led Andrew Collins to ever more ancient strands of forgotten humanity, that yielded such potent fruit back in the nineties when he immersed himself in the Nephilim mystery, had come to the Altai region and the Denisovans. I find it a poignant ache to ponder what rich strand of literature Storm might have been inspired to create by the material he is currently investigating.

Lost Tribe Eulogy:
A Wraeththu Mythos Tribute To Storm Constantine

E.S. Wynn

I was in rough shape when she found me. I don't remember much of that old life now, just pieces, just a vague sense of hell and dusty roads. Those old days already feel like another life, already feel like some story of something that happened to someone else. I've come a long way since then, become someone I never could have dreamed I would become, and at least some of that is because of her.

In my memories, in the sun-bleached hell that came before this life, the pain ends suddenly, gives way to cool shadows and smiling faces. Visions come of pastel sheets, of clean smells and gentle hands that were firm only when I tried to leap out of bed and run away. In those early days, I saw many of the faces of those who came to tend me and care for me, but it was *her* face that I saw the most. The other faces were har, but she was something else entirely. Not human, but also not Wraeththu. If there was a word for what she was, I've not found it, though I've heard whispers of others like her, far to the North and West, at the edge of the world. To us, to the ragtag tribe of hara she'd gathered around her, she was unique, and that's what truly mattered. She was elemental, like a force of nature given flesh. She was the eye and we were her storm, and everything we did and knew as a tribe centered around and came from her.

Only now, she's gone. Far too soon, she's gone, lost like a breath carried in a breeze.

Burying her felt like burying an elder. In a way, she was a mother to so many of us, a guide who taught so many of us who we were, who we really were, and what we could become. For many of us, she was the first one who ever told us that what we were was sacred. For many of us, she was the first one to show us that what we were was beautiful and right and wondrous. For many of us, she was the one who lifted us out of the trash and pulled us into our potential.

With her support, it was easy to find purpose, easy to see ourselves as being worthy of purpose, to see ourselves as being more than the filthy, shiftless freaks that the media of the dying world tried to cast us as. Through her eyes, we began to see that we weren't a cancer. We were the answer to the cancer that was eating our world alive. We were shining dehara *en natus,* the seeds of something great, sprouting like saplings from the ruins of man, and I think that it was only through her, through her stories and her guidance, that we all were able to actually see it.

I remember that we'd gather around the fire every night to hear her stories, and I remember that I always saw shades of myself in those stories, in the characters and the way they grew into their purpose. I think we all did. I think we all felt in those moments like we could live inside her words, like we could live inside the stories and be part of them, walk side-by-side with her heroic hara as they danced their way to greatness.

I remember how her stories whirled through my mind every night long after the fires had gone out, how they morphed into half dreams and quiet, excited reveries. I remember wanting to be Pellaz, wanting to live life for a day as Tigron of that far off nation we only heard about in her stories. I remember wanting to be Calanthe, to walk the world as he seemed to have, seeing more wonders than anyone else before. I remember wanting to be Cobweb, wanting to ride side-by-side on horseback with Terzian, living half in the world of the mystic, with a powerful warrior to lift me up like a pair of strong wings into an open sky.

But perhaps most of all, I wanted to be the Aghama, the first one of our kind. I wanted to know the deeper things that he seemed to be born entirely out of, to viscerally understand the things that he seemed to be so thoroughly steeped in. Late at night, I would whisper to him, whisper for his guidance, hoping he might somehow hear me, might visit me in my cot and teach me some of his deepest secrets. When I started dreaming about him, I started dreaming of his symbol, of sitting with him on a marble staircase, talking of things which seemed too ephemeral to stick in my mind. I went to our storyteller, our tribal mother, and asked her about the visions I was having, described the dreams and the symbol the Aghama had shown me. Her eyes grew wider as I spoke, like suddenly I was the storyteller, and as I reached the end of what I'd felt, what I'd seen and dreamed, she drew a long, pointed stick from one of her many woven bags and told me that what I had seen was real. She told me that my contact with the Aghama was part of a greater awakening, and that the time had come to wear his mark on my skin, if I wished to see and know more of him and his wisdom.

I remember that the ordeal of the marking was long, rhythmic, painful and yet full of visions. I saw the Aghama dancing in the lights that flashed before my eyes as I drifted in and out of consciousness, and I felt his touch on my back as she worked. In the end, the symbol came out clear and black on my shoulder, and even now, years later, I still look to it, touch it and think of the Aghama in times of difficulty. To me, the mark of the Aghama I wear on my skin is a reminder of all the wonder and potential I have within me. I may not be The First One, but a part of him lives forever within me, and that is enough. That is all I need to know; that I can overcome anything I might face now or in the future.

Even this loss. Even now, waking up each day and knowing that there will be no more stories except those that we write ourselves. The age of her great heroes has come to an end, but there is still so much powerful potential left in us, in the Wraeththu. We are the ascendant ones now, lifted up by stories of hara like Pellaz, Calanthe, Cobweb and Terzian, lifted up so that we might make our own stories, and inspire others to realize the power within themselves.

I don't know how many of the tribe have drifted away since she passed. I don't know how many have left to live their own stories now that we no longer have her to stick us all together like glue. I don't know what the future holds, I know only that right now it feels like the light has gone out of our tribe, like no one has stepped up to take her place. In truth, I'm not even sure we need anyone to do so. Maybe she was but a momentary teacher and this tribe has just been a classroom without walls, as ephemeral as sand in a windstorm. Maybe the drifting away is right and necessary. Maybe the entropy of it all is just another way of spawning new teachers, new classrooms, and all inspired by all that we learned in the years before she passed on.

There's a certain solace that comes with seeing her as a flower, and all of us as the seeds ready to be scattered in the wind, but in truth, I'll always miss her classroom. In truth, I'll always keep close all that she taught me about myself and what I can become, no matter where the tides of time direct my path.

THE GATE OF MOON

Dolores Ashcroft-Nowicki

There are gates of gold and silver
of horn and ivory.
There are gates that lead to earths and lands
that I shall never see.
There are gates of love and hatred
and a gate sealed by a rune.
But the gate that beckons to us all
is called the Gate of Moon.

The gates of moor and mountain
hold entrance to the earth.
The gates of man and womanhood
they are the gates of birth.
The gates of fear and rivalry
can cause a death too soon.
But oh, the gate I long to pass
is called the Gate of Moon.

The gate of life when I came through
it was a gate of law.
A gate of destiny for me
to match the fate I bore.
But now I watch the road ahead
from midnight to high noon,
and ask of those I travel with,
Where is the Gate of Moon?

I see it shining in my dreams
and in young lover's eyes.
I see it open up to me
in early morning skies.
Older, now, and wiser
I have found the gate of Rune.

But still I wander, searching yet
to find the Gate of Moon.

The gates of myth and fantasy
are pointing me the way.
The gate that leads to dark Annwn
away from light of day.
I wander through the darkness
There's a shining in the gloom.
Twixt pillars made of ebony
I find the Gate of Moon.

For Storm

I have been reading passages from your books... savouring them because they were/are/will always be a living part of you. Your words, like your name, defined you... quiet at first, but building slowly towards the spectacular, then the outpouring of energy building to a climax that leaves the onlooker or reader breathless.

When my beloved teacher, Ernest Butler, left us I wanted to find words that helped him to leave, and me to let him go. I feel the same way now, so I offer to you what I said then:

"To die will be an awfully big adventure."

This is said by Peter Pan in J.M. Barrie's book of the same name. Peter is marooned on a rock with the tide coming in and is contemplating the fact that he is facing physical death. His reflection is momentary, for he manages to escape from the rock in time. But such moments of reflection come to us all at odd times in our lives, times when we wonder what death will be like.

Storm had the ability to experience existence on many levels, and the verbal skill to share it with her readers. She lived, loved, and felt with all her characters and I am sure they gathered around her to welcome her into her 'Adventure'. As a writer myself, I know that we share the 'lives' of our fictional children and feel, suffer, and laugh with them. We share the world we build for them... and maybe they carry on that existence long after we have written *The End.*

Storm wrote from the head, heart and GUT. She made us feel, understand, and at times forgive, her characters. They in turn will have been there to welcome her, to thank her for their creation, and share with her the worlds she created for them. She is now experiencing **The Big Adventure.**

Dolores Ashcroft Nowicki

Serpent's Pride

Y.J.F. Cartwright

The city had stopped moving. This was no predicted terminus caused by a knot of pilot stones placed in its way by a group of terranauts. No abnormal shift had occurred to displace them in the landscape. No source of water lay nearby to entice the great moving metropolis closer. Nor had the city foundered upon sharp stakes of rock, or become bogged down in an unexpected plainswash, an infrequent menace whenever the city's path took it closer to the vast mountainous ring surrounding the Flatlands. This felt different, and Damarel thought she knew why.

It was a suspicion more than a working hypothesis, but her instincts had proven right many times before. It was how she had become a breakdown-diviner, her talent for solving the more intractable problems of the city having elevated her above the ranks of the typical engineer. Her mother, Lilane, would have been proud of her daughter's achievements having surpassed those of her own but she had not been there that day when the official had arrived to deliver the good news. Barely out of her apprenticeship, Damarel had been helping her mother repair a main spar when Lilane had inexplicably decided to leap from the walkway near to the main cataract that vomited unusable fluids to the lands passing by hundreds of feet below. It had been an unfortunate accident, she had been told, a hazard of the job and not at all like the one her father had caused which had burnt him to a cinder when she was only a child.

It had not been an accident, no matter what the Gyrean city officials told her. She had been there when her mother looked at her so strangely, with eyes so unlike her own, as if she could see straight through her whilst she held up the tool her mother had asked her for. They had stood there on the walkway, locked in that strange stare for barely half a dozen heartbeats before, without a sound, her mother had turned slowly, extended her arms and swan-dived over the chain railing still clutching her favourite wrench.

Maybe it was her intangibility that had given her mother such fear, a wave of it so profound that non-existence was preferable to its touch? Damarel had first felt it when she was very small. It was her earliest memory, the sense that she was not *really* there, that at least part of her, the part that was the most real, was somehow somewhere else, barely connected and fragile.

She had first voiced her concerns to her parents on the day of her eighth birthday, when she finally had the words to express them. Her mother had laughed as she tried to get her to sit still, combing out the knots in her chestnut curls ready for the celebratory gathering of friends. In stark contrast to his wife, Mirrit had not laughed at such a childish notion. He'd remained standing in the doorway of her room, looking at her almost suspiciously, before the first arrival to the festivities interrupted his thoughts. He hadn't lived to see her ninth birthday.

With both parents gone, her life as an orphan had begun too young, the wellspring of her soul poisoned by loss and the taint of unreality, and whilst these feelings came in waves as the years slowly rolled by, as she grew, their intensity only increased.

On the day the city became marooned, Damarel had been tasked with solving an intermittent problem with one of the main crankshafts that fed the myriad movement mechanisms that propelled the city endlessly over the landscape. Gyre was not an old city, not compared to others of a similar size, but it had developed fast from the primordial citykin that had launched upon the lands with such new ideas.

Unlike most such hamlets, the original masterplan for the city had not evolved from those grand dames that had tracked across the Flatlands for countless centuries. Gyre was to be unique, its very heart giving the city its name. All its motion to come came from the movement of the air itself. In its smallest state, rotating sails provided the initial force that first drove the ramshackle huddle of buildings onwards, then came the airvanes and airscrews that allowed the emerging city to develop and grow rapidly.

As their experience of harnessing the wind grew, the pioneering philosopher-scientists that had first begun construction conjured new devices: vortex tunnels and aerogenerators augmented the emerging city's towers, windstalks and spiralcatchers stretched into the sky, swaying like tall grasses in the breezes, or spinning in the sunlight. On the two-hundredth anniversary of its founding, miles-long windladders were launched, snaking high into the atmosphere, trailing their multicoloured kites in the city's wake. These moved in an endless cycle as their foils first lofted them high before angling to enable them to descend once more, all the while taking advantage of the ubiquitous high winds unavailable nearer the ground, their looped cables constantly turning turbines night and day.

Within a few generations, the city had become thousands-strong, helped by an influx of curious minds normally shunned by the inhabitants of the other insular cities. Gyre's maturing parts had been broken apart many times over the years with every new advance, either demolished, migrated out to its rim or built over. In time, a cyclopean new centre with gigantic twin animal-like fins had emerged. These were sculpted to channel the wind flowing between them into a vast air dam, its great spanning sail funnelling the accelerated air into a huge turbine, the largest by far in the city. From here, the energy was transmitted through uncountable gears, axels, cogs and chains down through the very strata of the city, feeding its dark underbelly of wheels, rollers, stickwalkers, paddles and skis. All other cities could claim a lineage of ideas that propelled them forth; but aside from the fabled floating city of Min, Gyre remained the only true original. Now, for no reason, it was static in the world, the greatest fear of all city-dwellers.

To be stationary on the Flatlands invited grave danger. This came in many forms but primary amongst them was the threat from other cities. Having a fixed location meant being easily hunted or harried by any roaming hostile city or other group intent on pillage or destruction, with no hope of evasion and little respite. Why the cities had started to move was a mystery. Perhaps it had been a great war or some form of plague that had only affected those close to the surface? Whatever it had been, there were no records of the cataclysmic events. No one from the ancient civilisations of the Flatlands wanted future generations to know their pain, the memory of the devastation, the near extinction. Now, combined with resources stretched thinly across the undulating plains, no large, static city could ever hope to survive for long.

With a suddenness in keeping with the lurching halt, teams of engineers were hastily dispatched into the rigging that underslung Gyre that allowed for inspection and any necessary repairs. Wheels were examined, lubricants and hydraulic fluids checked, changed or reapplied, the bearings on the giant rollers inspected for cracks or stubborn debris. Even the reticulated stickwalkers were given a thorough assessment although none could say why any fault in them would have led to the city's stubbornness to move. Nothing they did made any difference as they worked in droves into the night.

"I was worried about you," said Joh, as she lay in her lover's arms.

The bunk was barely wide enough for the two of them, designed as it was for a shift worker. Damarel gazed into Joh's liquid-blue eyes and saw the fear for herself. If it hadn't been for the increasingly desperate situation, they wouldn't have had the opportunity for a liaison in the corridor-like barracks. By chance, all the other engineers in the cabin were out tending to Gyre's woes and they had found themselves alone. Damarel's own lodgings were somewhat less basic and certainly more private. They were also in one of the oldest parts of the city that had earned it the name The Ramshackles from soon after the first great redevelopment. With Joh's next emergency shift imminent, they were also too far away.

"I'm fine," replied Damarel, lying as convincingly as she could. "I wasn't on the walkways when the city stopped." Physically, she was fine but inside her mind was a shadow of a returning fear that had been temporarily quelled by Joh's anxious lovemaking.

Joh's words were deliberately muted even though they were alone. "Several mechanics fell to their deaths," she said, not wanting to voice her fears aloud.

"Hush, my love," soothed Damarel, kissing her lover's mouth and forehead, smelling the scent of citrine from their communal shower. "The city will be moving again soon."

There was fear in Joh's eyes as she spoke. "But why has it stopped? It's not old."

The same question had barely left Damarel's thoughts. "I don't know. Maybe, it is the opposite problem? Some of the machinery is still quite new so there's bound to be some teething issues. Even the parts we are familiar with we can't be sure how long they're supposed to last for."

This was true and the uniqueness of Gyre's various novel propulsion systems had been causing problems for the city's engineers for generations. It was a grand experiment begun years before by a group of long-dead philosopher-scientists who had left their original city, a city whose name and history were both lost and irrelevant. The people they'd left behind must have believed them mazey-minded to consider leaving the safety of their original home city, to start again from nothing but their plan was easier, and quicker, to achieve from a blank slate. Revolution was like that.

"Do you get a sense of anything?" asked Joh hopefully.

Damarel thought for a moment, her fingers lightly stroking Joh's raven hair. "No," she lied again, "but we will find the answer, now rest. Tomorrow may be a long day."

How could she worry Joh further? She would think she was as mad as the calentured. How could she explain that she thought that she had somehow infected Gyre with her intangibility? As Joh's breathing slowed, she thought through the events of the day, unable to quiet her mind.

The morning had started as a completely ordinary day. She had diligently worked on her assigned task, tending to the ministries of one of the city's many massive crankshafts, trying to understand what might be causing the huge device to stick fast whilst the manifold machinery elsewhere kept Gyre moving at a steady slow walking pace. To diagnose the errant issue meant testing all the various parts, the rods, webs, journals, crankpins, counterweights, dampeners and flywheels, ensuring sufficient vegetable oil could reach it all from the passageways unimpeded, never too hot, or too cold, to be as efficient and trouble-free as possible. Hours had passed and nothing appeared capable of generating the anomaly.

In her mind's eye, she could picture the integrated machinery moving, turning, sliding, pushing; the sheer complexity of the interconnected whole that began even above the highest parts of the city, transmitting down to propel Gyre wherever across the Flatlands its city-soul decreed. Her ability to hold the abstract and dynamic nature of the city's inner workings in her mind had made Damarel the youngest breakdown-diviner in Gyre's history, and certainly the most promising one for generations. She turned the model over in her mind, trying to see all the angles, working backwards from the problem before her. So ingenious was Gyre's design and intricate implementation that it was hard to believe that any part of it could ever fail so completely.

That was when a thought struck her: what if the city itself, or some force beyond its lofty borders, wanted it to fail? Maybe it was her fault. Was Gyre like her mother? The more she grew into the world, the more she explored and diagnosed Gyre's inner workings, the more her intangibility spread to those beyond her, perhaps into the very heart of the city itself. What would happen if the city felt thin, as she did at times? Maybe its reality was somehow insubstantial or unreal, an invention of an inventive mind? What if they now both were? That was the moment when Gyre halted.

The next day brought more uncertainty and a growing sense of dread that pervaded down from the metal and glass fins that sliced through the city's hub and into the dwellings of the Gyreans. As Damarel and Joh got breakfast from the barrack's canteen, all talk was of the immobile city. Just down from their bench, two engineers were having a discussion that was turning heated.

"No, you're wrong!" exclaimed one of the men, banging his spoon on the wooden surface.

"I'm telling you, there's a bad air in this area," replied his companion, shrugging his shoulders. "We just need a strong mountain wind to clear it."

Joh glanced at Damarel who furrowed her brow in response but said nothing. "If that's true," started Joh, "then couldn't we just rig some of the larger airscrews in reverse, focus them back into the air as a disperser?"

Damarel shook her head. As powerful as the airscrews were, they were dwarfed by the sheer size of Gyre. "Unfortunately, that wouldn't be anywhere near enough," she said to those around her. A thought did occur to her though. If bad air really was the problem, there could be another way to achieve Joh's idea. "Of course, if that was the aim then you'd be better off using the air dam to pulse waves of air over the city."

That made several engineers nearby stop eating, their thoughts tuning into Damarel's fledgling plan. One was even smiling. Was that a good sign?

"That's an interesting idea," spoke up one engineer with butternut soup in his beard.

"Yeah, but how would you direct it?" asked a woman with short flame-red hair, her fringe failing to completely hide a thin scar across her forehead. It was a mark of the profession and the experience of the engineer often was judged on the number of such scars. Damarel herself had several, the most prominent of which was a slash across her left shoulder caused by getting too close to a spiralcatcher she thought she'd disengaged.

"The city will move when it wants to," interrupted one of the older mechanics to no one as he stared into his broth. This voice was Terryk's. Everybody knew and respected Terryk. He'd been an engineer for over sixty years and had done pretty much every mechanical job in the city in that time. Kinemechanic, megafacturer, ferrumer, aerorigger, even a few years in residuals.

"And we will help it," said a voice from behind Damarel. She hadn't noticed the arrival of Hirun, her chief breakdown-diviner and wondered if she was late for her shift. Twisting her body to face the man, she was relieved to see that he was carrying his breakfast. "This isn't the first time Gyre has stopped unexpectedly," he stated with some reassurance to his fellow engineers.

Damarel was pretty sure that it was having reviewed the scant information about Gyre's history in the city library. She wondered how Hirun could be so sure of his statement but decided against questioning her superior in such a public place. With their own breakfast finished, she got up to leave with Joh following suit, allowing Hirun to take her place. The febrile atmosphere of the canteen lifted as they exited onto the busy streets of the Chord District. Even outside, though, the usual good cheer of Lever Crescent was subdued. People seemed to lack their usual enthusiasm for a new day, either trudging disconsolately on their journey or simply sitting on one of the street benches, their faces melancholic and drawn with worry. As they made their way through to their designated sites for the day, Damarel and Joh could not fail to overhear the brief snatches of street chatter concerning the city's woes.

"But what are we supposed to do?"

"Leave it to the engineers," said his male companion pointing at Damarel and Joh as they walked past. "They'll sort it."

"Gyre is dead!" exclaimed one man dressed in black to a group of people standing in an arc in front of him. "We just don't want to accept it!"

"If it is, where would we even go?" asked one woman of her friend, who looked as forlorn as she did, as they listened to the doom-monger.

Damarel quickened her pace, not wanting to linger near such talk. At the entrance door that led to a service walkway, she kissed Joh, imploring her to take extra care before leaving her lover to her latest crisis shift. She would need to begin her own soon but before then, she had a sudden urge to head past her lodgings in the Ramshackles to the edge of Gyre.

There were fewer people around than normal. Usually, landseers enjoyed the views over the oncoming terrain, delighting in the new sights to come and any opportunities they might hold. Not this day. Most people were deliberately keeping clear of the walled rim, only in part in case the city was to suddenly move, risking the unwary pitching over the edge. Damarel, however, could guess the unspoken reason: looking out over the exact same landscape features and their unchanging relative positions was a visceral reminder of the citizens' approaching doom.

Movement through the Flatlands meant more than simply growth and prosperity, a way to acquire whatever the city needed, it was survival itself. Only the terranauts truly thrived in the Flatlands. Their nomadic peoples were held in an admixture of awe and suspicion by most city folk. They alone knew the secrets of the pilot-stones that guided the cities in their meanderings but could give no reason as to why they set lines of them across the landscape. Many in the cities thought of them as mad. It wasn't unheard of for rogue terranaut bands to occasionally wreck cities by leading them into traps of watery expanses or great seas of sand. Why they did this, none could say. The city-dwellers believed themselves to be metaphorically and literally above the terranauts in every way, but the truth of their semi-parasitic relationship with the land travellers could never truly be forgotten. Had their distant ancestors all been terranauts at one point before some schism or great cataclysm forced them skywards? It was a group of terranauts that had emerged from the soft morning light that now joined their efforts to overcome the city's inertia.

As a child, Damarel had always thought that each terranaut troupe must be quite different from each other given their small constituent numbers, but it was only when she was older that she realised how isolating each city was from all others, with very little interaction over the generations. Unlike the free-roaming terranauts, the city dwellers didn't just live-in walled gardens, they existed almost entirely within closed ecosystems, their development driven from within, whose original seeds were sown by the disparate minds of philosopher-scientists intent on new thinking, not common ways. All that the cities' inhabitants really shared was a language and an existential dread for what would happen without those walls and the movement. The movement was everything, that constantly changing vista.

From one of the main walkways gilding the underside of Gyre, engineers of various talents stared down at the approaching terranauts whilst mechanics busied themselves in the rigging. Damarel was in the group now descending one of the walkways to the ground, her team's talents the main hope for the city's inhabitants. It was strange to see Gyre from the surface of the Flatlands. It was, she realised with some incredulity, the only time in her life she ever had. Even the air smelled different like the earth had been burned long ago or formed from fire but now only held the faintest residue of this great conflagration. Looking up through the bright sunlight, she shuddered at the sight of the great array of movers, static, silent, lifeless. Quickly, she withdrew her gaze to focus on the unusual group in front of her.

She'd met only two terranauts in her short life, both apparently typical of their kind, driven by a carefree wanderlust, hedonistic outlook and a somewhat capricious nature that made them greatly fascinating to the staid city-dwellers. The first was when she was quite small. Her only memories of the man were him showing her a gleaming pilot-stone fragment set into one of his teeth, its surface glinting amber in the firelight from her parent's hearth. The second terranaut was a woman, Vela, a free soul and her first intimate, who spoke of living on the vast plains, steering cities with stones, trading with their populations, experiencing all those different cultures that emerged in isolation within their roaming walls.

Damarel had hoped to keep the exotic woman within Gyre for longer, using her body in newfound ways to barter more time to absorb as much as she could about life beyond the confines of the city. Their mutual attraction, though, was insufficient to overcome the older woman's roving spirit. Before the next new moon, Vela was gone, leaving an emotional, physical and ontological void in her wake. There were answers out there in the world, Damarel was sure of it, to questions that had plagued her since childhood, about the origins of the first cities, the mysteries of the great mountain ring at the ends of the earth, perhaps even to her growing feelings of semi-existence.

No two cities were alike, their peoples evolving in relative isolation behind their walls with different customs, cultures, traditions and conducts with other Flatlanders. In contrast, most terranauts were surprisingly similar given their nomadic existence. It was understandable that when the two groups met, there would be mistrust. It was Hirun that first spoke to the group of terranauts, greeting them in the traditional way.

"Hail fellow travellers of the land. What can you tell us?"

A tall woman with long, close-curled blonde hair that splayed over her shoulders and tumbled down to her waist approached. "I am Embar. I lead this troupe." Embar gestured with long delicate fingers at the front of the city. "We saw your city stationary against the sky and came to determine why. The stones are laid out correctly and none are damaged. We have tried replacing those closest before you but there is no change."

"Could it be bad air?" asked Damarel, still wondering if such a thing was even possible. There was a derisive snort from a young terranaut male who had a gold ring in his ear. "Or what about other disrupting influences?" she continued, willing her face not to redden.

There was a momentary pause as the woman appeared to be trying to decern the hierarchy amongst this city's engineers. "From other terranauts?" queried Embar.

Damarel felt all eyes upon her. "Maybe, but I was wondering if something external to the city, other than the pilot-stones, could exert some kind of controlling force," she glanced nervously around the terranauts, suddenly self-conscious in a way she'd never felt before, "or the city itself had chosen to remain here?"

Embar stared down at the peculiar young woman. "If this was terranaut work, we would know it."

Damarel pressed further, following her instincts. "Have you heard of anything other than the stones that could halt a city?"

Embar flicked her eyes between the assembled terranauts and the citizens, two peoples connected by the great cities. "Sometimes cities choose to end."

"End?" queried Hirun, unsure of what the woman meant.

"Yes," nodded Embar. "We do not know why." She looked over the landscape taking in the vast swathe of city strata before her that eclipsed much of the sky. "Maybe they have simply experienced the Flatlands for too long? Some think they grow tired of their own existence or grow too much, become too complex and break."

"We would be able to fix such an occurrence," stated Hirun somewhat haughtily.

"If you say so," replied Embar dispassionately. "Cities are wrought from the land, displaced from it." The terranaut fixed the chief breakdown-diviner with eyes as empty as a vacant grave. "They will return to it."

"What would make a city want to end?" asked Damarel. Her thoughts went back to the moments before the city shuddered to a stop. Could this all somehow be her fault?

"None can say for sure. Maybe over time, the shifts take their toll. As we travel, we sometimes see the lit-less corpses of their constructions."

Damarel felt nauseous. Was Gyre's malady a systemic problem? Everyone knew that it was the terranauts that caused the shifts that periodically affected the world causing changes in time and space, energy and matter. Why they did this, they would never say but perhaps there were other ways to trigger them? Either way, no engineer she was aware of had ever linked them to disasters on such a scale. All citizens learned from a young age to stay still during a shift when it occurred, accepting any changes to their consensual reality once the unnerving event had passed. Clearly, it appeared that the shifts had nothing to do with the city's current predicament and one had not occurred when the city abruptly stopped.

Whatever this event was, it was new and of a different cause than anything the current city's engineers had ever been tasked to solve. Had this event, or something like it, happened before in the Gyrean creators' former home, wherever that had been? Was this why she had found so little information in the city's archives that spoke of those first years and what may have come before?

Damarel almost didn't dare to ask the question everyone must have been thinking. "What happens to their citizens?"

"They abandon their homes and go into the Flatlands," replied Embar simply, without any obvious compassion. "Most die. Some find other places to exist, other cities sometimes. Few stay as travellers on the land."

Damarel could not conceive of ever leaving Gyre. The thought of being adrift on the plains with no city for protection or nourishment was unbearable.

"Can we offer the city another route?" asked Hirun. "Gyre has passed over many intersecting lines of stones in its past, sometimes moving onto a different path."

Embar considered the idea. "I do not know if this has been done with a city that has been stilled." She looked around at the older members of her troupe, but none suggested otherwise.

"But we can try?" entreated one of the engineers.

"*We* can," emphasised Embar pointedly.

For the rest of the day, the terranauts toiled beneath the great disc of the city, their work made more difficult by the implacable presence of the disjointed movement array. Shortly before dusk, Embar announced that their work was done. The city would either move or it would not, and nothing more they did could change its fate.

"We thank you for your efforts," said Hirun to the terranauts, "and would like to give you something in return. Perhaps you would like to see what Gyre offers?" He looked across his team of engineers. "I'm sure we can find suitable recompense for your efforts today?"

The terranaut leader looked at him through stony eyes. "We will not go into the city," stated Embar flatly.

"Why not?" asked Hirun with some surprise. Gyre had hosted its fair share of terranauts in its time, mostly those on one of their enforced solo wanderings but occasionally larger groups had climbed the visitor walkway and travelled the conveyor belts that led into the market area.

"Not all cities lie still when their end comes. Some undergo death-throes," warned Embar, her eyes glinting in the light of the dying sun.

The group of engineers exchanged nervous glances. They had all heard tales of other cities, ones whose end came abruptly. The tales were fanciful and told by plains-travellers in exchange for a meal or a drink at the many inns in the city. They were stories for the gullible, or those of limited intellect but, in Gyre's long travels, evidence of past catastrophes was infrequently chanced upon; wrecks of failed city-forming endeavours, the crushed remains of collapsed city-sections, the occasionally solitary wheel, crawler track or roller enigmatically positioned on the landscape, a discarded sentinel of a long-lost or now-distant city-culture.

"But Gyre is young!" pleaded Damarel.

Embar bent down at her with a sympathy reminiscent of her mother's. "If the city will not move, be sure to leave while you still can." The terranaut returned to her stiff pose as she addressed Hirun. "We will accept nothing while the city remains here, nor will we linger for long."

The group of engineers looked aghast. Was there so little time? The thought that they would fail was anathema to their very being. Without the city, what were they?

With that pronouncement, the terranaut troupe removed themselves in the direction of a distant copse of trees. Damarel followed the small team of breakdown-diviners back up the service walkway, trying and failing to imagine the city tearing itself apart in its premature demise. Before losing view of the terranauts, Damarel turned to see them setting up camp in the trees around a central fire whose smoke was already lost above the city's rim. She wondered what the older members of the troupe had seen on their travels, what they knew about cities that she did not. For its constant migration, Gyre favoured the lines of pilot-stones that kept it close to the mountainous ring where the winds were stronger, feeding its heart, gorging on the air. Who knew how much more there was to the Flatlands beyond, or if there was more to the great mountains than just walls of impassable rock that stretched into the clouds?

As she lay in her own bed willing the city to move, or at least display some sign of wanting to, Damarel realised for the first time that her whole experience of life existed entirely within a thin grassy ring, a littoral sea of green and yellow encircled by an impenetrable ring of rock. Was this why she felt incomplete in her reality? Would she only feel whole or substantial if she ventured beyond her small world, filling the spaces in her mind and body? Even if that was true, would her leaving allow the city to heal in time? The mere thought of it filled her with dread. Only the mazed or the exiled left their city for any length of time. What were the chances of ever finding home again, of seeing their families and friends? It was a nonsense, surely? Her mother had said so; the same woman that had without explanation or warning thrown herself from the only city she'd ever known, her body crushed and lost under the wheels she had worked to maintain her whole life.

No, they would get Gyre moving again! Embar's talk of cities destroying themselves was probably a ploy to get the citizens to leave if the worst came and they had to abandon Gyre. The terranauts would then be able to strip the city of anything they needed unimpeded. Had they truly tried to help the Gyreans today or was it all an act? What if they'd been the ones to immobilise the city in the first place, setting up an elaborate trap of pilot-stones, some confused arrangement that now lay hidden under Gyre's movers? Embar hadn't wanted any help, not that the city's engineers knew how to give it, but equally the terranauts had wanted to work without any oversight. What had they actually been doing all day?

That night, Damarel's dreams were filled with visions of the city empty, centuries of untended streets, buildings that had fallen into disrepair or worse, trees split through roofs, waterways green and stagnant. She felt utterly alone and responsible. It was eerie wandering there, the presence of Gyre absent, its heart dead. As she walked through the deserted districts, the recognisable streets and buildings from her youth morphed into those of another place, far away, a city that had never moved, its outer walls surrounded by high mountaintops like bright sparks edged in snow. This place had also been long deserted, its wan light an ashen grey but it had not fallen into disorder to be reclaimed by the harsh world. Instead, it appeared to be preserved as if in amber, frozen at the pinnacle of its glory.

As she ventured around corners and under archways, architectures shifted, so many different styles, a mix of ancient and contemporary forms, a fusion that could never have developed within a single city on the Flatlands. Beyond a row of homes whose continuous eaves silhouetted it against the sky, she turned into a wide thoroughfare bounded by shops that led to what appeared to be a theatre wrought in white marble. She stopped abruptly, thinking she was about to run into another woman who appeared to be inspecting something in a window.

Damarel opened her mouth to apologise before pausing. The other woman said nothing, nor did she even react to Damarel as she waved her hand in front of her face. Confused, Damarel flicked her eyes around the wide boulevard. Other figures dotted the pavements, all frozen in their everyday pursuits. On closer inspection, the woman she had almost barged into turned out to be an elaborate statue carved from some form of crystal, her scrutinising pose rendered so life-like by a skilled hand. She could have been real, so detailed was the surface of her skin, the delicate fronds of her hair, her eyes jewel-like and deep but there was no life within.

A cold dagger coursed down Damarel's spine. Was she like this poor woman, her own fate to become as stilled as a crystal statue, just like the city? As fear gripped her, she forced herself past the woman, trying not to catch sight of the unblinking eyes that watched her passage, and broke quickly into a run. She fled the street down a twisting alleyway, past the shattered remains of other people. Her foot suddenly skidded on the perfectly cleaved crystal face of a child. She screamed as she fell towards the cobbles, her face striking their shoe-smoothed surface. Lying prone on the ground, stunned by her fall, she felt another presence nearby, the hint of a mind, the mind of a man.

Damarel woke in her own bed, tears in her eyes, their salt-lines staining her pillow. Where was she? The white walls around her, the small tapestry of a wind-train weaving through a lush valley, the delicate vase containing vivid columbines on a small table near the only window, even the bed itself, none of it she could immediately recall. Her heart still thumped in her chest. The dream had felt so real, more real than the room she was in, the dreamscape's solidity greater than the sum of her surroundings. She could still feel the chilled mountain air on her face, the iron-rich taste of dirt and blood in her mouth, the scent of wintersweet masking that of the bell-shaped flowers Joh had given her. She looked at the gift as reality subsumed her mind, the flowers were to remind her of the sky whilst she toiled in the belly of the city. The dream imagery and sensations faded fast and the walls of her bedroom subsumed her thoughts.

From Unwen's Tower outside, its clock chords sounded, the jaunty peal yielding to a staccato of sharp trills. With shock, Damarel realised that she'd overslept with little time remaining to see Joh who must have been wondering where she was. Hurriedly, she dressed in her blue overalls, stuck on a protective cap to hide her unbrushed hair, barely pausing to grab her tool pouch from the table on her way out of the door. She ran through the Artificer's Quarter, passed the Guild Hall and down on through the narrow-cobbled cut-through that led to The Lost Compass, her favourite inn, all the while trying to stymie the recurring flashes of her dream. In the Crescent, she dashed inside Joh's section of the barracks, pushed her way through the bodies comprising the shift change and threw the door open to the cabin containing Joh's bunk. The berth where she'd shared many stolen moments of passion in their six months together was empty. Her lover had already left for her duties that day.

For Damarel, missing out on seeing Joh was just the start of a bad day. Not only had the city manifestly failed to budge a single inch in any direction but the increasing stress on the engineers was beginning to take its toll. Sleep for the strained workers had been snatched when possible but it held no succour. The city's officials now made hourly inspections, wanting the latest news on any progress or updates on backup plans that were now in operation. This was keeping Hirun occupied away from his team just when his experience was needed the most. Even the populace itself breathed tension as if the air that hung over Gyre was thick with crisis.

As she made her way through the lower levels, news reached her that several mechanics had been assaulted during a much-needed break, as if it were possible that they were somehow lacking in their endeavours or were at fault. There had even been a public demonstration at the lack of movement, the first Damarel had ever heard of.

Despite her labours, the hours passed fruitlessly. She'd been busy burrowing her way through the inner workings of more movement systems and their interconnections than she'd ever thought possible. Monumental mechanisms both new and ancient were weaved into a vast network to allow the city to progress across the Flatlands and still no one could deduce whether the problem had been brewing for centuries. Was it an imperceptible flaw that had grown systematically, or was it a fault in the constructions of newer technologies, perhaps one innovation too far?

She'd lost all sense of time, going further inside the more ancient areas of the city, losing herself inside a nexus of gears, armatures and torsion bars when, without expectation as her mind drifted in its own thoughts, she chanced upon what she thought must be the problem.

Above a massive twisting spar, twice as wide as she was tall, only one of several such momentum shifters connected to the surface, was a void. The gap was a palpable discrepancy amongst such god-like order surrounding it. Damarel was so shocked that she could do nothing but stare into the space in astonishment. She could barely move as she felt her heart thud in her chest. Her mind screamed at her; it couldn't be! The giant gearing that had to be attached in the high vaults was absent.

Nobody could have stolen it, that would be too large an undertaking for anyone outside a large team of specialist city mechanics and what would possess anyone to want to, so dependent was the movement of the city to its inhabitants? No outsiders could have removed it either, as none had access to such an important location. It was only as an afterthought that she'd requested that morning to inspect each similar colossal contraption herself, despite them being one of the first mechanisms to be checked over by the city's corps of engineers.

It was impossible. Was this why Gyre had stopped, affronted by such a reckless action; a surgical intervention into its daily routine, a theft or wanton act of destruction on a scale unprecedented? Certainly, there were enough supplementary movement systems to allow for the city to move if it wanted to. With a fundamental part of itself gone, was it simply that Gyre was angry?

In her confusion at the quandary above her, Damarel cast her eyes around the space holding the vast segment. The only prosaic solution she could conjure for the missing apparatus involved a catastrophic failure of the gearing mechanism itself, an event so calamitous that the gearing must have sheared off so abruptly and completely to have then exploded into a thousand shards, now scattered somewhere beyond where she was standing.

Damarel shone her torch in slow wide arcs across the dark recesses of the chamber but nothing, not a single metallic splinter littered the tiered floor; it was as smooth and untouched as it must have been when it was first sealed away by the early generations. In bewilderment, she returned the torch beam up to the missing gearing and her heart stopped. There was the faintest gossamer-like outline of a gear, its form only vaguely substantial due to the multitude of teeth cut with such precision into its rim. She'd heard ghost stories in her childhood, her fears falling away as her understanding of the world increased, but never once had she heard of ghost machines.

It wasn't real. It couldn't be. The gear, and its connected brethren, could not be disappeared yet visible, both existing and not. If such a thing was possible then why here and not in any other part of the city or its citizens who were as much a part of Gyre as anything else? Why not her, she realised with dread, her stomach suddenly queasy, her spine like ice. Had she finally found a clue as to her feelings of non-presence? Was the ghost-gear akin to what her mother had seen moments before killing herself, unable to face the existential truth as she gazed upon her phasing daughter?

Damarel dropped her torch. Its light was snuffed out in an instant, smothering her in an inky darkness blacker than any night. When she finally felt its firm surface, relieved that it too hadn't become incorporeal, she flicked it on and aimed it pointedly back at the spectral phenomenon. The gearing had returned. No longer was it as substantial as a light beam caught in dust, now it was fully formed, as solid and shiny as the day it had been cast.

She stared open-mouthed at the reformed mechanism, unsure of what to do next. She couldn't tell anyone. Who would believe her? Given the circumstances, there was more chance that there was something wrong with her. It was, after all, the simplest explanation for what she had seen. Maybe it was the lack of sleep, her sheer exhaustion that had fooled her mind into thinking that the gearing had somehow phased out of the world and back in again? It was just an artefact of her own disconnection with the world made manifest by stress. There was one person she could tell, however, someone she hoped would believe her.

Later that evening, as Joh returned from her prolonged shift, Damarel found her and led her away to the nearby park where they could be alone.

"You're kidding me?" replied Joh after her lover's short description of her weird day.

"I wish I was," stated Damarel as she looked down despondently at her shoes.

There were few other people in the park. Nobody seemed to want to take the night air, preferring the comforts of home or one of the many taverns to provide relief against the city's woes.

Joh seemed to be caught between disbelief and the faith she had in her partner. "But that couldn't have been real, what you saw, surely?"

In her mind's eye, Damarel could see the gear in all its intricate detail. "It was so vivid, not like I imagined it, or it was some kind of waking dream."

"You have been under a lot of stress these last few days," offered Joh.

"No more than any other engineer," countered Damarel.

There was a pause as Joh appeared to struggle to find the right words to broach the subject. "You're not thinking it has anything to do with the way you've been feeling, are you?" Damarel stared up at her. "You know, like you're not fully here?"

Damarel had only recently brought up the feelings that had been present her whole life, and how she'd wondered if her mother had seen the manifestation of it for herself before her suicide. Had she too turned into a wraithlike outline in front of Lilane?

"I honestly don't know." It was something of a relief to finally be able to talk about her disconnectedness, but it hadn't come easily to her. "I don't really want others to know though."

"I understand." Joh held her hand next to her breast then raised it towards her lips. "Look, we'll just say that you thought there was an issue with the main gear to Hirun and he can get it inspected properly. If there's anything unusual going on, they'll find it. "

Damarel's mind went immediately to the logistics involved in that venture. "They'll need winches or a platform to reach that area. Also, it might be an idea to tell them that there could be some sort of transient issue with it in case it all looks fine on first inspection."

Joh nodded then wrinkled her brow. "Do you think you should be there, you know, in case your presence could trigger it?"

Damarel's first thought was to refuse but Gyre needed her; Joh needed her. "Maybe. I'll ask Hirun."

Joh's visage brightened at her acquiescence. "Well, that's settled. I need some food and a lot of sleep, that I'm not going to get," she added impishly. "They've got me in at dawn tomorrow. Let's go to Marazane's, that's not far and she always makes my favourite!"

That night, she dreamed of the other city once more. She was walking through a long, narrow street having turned off from a broad marbled parade. It was evening and the city was preternaturally still. A sign in black bold letters on white jutted out from the nearest building; it read Womber's Yard. The street itself appeared to be lined with a series of boutique shops, the pavements neatly maintained with few weeds to break up their smooth shapes. Above the shops appeared to be the residences of the shop owners. All seemed lifeless.

She walked down the street, her shoes making clacking sounds that echoed off the silent walls. Inspecting the myriad architecture in wonder, she rounded a curve and thought she heard someone talking. At first, she couldn't locate the sound but moving her gaze up, she noticed a warm light sneaking around a curtain from several floors up inside a four-storey narrow building. Gingerly, she approached the doorway to the shop. On the front door was a brass plaque. It was hard to read in the fading light, but Damarel could just make out the words written in a larger font which read, Casmeer Brume, Rugmaker. She pushed open the door, hoping no bell would sound to warn the occupant of a customer and stole herself inside.

No one was present in the gloom, but a faint trace of light picked out a thin staircase around a corner. As she climbed slowly, all the while straining her senses for any hint of an inhabitant, she made no sound on the carpeted steps. The wall held a long rug depicting what looked like a king on a hilltop above a spectacular city surrounded by mountains, the robed figure staring through a telescope at the night sky, the stars picked out in silver motes that shone back at her.

When she reached the landing, she noticed another staircase opposite that twisted upwards to a higher floor. She peeped into the hallway. On a raised table near to where she stood was an intricately worked silver oil lamp that cast patterned shadows on the walls. No one was there. Then came the voice again from somewhere above. Were they talking to themselves, she wondered? Certainly, no one seemed to be responding to the man's voice. She passed the entrances to two rooms, one a bedroom, the other had its door closed, and slowly ascended the stairs.

On the third floor were several more rooms, the first had its panelled door open and she could hear mutterings from within. From the sheer number of shelves lined with books, she could tell she'd found the owner's study. A fire glowed hotly in the hearth, its light flickering off the spines of more books than she could count. Beyond a chair and desk was a pair of tall window doors that seemed to lead out onto a roof garden. In the chair sat a man, his back to her, his frame bent forward in the leather-bound chair as he scribed with his hand, the top of an elegant pen twitching with each new inner thought. He was muttering to himself. On the floor near her foot were several scrunched up pieces of parchment, presumably tossed there by the figure in front of her.

Silently, she crouched to pluck the nearest one up and carefully unfurled it. It held notes for what looked like a person or a character from a book. There was a thin outline of a face that was not unlike her own. She gasped audibly when she saw on closer inspection that the contents were about her. Written in a neat script were notes about her life, Gyre, Joh, her family. The man stiffened at the sound and slowly, he began to turn. Before his eyes could meet hers, she awoke in a cold sweat, Joh's warm body next to hers and the night still clinging to the sky beyond her window.

She couldn't fall asleep after that. The hour before Joh woke was consumed by her pulling apart every fragment of her dream that she could remember, trying to preserve the detail in her conscious mind. Was she dreaming the man, or was he dreaming, no, writing her? Was her existence a dream, or was she in some sense merely a part of the unknown writer? Had she found the God of the Flatlands and was he doing this to her, to her city?

When Joh woke for her emergency shift, she didn't say anything about her dreams that night or the one she'd had before about that strange unmoving city and its solitary occupant. It was enough that Joh had not thought of her as insane when she spoke of her experience with the ghostly gear. They would speak to Hirun together and maybe some sense could be gleaned from the new day, something that they could work on to get Gyre moving again. The day might be peculiar, possibly very long, but answers might be found.

Damarel froze, her hand still switching out the tool she held with one from her tool pouch. It was a vibration she could feel, coming up through her feet and her prone body as she half-stood, half-lay within the upper heights of the main gearing system she'd stood below the day before. If the city had been moving, with all its attendant whirring and clanking, not to mention the crashing ambulatory sounds from hundreds of feet below where she lay, she would never have noticed. Of course, if the city were to move finally and without warning then she'd be crushed by the giant mechanism she was inside, but this felt different. Whatever the cause, the sensation was intensifying rapidly.

She began extricating herself from within the tangle of vegetable oil tubes and gearing, desperately fighting her rising panic in her haste to remove herself from the narrowing confines. It was with a sense of dread that she saw the main gear, the one that had become insubstantial before her eyes before mystifyingly reappearing, had vanished once more. When she reached where it should have been, its spiderweb-like outline barely highlighting its position, she tried to touch it, her fingertips meeting air.

As she descended the scaffolding erected for the inspection, she knew something was terribly wrong with Gyre: they were out of time. The vibrations had amplified into a rumbling sound like thunder overhead. The other engineers in her team nearby had also stopped their work, each one scanning their immediate vicinity, trying to locate the source of the aberrant phenomena. They all held that same expression, a chilling realisation of an approaching doom. Some had even stopped to stare at the missing gear, their shocked faces frozen in horror at the spectre.

It was a tremendous crash like waves from a storm that broke the mounting tension. From somewhere high above, through interconnected crankshafts, complex gearing, spurs and transmission spindles came a deafening crescendo as chain teeth slipped, metal ground on metal and the awful rumbling sound of so much mass descending assaulted their ears, every new detonation closing in on them.

Her heart thudded in her chest. She had never been so aware of the vast weight of the city above her before this awful moment. Since her first days of working as her mother's apprentice, not once had she held the slightest concern for this aspect of her safety. Fingers of ice clenched her heart. With an awful dread, she could sense her insignificance beneath the belly of the rupturing colossus. If she died here, would anyone find her body or would it be pulverised to dust, her existence utterly ground out?

"Run!" cried somebody as bodies rushed past her, knocking her onto her knees.

She threw her head up and was met with chaos. Most of the engineers were fleeing towards the tunnel that led out to the walkways. Above her, arms and legs struggled with the swaying scaffold. Someone screamed as they fell, their lifeless eyes meeting hers from the cold stone floor. In terror, she fled into the tunnel.

She quickly reached the walkway that led to the ground, even as the connecting planks and railings shook and swayed through the contorted paroxysms of the city. The only other option was to head back to the surface, the one that sounded like it was hurtling towards her as each visceral second lurched towards the next. There was no time to rationally assess the situation, she was probably dead either way, but she knew Joh was somewhere above her and as terrified as she was. Damarel took flight towards the only route up.

Great rends split the metal sky. There were screams as a large cog bounced down onto a crush of bodies fleeing down a walkway, causing it to splinter, sending those unable to grip to their doom. More broken machinery followed; tooth, wheel, chain and beam fused by gouts of dust and debris, their features lost in the immense unmaking, crashed down like a waterfall, destroying all in their path. Some of the engineers hid under large storage tanks. Others had taken to the ropes or rigging, hoping these might prove a safer means to the ground but these routes existed in the wider underslung spaces and proved to be easy targets for the avalanche of material.

As she staggered along the access walkway, Damarel heard something vast screech its descent from above her. She leapt forward as a section of the city's bedrock hurtled past where she had been, its natural walls giving way to those of the Grand Market she knew should be over three hundred feet above. In a deafening cacophony, the combined mass dashed itself to pieces on a set of great wheels. They buckled and then broke, adding to the shaking from above and initiating an explosion of lethal shards.

She fled up the tunnel stumbling and crashing into the walls as it bucked and heaved. Service pipes had cracked sending vegetable oil and steam spewing into the spaces as Damarel fought for every few feet of progress. Behind her, the ceiling collapsed in chunks, killing instantly the few engineers that had followed her into the tunnel. Her vision narrowed just as the corridor had. She would die here, she thought but she scrambled her way forward, every second of extra life her most precious commodity.

When she couldn't see any more, she groped in the darkness and the stifling oppressive heat. Then her hand followed by her face hit a solid impasse and for one awful moment she thought she was trapped, doomed to die in the dark either through asphyxiation, starvation or crushed by the falling city. With ecstatic realisation, the blockage under her fingers felt wooden and familiar; she had found the door that led to the surface. Damarel fumbled in hope for the handle, twisted it and put her shoulder to the structure. It would not budge.

From beyond came the sound of crashing buildings and the

cries of dozens of people. Had the space behind the door become blocked with only an agonising distance left to traverse? Damarel started to panic, wrenching at the door again and again, all the while frantically calling out for anybody on the other side to help her. Just as she began to lose hope, the corridor shook violently, and the door split with a loud cracking sound before exploding outwards. She was free.

Her relief at surviving her ascent back into Gyre was short-lived. She had left behind certain death but all around, citizens ran or huddled together in the streets, children and adults crying as buildings crumbled, towers fell. Dust filled the air causing Damarel to cough as she fought for air, her lungs screaming in constricted agony following her desperate exertions. The noise was deafening as she picked her way through streets grown thick with debris, roof tiles skittering or falling in sheets, walls tumbling, places she had known her whole life disappearing around her as she had felt herself disappearing.

When she reached Lever Crescent, she stopped cold. The barracks Joh lived in was gone. In its place was nothing but whorls of dust. Damarel could see straight through to the line of shops and taverns in Wandsbeck Street, where she'd gone with Joh only the evening before. Marazane's had vanished. In its place was a ghostly tracery of its distinctive entrance, the wrought-iron railings that led into a wide welcoming oak doorway, a solitary window and half of its sign. The rest of its grand exterior was no more.

Sitting on a low wall opposite, where the entrance to the barracks should have been, was a man, unmoving in the chaos. She couldn't tell until she was within arms-reach that he was an engineer, his blue uniform turned ashen in the falling dust.

"What happened?" she screamed at him.

The engineer said nothing, barely registering her presence. His eyes were hollows, twin black pits limned with dirt. Like others she had passed by in the destroyed streets, he had accepted his fate, already dead bar the final act.

Damarel shook him, which brought him partially out of his vacuity. He half-twisted his head towards hers but his eyes were unfocused, their pupils like those of a puppet.

"Did anyone get out in time?" she demanded.

It was agony waiting for the dumbstruck engineer to reply. When he did, even his voice sounded distant. "Me… Only me…

No time."

Damarel left the man to his melancholia and edged over to the precipice that bounded where the barracks had once stood. Gyre's modular structure had proved its biggest weakness. Almost the entire building and the section of surface it was situated upon had fallen through more than just its foundation. Beyond the mirk, Damarel could make out the red-brick rubble of the barracks in a heap on the landscape of the Flatlands itself. Any hope she still held at finding her lover in the ruins dissipated. Joh was gone.

Still the city shook. Fires had started, sending up vast dark clouds into the blue sky, turning the day red and black, the air acrid on her lungs. She would have ended it there, thrown herself down through the gap just like her mother had done to die closer to where Joh must lie. Anger prevented her. This would be the end of Gyre, just as the terranauts had warned. Why it had happened was Damarel's one burning question and she knew it was connected somehow to the man in her dreams.

If she wanted answers, she would have to first escape the destruction of the city. There were few options, and none afforded her much hope. It was suicide to attempt to traverse the various passages under the city; she'd seen the grisly outcome of that choice first-hand. Winch-system elevators dotted the rim of the city, but these were all hand-driven, used mainly for lifting goods to and from the city-surface, and she doubted anyone would want to expend the effort in hauling her down to the ground just for her sake. That left the rope ladders. At select locations around the city's perimeter, these were a seldom-used backup, but would she even have time to climb down before the city's ultimate collapse? Probably not but what choice did she have?

Once she'd made her decision, no other thoughts rushed through her head other than keeping her feet moving towards the rim. Screams mixed with the noise of collapsing buildings. For every new corner rounded, she was met with turmoil. At one point, her path was blocked by escaped livestock, forcing her to take a longer route around. As she cleared the diversion, the tall side of a three-storey building collapsed towards her giving her no chance to evade it. As she threw her hands up over her head, expecting to be crushed any second, the wall turned to spectral spider-silk, surrounding her in a knotted web of ghost-brick. Without a moment for thought or shock, she hastened on in case the debris reappeared, trapping her within.

Damarel was part-way through the open spaces of The Idles, the parkland where she'd first gone with Joh as a couple, when a whole section of Two Waters dropped from in front of her. She barely stopped herself from falling into the new space, staring at the draining waterfall that had appeared in front of her, the waters arcing and roaring into the dark depths so far below. Damarel skirted around, heading for the edge of the administrative district with its towering monolithic buildings bordering the exterior of the two great glass fins of the air dam.

The squat building housing the great turbine seemed to be miraculously unharmed as she darted past fallen debris, deliberately avoiding any of the many large cracks that had appeared in the open paved area. In contrast to the central areas, there was less structural damage here, the giant forces shaking the city dampened by the tall civic buildings, but their glass frontages began to shower down on her, exploding from their storied heights as the city heaved in its death-throes. High above, the great guiding sail rippled under the harmonic motion of its swaying moorings.

She was breathing hard by the time she reached the middle of the district. The edifice of the central fountain had cracked, its marble contours jetting water in directions its designers had never planned, soaking her as she attempted to circumvent the spraying jets. No more did the statues in the fountain's centre of the city's founders fill her with pride, their faces rigid with the certainty of their environmental mastery; all that remained for Damarel was a sense of betrayal.

She was nearly through the worst of it, passing swiftly under the watchful aegis of the main courthouse when the steel anchorages of the overhead sail snapped, the steel cable whipping through the wide civic boulevard. She could feel the sail's shadow over her as she fled, her legs and lungs burning, believing that her heart must surely burst at any moment. Darker grew the shadow, her death shroud descending with every heartbeat. She was so close to escaping when it hit, knocking her flat, enveloping her in its deathly white embrace. The sounds of the dying city were immediately silenced. She almost felt like she was in a protective cocoon but for the shaking still reaching her through the slabs of limestone that spanned the district.

She wondered dimly if the destruction had started at the city centre before circulating out or if the rim had been affected first. If that were the case then she had no escape and may as well just lie there and accept her fate but from what she'd witnessed of the devastation so far, there did not seem to be a pattern. Whatever the cause, she had to know, she had to keep moving.

The sail stretched over her prostrate form, almost pinning her to the surface but passage through, though awkward, was not impossible. She pushed with her toes and clawed at the edges of the slabs with broken bloodied fingertips until finally, her head emerged into the air once more. It hadn't been more than a minute but the outside in that time had changed markedly. Facades had cracked, spilling their renderings into the wide street. Buildings had begun to pitch over, shutting out even more of the diminishing sunlight. Even the great glass fins were affected, their radial metal spines buckling under the extreme forces from below, their glassy skin fracturing in wide coruscations.

Damarel was on her feet once more and sprinting hard. She raced past a farm and reached the rim almost before realising it, so focussed on fleeing that she nearly ran through the fragmented perimeter wall itself. In minutes, she had located one of the rope ladders before realising the futility of the task ahead of her. The ladders were never used under normal circumstances or, for that matter, in a rush. Each one was housed in a small building that overhung the rim itself, but the ladders were operated by a large hand-operated crank. Looking at the hundreds of feet of rope curled up around the giant winding, Damarel knew she hadn't enough time to release it all, let alone the time it would take to climb down to the Flatlands so far out of her reach. She did briefly consider tying the end around herself and diving over the side before realising that her weight would never be enough to unwind the mass of rope. Maybe others had already unfurled one in another part of the rim? Perhaps she would find one that other people had already used to make their escape?

Minutes slipped by as she reached another ladder-house, then another, both in the same unused state as the first. The third one vanished suddenly as she reached it, the outlines of its walls vaguely still visible. On the fourth one, she found a crush of people all vying to take their turn on the descent down. Damarel looked over the quaking edge of Gyre. There must have been at least fifty people on the ladder already. In her mind, she knew instinctively the outcome of such a misadventure.

"Wait!" she screamed but to no avail as more bodies piled on top of the ladder with grasping hands and frantic feet.

In seconds came an awful snapping sound. The ladder held for the briefest of moments, untwisting its strands on the second of its two moorings before it too broke under the extreme strain of so many bodies weighing it down. Damarel couldn't look as the desperate screams of so many helpless people falling to their deaths filled the once-living space.

Instead, she ran. Where she was heading, she could not say but staying at the ladder-house along with all those other doomed people felt like surrender. Movement was her only instinct. It had been the only action that had kept her alive so far, even if it was futile. Through broken streets she darted, twisting in her directions as raging fires swept around corners, buildings fell into ruin and always that deep rumbling of destruction assaulted her ears. In the distance, the familiar form of the Ramshackles peeped its roofs over the tree-lined avenue before Unstan's Tower. As she fled towards the grand spire, she ran into another fleeing woman who fell to the ground before vanishing completely with not even a second to scream.

Damarel kept going and when she reached Sweethouse Street, the city made an ear-splitting sound and hurled her ten feet. She hit a wall, bounced painfully, and dropped to her knees as Gyre fell sideways before finding a new unstable equilibrium. After seconds of what she realised were her own screams, she stopped rolling in time to see Unstan's Tower falling, toppling into a fringe of houses, her home obliterated to the sound of discordant bells. Tears stained her face, the salt on her tongue mixed into a metallic brine from a cut lip. She was propped against a wall, its angle all wrong, staring into the ash-filled sky as the sun blotted out. It was hopeless. There was nothing else she could do now but await her death.

Damarel focussed on nothing. This was to be the end of her story. Since her mother's suicide, she had been living for a better future, seeking comfort or distraction in others, passing through time to an ever-receding destination, hoping to understand her existence as life threw mundane obstacles in her path. With her precious last seconds of life slipping by in chaos, it was like seeing her life from outside. There would be no history of Gyre, just another unnamed failed and ruined venture lain stricken on the

Flatlands, its people lost to time past, all their personal hopes and dreams, struggles, successes and failures not even a memory without anyone to remember them. What had been its point in existing? Had it even had a purpose? She thought it had, once, but that notion was as ephemeral as a dream. Maybe that's all her life had been. Would there be an awakening or simply a surrender to the void?

A line of sail-kites undulated in the thickening wind high above her. Damarel envied them with their protective distance from the city. Whatever else might happen to Gyre, the kites would likely remain to flutter high above the city's corpse for a time to come yet. Would passing cities see the kites at first on the horizon as they approached, their citizens marvelling at their graceful engineering before coming upon the smouldering ruin of Gyre, wistfully wondering what had befallen the unlucky unknown and unnamed citizens buried beneath before their own city drew them ever onwards, never to look back?

It felt like a punch to the head when Damarel realised that there might be a way to flee the catastrophe after all. With adrenalin surging through her, she sprang to her feet and climbed a remaining flight of stone steps. These led to the building that housed a windladder that drifted high in the air. She was inside in moments.

The windladder was a marvel of seeming simplicity. Rooted to the floor of the building was a turbine that intersected a large wheel through its hub. The wheel was strung with one end of a long double loop whose great length extended out of the building and up into the sky. At a distance much higher than the city-surface was to the Flatlands, the other end of the twin tether was looped around a duplicate wheel that was held aloft by a giant inflatable pilot kite. This kept the entire tether taught but what gave power to the turbine were the tether's rungs. These were the sail-kites whose shape allowed them to hang down on the lower half of the tether to catch the wind, pulling the tether up with it on a cord. When these sail-kites passed around the higher wheel, their clever shape meant they descended like a glider until they reached the lower wheel, where Damarel now stood, to cycle around once more. The windladder could operate throughout the day and night, required little maintenance, and provided more power than any windmill or spiralcatcher could, due to the much stronger winds available at higher altitudes. What the designers had never thought of, however, was its use as an escape system.

Damarel looked at the mechanism with new eyes as she formulated a hasty plan. The turbine, indeed the whole building, was now no longer level with the horizon and the tether had slipped sufficiently that it was in danger of coming off the wheel. When that happened it would pull on the turbine itself, probably destroying it, the windladder and her only means of survival in the process. With no time to study the likely lethal ramifications of her next action, she quickly donned a pair of work gloves from her tool pouch, climbed up in front of the wheel and waited a couple of heartbeats for the next sail-kite to whip around it. As it passed overhead, its gossamer-like surface brushing her head, she leapt up to grab the nearest of the two tethers. In an instant, it pulled her off her feet and out over the rim of the city. In seconds she was higher than the tallest of Gyre's buildings that still stood. Only the tips of the great fins of the air dam remained above her but not for long.

As the tether looped her higher above the city, she could clearly see the great destruction that had been wrought upon it. Large sections of Gyre had fallen away to smash upon the surface of the Flatlands, others were tilted oddly, still pitching as she watched open-mouthed. More of Gyre was being lost to the vanishing phenomenon, great sections eaten away into nothingness in moments. Then, the whole of Threemilestone containing much of the commerce centre fell away taking the grand beauty of the Guild Hall with it. The sound of unending devastation was deafening. Many buildings had toppled or simply crumbled in the all-consuming cityquake. Fires punctuated the districts sending up great clouds of choking smoke. Great expanding rifts put asunder the surface, and on them, knots of people stood frozen in terror as death took them.

Damarel could not bear to witness her city's death but forced herself to look upon the undoing of all she knew, searing all the soul-wrenching details into her memory, fuelling her fear into bitter anger. With one final massive tremor, the once-imposing fins of the air dam collapsed inwards. When they collided, their great shattering ripped the sky into shards of glass and steel. At that moment, Gyre's strength disintegrated and the remains of the city dropped like it had been floating on air, held aloft by nothing more than the shared will of its people.

As Damarel reached the upper wheel, she gripped the sail-kite next to her, gathering folds of it in her hands as it swung her over.

Without thinking, she reached out to snare a control cable to the pilot kite. Her original idea was to somehow cut the tether so she could glide free but Gyre's parting gift to her was to sever it for her in its own demise, cutting her off physically and spiritually from her home city forever.

She drifted free on the high winds, alone, her future dictated by the untethered winds. As Gyre disappeared into the distance, she cast one last look at its disappearing ruin, its location only apparent through the large cloud of smoke that denoted its resting place. Somewhere amongst its ruin was the body of Joh, lost to her forever. Maybe all of it, everything that had ever been Gyre, its buildings, its populace, perhaps even any memory of its existence would be consumed by the eventual, ghostly erasure, all but her own for as long as she lived.

She did not know how, but she would get revenge for her dead lover, and all the citizens of Gyre. One day, she would understand what had happened, and if anyone was to blame, however powerful, she would make them suffer for their actions.

Casmeer

He wondered about the character he'd conjured from his imagination. As he read back over his notes, Damarel felt real enough to him, but she didn't feel complete. He'd given her a role within an interesting city and imbued her with an inquisitive mind that would allow him to explore the Flatlands through her, so what was wrong? His doubts were manifold. It was just that he was still so new to being creative to feel sure-footed in his words. Writing for these past four hundred years had consisted of chronicling the history of Thermidore, the only city he'd ever known, but that academic writing process was very removed from his recent experiences of crafting fiction.

He knew he could describe imaginary places well enough, taking ideas from the fusion of hubward cultures that the various districts of Thermidore had been designed around but could he convincingly write a female protagonist? He hadn't spoken to a woman in centuries and found to his dismay how little of his wife Elini he could recall. Sometimes, it took him minutes to remember the sound of her voice, her smell, the touch of her skin. He had long since forgotten what colour her eyes were. There could be no forgetting the way she looked as he saw her every waking day when he visited the roof garden beyond his study. Like himself, she hadn't altered her appearance at all, save for the fact her entire body had crystallised, the cursed outcome of an immortality drug. This side effect had affected all Thermiddians; all except him.

No, he wasn't ready, not for that writing challenge. Other characters formed more easily and completely in his mind. One, in particular, he felt should begin his story again for him. Already he had a name for him and a role within the imagined vistas of the Flatlands. There would need to be a new city for his new protagonist to inhabit, something more exotic than the wind-powered Gyre, as interesting as he found that place to write but what? All day, ideas surfaced only to be rejected. As he ate that evening, his vexations suddenly abated with the realisation that he'd already thought of such a place; it would be a city unlike all others, a city that could fly, a city called Min.

He smiled to himself at his previous folly, but what of Damarel and Gyre itself? He could easily resurrect the city as another place if he chose, but he'd reached an impasse in his depiction of the young woman. In some ways, she was too mechanistic with her thoughts, a deliberate act on his part when he first pictured her, but this aspect of her personality was at odds with the fantasy landscape he'd originally conceived. Too much detail on its inner workings would throw chains over his imagination, binding him to a rigid meta-physics. This would negate the reason for writing his fiction in the first place, to provide an escape from the unending stasis of his own city and its cage of surrounding mountains.

His creation of Damarel had maybe come to a dead-end, he thought. It had been an experiment, an initial foray into his ideas that had ultimately failed to meet the expectation of his scrutinising mind's eye. Whilst other female characters would enter the story, he now decided that the focus would be on his male characters. With a surprising reluctance, Casmeer knew she had to be discarded. Damarel had met her end.

Tribute to Storm

Brad Carpenter

In the year 2000, a friend gave me their copy of the original Omnibus edition of "The Wraeththu Chronicles." He told me I should check it out. He had a feeling I would like it.

I marveled at the person on the cover – athletic, imbued with spirit, divinely erotic. I loved the look, the punkish hair, the way the person seemed to magically manipulate all the objects around him. I would indeed check out this book!

I opened it and was immediately drawn in. The story of Pellaz in a distant town who felt he had a bigger destiny ahead of him, harkened to my own feelings of having grown up in Des Moines, Iowa. I was raised by hard-working, caring parents alongside an older brother and sister. I had a happy childhood, but always sensed I was different. It was only when I came out to myself as a gay man, then moved to the west coast to attend college, that I began to sense how different (and bigger) my life was going to be.

Early in the book, Pellaz gets swept away by an intriguing and mysterious stranger named Cal. Pellaz is drawn to this person, but also terrified. He senses that Cal is part of something bigger, and he knows his destiny has taken a turn.

During my early days attending Stanford University, living just miles from the sparkling city of San Francisco, I met a handsome, blond muscular grad student named Lonnie. Looking back, I can see that Lonnie was the Cal of my day. He helped me realize that I was a part of something much bigger than I had ever dreamt of. I had left my humble beginnings in Des Moines to plunge full on into the magical mysteries of the vibrant gay community of San Francisco. Any kind of future would be possible. Those memories and feelings came flooding back to me as I read through Storm's pages.

As I read on, I loved following Pellaz and Cal's experiences in the foundling Wraeththu community of Saltrock. The town felt very much like what I had experienced in my years at Burning Man, the once-a-year arts festival also created on a salt bed. The people who founded Burning Man aspired to create a utopia where people of all backgrounds could form a different type of society, one that would foster self-reliance, gift-giving and unfettered creativity.

During my years attending Burning Man, I marveled at the surreal new worlds being created year after year. Art and performance blossomed everywhere, sometimes planned and built by whole tribes, sometimes improvised by single artists. The general sense of community and togetherness transcended anything I had ever experienced elsewhere. At Burning Man, they call that magical town Black Rock, named after the desert on which it's been formed.

The people who gathered at Black Rock, like the Wraeththu members of Saltrock, radiate an exuberance and optimism that is truly infectious. They celebrate rampant creativity and the radical change that comes with it.

Each new generation that enters our society has always strived to be like that, wanting to improve the world they were brought into, but never has it taken on such an intense urgency. The generations before this one had already squandered precious resources, polluted the planet, and killed off countless numbers of species. It's as though most of Humanity has no clue how fragile the planet's ecosystem is, and how close it's getting to the tipping point.

As a young writer just beginning her professional journey in the late 80s, Storm had somehow envisioned a post-apocalyptic world that would come to strongly resemble our "near-present." We are just on the other side of that crucial line, where we need to evolve as a species, or face extinction.

I devoured those first three books in what felt like an instant. I had never been so enthralled by a literary work. It wasn't long before I gave that omnibus edition a second read. I started writing notes in the margins, various thoughts about how to best develop each book into a mini-series. I felt each book contained too much story for a feature. It would take several hours to bring the viewer through the story properly. Unfortunately, at the time, the mini-series had begun to fall out of popularity. Most Broadcast networks had started phasing them out of their schedule in favor of full ongoing series. With a series you could take that initial investment and build upon it with subsequent seasons. No matter the format, though, I knew the richly detailed world Storm had created deserved to be shared with viewers all over the world, so I decided to figure out a way to make that happen.

After some research, I found a way to reach out to Storm, and we began discussing the idea of taking her work to the screen. Storm explained to me that the Wraeththu trilogy was so early in her writing career that she now viewed those books with new eyes. She would release updated versions, then follow up with three more books that continued the story of the evolution of Wraeththu, and its companion species, the Kamagrian.

In 2005, my attorney set the deal with Storm's agent, and our collaboration began. The next year, my husband and I flew to the UK to join Storm for her 50th birthday party. Our attendance was kept as a surprise for her, and surprise her we did. (I was grateful we didn't give her a heart attack!) The party was well underway by that point, so we decided to meet up the following day to discuss ideas.

Chris and I spent most of the next day exploring the lovely township of Stafford while we gave Storm the chance to recover. That evening, we all sat in her study, chain-smoking like demons as we discussed all things Wraeththu. Her many cats settled in all around me on the couch, making me feel most welcome. It was a dream come true for me. There is nothing better than having the chance to discuss the property with the creator herself. Those discussions still resonate with me today. I will treasure that evening with her for the rest of my life.

I created a treatment for the Wraeththu Chronicles that became a tool to introduce the filmmaking community to the world of Wraeththu. People were intrigued, but dubious about the reality of producing such a fantastical and potentially costly property dealing with gender identity as one of its main themes. Entertainment industry people tend to be forward thinking, but when it comes to spending the millions of dollars needed to get a property like this made, they can easily go from cautious to fearful. John Cameron Mitchell, for example, loved the books, but felt no studio would spend the money and let it be as Queer as he wanted. I remember being perplexed by that reaction. The world of Wraeththu wasn't "Queer" to me. I felt the story transcended all of that. This was well before the transgender community had started making their great strides towards visibility and equality, so even though JCM had written and starred in "Hedwig and the Angry Inch," his perception was that Wraeththu was too "other than" for the mainstream to handle. And you know, at that time, he was probably right.

The option lapsed before I could get enough of the right people interested, so I moved on and dove fully into my career of producing other people's work.

A few years later, I reapproached Storm with a new idea: instead of jumping full on into the post-apocalyptic world of Wraeththu depicted in the books, I would start by writing a series taking place in the present day, at the beginning, with the birth of Theide, the first Wraeththu. It would be an origin story, long before the time of Pellaz and Cal. My idea was that by setting the story in the present day, we could make it easier and less costly to produce, giving us time to grow an audience before we transitioned to the vast and mysterious kingdoms of the new Wraeththu world.

Storm liked the idea, and she generously gave me permission to create all the backstory I wanted, so we renewed the option, and off I went to write the pilot.

I set the pilot in the present day as an Urban Fantasy called "Raythu Rising." I wanted the name to be something easier for people to visualize. Storm had said in the novels that "The First" had been created in a lab, so I called the pharma company that created Thiede, Ray2Corp. The company's cell therapy research aspired to cure cancer and any number of human ills. The sturdy species they inadvertently created, would come to be known as Raythu, a phonetic variation of the company name.

After I felt I had a solid pass, I sent it to Storm and waited for her response. It was crucial to me that she approved of everything I was doing with her beloved property.

She read it quickly and got back to me. Storm loved all the backstory I'd created. She felt that setting it in the present day made the property that much more relevant and relatable. She even said the words I could only have dreamt of hearing from her, "I wish I had written it myself." And of course, when she said that, I knew she was mostly being generous, because that was her way. Storm was never precious about the magical world she had created. Nothing seemed to please her more than to see her work inspire other writers. Witness the extraordinary amount of quality fan fiction inspired by the world of Wraeththu. Storm thrived on the expansion of the property, and always encouraged contributions from other writers. The Wraeththu books inspired a deep passion in people, so they wrote from the heart, and writing from the heart was what Storm was all about.

With my Storm-approved pilot in hand, my conversations with people in the business became much more productive. It's one thing to have a treatment, but it's another to have a pilot script where creatives and execs can hear the characters speak and see how stories and themes play out in an episode.

My manager Stuart gave the script to his friend Silvio Horta to have an advance look at, hoping he could help us get it to industry people who might be interested in working with us. A few days later, Stuart forwarded me Silvio's email which simply said, "I read Raythu. Let's talk!"

Silvio loved the pilot and treatment so much he wanted to be the one to work on the show with us. He was just the type of successful showrunner/producer I needed, too. Silvio was riding high from his wildly successful adaption of "Yo Soy Betty la fea" into "Ugly Betty" for ABC, he had a studio deal at Sony, and a big power agency supporting him. If he got behind "Raythu Rising," we stood a much better chance of getting the show made.

Unfortunately, even as close as we were to sparking success, it was not meant to be. The Studio and his powerful agents were all saying the same thing. This property is interesting but didn't have nearly the profit potential of his three broadcast network pilots that had already been ordered. They told him to keep his eye on the prize. Silvio reluctantly passed on "Raythu," and in the end, none of his three broadcast pilots ever got picked up to series. It was one of those times where you couldn't help but wonder, "What if?"

Undaunted by this disappointment, Stuart started booking me for more meetings. I flew to the West Coast for a week to pitch "Raythu Rising" to various development execs. They were intrigued, but what I kept hearing was that the writing, the characters, and the story were all great, but the material didn't fit in with the other properties in their current lineup. In HBO's case, they had just had their first blockbuster season of "Game of Thrones," and this was too similar genre-wise for them to consider it.

Stuart got me an agent at WME who planned to get us to the

newly evolving SyFy network. Ironically, at that time, mini-series had begun to make a comeback under the new name of "Limited Series." My agent, as it turned out, was more interested in the next hit that could be told in one gripping season. The submission to SyFy didn't go anywhere, so she moved on to find the next great Limited Series.

I was reminded, once again, that timing is everything. The stars must align in so many ways, and there are so many obstacles that any project must overcome to be picked up and made. I've worked with many successful showrunners on big shows with lots of backing, and I've experienced those challenges playing out again and again. That's the biz, as it were, so you need to be in it for the long haul.

Eventually I had to let that second option lapse as well. My manager left the business, and I haven't heard from him in years. That whole whirlwind period seemed like an impossible dream. We came so far, but not nearly far enough.

I've thought of Wraeththu and Storm many times over the years. It devastated me when I heard of her passing. I had never stopped dreaming of the day when I could take Storm's incredible vision and make it known to the rest of the world. I had wanted her to get to experience that. Storm's passing felt like the end of that dream as well.

A few months after Storm passed, our good friend Rodrigo came to us with an interesting proposition. His family wanted to bring investment capital to the US so he could start a company and live and work here. He had worked in television in Mexico City, so the plan would be for me and Chris to create a production company with him. Chris and I had dreamt for 20 years of starting our own production company. We had wanted to call it *Long Point Productions*, named after Long Point Light House, our favorite landmark in Provincetown, Massachusetts. Now it was finally going to happen. With the fulfillment of that long-delayed dream, came the rebirth of another. The investment capital provided by Rodrigo's family prompted me to reconsider the idea of optioning "The Wraeththu Chronicles" to develop for film and television.

The world has changed so much since those earlier attempts to bring Storm's Wraeththu to a new audience. Our time is disturbingly close to the world Storm envisioned all those years ago. Humanity is being ravaged by viruses, pollution, inequality, climate change and the extreme weather it creates. Mother nature seems to be saying, "Get a grip, humanity. Evolve or face extinction."

The idea of evolving into a "post gender" species no longer seems far-fetched. If anything, it seems to be the natural course of things. Today, more and more young people consider themselves non-binary, and the struggle for transgender equality has been brought to the forefront of public awareness. That shift has translated into shows that can draw an audience. Witness the incredible success of "Pose" on FX.

In terms of a marketplace for "Wraeththu," we are now in the bountiful era of mega-streamers. Netflix, Amazon, Hulu, Apple+, Disney+ and a handful of others are all competing for content. There are now many more opportunities for fresh new content like "The Wraeththu Chronicles."

Storm may be gone, but her massive legacy is still intact. Maybe the time is finally right to make the dream of expanding that legacy a reality.

Now that "Game of Thrones" has finished its successful run, all the streamers are looking for their own GOT. When I describe "The Wraeththu Chronicles" as a gender fluid GOT, peoples' eyes light up.

This is the time.

Storm's vision from the 80s is suddenly very "now." It's time to bring Wraeththu to the world, because, truly, the world has never needed Wraeththu more than now.

Contributors
The Peacocks

Ian Whates is the author of seven published novels, the co-author of two more, and has seen some seventy of his short stories published in a variety of venues. He has also edited more than thirty anthologies. His work has been shortlisted for the Philip K. Dick Award and twice for BSFA Awards and has been translated into Spanish, German, Hungarian, Czech and Greek. His latest novella 'The Smallest of Things' was released by PS Publishing in October 2018. In 2006 he founded award-winning independent publisher NewCon Press by accident.

Danielle Lainton has been working for and with Storm for the past fifteen years. She now helps Storm's husband Jim with the running of Immanion Press.

(Danielle Lainton is so much more than she says she is! She is also a talented artist and designer who has contributed many covers to Immanion Press publications. She is an all-round wonder and, together with Jim, keeps Immanion Press up and running! No less important - she was also responsible for supplying Storm with many an amazing cake over the years.

Louise Coquio)

Wendy Darling has been an editor and author with Immanion Press since its inception. She co-edited the Wraeththu Mythos 'Para' anthologies with Storm. She likes to burn the candle at both ends, working in a demanding full-time job alongside delving into all sorts of projects such as historic preservation and probably far too much time obsessing over *Star Trek*.

Fiona McGavin is author of the 'A Dream and a Lie' trilogy, her first collection of short stories, 'Lord of the Looking Glass' is published by Immanion Press. Originally from the Scottish Highlands, she now lives in Buckinghamshire where she continues her lifelong love of all things strange and spooky.

Freda Warrington is the author of 21 fantasy novels. She started writing as soon as she could hold a pen, and in her teens she was inspired by visionary writers, especially Tanith Lee. Born and raised in rural Leicestershire, Freda has a longstanding interest in that most fascinating of kings, Richard III. Her 2003 novel *The Court of the Midnight King: a Dream of Richard III* was recently reissued in print and ebook form to celebrate the reinterment of the king's remains.

Liz Williams is a science fiction and fantasy writer living in Glastonbury, England. She is currently published by Bantam Spectra (US) and Tor Macmillan (UK), also Night Shade Press and appears regularly in *Realms of Fantasy*, *Asimov's* and other magazines. She is the secretary of the Milford SF Writers' Workshop, and also teaches creative writing and the history of Science Fiction.

Louise Coquio is a sometime writer, editor, teacher and cook with an impressive talent for procrastination. She founded Visionary Tongue magazine with Storm in the 90s, and they went on to write Bast and Sekhmet: Eyes of Ra together. She met Storm, like many of the other contributors, through her love of Wraeththu and they shared their interest in subjects as various as cats, witchcraft, ghosts, writing, cake and gin for over thirty years.

John Kaiine is an artist, sculptor and writer. Husband of the late Tanith Lee, he provides artwork for all the Immanion Press releases of her work. His much admired novel 'Fossil Circus' was published by Immanion Press in 2013.

Tanith Lee was one of the UK's leading writers of fantasy, horror and science fiction, who died in 2015. Immanion Press is committed to keeping her legacy in print, through rereleasing rare novels and stories.

Paula Wakefield worked as a journalist after graduating from university. Her short stories have appeared in numerous women's magazines over the last few decades. She says that all her work explores love, sex and power – the tales we tell and re-tell to express our desires, regret and revenge, our loves and losses.

Deborah Cartwright, a close friend of Storm's for many years**,** is an author on esoteric psychology and philosophy in the self-development genre. Founder of The Luciferian Society, she currently writes nonfiction articles on LHP and Luciferian topics. Deborah is also passionate about human origins and ancient civilisations and is an assistant researcher for popular history authors Andrew Collins and Graham Phillips.

Graham Phillips is an acclaimed investigator of historical mysteries, Graham co-wrote 'Zodiac of the Gods' with Storm Constantine under the joint name of Eden Crane. His latest book to be released through Immanion Press is our revised new edition of his much-admired work 'The Green Stone', co-written with Martin Keatman.

Justina Robson was born in Leeds on 11 June 1968, and studied philosophy and linguistics at the University of York. She worked in a variety of jobs – including secretary, technical writer, and fitness instructor – until becoming a full-time writer. Robson attended the Clarion West Writing Workshop and was first published in 1994 in the British small press magazine The Third Alternative, but is best known as a novelist. Her debut novel *Silver Screen* was shortlisted for both the Arthur C Clarke Award and the BSFA Award in 2000.

Neil Gaiman is an English author of short fiction, novels, comic books, graphic novels, nonfiction, audio theatre, and films. His works include the comic book series *The Sandman* and novels *Stardust*, *American Gods*, *Coraline*, and *The Graveyard Book*.

Nerine Dorman is an editor and multi-published author who currently resides in Cape Town, South Africa. Her book reviews and lifestyle editorials regularly appear in national newspapers. She has previously contributed to Storm's Wraeththu Mythos collections.

Ruby has been the official Wraeththu artist since the 1990s. She created most of Storm's book covers, but especially so for any Wraeththu mythos titles, as well as creating cover art for other authors occasionally. She also provided interior illustrations for Storm's books. Ruby is up for designing anything as long as it fits with her bohemian aesthetic and animal loving ethos.

Ricardo Pinto is a computer game programmer and fantasy novelist. He has said that his books include his most deeply held political beliefs. He also felt that, despite possible commercial difficulties, his novels should include gay characters as a reflection of his own life experiences. He acknowledged that his ideas on writing and creating fantasy worlds had been influenced by the works of J. R. R. Tolkien and the *Dune* novels of Frank Herbert.

Ian Watson graduated from Balliol College, Oxford, in 1963 with a first class Honours degree in English Literature, followed in 1965 by a research degree in English and French 19th Century literature. After lecturing in literature at universities in Tanzania and Tokyo, and in Futures Studies (including Science Fiction) in Birmingham, England, he became a full-time writer in 1976 following the success of his first novel, *The Embedding* (1973) which won the John W. Campbell Memorial Award and in France the Prix Apollo, and *The Jonah Kit* (1975) which won the British Science Fiction Association Award and the Orbit Award.

Andrew Collins is a science and history writer, and the author of books that challenge the way we perceive the past. He co-wrote *'SHE: Primal Meetings with the Dark God*dess' with Storm Constantine.

Fiona Lane is a wee Scottish author originally from Glasgow, but has lived in a field full of sheep for the past 20 years. She likes hats and gin, and can be talked into most things with a liberal application of the latter.

Kim Newman is an English journalist, film critic and fiction writer. Recurring interests visible in his work include film history and horror fiction-both of which he attributes to seeing Tod Browning's *Dracula* at the age of eleven-and alternate fictional versions of history. He has won the Bram Stoker Award, the International Horror Guild Award, and the BSFA award.

J.E. Bryant has worked as a journalist and PR manager for the past twenty-two years. In that time he has written for publications as diverse as the *Royal Pharmaceutical journal* and the *Fortean Times*, while also finding time to write in and around a career in video games.

When not reading or writing , he can be found cycling the by-roads of Stapleford, Cambridge.

Michael Moorcock is an English writer, best-known for science fiction and fantasy, who has published a number of well-received literary novels as well as comic thrillers, graphic novels and non-fiction. He has worked as an editor and is also a successful musician. He co-wrote *Silverheart* with Storm.

Paul Weston is an author, lecturer, Tour Guide, and general disseminator of an exceptionally wide range of transformational ideas from both western and eastern paths. He has a Degree in the Study of Comparative Religion, worked as a Hypnotherapist, become a Reiki Master, Priest of the Fellowship of Isis, member of the Druid Clan of Dana, and Osho sannyasin. He has also extensively studied and gained experience in the work of the two great twentieth century masters of western occultism, Aleister Crowley, and Dion Fortune.

E.S. Wynn is the author of over seventy books in print and is the chief editor of Thunderune Publishing. In his spare time, he spins stories, builds board games, runs a pair of magazines and encourages people to create new art constantly!

Dolores Ashcroft-Nowicki is a founder member of the 'Servants of the Light School of Occult Science', Dolores has written many books on occult subjects. Her first book for younger readers 'My First Book of Magic' is published by Immanion Press.

Dr Yvan Cartwright is an award-winning computer scientist currently working within the games industry. As a massive space nut, Yvan has a passion for writing character-driven sci-fi and fusion fiction. He is currently working on a series of thriller novels involving time travel, the paranormal and the end of the world.

Brad Carpenter is an American motion picture producer. He is a Co-Producer for *Boardwalk Empire*. He has worked on the fourth season. He worked with *Boardwalk Empire* star Steve Buscemi on the series *Nurse Jackie*. He has worked with HBO on the series *Sex and the City* and *Bored to Death*. He has recently started up a new production company called Long Point Productions with which he hopes to be able to bring Storm's Wraeththu characters to life with a television adaptation.

Storm Constantine 12th October 1956 – 14th January 2021

Immanion Press

Purveyors of Speculative Fiction

Breathe, My Shadow by Storm Constantine

A standalone Wraeththu Mythos novel. Seladris believes he carries a curse making him a danger to any who know him. Now a new job brings him to Ferelithia, the town known as the Pearl of Almagabra. But Ferelithia conceals a dark past, which is leaking into the present. In the strange old house, Inglefey, Seladris tries to deal with hauntings of his own and his new environment, until fate leads him to the cottage on the shore where the shaman Meladriel works his magic. Has Seladris been drawn to Ferelithia to help Meladriel repel a malevolent present or is he simply part of the evil that now threatens the town?
ISBN: 978-1-912815-06-7 £13.99, $17.99 pbk

Para Mort edited by Storm Constantine & Wendy Darling

Para Mort is the sixth Wraeththu Mythos anthology. Authors from around the world have contributed stories, exploring Storm Constantine's alluring and mysterious Wraeththu: the androgynous, enhanced race that have come to replace humanity upon earth. Within art, love and death often walk hand in hand into the velvet night of obsession, which in turn can lead the way to murder and self-destruction. While hara strive to overcome human weaknesses that linger still within their minds and bodies, they are not immune to the ravages of desire, and its darker cousin, infatuation, which can lead the heart into dangerous territory.
ISBN: 978-1-912815-13-5 £10.99, $15.99 pbk

Mythotenebrae by Storm Constantine

Mythotenebrae is the sixth volume of her collected short stories, containing fifteen pieces, many of which are previously unpublished. It's long been Storm's aim to polish up the juvenilia works she has stored away on various devices. For this collection, she's completely reshaped three of these stories, one of which she wrote during her O Level exam when she was 16. She's also included several recent pieces that were accepted for publication by other editors, but then their proposed books were cancelled, or their publishing houses closed down. So we trust there will be a lot of material that is new to the majority of readers, within a variety of genres.
ISBN: 978-1-912815-06-7 £10.99, $14.50 pbk

immanion-press.com
info@immanion-press.com

Megalithica Books

SHE: Primal Meetings with the Dark Goddess by Storm Constantine & Andrew Collins

The Dark Goddess is unpredictable, dispassionate, cruel, and often deadly. She reflects our deepest desires, fears, hopes and expectations. In this fully-illustrated book, Storm Constantine and Andrew Collins have selected a fascinating range of 34 goddesses, including some who are not so well-known. The pathworkings to meet them and explore their realms will offer insight into these often-misunderstood deities. (This title is also available as a limited edition, numbered hardback.)

ISBN: 978-1-912241-06-4 Price: £12.99, $18.99

Coming Forth by Day by Storm Constantine

This book explores the myths of Ancient Egyptian gods and goddesses – showing how their stories relate to aspects of our lives, hopes and aspirations, and how we can learn from these ancient narratives. Through 28 deep and evocative pathworkings and rituals, the author provides a rich and vivid system of magic that the practitioner – whether experienced or a novice – can utilize in the search for self-knowledge, and to help themselves, others and the world around them.

ISBN: 978-1-912241-11-8 Price: £12.99, $16.99

Sekhem Heka by Storm Constantine

Drawing upon her experiences in Egyptian Magic and the energy healing systems of Reiki and Seichim, Storm Constantine has developed this new system to appeal to practitioners of both magic and energy healing. Incorporating ritual and visualisation into a progressive journey through the seven energy centres of the body, Sekhem Heka can be practiced by those who are already attuned to an energy healing modality, as well as those who are simply interested in the magical aspects of the system. Sekhem Heka is designed to help the practitioner work upon self-evolution and self-knowledge. Each of the seven tiers focuses upon a particular Ancient Egyptian god or goddess, including practical exercises and rites.

ISBN: 978-1-905713-13-4 Price: £12.99, $21.99

CPSIA information can be obtained
at www.ICGtesting.com
Printed in the USA
BVHW080911020122
625302BV00005B/1115

9 781912 815159